FOOL'S ERRANDS

MICHAEL SMIT-DRURY

Tellwell Talent
www.tellwell.ca

ISBN
978-1-77941-899-9 (Hardcover)
978-1-77941-898-2 (Paperback)
978-1-77941-900-2 (eBook)

Prologue

THE CONFLUX

The woman lay in the deep grass, invisible in the fading light of dusk to anyone who might have happened to walk by. She wanted to make noise. It was all she could do to restrain a deep, raspy groan that demanded to leave her mouth.

Tumbling down that gravel slope had knocked the wind out of her. Somehow, she had remained conscious despite rolling head over feet and feet over head, again and again. The centrifugally charged woman had come to a rest at the bottom after glancing her chest, ribs, and solar plexus off a large boulder that, fortunately, also now occluded anyone's view of her from above.

She was awake enough to know it hurt like hell and aware enough to know she couldn't stay here long. But there was no air intake. She couldn't breathe. The collision with that boulder had compressed her lungs and spasmed those adjacent muscles so severely that she could only lay there, sipping at the humid, smoky air, trying to pull in what little she could. After a few suppressed hiccups and a muscular contraction that nearly pulled her head above the grass, she felt a breath provide deliverance to her lungs. Her chest expanded, her body fully inflating to once again fill the black, orange, and blue form-fitting compression suit she was known for.

As her senses resolved themselves with this fresh influx of nitrogen, oxygen, argon, and well-documented unavoidable particulate, the woman rolled to her front, raised herself ever so slowly on all fours, and peered above the surface plane of the tall grass. Diffuse area lights from above became more luminous, helpful enough for the woman to get a better sense of everything around her, yet very dangerous.

Damn it, they'll see me now.

She started shuffling through the grass toward a distant hill. Then she was caught, momentarily arrested by one spotlight, then another. She was the feature attraction in the convergence of two large directed beams that followed her as she got up to run.

People were yelling from above and behind her as she exited the grassy section.

Her strength was returning with every big gulp of air, and with every step, her stride grew longer and more powerful. Newly broken ribs were an annoyance, but nothing that couldn't be dealt with as she sprinted to the base of the slope.

A looming tower stood at the top, housing a big red beacon that shone far and wide and bathed the surrounding hill below it in a bloody sea. Bright white beams of the seeking spotlights became infused with a shade of ochre as they slashed through the tower's radiance in pursuit of this woman.

She sprinted, and so did her pursuers. They were not far off now, and her injuries were even more pronounced as she clambered up the hill. It wasn't steep to look at, but in that moment, it felt like a vertical wall.

"Get her!" a youthful voice called out as eyes watched the chase unfold.

With a final push to the top, she reached the base of the tower. There was a long-handled lever in a stylish brushed metal finish on each of its four exterior walls, and she pulled the one closest to her, using her body weight to expedite the movement. As the lever came down, a section of the wall rose, and she stepped forward to what it had revealed. A smile crept up in the corner of her mouth as she knew what she had to do.

"Oh yeah!" the watcher, a young girl no more than twelve years old, said, renewed with excitement at the unsurprising twist in what was unfolding.

The watcher swiped the thin piece of plastic she held in her hand, which served as a virtualized display unit for the not-nearly-as-thin and excessively awkward set of AR glasses she was wearing. Her control maneuver had switched the camera from the pursued to the pursuers, now offering a dynamic over-the-shoulder view of those who had only just arrived at the cusp of the top of the hill, very near to the woman they chased.

She wasn't the only one to have done that, the watcher's choice equally executed by many thousands upon thousands of other watchers, thereby outscoring the alternative choices made by others. Most were similarly transfixed upon their own nearly invisible slivers of plastic, which was important to do as everyone knew how easy those were to lose. However, many had also congregated in small groups to watch on public displays, an activity that was widely appreciated as a nostalgic nod to the past.

Millions of others were less compelled to involve themselves. Instead, they opted for a picture-in-picture video feed of the episode lightly overlaid on their other atomized viewing activities. Or, they may have preferred to listen to the real-time podcast via their bone conduction implants. No doubt they would be able to see it later, either through the traditional photo roll, automated video edits, or the fully immersive home projection experience. They couldn't avoid it even if they wanted to, and quite frankly, the coverage was great.

"Well, Althea, I've gotta say that Toto has shown us a level of skill that I would call generational—we're lucky to see this."

"Hmm-uh." Althea looked at Doug, nodding for emphasis while diligently posing herself at a three-quarter profile position on Camera One, which she knows is her best look. She was holding that longstanding sportscaster technique of being uncomfortably too close to her broadcast partner's face, staring at him with blinking eyes and looking like she gives a shit as to what came out of his mouth. Her actions encouraged him to keep talking.

"This is the kind of performance for the ages, the kind of day that makes us excited for the future of what we're building here." Doug was excited and nervous at the same time. That's also why he still held onto a microphone—an artifact from the past that served to calm his always racing mind. He surely didn't need it. Arguably, he also didn't need to be there, nor wear clothes, nor speak, nor exist—at least bodily.

"But Doug, it's not at all surprising. Nothing and nobody tells this woman what to do. She reads what's happening, and she acts. We see this every time Toto's involved. Well, maybe not exactly this, that's what we love about her, it's always different," she said, laughing awkwardly as she wrapped up her commentary, "it's her decisiveness and creativity. Just fantastic, right?"

The woman, Toto, had finally managed to address her pursuers. She had stopped them and, in doing so, proceeded to tear a strip out of them for their actions. Those many millions watching and listening already knew this was not limited to castigating them for their political views, denouncing their behavior amongst the community as disingenuous, or reminding them that no one cared for their other sordid activities. All those things were usually true, but this was by no means a metaphorical rebuttal, and it was certainly no debate. This time, the tower had revealed a directed energy projectile weapon for her deployment, which, to those few who hadn't yet seen the much-talked-about episode three weeks previously, was a new addition. It, for lack of a better description, was equal parts Taser and microwave, both of which Toto used to nearly instantly electrocute and molecularly disrupt her pursuers, leaving all three of them dead to rights and their skin peeling like juicy, overripe oranges when bits of flesh refuse to give up the safety of their outer enclosure and end up releasing from sections of the fruit in big meaty clumps.

"Right, Althea. Indeed." Doug looked at Althea and then at Camera One for those watching the traditional linear feed. He blinked, he looked on, and blinked again. He looked on again.

He blinked again.

One

CROSSING PATHS

Lecture Hall 4B was one part of a divided theater. Often used for performances, it also hosted many of the Communications and Sports Journalism programs at Spectra College. The acoustics were excellent. In fact, they were improved with the dividing wall in place through the middle of this massive vaulted room. *Surely, the architects who designed the building had not anticipated that,* Doug mused. He and his classmates simply assumed the improved auditory situation was a happy accident of the need to divide rooms to satisfy the ever-increasing number of student body admissions. Enrollment kept getting larger and larger every year, yet the expansion of the campus was continually delayed. And all this despite the relentless increases in tuition fees and living expenses.

Where was all the money going? There was constant discourse amongst the student body as to how they kept paying... and paying... and paying, yet only to end up jammed even tighter into the diminishing capacity of labs, study halls, and gyms. "The Fix Is In" was an eye-opening article penned for the online student paper and layered with controversy. Written over a year prior, in the fall of 2011, by Doug's former roommate Henrietta Adler, "The Fix" espoused several claims, chief among them that the Board of Governors of the college was conspiring to slow down investment into the school, all the while knowing that graduating classes were increasingly unable to find gainful employment in their fields of study. Henrietta had published

1

evidence that funds were being channeled from the college to companies that linked back to several key members of the Board. While there was some initial shock at her findings, they were quickly and summarily dismissed by university representatives. The controversy was but a blip in the timeline of the rote lives of these college students.

What remained unclear was what exactly happened to Henrietta. The Dean's Office had reprimanded her for publishing those accusations. Shortly after, she was approached by a mysterious new media company—some kind of secretive venture-financed startup business. No name, no names, and negligible details were provided. They had apparently given her an ultimatum to join them immediately, with a hefty price tag attached. And no one had seen her since. A new roommate moved in a few months later, a new school year commenced the next fall, and life continued.

While the seemingly conspiring minds of money-hungry, dividing-wall-installing Board members had indirectly led to a better-sounding lecture presentation, every time Doug shuffled alongside that temporary room partition, the gap she had left in his life kept invading his thoughts.

He would gaze at the perforated composite material boards that all hinged together to form this wall, space-gray in color with little dots everywhere, presumably to deaden wandering sounds or possibly just a result of the manufacturing process. Whatever the case, he could almost see those dots moving, reforming, and manipulating their own coordinates and those of the ones around them as if through a gravitational or magnetic force. Or possibly both, in a magnetically gravitational kind of way. The yin and yang of push and pull, all dots interacting with the other dots, all in different ways. Lines could be drawn, connecting related things, passing information, sending energy, or blocking other dots. This dot-network was running on the futuristic space wall of Lecture Hall 4B, in view of everyone who passed by, but all were seemingly ignorant to the threat. Doug was sure it all meant something, but he wasn't...

"What the fuck is this nonsense, man? Who they think we are... we gotta get out there and find a new sport to cover?" Ricky Templeton always had strong opinions, the potency of his commentary usually forceful enough to blast a hole through Doug's often meandering thoughts. They were walking side-by-side, shuffling up the gangway and through the large doors at the top of the lecture hall, now clear of the dividing wall and free of influence from Doug's enigmatic gray matter observations.

"Yeah Ricky, that's kind of a crazy brief to give us. Maybe ten years ago we'd be more likely to find something," said Doug.

"Yeah, like UFC. Can you believe they bought that shit for like a dollar?"

"Not sure, thought it was..."

"Now that shit worth like billions."

"Yeah, what a marketing..."

Cut off again, Doug was acclimated to Ricky's one-way communication style. It was quite apparent to Doug that Ricky—with his opaque and mostly ignorant understanding of the world around him—would do extremely well in broadcast. He was crass, direct, and punchy, not too dissimilar from the Ultimate Fighting Championship, which he had just offered up as an example.

That sport started as an underground blood-infused novelty almost twenty years prior in the early nineties. The first few seasons were almost as if someone had taken characters from the Street Fighter video game and thrown them into a fighting tournament with no rules, no law, and no real ability to distribute the content. As content and media became more ubiquitous, the appetite for all forms of it—especially more extreme forms of it—swelled amongst the viewing populations.

It was no surprise to Doug that as humanity marched forward with a news-media-propagated eye looking through the aperture of violence, a spectacle like UFC would thrive. Pervasive distribution and the power of personalities and brands were lighter fluid to an already roiling flame.

"But how we gonna find something else? Like what is left? There ain't no new sports that people don't know about," Ricky continued with his lamentations of the assignment.

"I dunno, Ricky, there's gotta be something we can find on the web, like some weird online Tumblr group or some shit. People seem to come up with all kinds of stupid ideas, and no shortage of stupid people to watch... that's all we gotta do."

By now, they had walked the length of a main corridor and passed through the open doors into a bright, brisk autumn afternoon. Leaves were starting to turn in the trees around them, but the weather was unseasonal.

Still warm throughout the day, the two young men found it harder now than in prior years to immerse themselves in their academics. The campus was active when the weather was like this, and being as close as they were to both New York and Atlantic City, there was always a healthy amount of social distraction at their fingertips.

The people-watching was exceptional as well. Ricky couldn't help but appreciate the late-season hanging-on of summer attire. Skin was showing, and fit bodies resided beneath it. He liked both of these things.

Doug enjoyed people too. He would stare, often getting lost in thought, often coming across as creepy, and often hearing just that from passersby. This didn't seem to bode all that well for someone pursuing a career in Communications, a vocation that demanded a couple of things. The first was curiosity, which he had in spades. The second was the ability to engender oneself with others, for which he had no measurable aptitude whatsoever. In the absence of having any refined communication skills or interpersonal intuition, Doug simply sought to put people in boxes.

Archetypes fascinated him. Through his late teens and into adulthood, Doug had constructed his own categorical framework which he applied to everyone he met or took a moment to observe, a system born from good intentions to mitigate his inherent awkwardness. It allowed him to neatly arrange his own segmented perspective on humanity, through which he could observe the patterns of their activities, behaviors, likes, and dislikes. For all these stacks of humans he sorted, he had developed his own architecture of engagement, a playbook for what he could say and do that would stand a good chance of being acceptable and occasionally even appreciated.

Needless to say, it took a lot of work for Doug to make new friends. He often wondered if this was why he felt more comfortable in front of the camera—it was cold, lifeless, a bit reflective, and above all else, it held no opinions or assumptions. Some people said the camera added fifteen pounds. Doug liked to say that even if it did, it never judged him for it.

Doug and Ricky approached an intersection in the campus walkway. A large formation of students crossed their path.

The lead group of four students had a determined head of steam. They were on a mission, their destination possibly unknown, but with resolute expectation that they would know it when they arrived. No periphery and no logos would slow them, clothed in plain garb and simple packs, most likely of discount rack or even thrift store acquisition. They counted four young men and women, two of each, all of them singularly focused on where they were going, these explorers at the head of the pack.

Behind them, not so far as to be completely detached from the overall procession, but far enough to ensure they were framed with adequate space and depth around them for anyone watching with a sense for composition, three girls walked in tight formation. One of them led the way, the other two slightly offset, reminiscent of the three-tiered orderliness of a podium. Small purses adorned the shoulders of their pristine, thin sweaters, and none held more than two books wedged between their torsos and arms. They were the heroes of their own stories, to be sure.

A trailing assortment followed with far less structure. Two engineering students, identifiable by snippets of a conversation that expelled quarks and hadrons into the air around them, shuffled along. Tangential to them were three assemblies of extra-baggy jeans and oversized button-up shirts of plaid and ironic striped variety, containing two guys with flat-brimmed hats and a girl with longer green-tipped hair. She carried a skateboard. The three of them must have walked in from the recent past of 2005 on their way to the more distant relaxed-fit fashion future of the 2020s. A few feet behind them, two of their semantic cousins trudged forward in the shade of their own black hoodies, large stringed cloaks floating above skinny jeans and unlaced high-top shoes.

Cutting across the grass and interfering with the unidirectional flow of this menagerie were several figures who couldn't help but stand out even more so than any of these other smaller groups. Mostly due to four of them being well over six-foot-six, which, interestingly enough, also commanded significant attention to the very short man who flitted in and out amongst them.

"Oh man, it's Brandon and Amare and those guys. I gotta catch up with them. Alright man, well, let's get back on this tonight. I'll hit you back later." Ricky walked off to fall into formation with his friends from the school's basketball team.

"Oh... yeah... later, man." Doug was again lost in contemplation of his people-studying.

Everyone's trying so hard to be unique, but aren't they really all the same?

Am I the only one who can see this?

The many semi-conscious thoughts in his mind were all crying out for attention and conflicting with one another, stealing from the clarity he would need to realize that answering both questions in the affirmative would be impossible.

Two

ENTERTAINED

Doug stopped at the campus coffee shop and sat down at an outdoor table. A refreshing breeze blew through the concourse, but it was still warm enough to be comfortable outside. He flipped open his laptop and turned to face the lower afternoon sun to ensure he could read the computer screen. As it came to life, the top right corner indicated a full battery charge, offering at least two hours of usage. Much like the sunlight he basked within, Doug's window to operate brightly was time-boxed.

[new sports]

He was auto-corrected without consent, and Google returned news articles covering the vast world of sports. *Not exactly what I want.* Doug looked out over the paved brick courtyard area. The materials used in creating the outdoor spaces of the campus were all very earthy and sandy. It suggested a Moorish or Roman aesthetic, no particular style other than a subtle homage to feeling ancient. The sandstone-inspired pavers all ran in non-standard patterns, curving to join walkways and around areas of landscaping. Doug could imagine that if those paths had existed centuries ago, they might have found their way through an ancient Roman village or perhaps led to the Circus Maximus or the Coliseum. How exciting it would have been to have lived in ancient Rome.

Other than the classism, poverty, famine, crime, unsanitary conditions, and untimely death, of course. Doug pondered how in many respects, things may not have improved all that much since then.

Did they have coffee shops? He wondered.

Inspired by these mostly distracting thoughts and having not yet been entertained, Doug adjusted his search strategy.

[gladiator sports]
[combat sports]
[chasing sports]
[redneck sports]
[white trash sports]

His thoughts were getting progressively more violent and ever darker, even while the sun shone brightly over the entirety of the campus. A slight breeze whipped a cloud of dust up and across the Roman courtyard.

Scrolling through pages of results, mostly regional sporting event coverage from the rural corners of America, nothing stood out. *Would any of these qualify for the assignment? Crash-up derby... that's an oldie but a goodie.* As a variation of this, he found some remarkable footage of a community competition in Alaska, the Cliff Jump Challenge. It was simple: older cars combined with a clamp on the throttle were ghost-ridden, one after another, over a massive cliff towering above an open valley with a small, pristine creek at the very bottom.

Similarly simple community members gathered on the other side of the creek, the "safe side." Food trucks, hot dog carts, lemonade stands, and American flags were only outnumbered by lawn chairs and trucker hats. With every car that leapt over the cliff edge, the hootin' and hollerin' would get louder. As one vehicle after another tumbled down the cliffside, everyone was in awe. The audience was hoping that just one of these cars would have the skill, timing, and fortitude to make it all the way to the creek, a stone's throw from where some of the front-row viewers were sitting as their children splashed in the slow-moving waters nearby.

[X] Doug closed the window.

This might just qualify, Doug's internal voice was saying. *It's pretty hilarious, too... would give me some good stuff to talk about in the class presentation.*

"Low power, your laptop will shut down soon," flashed across his screen. Time had flown by while Doug was detouring down the dead-end roads of the information superhighway.

What he took away from his research session was just how passionate people get about sporting competitions—in whatever format they take. Truly, since the ancient Olympics and the days of the gladiators, sports have always brought communities together in a celebration of competition that was itself reflective of society, from fights to the death in ancient times to feats of strength and culture of the Highland games to the ultramarathon races of African tribes. Soccer grew to prominence as a sport that can be played anywhere and everywhere. Baseball evolved from sandlots, and basketball and hockey were motivated by the need to keep active despite the daunting conditions of northern winters. Spelling bees, chess competitions, and debate clubs came about as competition moved from physical to intellectual. And the rise of social media, competitive memes, and gamification had already started to transform even the most mundane daily tasks into a medium of competition, and thus, something presumably worth watching.

The scoring system that Doug hadn't recognized and didn't fully understand was the one happening underneath his fingers. He didn't deserve to take any credit for whatever answers he might find in response to his homework assignment, as the work had already been done without him. The unstructured nature of everything on the internet was analogous to the battlefields, sandlots, and endless boredom that spawned all those competitive behaviors he had been thinking about. Similarly to his athletic career, he was merely an intellectual spectator.

In the early days of the World Wide Web, search engines became the de facto standard for finding anything that wasn't otherwise known or shared through the limited network of Bulletin Board Services (BBS), Multi-User Dungeon games (MUDs), or other primitive network configurations, all navigated through the iconic view of a two-color text-entry command prompt.

Some of those original search tools would simply index content, from which the small number of users dialing in to other remote computers would receive a list of prioritized results based on the system matching syntax to their search terms. In the early 1990s, this was functional enough and led to the glory days of Yahoo!, Excite, Tripod, Snap, and Altavista, among others. Microsoft saw this happening and tried to force its way into the game with MSN and bundled software, forging what would become a multi-decade battle between Microsoft, its users, and the industry watchdogs and antitrust authorities worldwide.

Meanwhile, internet users had a somewhat unacknowledged need for better-ranked pages in their search results. Certainly, the way it was working in the early days let people find the cure for what ailed them, as long as it was porn or gambling. Still, many were confident there could be even more utility for a near-infinite connected world of technology, content, and communications. Surely, they would say, there is a way for pages to be ranked better.

It seemed like divine intervention that a guy named Page would be the one to figure out a better ranking algorithm, who would then call it PageRank, the under-the-hood tooling of Google that had been doing all the competitive aspects of Doug's work for him. PageRank enabled a new way to discover everything ever known; it boasted the potential to have unbiased access to all things ever written down, ever codified in any format, and to facilitate the free flow of information from connected node to connected node on a universal global network. Pages and content were constantly ranked and re-ranked based on their popularity and the popularity of the pages connected to them.

In the same way Doug's meandering thoughts had been attributing the rules and formats of modern sports to ancient public spectacles, the network technologies he was reliant upon had their own ancestral body of knowledge.

In the 1940s, Harvard Economist Wassily Leontief could not have spoken of a sorting algorithm for navigating the internet, as no such connected technology yet existed and was still many decades of delayed and ignored efforts from becoming a reality. However, Leontief had, in those years, published a theory of measurement whereby he would iteratively rank a country's economic sectors based on the relative importance of each to the other sectors that supplied it, and vice versa. This framework demanded a continual re-evaluation of those sectors to accommodate the constant change of the relative importance and interdependencies amongst them.

His theory was proven to be markedly accurate in scoring economic activity, with the work being belatedly recognized with a Nobel Prize in 1973.

Over those same decades, a group of scientists and engineers at MIT and Stanford, with the backing of the Defense Advanced Research Projects Agency (DARPA), had begun stringing together remote computers in the very first edition of a wide area network. Based on the premise of packet-switching—sending packets of information from one discrete network address to another—the internet was born. Or rather, ARPAnet was born. Initially inspired by a network technology concept based on the principles of a decentralized architecture, of peers contributing to making something greater than the sum of their parts, ARPAnet had stalled in progressing from an existence in research papers to practical implementation. It only began to make headwinds and receive the necessary funding when the American military-industrial complex caught wind of a similar system being developed in the United Kingdom.

Like any self-respecting military-industrial complex with designs on guiding the sentiment of its populace, the risk of not being in control, of not being the central authority for an architecture that should have no central authority in its best implementation, was simply too much to bear. The Fear of Missing Out—FOMO—was, in many ways, the fundamental human decision-making criteria that led to the very creation of the internet.

Another thirty years of military governance delays, romantically masked as "incubation," would give way to another seismic event: the first web page on the World Wide Web, conceived and authored by Sir Tim Berners-Lee. That first web page was a page—lowercase p—about the World Wide Web and served as an index to other web pages as they came into existence.

As web pages about web pages began to proliferate, now 25 years after Leontief's Nobel Prize and over a half-century since his initial published thesis on the matter, PageRank would finally go live in the form of a website known as www.google.com, managed and operated between Stanford and a suburban Bay Area garage. While participating in the very friendly-sounding Massive Digital Data Systems program sponsored by the neighborly CIA and NSA, Google's founders—Page and his chief collaborator Sergey Brin—were steadfast in creating a search engine that would not be connected, influenced, or affiliated with advertising, even authoring a paper on the topic, stating that, "We expect that advertising funded search engines will be inherently biased towards the advertisers and away from the needs of the consumers."

Doug, like most of the now hundreds of millions of internet users around the planet, did not know of the more lengthy backstory nor murky origins of many of these helpful technologies. He most likely would have elected to skip over it had he been presented with even an abridged write-up of this history, instead choosing to give his attention to the top of his ranked results and the prominent ad directly above them.

***

"Oh shit, look at that, man, that thing looks pretty sick!" Ricky was staring out the window from his high-table perch in their local Burger King. Whopper juice was on his chin, and bits and pieces of mystery meat flew out of his mouth as he exclaimed his surprise.

"Yeah, that's bonza, mate. That's the first Tesla car... from the electric car company. I heard Travolta got the first one," offered up his friend Jason in a combination of Australian slang, Down Under twang, and a southern drawl. Jason Kim was one of Doug's roommates and a frequent burger-devouring companion of Ricky's. He stood out on campus for his sharp humor and notable accent, provided he spoke loud enough and no one else was too close as to block the view of the short Korean-Australian who had attended high school in Texas before moving to New Jersey.

Through their greasy and dusty lens on the world, Ricky was remarking at a car he hadn't seen before. The Tesla Roadster had been in limited supply since its unveiling a few years earlier, and with the public consciousness of electric vehicles in 2012 even more scarce than the cars themselves, a Roadster showing up in Valemont, Tabernacle, Chatsworth, or any of these nearby small towns was a rare enough event to justify their surprise.

"Some PayPal guy stuffed a battery into a Lotus... I heard it goes like a rocket. Looks pretty cool, too, but I don't know about having to plug this thing in," Jason added.

"Hmm... yeah..." Ricky was clearly lost in thought, "that's a damn good point, Jay. But for us broke-ass motherfuckers, that seems like the right kind of ride. We roll like we bad-ass, and then just get home and plug it in for free."

"You know you have to pay for electricity, right, Ricky?"

"Nah, man, not me, it's included in my rent. Negotiated that shit up front. Smart, right?" Ricky tapped the side of his forehead, letting Jason know that he, Ricky, has complete command of his financial situation on the strength of a monthly payment of five hundred dollars. What he's choosing to ignore with this ode to his intelligence is what he gets in return for his discount rent, the unwanted space under the stairs in a shared house with six other students. He has a mattress wedged into that little piece of real estate, the end of said mattress buckled over against itself as it doesn't quite fit between the wall and the lowest step, such that his six-foot-three frame requires a diagonal sleeping orientation. His situation resembled most of his written homework assignments from high school in that there was no thinking involved when he started, the idea was much grander than the execution, and he eventually ran out of room on the page when he finally got inspired to get to work.

"Okay, man, you go ahead and get that car. I wanna see you park that under the stairs, too." Certainly, that wouldn't happen anytime soon, he thought, as they were still a year and a half from graduating and god knows how long before having a chance to start careers.

"Whatever, my man. You will see!" Ricky slurped his fountain drink down and stuffed a handful of fries toward the front of his head, skillfully shifting the focus of his mouth from straw to hand, just in time to receive the oversized delivery of deep-fried potato-themed product.

"I'll tell you something though, it's companies like Tesla that will fix the world. Everything's burning up everywhere. Factory farms releasing all the CO_2. Oil companies spilling their oil everywhere. We need more innovation to make it right. Sign me up!" Jason waxed philosophically as he took a big bite of his crispy factory-chicken sandwich. The batter, he noted to himself, was excellent.

Three

THE CLASSICS

It was after nine o'clock in the evening. Doug had cleared space on his makeshift desk to get back into his work. Strewn about were his usual rat's nest of hastily written notes, illegible scribbles, crumpled-up receipts, candy wrappers, books, paper, pens, some dirty laundry, Polaroid snapshots, a few pairs of shoes, a few single shoes, and empty plastic bottles of Coca-Cola Classic.

He was addicted to Coca-Cola Classic. To his own knowledge, Doug had never even had Coca-Cola before it was classic, though he had heard about New Coke. When he started drinking it religiously, it was already the accepted doctrine of Coca-Cola Classic, but he was certain he agreed with the cumulative uproar and dissatisfaction around New Coke. In fact, there was no doubt in his mind that he hated New Coke.

Doug's room was on the main floor of the house. It was a classic American foursquare house, not to be confused with the mobile city guide and check-in app of a similar moniker which had been busily programming the behavior of hundreds of thousands of college students around the country.

The house had much simpler ambitions. Walking in the front door led to an open foyer. In this particular foursquare, the roommates most often kept their shoes on, and the floor was empty but scuffed. In homes like these that housed families, this is where the accumulation of shoes would typically be.

Straight ahead through the foyer led to the kitchen, and then off to the right of the kitchen was an old oak door with a brass handle. Originally leading to the drawing room where people would read, it was now a bedroom where Doug would draw, and often type.

Many would question the choice of that room for a bedroom, especially given Doug's seniority amongst the roommates who shared the tenancy, but it had some things going for it. Well-situated windows looked out onto the backyard and over toward the neighbors' house. On a clear day, his room received plentiful morning sun, framed by a taller sycamore tree just out and left of his window that offered privacy without obstructing Doug's exposure to the burning heart of the solar system.

A different kind of fiery energy—and exposure—was visible through the other window, which faced the house next door. This viewing portal doubled as an analog livestream feed of the lives of Mr. and Mrs. Doncaster, as well as Mr. Graysuit, who had a habit of showing up at the Doncaster household quite often, coinciding with when Mr. Doncaster was not there. Doug was well aware that he'd lose his viewing access if he revealed his unpaid subscription, so he only tuned in after dark, when the Doncaster lights came on and prevented the detection of external surveillance.

After all, there hadn't been any notable action in his own bedroom for over a year that might otherwise keep him occupied, and like other aspects of his life, he was more comfortable as a spectator.

He could also hear most everything that happened in the kitchen on the other side of the door to his room. This audio surveillance allowed Doug to participate in much of the household's social activity without actually having to contribute. Though after nearly two and a half years of blissfully ignorant vicarious existence in his friends' lives, he had recently learned the hard way the social importance of concealing his vast collection of overheard and non-participatory memories.

"Hey Elise, how did your doctor's appointment go? Hope everything was okay," Doug inquired and offered one day, with care in mind for his roommate and friend.

"What? What are you talking about? Who's been talking to you?" Elise had said.

Later that week, Doug was posting "Room for Rent" signs, and as time went on, he was frequently reminded to mind his own business whenever he encountered his old roommate and former friend Elise on campus.

[competition between people]

Doug picked up his efforts from earlier that day, now trying different search terms that weren't just about *[sport]*.

He was soon led down the grassy, steep, and irregular path of learning about the cheese rolling competitions in Gloucester, England. Doug was fascinated by how the judges and locals pronounced Gloucester—rhyming with imposter—and by the event itself. It again seemed like one of those things that no one would ever do by themselves. For one, if you had a nice wheel of cheese, rolling it down the hill seems likely that it wouldn't be such a nice wheel of cheese by the time it got to the bottom. For two, the breakneck speeds some participants get up to are actually... breakneck speeds. It looks insanely dangerous. Yet every year, up to one hundred inspired competitors show up to throw themselves down this hill.

Look at these lemmings! Doug thought to himself. As Doug knew, lemmings were a species of rodent with natural urges and tendencies to follow each other without any thought as to where or why, often resulting in mass deaths of these helpless, simple-minded creatures. He knew this to be fact, as he had seen it as far back as an old documentary that would air during reruns on Saturday morning television. And, of course, the video game.

Doug didn't know that in the pursuit of making a popular film, the producers of the original 1958 *White Wilderness* Disney documentary had actually shipped in a large quantity of lemmings by truck for the purposes of throwing them over a cliff, en masse, to record the infamously misreported behavior of the poor, unsuspecting furballs. An Academy Award for Documentary Feature rewarded the efforts of these producers, validating their own poorly directed behavior. To no real surprise, they had confidently built the vision for their documentary based upon what had come before them. Older legends had survived in public canon, certainly much longer than any supposed lemming had ever lived for, such as a *Popular Science Monthly* article in August 1877 which postulated that lemmings followed each other in droves into the Atlantic in pursuit of the legendary submerged continent of Lemuria. Befitting the source, these archival stories were never questioned on the merits of their scientific credulity due to their popularity.

The cheese roll chasers of Gloucester certainly fit this false profile of lemmings—these helpless creatures and their inconsequential role did not matter so long as they created entertainment.

[david bowie]

Doug needed to get into a healthy exploratory mindset, and for this, there was no one better than the artist who had for a while been known as the liberated androgynous alien Ziggy Stardust. Unfortunately, Ziggy had not yet landed in Doug's mp3 library.

Opening up SongShare, his favorite torrent-download application, he initiated a peer-to-peer search for more music from the famous musician. No meaningful results came back, but this seemed to be the order of the day.

Right, VPN! Oh shit, I hope firing this thing up without it won't get me booted off the university network. Their home internet service was provisioned by Spectra College, necessitating their use of VPN to access just about everything they liked to do, like downloading music, shows, and games, watching porn, and other similarly productive activities. Doug's paranoia had already convinced him that his torrent search had stepped on a digital landmine, and he was certain that the university's IT administrators and their private security forces were coming for him.

The VPN software on his laptop was a short double-click away from his desktop. The icon for HyperGoose was, fittingly, a caricature of a little goose with bloodshot eyes and a creepy smile. He trusted this strange bird. The menu in the software let him choose which remote server to go to, and as far back as he could remember, they had been choosing the Netherlands Antilles.

***

"Pass me some of that," Ricky said. This was the culmination of a vision that Ricky had all the way back to before their senior year of high school. Ricky proposed they work hard all that summer and pool their money for two plane tickets to Europe, with their objective heavily driven by the plentiful and sordid activities known to transpire in this beautiful city of Amsterdam. And here they were, a year after that decision and a few years before Doug would be in his messy kitchen-side bedroom virtually seeking out David Bowie's binary existence by way of small Caribbean nation-states.

Pooling their money the previous summer had gone much as Doug had expected, in that there was a deep end that Doug filled with money and a shallow end that received occasional tithes from Ricky.

And now he was out of breath, submerged in tourist culture.

Doug passed the joint to Ricky and started exhaling. Without fully knowing what he was doing or being ready for the complexity and fullness of an expertly hand-rolled Amsterdam joint, he started coughing. The small inhale he thought he had taken had brought with it a tightly-packed cloud of THC-infused smoke, which, after revealing its true self, had exploded and expanded into a cloud more similar to what he'd seen through the scratchy offset window of their discount airline economy seats than what he could have expected to form from the burning end of that perfect paper cylinder packed with marijuana. Smoke billowed out of every opening, every orifice—his mouth, his nose, his ears. He felt pressure in his sinuses pushing on his eyes. Doug was pretty sure smoke was peeping out of his asshole as well.

What the heck was this? This was what I worked so hard for all last summer? Where the hell are we, anyway? What should we do later? I'm hungry! No, I'm not.

Doug was seriously baked. Another victim of European history, his own circular stoned logic every bit as mysterious as a more famous megalithic structure in southern England.

"I tell you man, anything goes in Amsterdam... this country is crazy!" Ricky offered up his worldly opinions. While he was wrong in thinking that Amsterdam was a country, he was correct in his observation that, indeed, anything goes. Everywhere they turned in their hazy, stuporous wanderings that afternoon, the same was confirmed. First, the map. They had no roaming data available on their not-very-smart mobile phones. This necessitated a paper city map, a puzzle that revealed an endless convolution of folds that soon became perforated tears in the fabric of their intoxicated time and space. It seemed to transport them every time they unfolded it, held it aloft like a kite, studied the twists and turns of streets and canals, disagreed about their location, and then folded it up again.

A man juggled spinning chainsaws. This was too much for two young men with one singularly focused common brain, its cells of diminished capacity. The longer they stood watching, the more likely that man would sever his arms and legs. It was a certainty that they left behind as they reopened the map-portal.

A woman and a man were trapped together, embedded into the side of a building. But only when Doug and Ricky would look from directly in front of the wall. As they moved to the side, the two performers extruded from the wall and simply remained posed in the shackles, chains, and torture paraphernalia that had seamlessly blended into the dungeon mural behind them. These shifting realities begged the travelers to move on as well.

Now inside a dim space with a brilliantly lit small stage, another woman and man were trapped together, but no longer as a static piece of art. The boys were in the front row of a sex show, and this time, "Doug, we ain't leaving til they finish," Ricky had said, and finish, they most certainly did.

***

It was that original experience in Amsterdam that would help decide the location of their VPN server some years later. Without any better reference point, their experience participating in the free lifestyle of Amsterdam had convinced them to go with the Netherlands as a logical endpoint where they assumed freedom (of musical piracy) would prevail. Yet one better than that, here was an option for the Netherlands Antilles, the former colony and present tropical mystery, which had sounded close enough. Doug theorized it might also be a good place to catch a glimpse of a famed X-Wing pilot if anyone were to open a dimensional-crossing map-portal to the Star Wars universe.

Finally establishing connection to the trusted server, which the myopic roommates imagined was powered by a generator in a sun-drenched beachside cabana, his trusted SongShare application started spitting out various options for Bowie tracks. Doug clicked on a few of them, knowing even one song might take a few minutes to download.

He flipped back to researching his project. After all, multi-tasking was what Doug continually stopped to remind himself he was great at whenever he was thinking about doing more than one or two things at the same time.

[competitive spectacle for sport]

He couldn't help but be influenced by some of the memories of Amsterdam. He literally couldn't, as ever since he had gone there, his own flight itineraries, emails, photos, and social posts had been redefining his search algorithms, constantly shuffling the invisibly iterative ranking of pages in the background cloud of his efforts.

But that doesn't explain why so much of this is in Dutch! Weird...

He scrolled through a few of the results, many conjuring more flashbacks of that trip to Amsterdam, a trip that had also taught him the important lesson that any memorable experience is better when shared.

"Yo, my man, what's good?" Ricky answered the Skype video call from his laptop.

"Hey man, looking good, put some fucking clothes on, would you?" Doug responded, commenting on his view of Ricky's bare chest, neck, nostrils, and downward-looking eyes. He had watched this show before and knew what the exposed lumber and the desk lamp held up by a bungee cable and connected to an orange hardware store extension cord indicated. Ricky was lying down on his weird bed under the stairs. The perspective of everything was skewed by a few degrees, a result of Ricky's diagonal fit in the space, with his head sort of wedged between the corner of the vertical post supporting the stairs and the unpainted peeling drywall that ran alongside.

"You know you like seeing this. All of this!" Ricky draped his hands up and down his bare torso and chest. While Doug didn't especially care for it, his life had already been exposed to more of Ricky than he ever would want to admit. Mostly, he was glad that video calling was still such poor quality that even if Ricky tried to put things in front of him that he couldn't unsee, they would remain a distorted unfocused mess.

"Never heard that before, so funny, dude. Do you have that written on the bottom of the steps so you nail the delivery of that joke every time? Cuz it's fucking hilarious."

"You know it."

"Okay, well when I'm done, you can go back to rubbing one out or whatever you were doing down there."

"Ha ha!" Ricky laughed. He loved this kind of juvenile talk.

"Ah shit, why did I go there? Just keep it off-screen!" Doug lamented being pulled into the abyss of Ricky's humor.

Doug brought his friend up to speed, "Anyway, Ricky, check this out. I was looking for some more ideas for the sports project. I looked for a bunch of stuff earlier and didn't really get anywhere, but just tried now and I started to find some stuff from our favorite place!"

"Huh? Burger King?"

"No, jeez... c'mon, man. Amsterdam!"

"Oh... damn! What'd you get? Was it like that crazy sex club we went to? Shit... there any footage of me?" Ricky was always proud to share the story of his disappearance for nearly a full twelve hours. He claimed that he went off with a few of the staff from a sex club they had stumbled into in the Red Light District. Doug wasn't sure what to believe. He sort of felt like Ricky, without the benefit of the map-portal, might have just gotten lost trying to find their hostel and slept outside somewhere.

"No, Ricky, not yet," Doug placated him. "But check this."

He shared his screen of the list of search results along with thumbnails for them to look at.

"Some quality footage here, looks like," Ricky said, his description assuming that one did not apply any maturity, decency, or production standards to their criteria.

Ghost Riding Dam Bikes was a fortunately innocuous collection of videos and photos of those classic Amsterdam bikes being held up alongside moving vehicles and set loose on some of the smaller hills and downslopes of bridges woven amongst the city's canals.

Biggest Bong Hits featured a group of five traveling stoners who had attached a large metal colander to their water bong to facilitate what looked more like a bonfire of cannabis with a glass chimney attached, connecting said fire to said stoners' lips.

"Oh shit, look, it's the guy with the chainsaws again!" Doug exclaimed as he clicked on another link, as the same wave of trepidation crashed over him, a flashback of watching the man perform live.

He continued scrolling. He saw something a bit abnormal. A listing popped up at the bottom of the page without formatted titles, just a filename. He couldn't even tell where this result was linking to as it didn't appear to be a web address, but the cryptic nature of it intrigued him. "2010-04-21 first comp TC1 uzbk dv."

Clicking the link spawned a notification on his VPN software—"connection secured"—as an .avi file began to download. AVI stood for Audio Video Interleave, which the boys did not know, and, as the boys knew, was the dominant video compression codec for the web, the format of choice for reducing complex information down to shareable file sizes.

"AVI, that means it's porn, right?" Ricky asked excitedly.

"Not sure what this is, Ricky... haven't really seen this before."

Doug found that his ability to combat and even disable Ricky's overbearing conversational skills was a lot stronger over a video call. It felt like they were more at parity and he supposed that, from Ricky's standpoint, the communication format also made him behave as a viewer. Sure, it was as a viewer of Doug, but it seemed Ricky was more obedient to a subject on a screen than when conversing in person. Doug noted that many of the archetypes he observed behaved in the same way.

This banter continued for a while. They continued their discovery into the dark underbelly of user-generated content, skewed by Doug's search terms and the hidden sorcery of Google, finding more and more things that were interesting to them, if not relevant to the assignment.

DING! The download was complete.

Acting on his curiosity, Doug furiously alt-tabbed and double-clicked on the file at the top of the list. Nothing happened. Another file appeared. He double-clicked again. He realized the application focus had shifted and something was playing, but nothing was seen or heard. He bashed the volume button a few times and then a few more times again as faint noise through the speakers became louder.

The iconic guitar of Ziggy Stardust could be heard, helping to cut through the suspense. The soft words of a classic song dispensed an air of calm.

Didn't know what time it was the lights were low

Almost on cue, the video player app on Doug's screen opened. On the other end of the call, Ricky was still lost in his thoughts, flitting between different browser windows until the flickering frames of a new video playing brought him back.

I leaned back on my radio-o-o

The screen was dark. There was faint light above wherever this camera was recording, as if it were dusk or dawn, still very dark blue with black clouds. At ground level, at some distance from the camera, a few fires were burning.

Some cat was layin' down some rock 'n' roll

A few trees lined what seemed to be a path leading down to the contained, vertically-oriented fires. Possibly barrels, but impossible to confirm.

"Are those tiki torches?" Ricky asked, his primitive mind's attention captured by the sight of fire. "Is this a beach party? Yeah...!" his volume drowning out much of Bowie's opening verse.

... weren't no DJ that was hazy cosmic jive

"Hold up. I don't know, I don't think so..." Doug responded. He was looking closely at the video, trying to determine what he was seeing. The camera perspective didn't move. It was "locked-off" as they knew from their film production course work. But it had some overlaid superimposed text: *"Apr-21 TC1 UDV"*.

Then a rustling sound came from the playback, layering in over the lyrics as they hit the delightful chorus.

There's a starrrr mannnn.... waiting in the sky

From behind the camera to the left, there was some movement. The sound of steps at a running pace could be heard, heavy shoes running over gravel with an audio layer of dry sticks that would snap with every second or third footfall.

He'd like to come and meet us

Now, from that same direction, a body quickly sprinted from behind and continued on in front of the camera, moving toward where the fires burned. As the feet moved past, a yellow overlay rectangle appeared on-screen, as if someone had marked the location of the running person with the outline of a postage stamp.

But he thinks he'd blow our minds

Bap! Bap! Bap! A series of quick, explosive noises could be heard. Gunshots.

While the footage was dark, and it was hard to make out anything identifiable about the running person, what had happened was apparent. He or she had been shot and fallen to the left side of the trail. Based on the height and perspective of the camera, it looked to be approximately twenty feet in front of their position. The yellow box that followed the runner had also stopped in place.

There's a starrrr mannnn.... waiting in the sky

More rustling could be heard behind and to the right of the camera. More running people!

He's told us not to blow it

A multitude of footfalls could be heard, getting closer. As they passed, this time from the right side, the motion jostled the camera, causing it to tilt down and to the left.

'Cause he knows it's all worthwhile

A few leaves and pebbles could be deciphered from the trail floor, but the path, the original runner, and the new runners could no longer be seen.

And he told me

The clip abruptly ended.

> *Let the children lose it*
> *Let the children use it*
> *Let all the children boogie*

Guitar solo.

Four

HOPE

Bex had again been on the move for much of the past year, displacing her far from her former life—or rather, her former lives—and all the traps and trappings entrenched within. As her sense of stability, if one could call it that, had started to strengthen, she felt renewed, reborn, and ready to take on the world from her new home in Los Angeles, much like the city itself and its many millions of resilient residents.

It had been a hard year on top of a hard life, but could she really expect anything different? Certainly, she could not ask for sympathy, not from this population only a year removed from some of the most devastating wildfires to ever hit a major modern city. The change in the amplitude of changes—of the range in extremes—seemed to offer one measure in how she might find common ground with this place. For a few winters before the one before this past one, the LA skies and street-level conversations had been surprisingly dominated by unseasonable rain and cold. Some leveraged these unexpected patterns to decry climate change, with others pointing to them as supporting evidence, all while the undrainable water washed away hillside homes and spurred the fast growth of alien brush and fire-friendly foliage. From all sides of the argument, all were in unison, running together when everything burned.

Yet in this new beginning, in this new place, she, more so than the many millions of established Southern California residents, was familiar with the palpable shift to the smells and colors of spring. Having never found it necessary until those more recent unseasonal seasons and a horrific, fiery, crash course in early 2025, all those Angelinos were still learning how to talk about the weather.

Like the few standing structures amongst the many burned-out lots where homes once stood up and down this Pacific coastline, the journey of her still-young life had woven through tragedy, offering only just enough respite to keep going, to keep running. First, growing up in Saskatchewan in the middle of the Canadian prairies, and then, after she dropped out of school and left her childhood home, the destitute conditions of living on the streets in Vancouver. The difference between those two places was stark. On the one hand, the flat, endless lands of her childhood were rural, sparse, empty, vast, cold, and lifeless. Yet after finding her way to the most temperate region of that great big country in the north, to the west coast in the dense urban setting of Vancouver, she could have used some of those same words to describe the half-decade she had spent there.

In many ways, what Bex felt now was similar to the first time she meaningfully took control of her life. That's also why it was impossible to shake the massive subcurrent of caution that was running circuits throughout her body.

On that decisive day in 2019, trauma and tragedy had been numbed by a strange sense of solace, delivered upon her in waves that started with getting on the bus at the local station with a one-way ticket in hand and not enough money in her pocket to accommodate any second thoughts of a return fare. Leaving the town of Milestone, Saskatchewan, behind her gave the very name of the place a greater meaning. The sixteen years spent growing up there had felt as if nothing had been achieved, nothing had been gained, and truly, no milestones garnered. Leaving, on the other hand, was a seminal accomplishment.

Fourteen hours later, and after a few stops along the way to pick up other western-bound travelers, the bus had covered hundreds of miles of endlessly straight roads. Another dose of relief washed over Bex. Those long, unchanging roads seemed at the same time to be infinite and to be nothing at all. By traveling along them, she continued to put distance between herself and those things she hoped never to think of again. Yet it seemed that the road was simply a long, taut string, and if someone were to pick it up and loosen it, wherever you were and wherever you came from might end up being the same. The paranoia was palpable. The string-holder was back there somewhere, and in front of her as well.

As they began to climb into the foothills of the Rocky Mountains, the ambiguity of time and space finally started to diminish. Up through the forests and hillsides they went, diesel engines powering the large bus over terrain that historically had proven such an obstacle for those traveling east to west.

"Amazing, isn't it?" a croaking voice asked from the seat behind and to the right of Bex.

She turned around, more out of surprise at the harshness of the voice and the break in silence this long into the trip than out of genuine interest to converse. In fact, she had absolutely no desire for a conversation, not the least of which was due to the difficulty in turning to face backward at an angle. A pinched nerve in her neck that she had suffered a few years prior affected any kind of asymmetrical upper body movements, with the impingement only further magnified from being constrained to her seat for over half a day.

The voice belonged to an old woman. Wispy, scraggly gray hair crept and poked out from around a brown, crocheted skullcap. Bex wasn't even sure if it was a hat, but it did reside on the woman's head. Her eyes were piercing in Bex's direction but not exactly navigating the right path, as they seemed to be fixated upon the empty chair beside her. At the same time, they were intensely focused and as murky as the air left behind after a sandstorm on the prairies.

"The mountains? Yes. I've never seen it before," Bex politely offered. Despite her gruff nature and dour perspective on the world at large, a sweet, honest, polite young girl remained inside.

"No, not the mountains. Well, indeed they are, and you should take them in."

Curiosity got the better of her. Even though the easiest thing to do, physically and conversationally, would be to simply nod and turn back, Bex found herself compelled to ask, "Okay, what's amazing?"

"Up. We keep going up from here," the response offered no more clarity.

"Right, the mountains," Bex asserted.

"No, not the mountains," came the response, threatening a recursive loop.

"I'm not sure I understand," Bex admitted, confused.

"You will. Yes, that is for certain. You will," the old woman countered.

"Hmm, okay, thanks," Bex politely replied, now more certain that this old lady was crazy at best and likely senile. The old woman, on the other hand, was now seemingly convinced that she had made it all so clear for Bex that no further explanation was required. Her hearing was a far cry from what it had been in her youth, though as she had gotten older, the woman had become more and more comfortable with hearing less and less of the outside world.

Bex turned to look forward again, releasing the pressure on her pained neck, and allowed herself to peer out the window to her left, as the landscape continued to roll downhill behind her.

Hours later, after cresting the highest mountain passes amongst the Rockies, the initial descent felt like it was blocking the past off behind her. She could imagine the very highway collapsing, the mountains falling upon it and closing off any chance of retreat. Yes, she was starving, having only had a bag of potato chips from a rest stop and a cookie offered by another traveler who had intuited her hunger, but she felt more full than she had ever been.

Having left early that morning, they were chasing the sun. The bus had already jumped two time zones traveling west, and it was now getting on to about eight o'clock at night. The sun was low in the western sky, and it started hiding behind the taller mountains and cliffs as the bus kept winding down the highway with many hours remaining on the journey to the coast. Whenever the sun appeared around a turn or blasted its rays through some of the tall trees thinned out over the years from fires and logging, Bex felt it burn off more of the layers of her past.

Through mountain ranges, sweeping river valleys, forests, the semi-arid desert landscape of the central high desert of the province, and the twists and turns along the majestic Fraser River, her sense of belonging grew, even as she moved further and further from everything she had ever known.

It all led to Hope, the small town of that name, which served as the gateway between the mountainous highway travel and the lowlands of the coastal farming communities.

The river valleys tilting toward Hope also contributed to the city being almost constantly under a low-hanging rain cloud at this time of year.

Many have seen the town on film without realizing it. It was the shooting location for *First Blood*, the very first Rambo film featuring Sylvester Stallone, creatively set in Hope, Washington. Those wet, muddy trails and mountain slopes filled with massive cedars and Douglas firs had become a familiar place for John Rambo, the fictional Vietnam War veteran. The impenetrable terrain had provided comfort, a solitary place where he could control his own outcomes by hunting people in the woods, rather than subjecting himself to the world that had taken advantage of him, asked him to kill, taken his friends, and refused to welcome him back.

While Bex had never seen *First Blood*, she could certainly relate to many of those same feelings of loss and of a world that had betrayed her. But the oppressive mountainscape did not offer respite as it had for Rambo. The last five hours of feeling partial relief and a lightening of her mind, body, and soul seemed to be crashing around her. Questions flooded her mind, challenging whether she had made the right choice and demanding to know where she was actually going, beyond just the destination printed on her ticket. It seemed more likely that she, too, would hit a wall of mountains, mist, and cloud and be refused entry.

And then, it opened up. The skies raised up tens of thousands of feet, the lands cleared around her, and the mountains started shrinking and walking backwards, further and further away. The road became straight and true once again, and the bus continued on.

Hope remained. Though had she blinked, she may have missed it.

Five

WHAT WE CAN'T CONTROL

That bus ride was so far in the past, almost six years ago now, yet everything Bex felt was so uncomfortably familiar, in too many ways. That was all behind her, she thought, all of the tough, cold, violent life in Milestone, the wet, miserable, destitute existence in Vancouver, and her paranoid, explosive journey to southern California. She had to figure out a way to jettison those other component pieces of her life, those histories that she didn't want recorded and didn't want to remember.

Los Angeles, on the other hand, was an almost mythical place. Throughout Bex's childhood, it was simply two exotic words that she associated with glamor, fame, and celebrity. It didn't mean much more than that and didn't even seem or sound like a place where people would actually live, work, eat, and do normal things. If she had known then, as a child, what a Hollywood studio lot looked like, her vision of Los Angeles probably resembled that more than the sprawling, charcoaled, hazy urban cauldron it manifested once she arrived here.

She gazed out the window, looking out over the ocean, the infinite blue sky stretching beyond the horizon line. It was a tease, a distraction, this blue canvas holding a shiny golden false idol that was so welcoming and warm to those in worship. It was fake news that made for easy reading, especially when one was enjoying a day at the beach and didn't care to look at the blackened hills and burned out neighborhoods still waiting on clearing crews and insurance claims. Bex couldn't help but wonder just how it was that she was where she was, that she *was what she was.*

The city had been pummeled these past few years. The populace had been bruised, battered, buried, and burned, yet they kept fighting back. Everyone she met in LA was calling it the "new normal," which was pretty easy to agree with considering it had all started on the tail-end of the COVID pandemic. If anything, to Bex, it sort of just felt normal, in that the only true normality in life is that most everything is never as you would expect it to be, that all things not completely understood or controllable were usually fucked up beyond understanding. More likely than not, they would eventually turn on you.

That's really what it was. If things were meant to be, that's what they were gonna be.

Running was no longer good enough. She had repeatedly proven to herself that she couldn't escape what was predetermined to catch her, and if stopping and facing that destiny needed her to stand up and be ready to fight that good fight, then so be it. It was a decision not unlike one she had made before in a different place under very different skies.

***

The rain was insufferable. The clouds above had not ceased to deliver heavy, thick precipitation for days on end. The roads were littered with potholes created by the massive amounts of water eroding at their base materials. In the same way, street life in Vancouver was hard. It weighed heavily on everyone in that situation, all the while tearing away at their base, stealing their pride, and casting a shadow around them that prevented passersby from offering any benevolence.

For a few weeks now, Bex had been set up in a tent underneath an overpass in the east side of the city. She had a small area of grass, a triangular section of real estate between an onramp and a connecting side street. Freight trains and overpass traffic were just about the only things that would cut through the heavy, wet air, with the mechanical sound of engines, brakes, and metal smashing into metal composing the soundtrack of her days.

The tent was a mass-produced "4-man" designation, Made in China and well-used in Canada. In its younger, stronger days, she could imagine it would have traveled around in the back of a family's SUV, unfolding and erecting at beautifully manicured campsites across Western North America. This tent had probably seen some of the biggest mountains, deepest forests, bluest crater lakes, and most beautiful Northern Pacific beaches. It would have protected families from the elements while they sat inside under candlelight—or more likely lithium-powered LED candle lamps—while they poured through books, played Monopoly or crib, and bundled up in plush warm sleeping bags.

Drip. Drip. Drip.

The leak in the roadside corner was usually out of reach from the rain. Bex had taped it up with that bright red Tuck Tape. In fact, a healthy percentage of the tent's material had been usurped by Tuck Tape ever since she was lucky enough to find a box of it in the back of a builder's truck. Similarly, her boots had become red over time, first from the blood from open cuts and blisters on her feet and later from a similar adornment of that same tape, which, when layered the right way, would provide a very strong waterproofing treatment.

In fact, that tape had such a commanding grip over everything it touched that whenever Bex used it, she could feel it cleaning the dirt and crud from her hands and fingers. Whatever it attached itself to, it pulled the facade away and revealed what was originally there. Careful to apply it to things she was fixing, like her tent or her clothes, she was more liberal in how she handled it, as the satisfaction of shedding a previous veneer from her own hands or body—an old skin—allowed her to envision a restart, a clean beginning, every time she did it.

Drip. Drip. Drip. Drip.

It was like clockwork. She had determined the tent had achieved "max drip" as it couldn't possibly be raining harder, and the ingress of water surely was flowing as strong as it might. The problem was, with the placement of the tent on a slope next to the overpass, that top-side drip would course its way right through the middle of her otherwise habitable space, soaking everything in its path.

What little she had to her name—her clothes, a few books, a small wallet that she carried with her identification—was all in that tent and, like her, waged a constant battle against the rain.

She zipped open the door to her home and stepped outside. Her feet were immediately challenged by the once grassy surface. It attempted to pull her down the slope. Zipping up the tent behind her, she began carefully stepping around its flailing canvas walls. Bex moved in the direction of where the side street below met up with the onramp above, as there was a large streetlight that at least offered a semblance of visibility. The intensity of the rain combined with the darkness of mud, concrete, and metal railings created a surreal effect, almost as if she were underwater, walking the ocean floor through reefs made of forgotten artifacts of humanity.

Through the fluid drone of water, she could hear someone yelling from just above on the small sidewalk that adjoined the onramp and overpass.

"Stop! Stop it! Leave me alone!"

It sounded like someone needed help. If Bex had learned one thing in life, it was that help is never offered. It was something one had to find, or create, for oneself.

Her next actions started out of self-interest and self-preservation, not out of any motivation to intervene. She moved uphill from her tent, closer to the end of her triangular plot of land where the street and onramp conjoined. She was still downhill from the goings-on but could now better interpret what was happening.

"Why are you doing this? I don't even know you..." the screaming man was saying. He was entangled with another person, a woman. In the rainy darkness, it was hard to see what was happening—just a mess of dark clothes and arms. As they turned, a glint of metal reflected in the light from the lonely streetlamp above.

She could now make out that the man was trying to reach for the woman's right arm, in which she held a knife. He had one hand tightly gripping the arm of her jacket and was trying to get his other hand involved. In turn, the woman—the attacker—was holding back his second arm. Currently, a stalemate.

Bex had seen this before. The roles were different, but the actions and outcomes the same. She started to step closer, now on the sidewalk just a few feet from them. At this point, curiosity was no longer leading her, nor was reason, nor did she have any clear thought as to what she was doing or why she was getting this close. It was as if her being here in this submerged aftermath of humanity, with these battling strangers, was not real and was not now. The victim and the attacker were versions of her and those who had hurt her so many times before.

They were a twelve-year-old with an alcoholic father who couldn't help and a drug-addled mother who could only hurt.

They were a group of kids just a few years older who wouldn't hesitate to make your bad experiences become your worst ones.

They were the teachers and adults who refused to help and would turn away.

Her intense and wandering thoughts were jarred. She could see another figure running toward them on the sidewalk, a larger man dressed in black. He, too, carried something in his hand, a long black bar of some kind. As he got closer, Bex could see that the entire left side of his body, the side facing the road, was encased in mud and grime. More than just being drenched from the rain, something had happened to slow him down. This must have been a chase. A strip mall, gas station, and a pub were at the intersection on the other side of the overpass. It must have started there.

But who? Two men, chasing one woman, and now she was fighting back?

Despite her inclination to think so from personal experience, it didn't fit. The woman was attacking the man whom she was locked in arms with. *Was the second man coming to help the first man?* That didn't fit either. It didn't seem plausible that the woman would have subdued one, let alone both.

The first man also seemed out of place. Here Bex was, drenched in the rain, holding a small piece of vivisected innertube and the aforementioned Tuck Tape to fix a broken tent that she called her home. Wet and dirty herself, the scuffling woman did not look as if the situation materially altered her. Her clothes were well worn, and the rain looked more likely to wash them than spoil them. The man running to join them, face hidden behind a long beard with a hole in the upper portion of it through which a maniacal scream—almost a warcry—escaped, seemed in his element. He was wild, an animal pulled from the furthest reaches of the natural world and placed here in a polluted concrete jungle where the rain sought to wash it all away and return it to its—to his—desired state. Indeed, it was the first man who was alone. As Bex continued to take it all in, the man's collared shirt, the black designer jacket, and the leather shoes made his isolation even more apparent.

The second man was almost upon them. Bex couldn't even tell if he had yet seen her. She knew the other two were so locked in battle with each other, groping for hands, for clothing, that they had not even been aware of her standing where she was, transfixed by their fight from only a few feet away.

Lights! Headlights appeared out of nowhere, cresting the curvature of the overpass. Traffic hadn't been very busy that night, and with the time now well after midnight and the weather this poor, it stood to reason that there were so few cars on the road.

Bright LED headlights tapered toward the middle of the car's hood. They were watchful eyes out of the dark. Bluish and cold, the lights exposed everything and everyone, for just a second.

The combatants were equally surprised. They both looked up at the car, still locked in a deadly grasp over the weapon in the woman's hand.

In that instant, Bex's subconscious acted. Whether it was her fear that being seen would involuntarily enlist her into the fight or triggered by a gut reaction spurred on by past injustices to her life and liberty, she would never know. Everything that followed happened so quickly as to be beyond an accurate recollection of events by anyone present.

She screamed. A noise, something between a high-pressure machine release valve blowing its top and the effortful grunting sound a tennis player makes when delivering a powerful groundstroke, emanated from her.

The world was erupting around the man and the woman. First, those lights had caught them by surprise. Both had looked back down the street from where they came, holding each other's arms, yet their weird and awful choreography would not stop for that. In doing so, the two of them caught sight of the second man in full sprint toward them. A wry smile appeared on the woman's face, countered by a fallen expression from her dance partner. But then, this otherworldly scream erupted from just behind them both!

As they turned, Bex had already lunged forward. She jumped, kicked, and threw all parts of her body into the coupled fighters. The combination of Bex's unplanned ferocity and the imbalance of her targets caused them both to bounce away from her. She was a momentary bowling ball, and they were the 6-10 split picked up by a right-handed bowler with a mean curve.

The woman flew backwards and to the side of the road, falling hard against the sidewalk railing. Her torso and head were bent over the railing for a moment, and as she collected herself, she was staring down upon an old tent propped against the underside of the overpass. Rain and dirt dripped off her nose and fell toward that canvas structure, nearly missing the closest part of it, which, unbeknownst to this aggressive woman, still had a leak.

A moment of calm swept over the man. In one instant, he was fighting for his life, and now, here was a savior—a stranger out of the dark, unexpected, who had intervened and separated him from his foe. Why they had attacked, he had no idea. Just thirty minutes before this, he had been at the pub with his friends.

***

"Damn, Trav, that was a heck of a performance. Your fingers are like magic!" the man in the collared shirt, black designer jacket, and leather shoes had told his friend Travis.

"Thank you, sir. I do what I can!" Travis replied.

"Well, here's to more like this," the man held up his drink for the other five guys around the table to toast their friend's success. Travis Mathers had played guitar as a hobby all his adult life, but always by himself. It was a nice distraction from his work and helped him find a sense of balance. He played by himself through the various periods of economic turmoil in 2000, 2007, and 2016. He navigated the events post-9/11 and the fluctuating political landscapes in North America by taking solace from his solo unattended performances. And through the almost daily news of mass shootings, the Highway of Tears, protests and riots, and the deplorable misogynistic behavior of many, far more famous, musicians, he kept on keeping on, playing his guitar by himself. And he'd be damned, when COVID hit, he just doubled down on what he'd always relied upon for salvation. Finally, once the world had opened up, even while people were closing themselves off even more, he thought it was the right time to play music for others, and with others. *Free Age Ants* was the name of the band, a play on words that had come into existence of its own accord one day when Louis asked how Travis had assembled his bandmates, all of them similarly longstanding solo artists.

"Free agents," Travis had said in response while strumming his guitar, the cadence of which had him break up his syllables and prompted Louis to closely echo, "*Free Age Ants*? That's fucking cool, man, like little hippie peons, I get it."

They'd been playing for a couple of years now since pubs and restaurants had begun to operate with no pandemic restrictions. Initially, the venues were desperate for acts that would show up to nearly empty crowds for the promise of a miniscule payday. That was the perfect formula for Travis and his bandmates—low pressure and even lower expectations. But over the course of a few dozen performances, the crowds picked up, the chemistry of the band caught up with their energy, and the shows were being raved about.

And that's what brought them to this pub tonight.

"Cheers!" were stated in unison by the group—Travis, his three bandmates, and the traveling fan club, which consisted of the black jacket man—Louis—and their friend Iqbal.

As most everyone knew, raising a glass in a toast brought with it several requirements. Look the other toastees in the eyes, one by one. Hold the glass up while doing so, and make sure to establish eye contact before moving on. In some customs, a slight nod is to be expected, but that would be excused if the eye contact and acceptable time spent gawking were observed. This group was well accustomed to it, and as a result, their mutual *cheers* would often take a few minutes.

To an observer, it might look like a table surrounded by human-chicken hybrids. Human in that they were sitting on chairs, wearing clothes, and holding glasses of consumable liquid in front of them. Chicken in that their heads were pivoting and darting around from one direction to the next, holding their bearing for a moment and pecking down to the ground in a robotic motion before lifting and pivoting elsewhere.

Critically important to finishing the ceremonial toast, a drink must be imbibed before breaking the last mutual eye contact connection. In a more amateurish operation or an odd-numbered group of human-chickens, someone would often be left out. An even-numbered group with experience such as this one would result in matched pairs of heads, each of two pairs of connected eyes, and none left wanting.

"I'm gonna step outside, fellas," Louis said after finishing his perfectly executed post-staredown gulp.

The others knew what this meant. Louis and his cigarettes.

"Lou, when is this gonna end, man? Everyone else stopped this shit when they started making bread at home... what's it gonna take for you?" Iqbal was always the first to jump on Louis for his habits. His theory was that the COVID pandemic delivered the knockout blow to smoking, as without an office to go to, there was no need to have a smoke break. He was often quick to blame Louis' obsession with trading crypto for maintaining his addiction to nicotine. Iqbal surmised that when at home, Louis needed smoke breaks from his round-the-clock crypto trading, and conversely, in social settings Louis needed the same excuse for the opposite reason: to get away from others and put in a few minutes of trading on his phone.

Iqbal's contention on smoking's broader demise was a little misguided and heavily influenced by his membership in the upper-middle-class of society, where "work from home" became a de facto standard. His isolation at home served to remove him even further from those who still had a location-based job from which to take smoke breaks, like those in frontline emergency work or essential services industries, as well as those many other needy souls who no longer had the job-part to get in the way of the smoke-break-part and started smoking a hell of a lot more in response.

His assessment of Louis' smoking was much more correct and insightful.

Louis stepped outside, remarking the heavy rain would make it hard to light his smoke. There was a covered area in the strip mall just on the other side of the parking lot, a trail of cigarette butts illuminated by the flickering streetlights above indicating he wouldn't be the first to be drawn there by his habit.

Bitcoin had been on a downswing of late, though it had remained more stable than most of his holdings. The past year or so, any time spent reviewing his crypto portfolio had necessitated a lot of smoking. He would gladly burn anything he could to warm up the crypto winter that had settled upon him and his kind.

Louis had always enjoyed speculating on new investment opportunities, yet his timing had never manifested in a huge financial windfall. His payoff had come in smaller wins and in the incessant maelstrom of emotions, spurred on by the round-the-clock fluctuation of "trading pairs"—the shorthand for being able to shift one's holdings from one cryptocurrency, such as Ethereum (ETH), for another, perhaps Golem (GLM), in this example.

Louis had been in and out of positions on both tokens over the last few years. Each had caught his eye as representatives of a decentralized vision for technology. The blockchain supporting ETH had extolled the potential of enabling smart contracts for anything and everything, of defining the provenance of a thing, with an essentially immutable record of ownership, only updated to reflect the conveyance of that thing from one owner to a new owner. He could imagine the possibilities of using this technology for property deeds, insurance, and even the gold fillings in his mouth. But for the time being, people like him wanted to buy and sell it, "it" being records on that blockchain, and it was making people rich.

GLM had garnered some attention, and Louis' specifically, as it promised a way of ensuring access to distributed computation. Perhaps best thought of as a library of computational power, whereby a blockchain transaction might enable anyone to "sign out" and borrow said computing resources. No doubt it was this idealistically fantastic democracy of enhancing the world's access to intelligence that encouraged people to openly trade GLM tokens for, as an example, invisible meme coins commemorating arbitrary species of smiling dogs.

Louis knew that with crypto trading done right, one could soak up profits and make themselves rich beyond belief well before any of these technology visions need come to fruition. You just needed to know where the "new money" was flowing in.

After all, there's a sucker born every minute.

He noticed a dip over the last few minutes in the price of GLM and snapped up over five thousand dollars worth with the swipe of his thumb, taking a deep inhale of his damp smoke as he did so.

Louis absent-mindedly swiped over to his NFT library.

Can't believe I bought this stuff, he thought, as he looked upon the caricature drawings of some of his favorite *Fastnite* contestants from the popular arena-battle reality show of the same name. Most of these hadn't cost him more than a quarter-ETH, or close to five hundred dollars at the time. Still, he felt an air of regret every time he looked upon the prized possession in his collection, a "limited edition Big Mr. Z" that showed a sketch of a massive shirtless man holding a dead bird in each hand, his fingers squeezed tight around their necks. This one had cost him nearly twenty thousand dollars when he bought it over two years ago, on September

16, 2022, with the exact time stamp of his expenditure memorialized for eternity on the blockchain.

Those things were going up by the minute back then. It's got to come around again. It's got to.

Louis often reminded himself that crypto markets had seen this before, and he just needed another wave of uncertainty to push through society, floating more of those loose, speculative investment dollars to the surface.

He closed the app, rain now blowing sideways into his cover and making it harder to trade crypto with certainty. Louis placed the phone in his dry front pocket and took another long drag of his cigarette.

"Hey, got a smoke?" a female voice asked.

He looked over toward the darker area of the strip mall, and a woman stepped into the oddly purple-hued light he had been in reach of. "Sure, here," he said, offering the pack of cigarettes fully opened in her direction.

"Thank you," a voice said. But it wasn't the woman's. A large figure with a long beard had assembled out of the shadows, his claw-like hands closing on the pack of cigarettes. Louis could feel the roughness of the man's large fingers as he conveyed the smokes from Louis' possession. Had it not been for the surprise and fear instilled by this couple, the active trader may have thought of this as another viable use case for blockchain transactions.

Louis was stunned. The man and woman stood before him, scanning him up and down with their eyes, their fingers and fists not far behind.

"Nice jacket," the man said.

Louis turned to run. The woman reached out and grabbed hold of the open right side of his jacket, causing him to spin and pull her with him. As he broke free of her grip, she slid into the big man with the beard, who, like the cumulative demand for crypto, slipped and fell. Louis was now facing toward the intersection, with the man and the woman temporarily slowed but directly between him and the pub. No one else was nearby, and the rain and occasional fast-moving traffic would only drown out any noise he could make. He ran for the intersection.

Six

CARNAGE

This other woman had come out of nowhere, not dissimilar from how he had met the other two strangers. But she was on his side, this hero from the shadows.

Louis had fallen in the opposite direction from his female assailant. He took two dizzy steps up the slope of the sidewalk and then one step back away from the guardrails. That step landed right on the edge of the curb.

One moment ago, his only thought was that this was over, that he had been saved by this third stranger. In the next breath, he was brought back to the situation. This being an industrial vehicle route, the drop down to the asphalt was much higher than he expected. His left foot failed to gain purchase on the sidewalk, twisted, and slipped off.

With a crunching sound, his ankle collapsed in the gutter of the road.

"Fuuuuck!" he screamed.

His right foot was still handsomely dressed in a leather shoe and firmly placed on the sidewalk. The incompatibility of this situation could not be overcome. Louis started to fall. The only thing going through his mind now was that he'd be unable to run, or even stand.

Could this stranger save me again? Was it one person, or more? Did the boys at the pub notice I'm missing yet? Would they come in time?

He kept falling sideways, but the height of his right foot was causing his body to turn. Louis realized that if he didn't act fast, the rotation would initiate a whiplash action through his body, risking him striking the back of his head on the asphalt. Despite the pain in his left foot, he over-rotated to his side and managed to get both hands up in a crash position on the sides of his head.

It didn't matter.

The headlights that had sparked the last few seconds of events belonged to a dark sedan traveling in the lane closest to the sidewalk. The arched shape of the road, the rain, and the poor lighting conditions made it just about impossible for the driver to react.

As Louis rotated to the right, he took in his last sights—those same headlights connected by a chrome grill, a Nissan logo right in the middle, running lights below, and two dark spinning orbs between this large Newtonian object and the road onto which he was falling. But he wouldn't even make it that far.

The vehicle, now with brakes fully activated and the driver ratcheting the steering wheel in avoidance, shifted its orientation ever so slightly to the left. This resulted in an off-center collision between the right side of the vehicle's grill and Louis' head. He was killed instantly, his face at first receiving an immediate engraving of horizontal lines reminiscent of the chrome grill bars just to the side of the Nissan logo before being obliterated by the momentum of the vehicle. His pulverized upper half then snapped back, allowing his entire body to be smashed by the corner of the car, with the lifeless corpse launched up and to the right side of the road, coming to rest on the downslope toward the lower onramp road. A golfer such as Louis would call that type of strike a fade, and when done so with a club and a ball in the confines of a course, he would eagerly take credit for it on a dogleg hole to the right.

There would be no such claim nor credit received today.

The other three had somehow escaped this carnage. Each of them shaken and shocked, but in their own ways, it perversely and universally felt like the kind of thing they had come to accept in their lives. Bex, still coming to terms with her instinctual interjection into the fight, had not yet even contemplated the resulting outcome of her action to separate the man from his attacker.

The running man had been winding up his weapon, the long black bar that he had carried, as he was advancing toward Louis. In the same moment he had taken a Ruthian swing for the fences, Louis had half-stepped that fateful half-step with his left foot. As he fell and the car advanced, the running man, who was now a swinging man and soon to become a missing man, had swung and missed the man who was no longer standing.

The attackers had now failed on at least two attempts to harm the now-dead Louis. Not that it was helpful for Louis by this point. Their sights shifted to Bex.

"Who... who are you?" the unknown woman asked. She was surprised by Bex's appearance and confused over the finality of what had just happened. The intensity of the carnage did not bother her so much as this strange girl who had disrupted their efforts at taking what was rightfully theirs. Her mind was instantly dwelling on how hard it would be to pick through the pieces of the dead body and find things of value. She had seen him using an expensive phone outside of the pub.

I bet that thing is smashed up and long gone now... dammit. She looked to her partner. *Glad he got the smokes already.*

"I... dunno... what..." Bex was stammering. It's not like she actually wanted to intervene, nor did she really care about what was going on between the woman, the formerly running man, and the formerly living man. *I sure as hell didn't want him to die! How the hell does that happen? Oh my god...*

"You're gonna pay for this, bitch. You do not fuck with my shit!" the other woman was yelling now. She had determined that her space had been invaded, and payment was due.

She punched Bex in the face. Not a very well-thrown blow, but it still hit Bex in the nose and glanced off her cheek, stunning her. She took a swing in retaliation, but the woman had already dodged to the side. Bex lost her balance and fell forward to the railing.

The woman pivoted to where she was now standing behind Bex and slammed both hands into the vulnerable lower back that presented itself. Bex felt her midsection and pelvic area mash up against the guardrail. Hard metal slammed against the pointy bones along the front of her hips.

By now, the woman's partner had recovered from his strikeout. He took two more big steps and slammed the weight of his frame into Bex. Crushing pain infiltrated all parts of her body as she was forced hard against the unforgiving guardrail. Her head shot back as if being rear-ended, and her torso went forward.

Weightlessness. She flipped over the railing, head first and pointing down, her legs catapulting up and then over. She rolled to one side in mid-flight, seeing the ground, the side street, and then the black cloudy sky above. The silhouette of two heads looking over the railing hovered above her as she lost all sense of verticality. Rain hit all of her, like going through a car wash without the fluffy brushes and colorful wax.

Time had chosen to offer parallel tracks, minutes of activity that were being consumed in fractions of seconds as she floated, hardly falling. Until she crashed, landing on her back and directly on top of a tent held together by zap straps and Tuck Tape, which she knew to be a very reliable product. The tent material ripped apart at the seams, poles snapped, and she felt the hard but somewhat forgiving thud afforded by her worldly possessions on top of a subfloor of mud and grass. Air was forced from her lungs, and her arms and legs splayed out, wrapped and covered by a crumpled heap of fabric and fiberglass. Pain shot into her back, an offset to the pelvic frontal bruising she had experienced from the woman's attack before her fall.

Everything went dark.

In that same infinite moment of Bex's weightless journey home, there was yet more to unfold on the cold, wet road surface above.

The Nissan sedan had veered hard left after it had disintegrated, destroyed, and launched Louis' head, torso, and body, respectively. The vehicle started hydroplaning on the downslope of the overpass as the high-quality engineering of its anti-lock braking system failed in its duty. The slide, however, likely prevented the driver from being seriously injured.

By the time it came to a stop, it was perpendicular to the two lanes of traffic, having left over one hundred feet of damage along the meridian fencing that separated the two eastbound lanes from its dark, drenched, barren siblings going the other way.

The driver, an older Asian man, was disoriented but unharmed. He wasn't even sure what had happened, but felt like he avoided whatever had fallen into his lane, trading it for violent contact with the concrete divider in the middle of the road. In retrospect, he had closed his eyes to allow for this version of events. He could imagine the front end of his car was damaged, but he wasn't yet sure whether it was drivable or not.

Looking to his left, back up the road, he could see two figures on the sidewalk who seemed to be looking over the guardrail. *Oh my god, there were people there. What happened?*

"Hey! You! Is everything okay?" he had now gotten out of the Nissan and was walking back to the two people, waving his hands and yelling for their attention. He still had no idea the severity of the accident, but given the conditions of the night, he wanted to be sure before checking his car or calling for help.

The man and the woman turned to face him. What for them had started as a simple shakedown of a deserving target had now compounded into something much more than that. The two attackers had failed in their initial plan but perhaps had redeemed their efforts by dispatching the strange woman who ambushed them. Whatever this man in the car had seen or understood to have occurred was more than he was allowed to know.

As the driver walked closer to them, he held his hand above his eyes as a shield from the rain, striving for a better view through the limited light available from the overhead streetlamp.

Everything was bathed in purple. This was a result of a failed supply-sourcing contract by the city a few years earlier. An initial upgrade plan to LED lighting for all major roads had promised significant replacement and energy cost savings. What hadn't been factored into this upgrade were the failures in production quality at General Innovations Lighting, the manufacturer behind the sourcing deal. Thousands of lighting units shipped around the world had begun to suffer from a delaminating phosphor coating on the light fixture despite recently implementing factory floor gamification. Workers had been given an extra boost of 3.6 star-points per coating applied within the top ten percentile of completion time, and if they met the daily threshold of 260 star-points amongst their work group, they would still be allowed to have their usual Friday pizza parties. Production volumes were up, everyone was having pizza, yet even the brightest managers at GIL had been in the dark about these production issues.

"We need help!" the bearded attacker called out.

"What's wrong? Are you hurt?" asked the driver. It would have led to a very different answer if he had asked the question a few seconds later. The problem, however, is that a question needs someone to ask it, and an answer needs someone to reply, and neither would be imminently available.

***

Somaya Patel had landed at YVR, Vancouver International Airport, late that same evening. Her plane had been "wheels down" around the same time Travis and *Free Age Ants* had started playing. After another exhausting business trip, she had elected to fly home that day rather than stay any longer. São Paulo was, at best, a full day of travel, provided the itinerary routed the layover stop in Houston. If the flight needed to go through Mexico City or, god forbid, anything on the East Coast of North America, it quickly became a multi-day trip and a week of jet lag. As the CEO of Computer Vision Infosystems, Somaya had been requested by their biggest customer, the state electrical agency in Brazil, to visit and provide an update on their recent product advancements.

Experience had taught Somaya that being fleet of foot at this time was important. International flights coming into YVR were confidently managed through a compendium of people, processes, and technologies. After all, the airport was routinely awarded "best airport in the world" or something to that effect. Somaya had shared that anecdote often with her colleagues around the world, which inevitably led to discussions as to what makes a great airport and who exactly is out there doing all the airport judging.

Whoever those people are, they must fly even more than me, so credit to them, Somaya often thought.

Given the choice, she would have taken a video call over a flight every single time. After the pandemic broke out, the global white-collar move to virtualization meant that her work and life fit just about perfectly into a formula of how she liked to operate. Somaya was an effective leader, but despite making a point of ensuring she was available for her customers and staff more often than not, underneath it all, she disliked wasting time with people. Small talk and wasteful meetings were the bane of her professional existence. If you caught her on a weekend or a holiday, often spent at her family's estate in the outdoor resort town of Whistler, contemplative silence was one of her preferred activities.

In this, the world's best airport, she knew it came down to a footrace. Those who knew, knew that your seat selection on flights to YVR should be primarily concerned with getting as close to the front as possible. Somaya, fortunately, was in business class, placing her in Row 3 and starting position number seven in the middle-distance event that was just about to begin.

The aircraft taxied into the arrival gate. With her backpack draped on one shoulder and positioned just so to sling around and catch the other shoulder in stride and the small carry-on she relied upon placed on the floor in front of her, leaning against her leg with its handle in her grip, Somaya was ready.

The aircraft door opened, and they were off. Slightly up and straight through the gangway. Veering right, then left, and then straight through the boarding gate. Into the carpeted node of the US departures hub. A long stretch past the boarding gates, with a floor-to-ceiling bulletproof glass wall separating her from those few poor souls taking the late flights out that evening. Escalators to an elevated walkway, soon conjoining and merging with one, two, four, and eight more of the same type of walkways. She darted ahead just in front of arrivals coming in from Denver. She was fast but wasn't running.

Somaya knew if you sprinted, you would tire and quickly fall off the pace. There were still a few hundred meters to cover, and she needed to maintain cruising speed. The Denver arrivals poured in from their tributary walkway into the central elevated corridor, a mass of humanity throttled by the limited size of its initial walled-in space, then exploding as it reached the main thoroughfare—reams and reams of rolling luggage attached to people spilling over and contaminating the uncovered carpet much as a virus invades a host organism, through its weakest, most accessible spaces.

Finally, she came to the end of this initial contest, a champion of the first leg. Staring down, she now towered over endlessly flowing streams of pinstriped heavy metal cubes—the escalators down to the Canada Customs hall. Looking across the first valley below to the peak on the other side, her heart skipped a beat.

China!

The incoming Cathay Pacific flight from Hong Kong must have just landed. Predominantly Chinese passengers had just arrived at the top of the escalators across from her. The two spaces were symmetrical in every way except that she was alone on her side, having left the Houston and Denver-origin travelers in her wake, whereas an almost endlessly streaming population of Cathay Pacificers started descending the opposing moving stairs.

Two at a time, I can do this, she thought to herself about navigating the large toothy metal steps of the escalator. Down to the mezzanine concourse. *One more escalator flight to go.* Throwing caution to the wind, she pushed her tired legs to engage this final descent. To her luck, all the Cathay travelers had elected to take the escalator on their side of the mezzanine, with none of them stepping out of line or taking the extra three steps to use what was now Somaya's private powered staircase. *And just like that... humans keep their heads down and get in line.*

She would often remark on the insanity of people to just do what they were told, or in the absence of instruction, to follow what others were told to do, until it simply becomes what they do without having been told to do it. Her ruminations were notably similar to those of an awkward college kid across the continent watching cheese-wheel races on the internet over a decade before this moment.

"Where are you coming from today?" the customs official asked. He was a young, cleanly-shaven Caucasian. She could tell he had an athletic build even through his collared uniform and V-neck navy blue sweater.

"Houston," she answered, not wanting to offer anything else up. Somaya had learned through trial and error that in these situations, you answer just the question and nothing more.

"Purpose of your visit?" he asked.

"Sales meetings." She knew that sales activities were easy to defend, whereas a more generic response such as "business" risked the conversation detouring into imports, duties, and whatever else the handsome ignorant man in the V-neck sweater might think she had been doing.

He looked down at her passport, up at her face, and then down at her body, as if trying to ascertain what kind of shapes and curves were hidden underneath her somewhat crumpled suit jacket. Then back to her eyes, he had an expressionless grin. She flashed an ever so subtle smile, mouth just slightly open. Despite the dehydration of traveling for the better part of twenty hours, her lips were still as moist and fulsome as they always were. She knew they were a secret weapon, and, as expected, his eyes beamed.

The border agent's defenses were overcome. He looked back down at the passport, closed it, and handed it to her.

"Have a nice night, ma'am," he said with a friendly smile this time.

I would fuck your brains out if I had the time to take you with me and the energy to do it, her internal voice replied. Her external voice said, "Uh uh."

She took the passport, placed it inside her pocket, and moved quickly through the baggage claim area and out the doors to the parkade.

Halfway home in her Tesla Model Y, Somaya felt the waves of exhaustion wash over her. The rain outside reminded her of where she was. Looking out the driver's side window of the car, she could see one of the larger, newer towers that had gone up in this part of the city. The penthouse had a glass-bottomed pool. Every time she drove by, she looked at that pool, and not once had she seen anyone in it. She was sure she had met the owner of the penthouse before but couldn't recall where or when. A property developer, she was certain.

In a tired and dreamy state, her thoughts drifted. The car kept moving along on autopilot. Somaya had come to rely heavily on the self-driving technology in this car and automation in general. Given her company was a market leader in computer vision systems, it felt like the right thing to do, even with the general skepticism and distrust she had developed for most of these other technology companies and, of course, their founders.

She imagined being in that pool, relaxing and floating. She blinked. She could see the face of the border agent. She could see him standing with her. *Where were they? Oh, the pool.* They were both naked, standing in the shallow end of the pool. He picked her up, brought her to the edge.

Her right hand had unzipped her trousers. She was touching herself. Her car drove on, and her fingers kept moving as well. Her vagina had taken on the same sensual properties that her mouth had leveraged to its owner's advantage at the airport. She was moist, her lower parts sensually writhing around in her seat. Somaya's knees were slightly bent, and her legs pressed against both sides of the driver's cockpit walls. In the pool, they were wrapped around the border guard, her heels in the backs of his thighs. In that moment, she was wishing for a larger car, among other things. Maybe a Model X. Somaya smiled. Her thoughts had just taken her someplace else

completely, and she liked it. She leaned her head back, knowing this stretch
of road was long, dark, and straight.

***

"What's wrong? Are you hurt?" the driver of the Nissan shouted at the
two figures obfuscated by the rain and the overwhelming aura of purple
light.

"Yeah," the man let out a guttural noise in the affirmative. It was his
finest acting, the blatant fibbery lost amongst the terrible conditions. In
truth, the man had only suffered wounds to his pride.

At first glance, he had considered the Nissan driver a necessary victim,
given what had transpired. In a matter of a second or two, he had crafted
a bigger rationalization. This driver, an Asian guy wearing glasses, coming
from the nice, shiny car in his clean sweater, just deserved to die. Whatever
he had, he had surely taken from others. And in the moment, he had taken
a kill that the man had decided should have been his. Whether he even
would have killed Louis in the first place is doubtful, as they had only ever
wanted to steal from him. But the situation had escalated, and so had the
man's dark intentions.

As the Nissan driver came closer, his expression changed. The assaulting
man realized that the Asian man realized that he was not looking at someone
who needed help, but rather someone who needed no help nor was intending
to offer any.

In response to this, the metal pipe realized itself out of the attacker's
sleeve and into his hand. He grabbed it with both hands and started his
clockwise backswing. *There would be no mistake this time.*

The Asian man lifted his hands in a defensive posture. He couldn't tell
what exactly was happening or what was coming, but he knew it was bad.

Somaya was coming. The car's motion at speed was only adding to the
physical sensations coursing through her body. She bit her lip, pulled her
hands out of her pants, and with wet, warmed fingers, she braced against
the sidewalls of the door and the console that cocooned her seat. Her body
pushed down into her seat, and the car pushed up as it went over a shorter,
raised overpass. She moaned and looked up.

The internal sensors of the Tesla had been tracking the road for most of the drive, with the vehicle doing much of the heavy lifting for the last few enjoyable minutes. As the car poured over the summit of the overpass and Somaya achieved her own sensory peak, almost a dozen external cameras were hard at work, scanning the exterior of the car and fueling decisions made by the self-driving AI systems to ensure the car maintained a safe heading.

These systems had been trained with millions upon millions of miles of driving telemetry and dashcam footage interrogated by computer vision. Furthermore, there had been an enormous undertaking at numerous machine learning labs around the world to simulate additional telemetry and real-world traffic behavior. Still, many challenges remained in being unable to predict the multitude of possibilities of what could happen on the road and what was happening at any given time in the driver's seat of other vehicles. Both of those issues were at play in this case, Somaya perhaps more at play than the driver of the crashed Nissan.

This car, the 2025 Model Y, finally could take in the entirety of the scene in front of it. Systems were crushing algorithms at blistering speeds. The logic processors in the car were running hot. *What could it see? Two lanes going east. Or was it four? Marks on the road were unclear. Extrapolating the computer vision image with map data should confirm two lines. What was that third road? A black Nissan facing south. Or was it north? Check the vehicle silhouette. Too many lines, too much rain. Poor light spectrum. Turn right or left to avoid the Nissan? Human silhouettes, or are they? Yes, a woman on the sidewalk, now looking at the Tesla, that was clear. Two others in the right lane, or was it one? Another shape, but with an exceptionally long arm. It didn't compute.*

As the numbers crunched, the vehicle made immediate decisions based on the statistical probabilities of different outcomes. Steering clear of the Nissan and avoiding the meridian for the safety of its driver forced it to make a hard right. But the larger mass of people—*two humans maybe?*—in the right lane forced an additional hard right, navigating toward what it had determined was a third road, the side access road below the overpass.

All this horizontal motion had captured Somaya's attention by now. Just as the autopilot AI was trying to make sense of it, so was she. She grabbed the steering wheel, the enhanced grippiness of her fingers now providing an advantage the AI did not have, and she pulled back to the left to stop the automated vessel from blasting through the guardrail and launching into the air.

In doing so, the car had lined up in a horrifically perfect bearing toward the three humans still on their feet. Somaya's car screamed as it scraped along the guardrail, pushing hard against the solid barrier just as her body and mind had done so inside the vehicle a few moments before.

First, the assaulting woman. She was quickly reduced by the car as it wiped her lower half against the heavy steel guardrail that had previously helped Bex return to her tent. The woman was killed almost immediately, thrown far to the side of the road against the chain-link fence across from the onramp.

Next, the man. Once again, he would be foiled in his attempts to swing his mighty metal stick. As he had turned to load up for another homerun attempt, his peripheral vision caught the headlights of the Model Y coming over the hill. *Not again!* The front of the Tesla hit him squarely in the left hip, immediately fracturing almost everything down that side of his body and nearly severing the man's torso from his legs. The gelatinous substance of his shattered body wrapped around and under the front of the car, forcing it to pop up ever so slightly as it dragged him toward the next obstacle.

Namely, the Nissan Driver, who, sadly, will never be known by another name. If he hadn't been bent over with his hands in the air trying to shield himself from the threat of the man's metal pipe, he might have been able to react to this new threat. Indeed, as a 2025 model year, it was extremely new. It had just been delivered to Somaya and her husband Warren a few weeks before.

It was also extremely new to the Nissan Driver, and in the half-second at the end of his life that he became acquainted with the car, it had made quite an impression. A negative one, in fact, compressing most of the front of his body as it smashed into him before he slid across the frunk, against the windshield, and up over the roof of the car.

He landed in a crumpled heap not far from where he had just been standing in his defensive posture and still relatively close to his namesake sedan, the Nissan, which still posed an obstacle for the deathly wayward electric crossover SUV.

All of this had happened so fast. Somaya's eyes darted up, down, left, then right. The car had bounced and smashed its way through this scene of carnage, swerving left, right, and left again. Going over the curve of the overpass, hitting the sidewalk, and popping up and over the bearded man had all added to the verticality of the motion. If this had all been nonviolent, the intensity and forcefulness of these moves might have taken Somaya's self-pleasure to stratospheric levels. But that was not the case; she was no longer in the mood.

With two bodies having been relocated by the front of the car and one still being dragged along by the undercarriage, it now bore down upon the Nissan, still taking up both lanes and just far enough down the road for Somaya to attempt to miss it. She pulled heavily to the right on the steering wheel and, as she did so, released the bearded man from his attachment to the bottom of the vehicle, depositing him on the road up against the same high curb Louis had also had difficulties with just a short time ago.

The car was now past the guardrail and the streetlamp and careened down where the onramp met the side street below Bex's tent.

It smashed into the far curb, colliding nearly perpendicular with it and still at considerable velocity—the black box in the vehicle would later show that the car and its occupant hit their respective peaks on the overpass at over 100 km/h—almost 70 mph—and likely launched off this curb at closer to 60 km/h. The SUV bounced up again and twisted sideways as it plowed through the chain-link fence. The fence went soft, a crosshatched metallic blanket that cushioned the vehicle but also caused it to flip into the train yard.

The Tesla rolled forward and sideways at the same time, conducting a gymnast's round-off maneuver. It landed on its passenger side and slid, bouncing over a few train tracks before finally coming to rest nearly one hundred feet beyond where the fence had recently stood tall and undisturbed. The fence was a barrier designed and erected to keep undesirable elements out and, more generally, to protect the broader public from the risks and dangers of the railyards. It had stood for over fifty years until this terrible series of events that unfolded in less than fifty seconds.

No longer standing tall, this demarcation line in front of infrastructure from the Industrial Revolution had been unceremoniously flattened and rendered immaterial by the speed, weight, momentum, and catastrophic failure of modern automation.

Seven

INCENDIARY

The package looked normal in every way. While the ubiquity of those iconic cardboard boxes delivered to nearly every doorstep nearly every day was still a few years away, Henrietta's individualistic style would often have her sourcing books, music, and artifacts from obscure locations on the web and around the world. She was, in fact, a great example of the premise of the "long tail"—a distribution concept that was historically the domain of statisticians but would become popularized by the bestselling author and accomplished entrepreneur Chris Anderson.

Anderson's work on the subject was born from his longstanding authorial roles at *The Economist* and *Wired* and came to the public's attention first as an article in the latter, and, a few years later as a book. The basic premise behind the long tail is that obscure products in low demand can collectively deliver more market share than more popular individual rivals. An example might be how thousands of relatively unknown books by thousands of unknown authors could be a stronger singular market force than any one bestseller such as, ironically enough, *The Long Tail*. This theory hinged on the removal of friction in inventory management and distribution, such that all obscure products could easily find the individuals that desired them, wherever the products and said individuals might happen to be.

The internet was exceptional at facilitating the long tail economic theory, with Amazon being the best example. Primarily operating as an online bookstore throughout its first evolution, the company had continued to expand into new categories of offerings over the past decade as its statistical understanding of consumer preferences would indicate latent demand. It was a data-driven exercise of matching long tail products with long tail buyers.

Four years earlier, just in time for the 2007 holiday season, Amazon had introduced the Kindle e-reader, of which Henrietta was at first skeptical but ultimately came to thoroughly enjoy. Now, she and her Kindle were rarely separated by any meaningful distance. Not only did it give her more immediate access to some fantastic and hard-to-find books, but she also liked that everything in the supply chain was digital. She still loved a good physical book—Henrietta truly believed that the tactile feeling of turning a page would never be replaced by technology—but the advantages to her voracious appetite for consuming information and the benefits conveyed to the environment by digital delivery were hard to argue against.

"Hen, this box is for you!" Doug bellowed as he stepped back from the front door. A courier had just delivered a package, taking Doug's signature in the process. Doug marveled at the digital terminal the delivery guy had used. It let him sign with a stylus and then confirmed with a flash of light. Doug could imagine this device working much like a tricorder from one of his all-time favorite series, *Star Trek*. Though Doug really liked *Star Trek: The Next Generation*, or "next gen" as he and his Trekkie cronies called it, his preference was for *TOS—The Original Series*. Tricorders were a staple tool in the exploratory quiver of any self-respecting Starfleet officer or disposable redshirted ensign. A timeless device from the future, it would quickly and continuously analyze the world around its holder, reporting back on any chemicals, structures, and lifeforms. Fascinated by this concept and its numerous fraternal fantastical literary creations, Doug was awestruck by the creator of the show, Gene Roddenberry, and his writers, who had come up with these ideas for mobile communication, video calling, spatial analysis, and other wondrous inventions. At the time of their imaginative inception—in the 1960s—none of them would have had foundation in the real world.

Life imitates art, he liked to think to himself, as it made him feel very observant and worldly.

"What is it?" she called out.

Despite her more recent commitment to literature served digitally, Henrietta still received more packages than her roommates. Certainly more than Doug, who rarely had anything—or anyone—show up at the house for him.

"Oh, it must be that new set of shading pencils I ordered." Henrietta was in the kitchen making a late lunch. She had been at the university for most of the last thirty hours, first dealing with a round of blowback on the article she had recently published, and then pulling an all-nighter trying to keep up with her coursework. When she finally got home, she was starving and exhausted.

How the hell can they expect me to legitimately pursue my journalism degree if they tie me up and cast stones for doing a bit of decent reporting? While she took a lot of pride in her work and the research she put into writing "The Fix Is In," she was also mature and smart enough to know that it was far from a complete story. *Why are they so up in arms that I busted them on taking some profits from the college? Especially when they're supposed to be teaching me how to do this exact thing as a professional... Jesus!*

If the school administration hadn't taken so much of her time over the last week on the matter, she might have appreciated the irony. The Dean's Office was upset and concerned that her exposé would inject an unneeded sense of strife amongst the student body. Their argument was that, as a private institution, it was entirely appropriate for the school to be generating profits for the benefit of owners and investors as long as they met the duty of the school and maintained a healthy and replenishing student body.

Henrietta thought this was somewhat short-sighted. *Sure, they may be able to convince another decade of students to keep coming, but if they don't start improving the overall state of things, it's a path of decline.* And for the present student population, they were left to deal with the literal and metaphorical cracks in the institution.

She was, and self-admittedly so, very idealistic. She was studying first and foremost to enrich her own education. Journalism aligned with her inherent curiosity and her self-belief that she could be an "agent of change," as she liked to say, for the betterment of the world, just as so many other empowered and opinionated Millennials had anointed themselves.

It was Friday, late afternoon, when she had walked in the door. Doug had been in the living room playing Xbox, which was not a surprise, given that when she had left on Thursday morning, Doug had been in the living room playing Xbox. From what she had come to know of Doug so far this year as roommates, she fully expected that tonight, Friday night, Doug would also be in the living room playing Xbox and would continue on through most of the weekend. Their other roommates were likely out for the night already. In fact, Elise was already sort of annoyed with Doug and was spending as little time as possible at the house. Doug was oblivious to her perception of him, however.

But, first things first, she needed to eat. She had put in enough long days and nights over the last few weeks and knew from experience that if you didn't fuel the body, it would protest when you tried to put it to sleep. On the other hand, her mind would never fully switch off these days.

***

"Can I open it for you?" Doug asked. He was a child, and it was Christmas morning. Henrietta was momentarily annoyed but then caught herself. She realized just how innocent his question was. *What a simple guy,* she thought to herself.

She also considered what might be in the box and was steadfast in thinking it must have been those shading pencils she had ordered. Henrietta had always been known for her creative mind, though many who knew her didn't realize those traits extended to a competency in visual arts. She was an exceptional sketch artist. She rarely had time for it anymore but often took to sketching out scenes that were playing out in her mind to help visualize them. It helped to exile those thoughts to a jail of graphite and paper, thereby freeing up mental energy.

It would be, she surmised, mostly harmless to have this simpleton rummaging through her package of new pencils as long as he didn't drop them. A wooden exterior could only prevent internal damage up to a point.

"Sure, Doug, go for it," she called out as she chopped up some multi-colored peppers for the salad she was making, a confluence of nutrients, textures, shapes, and flavors. She couldn't help but think about how a little bit of effort like this went a long way and how so many other things in modern society could similarly benefit from different colors, textures, shapes, and sizes. *If only people were willing.*

"Thanks, Hen!" replied Doug. He had heard Henrietta speaking with a family member a few weeks ago, and they had called her by that endearing nickname. He sort of liked it and started to introduce it in the rare times they would speak to each other. Rare, because they were still getting to know each other, having just been roommates since September. With how busy Henrietta had been and how introverted Doug was, they only had fleeting moments throughout any given week that would lend themselves to conversation. Even then, it was the smallest of small talk at best.

For her part, Henrietta hated that nickname. Her mother and siblings used it, and she was fine with that. But it had been nothing but trouble otherwise. She had natural curly hair and angular, thin features, though somewhat of a pointy nose. Growing up, she was a skinny girl, usually shorter than the others, and her finer features were seemingly always not yet fully developed in comparison to other girls. Somehow, her nose was always a couple of years ahead of the rest of her, a condition of incredibly subtle and unrealized irony that would never be appreciated by her younger self, too busy looking for flaws in the mirror, nor her older self, obsessed and occupied with sniffing around the future. In elementary school, she was "Henny," which she liked. But nobody called her that anymore.

In her first week—possibly the first day—of high school, her mother picked her up at the end of the day. A bunch of her classmates, most of them as yet unknown to her, were standing nearby—some waiting for the bus, most of them just waiting around trying to be the last ones to leave, a show of defiance to parental instructions. When her mother called out, "Hen! Over here!" it set the stage for five years of torture. She was the skinny, short girl with a beak-nose named Hen. *Cluck! Cluck! Cluck!* She could still hear those taunts and see the other kids walking around with their hands behind their backs, bending over at the waist and clucking as if munching on teenage-snack-sized ants and grains floating a few feet off the ground.

The box was rectangular, about the size of a picture frame, and maybe as thick as a countertop. He peeled the shipping tape off the package. The tape was that fiber-infused industrial-strength material that was nearly impossible to tear and wasn't nearly as enjoyable to pull off as traditional packing tape. By yanking at the unrelenting wrap, Doug was causing the cardboard to pull apart materially, leaving the scene of the unboxing in a complete state of disarray.

The center divide of the box's two top flaps was now released from the restraints of its fibrous captor. But the flaps remained in place, fixed in dutiful, parallel formation by the remaining strips of tape along the ends of the box. *Now, these... these ones give me some satisfaction.* Doug's subconscious self was having an internal monologue. Or possibly a dialogue, though he hadn't been asked to participate so he was unable to confirm how many voices there were. He pulled from the middle of the two flaps. *POP!* The tape on the edges released, and with that, the flaps came to full vertical attention, standing tall and proud and extending a welcome to any hands that chose to explore within.

Doug chose to. This is what he had been waiting for. Within the box was some kind of device—maybe a tablet or a laptop. It was held in mid-air within the volume of the box by two perfectly shaped pieces of Styrofoam. Not only did those pieces of foam allow for safe travel, they also created this beautiful harmony of the device in stasis, floating as if by some magical force, waiting for human hands to slide in and fit alongside the device to grasp and extract it, decommissioning the prize from its hovering obligations.

Schlooooppp! The sound of the Styrofoam sliding up was quickly followed by the box falling away and hitting the floor as the crescendo of the operation. He now stood alone and happy in the middle of the living room.

Anyone looking through the window from the street outside might have remarked at this very strange reincarnation of that famous sequence under a sunny blue sky where a certain mandrill monkey lifted a young lion cub high into the air for all the kingdom's followers to adore and celebrate. Except in this case, it was Doug, frontally bathed in the blue glare of a plasma TV, holding up this mysterious object and shaking it to release itself from the protective womb of those two symmetrical pieces of foam.

"It's a monitor! You ordered a monitor, Hen? Looks pretty cool, a bit small, though," Doug called out.

Henny was confused in the kitchen. She had cut up the peppers—red, orange, and yellow—and added some sprouts and fresh broccoli to her plate but wasn't sure what to do with the falafel balls she had bought for dinner. Fry them or bake them? No instructions. *What the heck was this? It really shouldn't be this hard,* she thought to herself. She was too hungry to overthink it. Her salad was ready to go, as bright and as colorful as anything she had seen all week, so she turned on the stove and set the falafels to fry in some coconut oil.

Then she heard Doug call out what he had found in the box.

"What? A monitor? I didn't order a monitor..." and with that, she put down the falafel packaging and spatula next to her salad and walked into the living room to inspect. Henny still had coconut oil on her hands from her dinner assembly. One of the reasons she liked cooking with that natural ingredient was that it served a few parallel purposes. Not only would coconut oil in the pan prevent anything from sticking, in this case, the falafel balls, but it also added a very subtle sweet flavor. Perhaps the most pleasurable benefit is that if she ended up with coconut oil on her fingers, no cleanup was required. Henny would simply massage it into her hands and then apply whatever excess to her face, lips, and arms. She liked to think of it as dinner and a spa treatment all to herself.

After lowering it from the heroic unveiling pose, Doug had inspected the monitor.

"It's sort of confusing. I don't see any wires or plugs anywhere. Not sure how you're supposed to use this thing?" Doug offered his analysis as he handed the unit over to Henrietta. She took it from him, carefully wrapping her fingers around the side of the very polished, hard, shiny material.

Strangely to her, it was glossy and glassy on both the front and the back. It was like some massive touchscreen phone, but for its size, it was quite light. It was sort of like her Kindle, she supposed, although seemingly much, much fancier. Upon closer inspection, she could see that Doug was correct. There were no visible ports, plugs, or anything of that sort.

Looking down at the carnage from Doug's unraveling of the wrapping tape, she noticed an envelope poking out from underneath one of the prone Styrofoam pieces.

"Doug, you might not want to be so manic with how you do things," she gave him some admonishment poorly wrapped in advice as she bent over to pick it up. She liked Doug, or at least tolerated him when she knew the other roommates struggled much more than she did with his oddities and idiosyncrasies. What was more odd to her was that, generally speaking,

Doug was normal. He was not, in her opinion, bad-looking at all. He wasn't short, wasn't tall, and had a slender build. That was a bit surprising given how much sugar he seemed to consume and generally how inactive he was. *Must be good genes. At least he's got that going for him*, Henny thought.

The envelope was neatly assembled—very crisp and heavyweight cardstock, machine folded and glued. There was no formal address block, but on the front side, printed in lightweight sans serif typeface, was simply, "Ms. Adler."

"Well that's kinda cool. Look at this, Dougie," she said. She had called him Dougie a few times recently, as it occasionally seemed fitting. He was still quite innocent and youthful. When she said it, the smile at the corner of her mouth belied that she was simply and subconsciously responding to the formal, thoughtful, monogrammed envelope. Despite having been through the wringer over the last thirty hours or more, being dead tired, hungry, and feeling the stress of the week's activities, the endorphin rush of reading one's own name in handsomely printed font on a letter was enough to melt much of her compromised state away.

The sheer enigma of this glassy device and her curiosity of its provenance also piqued her emotional and intellectual state.

Doug beamed. *She called me Dougie!* His eyes lit up, and a smile came over his face. He felt incredible. Hearing niceties from anyone was rare for Doug, and while this wasn't exactly a compliment, it was endearing enough that it lifted his spirits. Quickly, however, the feeling gave way to a wash of old memories.

***

Tori McCandless was the coolest girl in fifth grade. She always seemed to catch the attention of other kids, of the teacher, and of other parents. To be the apple of everyone's eye had instilled a strong sense of esteem and confidence that would surely serve her well as she grew older. With this optimistic and affirmed sense of the world, Tori was always looking forward. What was next? What was fun? What was exciting? What could she get away with that her peers couldn't? Knowing that getting in trouble was hard for her, she often made decisions that left others scrambling in her wake. On this particular day, she needed some help, and she knew where to get it.

"Hi, Douglas! Did you make a clay thing?" Tori asked her classmate. It was before school, and they were outside the gym with other children playing a game with a bouncy ball and a concrete wall. She had strategically positioned herself near a ten-year-old Douglas Everett Watson. He was on the periphery of the game, trying to figure out how to insert himself into the playing space. He still had the asymmetrical dead weight of his backpack looped over his left shoulder, the result of indecisiveness as to whether he was playing, staying, or going. The awkwardness that would become his hallmark in university was clearly not a learned behavior. This was simply who he had always been.

Douglas was transfixed by Tori's curly brown hair and blue eyes. They had been friends since they were toddlers, and Douglas often wondered why it had been so much easier for him to communicate with Tori—and everyone for that matter—when they were younger. Older Doug would often have the same thoughts, silently reminiscing of his glory days as a three-year-old social butterfly.

"Yep!" he stammered in response.

The game going on around them wasn't concerned with their discussion, nor was the small rubberized ball. It had caromed off the wall and was now heading directly for the side of an unaware Tori's head!

Douglas leaped forward, his actions now guided by intuition and instinct. He jettisoned the backpack behind him like a rocket ridding itself of depleted fuel tanks, his outstretched arm reaching through space to protect his crush from the orbiting junk that maintained its dangerous trajectory.

He overreached, as he was wont to do in many other ways as well. Douglas' calculations had been incorrect. His hand flew past Tori's head, generating turbulence that wisped some of the curls in her hair. His arm followed behind and brought a neck and head along with it, the latter replacing the original intended target of the high-speed sphere.

WUMP!

The ball completed its flight plan, connecting squarely with the center of Douglas' forehead. Upon collision, it expelled one big vacuous sound as it instantly compressed into a flattened disc that attached itself to the boy's youthful skin like a patch on a bicycle tire. Just as quickly, it pulled away and reclaimed its original shape before accelerating back toward the wall.

In its wake, the red rubber orb left a reverberating *wump, wump, wump* inside Douglas' head and a telltale circular stamp on his skin that quickly took on the same color as its maker.

The half dozen kids playing the ball game stopped for a moment, looked at Douglas, and, as often happens when kids are playing a game, started laughing.

Ha ha ha! Ha-ah! Ha ha ha! Ha-ah!

Then the ball, back in play, continued to hit the wall, ricochet toward the ground, and bounce once or twice before meeting the fleshy young hands of whoever was catching it next.

Thud! Thup! Thup! Slap! The sound repeated and repeated.

Wump, wump, wump! The echoing resonance of the ball bounced around inside his skull. *Ha ha ha! Ha-ah!* The combination of noises filled the audio spectrum, his own internal orchestra amplifying the humiliation that had taken hold. *Thud! Thup! Wump! Slap! Ha ha! Wump, ha, wump! Ha-ah!*

"Douglas! What was that? Are you okay? That was crazy!" a loud, confident voice called out. The angelic notes of Tori's words had cut through the cacophony.

"Uh. Yep. I'm... okay."

"Here, come over here, let's sit down. I wanted to ask you something," Tori said, signaling toward a big concrete planter in the schoolyard. They sat down together, and she looked at her young Cyclops friend, unable to move her eyes from the massive red welt that had formed an inch above his nose.

"The clay project, what did you make?" Tori said, with a sparkle in her eyes that suggested a genuine interest in whatever Douglas might have created.

"Oh, it was a mushroom! Like in Super Mario, you know?" He was thrilled that she was interested in his project. For a single beat of a smitten heart, he was ecstatic. Then came the realization that he had taken it home yesterday to paint it and brought it to school this morning. In his backpack.

"Oh no..."

"What? What's wrong, Douglas?" she asked, still very interested.

"Oh no! Oh no!" He scrambled to pick up his backpack and put it in front of him on the ground. The jingle of small shards of hard material could be heard as they meshed and scrambled against one another, perhaps like a faint rattle of maracas. Opening the zipper revealed what he expected, peering in to see the shattered results of his efforts.

"That sucks!" Tori said. As she watched Douglas in distress, she thought over the situation. The blue eyes that captured Douglas' heart were veils to the machinations of her true intentions.

"Dougie, let me take it inside. I'll see if I can fix it," she offered. *Dougie!*

It was that moment of hearing it that way, from the lips of someone—a girl, a woman—that he admired, that connected those moments. Here Doug was, in the living room, opening a package for his roommate, and at the same time, he was sitting on the ground almost ten years before that, holding back tears and sifting through the rubble of his imagination.

What his selective memories as a young adult chose to redact was that Tori had then proceeded to take the broken earthen mushroom pieces to the school office and reported that young Douglas had pushed her on the playground and smashed her clay Super Mario-themed statue. She was beside herself after painstakingly working on it in secret for days, only for her uncaring classmate to destroy it the same day the assignment was due in class. The imbalance in Tori's world could only be partially set right with an A+ for her, and, as an offset, a failing grade and detention for Douglas.

Doug didn't care. He would gladly trade a hundred mushroom statues or get blasted in the forehead by a thousand rubber balls for those rare glimpses of recognition, those moments of appreciation or endearment from someone he liked and admired.

***

Henny stood in the living room with the handsomely crafted envelope in her hands. The fold was crisp, with the triangular flap obviously glued down by machine, forming a geometrically perfect segmentation of the top and bottom half of the envelope. It was ever so slightly bubbled underneath in support of the top-quality cardstock within.

She slid a thumbnail under the crease of the triangular flap, releasing the line of glue that held the envelope secure. It graciously peeled back and flipped open, with minimal tearing along the join of the two halves. A light blue card showed itself as the sole occupant of the envelope.

"A card! What do you think this is?" she spoke out loud, mostly to herself. Doug heard it but didn't have a strong opinion and, as such, was bereft of an answer as he tried to assess the meaning of all that was in front of him. *What could this card be?* he innocently wondered.

Pulling the card from its secret enclave, Henny's temporal anticipation continued to build. She had no idea what to expect. A pastel hue made the card feel very approachable, presented in a matte finish that prevented the overhead dome light in the living room from creating any glare. It was a one-sided card.

"People like you belong with a team like us," the card read, which she shared aloud. "It takes a special sensibility to see the world as you do. We would like to share our story with you and hear more about yours."

As Henny processed this message, her first reaction was that it was so ambiguous as to not say anything at all. Yet it was so interesting and curiosity-generating. Who had sent this beautiful monogrammed envelope, the mystery device, and this spellbinding message within?

It was generically signed by machine: "Your friends at EMC."

No phone number. No website.

"This is pretty wild, Dougie. What do you think this means?"

There it was again. *Dougie!* He looked directly at Henny when she said it. Their eyes met ever so briefly, and in that moment, it seemed to Doug that anything was possible. And truly, it might have been one of those fleeting nanoseconds where two people realize the endless possibility and potential of making decisions in their lives. As quickly as it arrived, it faded. Doug had felt the transcendent nature of their connected gaze. His eyes widened to take in more than just Henny's eyes. Her skin was radiant from the coconut oil. Even with the exhaustion she was facing from her very long week, her young visage was indeed bright and alive, mesmerizing to Doug at this proximity. Her thinner face, graceful cheekbones, pointy nose, sharp eyebrows, and penetrating eyes all contributed to the overload on Doug's internal circuitry.

He looked down as if to shield himself from the glare of beauty right in front of him. A moment ago, he was about to formulate an opinion, but the connection between his brain and his voicebox had since been severed by her deployment of that whimsical version of his name. If he could speak, he might have shared his innocent interpretation that this was somehow related to her recent article, given all the attention it had received.

Henny had not quite arrived at that conclusion. Not because she was slow to interpret things but rather due to the greater worldview she held and her intimate awareness of the situation of her article. She just felt it was a bit... small. In the sense that, admittedly, there had been some local media coverage of her work. But could her hastily-written analysis of college spending and the ten-second sound bite she offered up on the local five o'clock news coverage last week have resulted in whatever Spy Kids mystery package had shown up at the door? Not likely! She couldn't even be sure that her article, "The Fix Is In," was completely factually correct. Hell, she didn't even like the title. She had been convinced to go with it by the editor of the student paper. While she had been diligent in her research and used all the resources she had access to, this was essentially a first-time publication in a school rag from a nineteen-year-old college kid, replete with inconsistent tone and tense, too many run-on sentences, and probably a few statements that would have been removed if she had sought the advice of a lawyer.

More likely, she might've thought she had been the target for some kind of mail-out promotional campaign, which she knew came with the territory of being such a consistent online shopper. Long tail junk mail, as it were.

Now her attention turned to the device. Carefully placing the card and envelope down on the coffee table, she picked up the mysterious glossy, glassy black object.

"Not sure what this is, but if it's an advertising thing, that's an expensive piece of glass!" she shared her suspicions out loud.

BEEP! BEEP! BEEP! A piercing sound shot through the house. Initially awestruck in admiration for his roommate, Doug's eyes widened even more in fear as his internal voice took on the personality of a serial cliffhanger. *What was this god-awful noise? What is this sinister device? Will we be blown to smithereens?*

"Hen, put it down!" he yelled, reaching forward and slapping the device out of her hands. With a heavy thud, it landed on the floor, one corner chipping into the original oak hardwood flooring of the foursquare. The device held itself in a standing position for a beat, like a figure skater posing on the very tip of a single skate. Similarly, it started to pirouette, but instead of maintaining a spin and holding its balance, it turned only slightly and fell to one side.

"Doug! Jesus... it's the smoke alarm!" Henny yelled in reactive anger at what had just happened but with a layer of urgency to take care of the problem at hand. She ran into the kitchen.

Thick white smoke was pouring upwards from the frying pan like an industrial factory exhaust stack, filling the upper three feet of the high-ceilinged kitchen with an opaque cloud. The falafel balls had burned to a crisp on the pan-side down. The splatter of overheated coconut oil was all over the metallic surface of the stove and the surrounding countertop.

Doug was following sheepishly behind. He may as well have just smashed Tori's Super Mario Bros mushroom statue all over again, even though he never actually did it in the first place.

"Open the windows and the door," Henny commanded.

"Uh, okay!" Doug responded quickly. He opened the back door to outside and the door to his bedroom, then ran down the hallway to the front door. Henny didn't try to stop him. A part of her thought it would be perfectly fine if he just opened it and kept on running.

Henny had managed to climb up on the countertop and turn off the smoke alarm. It was an old unit, still wired directly into the house, and likely a decade or more past its expiry date. The fact that it worked should have been more of a surprise than the sound it had made. From this elevated position, she could also reach and open two higher windows in the kitchen, with her slim frame and long arms leaning out over the dining area much like a mountain climber stretching for a new handhold at the most treacherous point of an uphill journey.

Doug returned to the kitchen. "I'm really sorry about that, Hen. I thought that thing, when I heard the beeping, whatever it was, had some kind of bomb in it. I swear."

She placed a hand down on the edge of the countertop and jumped down to the floor. Sweat and grime now clung to her from time spent in the smoky upper altitude of the kitchen.

"So, you thought it had a bomb in it, and your first reaction is to knock it out of my hands onto the ground? What the hell were you thinking?" She was upset. This was a culmination of her ordeal over the last few days, and now she had to deal with all this nonsense, in addition to her dinner which had burned half to a crisp.

"I dunno, I just was looking at you, and then the thing, and then the sound... I'm sorry," he continued with his apology.

"Oh, whatever, Doug. Can you just get the thing and bring it in here? I've gotta clean this up." She turned back to the scorched frying pan and the blackened falafels. With a knife, she quickly cut them in half and placed the lesser burned half on her salad plate, a semblance of a meal that Henny carried to the dining table and sat down to eat.

Doug was slow to get back to the living room. He was held for a moment admiring this authoritative and opinionated woman. Sweaty, smoky, and oily, her tired eyes were overseeing a remarkably savage and efficient dissection of those crispy balls. He then retreated to where the device lay.

Picking it up, he flipped it around and held it carefully, inspecting for damage. The glass had been nearly completely smashed. The front side of the device was now bearing that telltale spider web pattern, growing most intensely from the corner that hit the floor and expanding outwards to consume nearly the entire face of glass. The paths that could be traced along those interwoven networks of broken lines of glass were infinite and, in many ways, resembled the random patterns marked upon a particular soundproofing wall that Doug often found himself staring at in Lecture Hall 4B.

He was frozen for a moment, not sure what to do. She was upset with him already, just for doing normal Doug stuff. He didn't want to think what she might do when he brought this unintentionally kaleidoscopic mystery glass to her in the kitchen.

Jesus, does she still have that knife in her hands?

Eight

PROLIFIC

Faria Lima B32 was a sight to behold. With an all-glass angular facade, it struck a unique pose in the São Paulo skyline. The building's geometry ran non-parallel to the streets, thus creating large, wide-open spaces at the ground level, standing apart from the otherwise intensely dense city life in every direction around it.

The country was still reeling and recovering from over a decade of exposed corruption, with still more sordid goings-on known by the populace but having yet to come to light of national or international attention. Faria Lima B32 filled a few roles in society since its completion in 2020. To many, it was a sign of prosperity and progress, a glassy proverbial phoenix rising from the ashes of exposed political backroom dealings and wanton theft from the economy. To others, it demonstrated all that was wrong with the Brazilian economy. Those detractors couldn't understand how such a massive, beautiful country, filled to the brim with the riches of resources and culture, still struggled to provide a consistent quality of life for its citizens. They were able to construct remarkable buildings like this one and numerous soccer stadiums almost ten years earlier for the World Cup but could not provide adequate housing or community infrastructure for millions and millions of people.

It didn't help that several of those World Cup soccer stadiums were now effectively defunct and unused, in some cases hosting less than a dozen matches before being switched off, save for the occasional concert. Signs of wastage and political profiteering were everywhere in the country, and most citizens were very unhappy about it.

Somaya had flown in the day before, landing at Guarulhos International Airport early in the morning. Typically, she wouldn't have chosen to arrive so far in advance of needing to be somewhere. On this trip, Somaya knew that the return flight after today's agenda would be grueling, as would the meetings themselves, and had decided to give herself a day on the ground to prepare. Given the choice, she would always elect to get in early and leave no later than the soonest opportunity rather than the other way around. Her feeling was that, especially in the context of business meetings, if you lingered, you took away from whatever thunderous delivery you might have brought to the meeting in the first place. Somaya's default strategy was to shine her brightest at the absolute peak moment of an activity, and then get the hell out of there as quickly as possible.

***

"Prolific, Somaya. You gotta just be absolutely prolific," her supervisor and mentor Jeff Christiansen had said, introducing a word that she would eventually abscond with as her own personal mantra. They had been at the telematics industry's big event, "DATA METRICS 2006," a future-friendly conference that touted itself to be "ahead of our time at the cross-section of nature and numbers." It was November 2005 on a beautiful day in San Francisco.

Sunlight streamed in through the big four-story eastern windows of the Moscone Center, bathing the entrance area exhibits in more direct sun than might be anticipated. It made it hard for these booths—if one could be gracious enough to call them that—to capture anyone's attention, as all of their presentation materials were washed out in the light. Standing there in any kind of conversation would quickly get uncomfortably warm—sweaty even.

Regardless, Warren had been dutifully working at his entrance area exhibit for the last two days. He had managed to obtain floor space that, on face value—and it was expensive—should have been a great location. His table was wedged between a new gamified-rewards credit card startup and the registration desk for the conference. Most everyone passing by had little interest in stopping to talk as this area was deemed "in transit" and not formally a part of the conference, though the credit card company seemed to be getting a lot of signups. Apparently, they had offered a promo code for three months of ad-blocking on MySpace.

"Do you have any drinks for sale?" a raspy female voice asked, startling Warren. He had been replacing the batteries on the cameras mounted inside his demonstration fridge. The batteries kept getting cold and failing, necessitating a replacement every two or three hours.

"I'm sorry, I'm not the concession," he started to say until he turned and could find no more words.

An attractive young Indian woman stood before him. The raw, dusty, gravelly sound of that voice did not fit the beauty and youthfulness of her face, though her eyes looked a bit tired.

"Oh, I didn't realize. What do you have in there then?" she said, beckoning toward the fridge.

"Well, I've installed a mesh of three little webcams, with the feed integrated with a proprietary computer vision image recognition algorithm I've developed, for purposes of interrogating the picture with a high degree of confidence and extrapolating enough data to be exposed over a reliable stateful inventory API," Warren said, proudly sharing what he put together for his lonely exhibit.

"Ah, I meant, what do you have to drink?" Somaya replied, clarifying her request. "I'm dying of thirst, and the registration line is super long right now."

He noted that she sounded especially dry, which is also how someone might have chosen to describe his technical explanations if anyone had actually been stopping to ask for them. He opened the fridge, looked inside, and pulled out a chilled plastic bottle of green sports drink.

"Here," he said, "have this, it's my favorite."

"Thank you so much," she said as she opened the bottle and took a big swallow of the electrolyte-laden potion. Warren, now a mesmerized props assistant for this impromptu sports drink commercial, looked on as the star performer, her presence illuminated by a halo of luminescent energy from the large bands of sunlight in the room, quenched her thirst fully before slowly lowering the bottle from her shapely, succulent lips.

"So what exactly are you doing here with all this stuff?" she asked, thankful for his provision of liquids.

"Okay, I'll restart from the top," Warren said, elated to be given the stage again. "We all have the issues of not knowing what's in our fridge, what we can make for dinner... whether or not we have anything to drink, right?" he said with a gesture toward the bottle in her hand. "So, what I've got here is a way to get a real-time view of everything in your fridge, with an itemized list and even details like how full a bottle of ketchup is, how many of them you have in your fridge, that sort of thing."

"With... camera recognition? You mentioned the cameras?" she asked, genuinely interested in that aspect of the work. She was a sponge for information, especially anything related to the commercial business of camera technologies.

"Yes, so these little guys here," he said, pointing to miniature webcams he had mounted in several places inside the fridge. "With them, I'm capturing high-quality images every time the door opens. The images are then sent to a server, where I can process the information with my computer vision algorithm."

Warren felt like he had impressed her. He almost finished his explanation by saying, "Ta-da!" but thankfully, he thought better of it.

".. and I presume it generates some kind of output?" Somaya asked, her intrigue still yet unsatisfied.

"Right. Yes, see here." He pulled up a tabled report in a web browser on his laptop. "Actually, look right now. We can see the fridge contents a few minutes ago, and the fridge contents now."

On the screen was a two-column view of data with a corresponding timestamp at the top of each list. The rows were mostly uninteresting, containing an ordered list of everything inside. "Even the stuff at the back! But look, ketchup, ketchup, ketchup, cream soda, water—four of them, a ham, cheese, and tomato sandwich, it doesn't yet know to read mustard, potato salad, six bottles of SportAde, and a T-shirt."

"A T-shirt?"

"Yeah, it gets hot out here in front of these windows," he admitted. "But look now, in this column, see how it's only five bottles of SportAde?"

Somaya smiled, amused by the quirkiness of this odd man, who she happened to think was also very cute. She agreed as well; it was hot standing there, and she took another long, cooling drink from her SportAde, wondering with a passing thought if the security cameras in the Moscone Center could similarly interpret how full her drink was.

"So, what do you do?" Warren asked.

"Oh, god. Me? Well, I'm here with my company. We are in the security camera business. It's actually my first conference. And Jesus, we went out last night after the opening reception, and those guys, holy cow, do they drink." Somaya felt comfortable enough around this friendly man to share far more information than he had expected to receive. "I don't think I was ready for that, but it was with a big new partner of ours, and they just kept going and going. Dinner, and then karaoke, and then some crazy dive bar. But I think I did okay, for what I can remember!"

"Well, that sounds like fun... I guess." Warren didn't care too much for the nightlife, though he was a self-described karaoke fiend. "Definitely the karaoke, what'd you sing?"

"All of it terribly, I'm sure," she joked, then admitted, "I did GoldenEye, if you can believe it?"

"Oh my god, like Tina Turner?" he asked. She nodded before he'd even completed the question, so he continued, "That's like one of my all-time favorite movies."

"Why am I not surprised? Here you are playing with Brosnan's night vision transmitting cameras in your fridge!" Somaya caught him off guard with her wit and her immaculate reference to some of Bond's surveillance work in the film.

"Wow, yeah, you're bang on. Life imitates art, you got me there. And you're now one of my favorite people too," he blurted out, saying what needed to be said in the moment.

"Oh. Okay," she recoiled ever so slightly, only out of a subtle layer of nervousness that had set in. "Well, I don't think I was anyone's favorite last night. I think I was too drunk and yapping on and on. Even told the Omniwatch guys—the partners—that I was still an intern 'cuz I wasn't sure if the company had enough money to pay me a salary, and Jesus, that we could hardly afford to be at this conference. Not sure if that's the best look, you know? Like, why did I feel the need to say so much?" she said.

He smiled at the irony of her words. "I'm sure it's not a big deal. Crazier stuff than that happens at these things all the time."

"I dunno. Anyway, today, I just hope I don't puke," Somaya said, before having another sip of the green liquid. She started giggling, thinking about how juvenile of a comment that was, and the air pushing up from her rib cage forced an involuntary snort from her nose, re-dispensing some of the bright green drink onto her upper lip.

Warren laughed as well and, with no other option readily available, offered her a brochure from his booth table. "Here, wipe it with this."

She did so, wiping the mess from her nose on his branded materials. The oddity of it all caused them both to laugh even more. The brochure was printed mostly in black and white but with the logo and tagline in an intensely bright blood red.

"Rotten Tomatoes?" she asked, the name of his company provoking a common response, "Like the film website?"

"No, it's not that. It's from the idea that you can use this to know how much stuff is in the fridge, even if it's gone past its expiry date, provided the camera can see it or if it just looks rotten. I've even got an algorithm for that! Anyway, rotten ketchup didn't seem like such a good idea, as I don't think it ever goes bad, and then I had the lawyer do all the work for the company name like this, and he never once asked me about the film website. So yeah, that's why," Warren said in reply.

It's always such a damn long answer. I need to change the name.

"But you're a big Bond guy? Doubly ironic that you don't know about the film website you're named after then, right?" she said.

"Yeah, yeah, you got me," he admitted. The truth was, he had never much cared for the internet, outside of using it for working with other developers and now, for the facilitation of data transmissions from his Brosnan-era MI6-worthy camera fridge.

"Hey, I get it. Look. I have to go," Somaya said. "But I'll take this," she added, indicating the brochure in her hand, which contained his blood-red lettering and her bright green nasal expellant. She confirmed that it also contained his email address.

***

Certainly, this Somaya, the forty-something experienced CEO arriving early for executive meetings at Faria Lima B32, had grown considerably since that eventful day almost twenty years earlier.

She had been hopeful that a good night's sleep would also help overcome the exhaustion from the long flight and the jetlag. Somaya liked to keep an active life, and she knew that no matter what she did during these long-haul flights, her body and mind would suffer from the lack of movement. Even the relatively small four-hour difference in time from origin to destination made it feel like it had been one extremely long day that went by quickly, with nothing happening in between.

As she crossed the green outdoor space and walked through the massive glass entry doors into Faria Lima B32, the juxtaposition of her orderly presence in this purposeful building versus the chaotic outside world of the streets of São Paulo couldn't have been more stark.

The big doors closed, emitting a suction sound that indicated the hermetically sealed volume inside the building had been re-established. Everything else had gone silent, from the lively ambiance of traffic, people, and machinery fueling the resounding din of this massive city, to nothing.

"Wow, that's pretty wild," Somaya commented.

"*Olá, senhora?*" the security guard behind the desk stated, with an inquiring tone.

"*Olá, tenho uma reunião com ANEER,*" she replied, communicating her scheduled appointment that day. Her ability to switch languages was remarkable, and it allowed her to very easily navigate and understand the world at large and individual people in general, even though she often held back from using those skills in conversation. In this case, she had thought nothing of it—a question in Portuguese would be met with a Portuguese answer, expediting the desired outcome for the situation.

But often, she knew that her control of languages was a strength to keep under wraps. As a woman, she had already faced enough obstacles in establishing herself as an industry leader and respected expert. As a South Asian woman, even more work had been needed as the hurdles had been taller and more plentiful. Somaya's personality did not lend itself to being limited, labeled, or held back by any of this. Over time, she identified and took control of numerous superpowers, which, in addition to her multilingual expertise, also included being South Asian, and being a woman. The element of surprise was often in her favor.

"Okay, *senhora, só um minuto,*" the guard replied and picked up the phone. This routine was a global one, a standard in the unwritten universal rules of office building meetings, albeit having been interrupted for a few years during the COVID pandemic. Now she could retreat to the waiting area in the lobby to observe the last ritual in silence.

While she waited, Somaya went through the inbox on her smartphone. She was quick to perceive the count of unread messages, the bright white number of 182 tidily wrapped in a small red bubble. Despite its efforts to ensure it was perceived as friendly and desirable, the number and everything it stood for was utterly disgusting to Somaya.

So many people wasting so much time on their keyboards, just looking for acceptance and validation from others.

She was quick to realize that with it being just after 8:30 a.m. local time, it was still 4:30 a.m. at home. Typically, her inbox was filtered and cleaned up by seven o'clock Pacific Time, so she was willing to absolve everyone responsible for those 182 symbols of wasted time in her inbox, at least for a few hours.

Her processing efficiency was top-notch. Although she typically didn't succumb to dealing with email bloat such as this, Somaya was still uniquely talented with her fingers and thumbs, such that when the need or desire presented itself, she would put them to work. She opened the email app and started scrolling through it.

- New manuf template facility in Kansas
- Quarterly bookings forecast - Q3 FY24
- Bangkok Data Center - power supply
- Energy Sector - pitch updates
- Investor update - latet deck
- Hiring updates
- November town hall

Goddamn it, if people are going to send me stuff, at least spell the subject line correctly.

She had zeroed in on the typo in the Investor update. For a moment, she was more concerned that it would reach her inbox at that level of carelessness than she was about the contents of the email itself. Somaya wasn't downplaying the importance of those materials, especially given the recent surge in sales bookings and a new round of capital she had just agreed to with the company's biggest investor, EGF, the Energy Growth Fund. Her reaction was more a reflection of how she compartmentalized her time.

Lots of time on the flight home to review that work. Just don't distract me with mistakes like this.

She ignored the rest of the messages, as none of them had been so rudely constructed as to invite her ire, and all of them were likely equally important and deserving of more time than she had now. The common thread across all the work in front of her for the months and quarters ahead is that it would be as pivotal as ever, a balancing act of sales growth, operational expansion, investor relations, regulators, dozens of new customers, hundreds of new hires, millions of dollars of capital to deploy, and likely as many points of failure.

People. *It all comes down to people.*

She looked outside through the high, angular windows. People were milling about, moving up and down the sidewalk as if they were riding conveyor belts, many of them crossing through the middle of the open block like wayward pieces of machinery. In the central concourse area, there was a massive polygonal whale sculpture, an enormous outdoor art piece of reflective glass and metal that likely rivaled the cost of many other far more useful public works.

Scattered around that big glassy whale were several tables and chairs. Nestled amongst the constant fluidity of human movement, people were sitting, eating, working, and laughing. The streets beyond were even more busy. Vehicles of all shapes and sizes were battling for pole position in the perpetual urban race, each with their own finish line. Somaya couldn't help but extend herself into a mental projection of the street scene, her own internal Google Maps. As the CEO of a computer vision company, she often found herself slipping into this type of imaginative reincarnation of her own products and how they might see the world. People, machinery, systems, language, communication, commerce—it all seemed to glide together, to flow around, over, and through, in total, beautiful, chaotic synergy.

The patterns are there, if you choose to see them.

"Ms. Patel? You can go up now. Please follow me." The security guard had come over to where she was sitting. To Somaya's significant surprise, his English was crisp, perfect, and very pleasing to listen to. *Well, I'll be damned,* she thought to herself. *I did not see that coming.* For someone who took great pride in her ability to cloak her most special attributes, she would almost take it as a personal affront when something didn't neatly fit into the little box she had mentally ascribed it to. In a very contradictory way, her analytical and structured view of the world and of other people was something that she wanted—needed—to be as she saw it. Yet, her own role in that world was one that she insisted was entirely up to her at all times, to shift and change at her infinite and often arbitrary discretion. Often, people with this type of personality would only remove those binary limitations on what they saw with the benefit of experience or the influence of tragedy.

She followed the security guard as he swiped his clearance card on a pedestal scanning device next to a set of glass security doors. He stepped to the side, held a hand forward, and offered, "After you, Ms. Patel."

"Thank you," she replied, still shaken by this surprising man. She would guess that his ethnicity was Brazilian, though his skin was darker than most of the men she found herself surrounded by in her work. Did that indicate an indigenous background? Perhaps an African influence? Or something else? She couldn't be sure, and it annoyed her that she wasn't.

Whether it was his ethnicity, his command of English, his mannerisms, or the smooth gait by which he walked, she was struck by this man. *He simply did not fit where he was. Yet here he was!* Regardless of Somaya's opinion, just about anyone would think this was a handsome man. The best reference point most anyone outside of the country might have would be that of a soccer player—a Brazilian national team footballer—paid massive sums of money to play in Europe and with occasional travel to corruptible host nations to seek glory within exotic financially-stressed stadiums. Billions of fans around the world would tune in and log on to watch the broadcast and presentation of those matches delivered under the authority of some of the most publicly corrupt organizations humanity has ever seen. Indeed, if you put this same helpful man, who took pride in his security work at Faria Lima B32, in an iconic yellow national jersey, he might be worshipped as an idol.

She continued walking ahead toward the bank of elevators. The security guard was now following her. Somaya could hear his footsteps and feel his eyes moving ever so carefully up and down her body. He was a skilled observer, careful enough never to overstep his boundaries yet still able to exude the intrinsic human energy that comes from mutual physical interest. Similarly, Somaya was adept at body language, both reading what came from others and speaking with her own. Her fitness was excellent, her body was very shapely, and with the benefit of the extra day to recover from flying, she felt very rested, refreshed, and confident. With an ever so subtle side-to-side shift of her hips, she was saying all these things over that short walk to the elevators, though her intention to use her superpowers to control the situation had been usurped by his charisma.

"Here we are. Please get off on the twenty-seventh floor. Your hosts will be expecting you," he said as he again swiped his clearance card on the elevator control box and selected the corresponding button for her destination.

"Thank you... *qual o seu nome?*" she replied, realizing that this sensual little sojourn was about to end, and she did not even know this man's name. The mystery of the unknown was controlling her. After all, she had given herself to him in that discrete shared moment, and it was imperative to claw back that slip and regain that loss of authority before departing.

"Estevão, Ms. Patel," he responded politely.

This gave her the opening she needed. Somaya rotated ever so slightly to face him more directly. She was still facing the elevator door but turned to her left. Her strongest side, she was certain of that. It would also allow him to take in her three-quarter profile from head to toe. She was confident in that look and in the shapes and curves that would escape confinement of the somewhat classical business suit she was wearing. Her rested face was covered with some of the softest, clearest skin that Estevão might ever have seen and contained those full, moist, succulent, shiny lips that were often a focal point for wandering eyes. Brown pupils shot toward Estevão, locked with his for the smallest moment in time.

The elevator doors had opened.

"Muito obrigado, Estevão." Somaya delivered her gratitude in a soft yet rangeful voice, perfectly hitting the intonations of those two words and his name.

He smiled and began to turn back to his post. She stepped inside, and his professionally trained and personally curious eyes took one last quick look at her as the doors closed between them. Estevão retreated to the front desk. *"Ah, linda... amiga da onça,"* he muttered under his breath, admitting to himself that yes, indeed, Somaya was quite beautiful, but her personality and intentions were as fake and transparent as he anticipated they would be the moment she entered the building. It would take far more than that to unseat Estevão's wife and two beautiful children as the true objects of his appreciation. They were why he went to work every day and subjected himself to the disregard of so many false personalities that walked in the door. To help him through the monotony of the day and as a natural exercise of his intuition, Estevão had come to treat it as a game, to guess the archetype of the incoming humans and then engage them just enough to check the accuracy of his assessments.

In fact, earlier that morning, he had been presented with two more fascinating character studies. A handsome but average-sized white man in a finely pressed blue suit had entered. He was British before the door had even closed. Shortly thereafter, a tall, impressive Brazilian woman arrived, perfectly appointed in a light pink tweed skirt suit, covering the lobby floor with powerful strides that clipped and clopped in her high heels. A Brazilian of German descent, Estevão was sure, just as he was that the overt efforts the two of them made to say hello had broadcast even more clearly that they had only just said goodbye a short time before.

As well, Estevão didn't care for football. He was a Formula 1 fan through and through.

Nine

VISION

The doors opened on the twenty-seventh floor. The elevator lobby was separated from the office space by floor-to-ceiling glass walls on each side. In the middle third of those walls, the glass was separated and hinged just right to allow passage through security-controlled doors. As she approached the doors on the north side of the lobby, the security panel switched from red to green, and the door began to open, remotely managed and mechanically powered.

Somaya smiled as she thought of how Estevão was likely watching her through his live monitor feed at the front desk and that he had been the one to approve passage to her recognizable silhouette, validated by the side-to-side sway of her walk from elevator door to glass wall. With the last two steps through the door, she consciously flexed the gluteus maximus muscles in each leg as the respective attached high-heeled shoes made footfall, certain that the extra tension in the backside of her trousers added some visual appeal for her gatekeeper far below, and with it, an extra boost of confidence as she continued toward the board room.

It was yet another room predominantly filled with men, as the self-satisfied executive made entry. The aura of her sultry charms were activated to full effect as she walked around the boardroom table and took a seat near the back of the room. Hugo and Rafael, two executives from the state energy agency, ANEER, were on the far side of the table, the windows behind them looking out over a smog-filled view of the bustling São Paulo city center.

To Somaya's right, seated in chairs that fronted the glass wall on the other side of the secure hallway from where she had just entered, were another four people.

"Hello, my name is Somaya Patel," she said as she extended a hand to the lone woman on that side of the table, the only other female in the room. Somaya made a point of engaging her first to show preference and to demonstrate priority to the others in the room, even though she didn't know who this woman was and hadn't yet said hello to her two primary customer contacts on the other side of the table.

"Hello, I'm Valeria. Valeria Almeida. I am here from the strategic task force in the president's office," she said as she looked toward Somaya, released their handshake, and then glanced to her right and left, sweeping her now free hand as she made introductions. "This is Rodrigo Carvalho, David Gomes, and..."

"Damian Worsley," the third man said as he interrupted Valeria. He stood up to greet Somaya. "I've heard much about you. It's a pleasure to meet you," he said with a strong British accent. Somaya could tell from his accent that he was from a higher caste of society in England, perhaps Surrey or Windsor. Most likely, he was a private school and Oxbridge alumnus.

She shook his hand politely. This man was dressed the part, wearing an expensive and well-pressed suit that hinted at being a Canali. He was perfectly manicured, with a mid-length haircut that allowed his bangs to sweep down, interspersing his forehead and falling toward his face before turning to the side, just long enough to catch and grab a statically charged hold of the shorter-length hair above his ears.

"It's a pleasure to meet you, Valeria," she said as she looked to the woman, who had taken on an even more serious countenance after being interrupted by Damian. "Thank you for joining with your team today. I am the CEO of CVI. We are very pleased and thankful to be working with your country," she said, ensuring that she had completed her introduction even though it was most likely not required. Somaya had made a point of extending her gratitude as well. The contract with the Brazilian government was one of the biggest in the company, last year accounting for over thirty-five million dollars alone.

"Your name precedes you, the work you have done for us is fantastic. I'm very interested to hear what you have to share with us today," Valeria responded.

Meanwhile, the finely manicured man who had interrupted the conversation was still standing at the table. The handshake he had forced with Somaya had started very professionally and cordially but quickly deteriorated to an awkward, loose, cartilaginous clasp. When Somaya turned her attention back to Valeria to complete the introduction with her initial target, she allowed her hand to go mostly limp, even as Damian had sought a firmer connection. As was Somaya's way, this tactic was entirely intentional, a very soft indicator to Damian that he might take caution in trying to command the attention of this room—or any room—when Somaya was present.

He released his hold on her flaccid digits, which returned a small dose of victory to Somaya.

"Thank you, Valeria. I trust what we have for you will continue to strengthen the work we do together," Somaya said.

"And you, Mr. Worsley, I don't believe you are with Valeria's team, correct?" Somaya asked after finally turning her attention back to him.

"Indeed, Ms. Patel," he said, addressing her formally in a way that he did not expect from himself. "I am working on contract with ANEER from Andreesen Consulting."

"Oh right. Okay, that's good to know. And your remit here?" she inquired.

"We are conducting a statewide security audit across all key infrastructure systems, so I've been working with Hugo and Rafael," he said as he nodded toward the two men on the other side of the table.

It was now Somaya's turn to interrupt. "Hi guys, great to see you both again." She walked over and delivered a more informal kiss on each cheek of the two ANEER executives she had been working with for years. She was always glad to see them, as they offered that rare combination of being exceptionally enjoyable to work with as well as representing a large stake of revenue for CVI.

Damian tried to reclaim the ownership of the discussion, "And I've also been working with Valeria and her team outside of energy-specific sectors, though there's an entire manor's worth of overlap between what you're doing and what we've been up to." As he said this, he looked to Valeria, with her gaze back at him reinforcing his attempt at taking a more authoritative voice in the room, if only to help justify why he was allowed to be there.

In that instant, Somaya could glean that there was more than just a professional relationship between Damian and Valeria. The connection between them when they glanced at each other, even though it was only for a fraction of a second, was communicative beyond the dimension of time and without the necessity for words.

I can use this, she thought to herself. *Just need to understand who these people are, what role they serve for us, what their real lives are like, married, kids, do they both live here?* An endless stream of questions populated Somaya's mind as she took this sub-second inference from the human dynamics in the room to build out an entire plan of attack as to how she could best manipulate these two people.

What this observation also allowed her to do was forgive Damian for his interruption up front. Especially as she watched their interaction throughout the meeting, she realized very quickly that he had not done so out of ego or myopia to those around him but mostly due to a certain amount of comfort in being in the presence of Valeria. What she had initially registered as an offensive position had now become a weapon she could redeploy against its source. Somaya thrived on the anticipation that came with recognizing when people showed up with a predisposition to be overwhelmed. It was a definitive aspect of her now well-honed strategy to *always be prolific*.

The meeting shifted from introductions and niceties to the matter of the day. Somaya took the lead, moving from her seat at the far end of the board room to the front of the room near the presentation wall, and began to speak.

***

As there were new participants in the room, she decided to give a complete introduction to Computer Vision Infosystems, or CVI, as it was now most commonly known. The company was founded in early 1998, during the dotcom boom. The original focus of the business was security camera installation and management, initially operating out of a small semi-industrial warehouse facility in Redmond, Washington. Microsoft and

Nintendo were two of the earliest customers for CVI, or *Camera* Vision Infosystems, as it was known at the time.

The company had quickly signed on several corporate clients in those early days due to the rapid expansion of other technology businesses and the growing concern around security. Y2K was a fantastic fearmongering movement that increased security budgets across the board. Yet, ironically, because most of the fast-growing companies had extremely nascent IT and network policies, the easiest thing for them to spend money on that could sit undeterred on the balance sheet was security camera infrastructure. It didn't require broader IT upgrades that usually came with much longer procurement cycles and extensive audits.

They had been beneficiaries of those heady economic times that had been famously remarked upon by the cautious words of Fed Chairman Alan Greenspan, words that seemed irrationally exuberant to those riding the crest of new website ideas, new companies based on those ideas, new venture capital to fund those companies, and new agencies to help spend all that money. This feedback loop fueled the early growth of CVI, but in yet another example of how all good things come to an end, as fast as those markets had grown, they unraveled even faster. The company soon found itself chasing down cash receivables owed to them from non-paying customers after the dotcom crash began in March of 2000.

As a result of a number of CVI's customers going out of business, the company was left holding the bag in many cases. Or, more aptly put, left holding enormous quantities of office surveillance footage that, as a result of bankruptcies and forfeitures, belonged to no one. With network infrastructure in place for a large customer base that no longer existed, they chose to store and maintain all that extraneous footage, even without any justifiably good reason to do so.

It was a few years later that Somaya joined the company as a marketing intern, in 2005, while CVI had still been limping along. The finances were only kept afloat by maintenance contracts with some of its largest customers, which, fortunately, still included Microsoft and Nintendo.

Within CVI, there had always been very little attention or understanding placed on the role of marketing, the entire department of which consisted of Somaya and her boss, Jeff Christiansen. For years, Jeff had been receiving blame for the fortunes, or lack thereof, of the company. The company's founders were all technologists who refused to accept that broader market conditions were behind those austere times. Somaya's addition had only been approved with the ulterior motive that it would prove once and for all that Jeff was responsible for the problems of CVI; that if he had what he needed to succeed, then succeed he must.

How could one person influence the state of the entire company? Somaya wondered after a discussion with Jeff shortly after her joining had exposed those frayed relationships.

The day after divulging the teetering state of the business to Omniwatch during that fateful drunken night in 2005, Somaya had also found herself in a boardroom filled with men. She was hungover, tired, dehydrated, and just wanted to go home to the contained accommodation of her spartan one-bedroom apartment in Bellevue. All they needed from that meeting was a handshake on the deal for CVI to take on hardware updates and maintenance of five Omniwatch customers. Both companies had been struggling, so it seemed like a ripe opportunity for the partnership to collaborate.

"We have a change to propose," announced the lead negotiator from Omniwatch.

A change to propose. Those words that pierced the meeting are still as fresh in her mind now as they were back then, almost eighteen years ago.

"We have decided to adjust the terms of our proposal. We still want to offer you the five customer contracts, but now for a limited two-year term. In exchange, we receive the primary position on the two discussed contracts from CVI, and we'd be willing to license those back to you for the same two-year term."

Oh... my... god...

This was a terrible outcome. Somaya felt sick to her stomach—not from the hangover, but from the immediate realization that the information she had shared with the Omniwatch team was the catalyst for this change in deal terms.

She had spilled her guts, and now she felt like throwing up.

CVI had been backed into a corner from which there was no obvious escape, essentially being forced to give up the Microsoft and Nintendo contracts over the long-term in exchange for a two-year grace period—a grace period that was akin to walking a plank.

She hadn't been prolific in her efforts that week at the conference. Far from it, she had been prolifically stupid. A prolific disaster.

Two things came from her unintended near-sinking of the company. The first was the last lesson she would learn directly from Jeff, a study on accountability. He took the fall for her mistake, recognizing that he should have been a better mentor to his freshly-minted intern. His experience and intuition also told him that if he assigned any blame to Somaya, they would both be fired, so he gave her the option to stay.

"I'll vote myself off the island, Somaya," Jeff had said, invoking a theme from one of his favorite shows. He admitted, falsely, to the company's leaders that he had been the one to share too much information with Omniwatch, thus leading to them making the predatory change in their proposal. With his flame shortly thereafter extinguished, Somaya, the intern, became the sole remaining non-technical team member.

The second outcome from her loose lips became the best lesson she would ever teach herself. As a sports fan, Somaya had been well aware of the importance of having a "short memory." Not in such a way that it would degrade one's ability to remember or prevent them from building a deep bank of knowledge, but from the standpoint of not allowing recent mistakes to cloud one's judgment on the next decision or to diminish one's confidence. The best baseball pitchers give up home runs. The best quarterbacks throw interceptions. The best sprinters stumble out of the gates. Even Serena Williams hits double faults. It's not what they do in that specific moment that defines them, but rather, what they do next. Or, in the case of a double fault, what they do next, next.

To her benefit, a short memory was made that much easier by how blindingly and forgetfully drunk she had been.

With a second lease on her professional life and now effectively in charge of business operations at CVI after Jeff's unceremonious dismissal because of his "error in judgment," Somaya had decisively facilitated the defining move that would set the course for CVI over the next two decades.

She chose to look at the Omniwatch deal not as the disaster it was, but as a pivotal moment to completely change what the company was and what CVI was trying to do. Gone was the company that was a ghost of its former self, selling cameras and wires and a few computer systems to store data to the few healthy companies they could convince to take it. In place of it, she was able to articulate a new plan to rise from the ashes, an organization of stubbornly brilliant technologists, an ambitious businessperson, several petabytes of surveillance data, and as the last piece of the puzzle, a new partnership with Rotten Tomatoes, Inc. (not the film website).

What Somaya had done—perhaps taking a cue from the blood-in-the-water deal architects at Omniwatch—was negotiate a licensing arrangement with Warren Simpson that gave them access to his computer vision code libraries, with the important provision—important for Warren—that they would not compete in any industry particular to surveying the expiring contents of refrigerators. Also partial to the deal was the option to acquire Rotten Tomatoes, Inc. (not the film website) on conditions that were generally favorable to CVI. And with that deal in place, Camera Vision Infosystems became *Computer* Vision Infosystems.

Now, in her presentation in the Faria Lima B32 boardroom, Somaya didn't share this much of the backstory of CVI, nor did she talk about her drunken night at the conference after-party, nor the fact that she had given away terribly sensitive confidential information that nearly shuttered the company. Instead, she opted for the preferential revisionist history of how she had seen a wave of Artificial Intelligence coming and realized that CVI was on the cusp of using visual knowledge for the benefit of many. It was also an easier and more inspiring story to share if she talked about how they had built and architected all of CVI's systems internally, from the ground up, rather than divulge the myriad other acquisitions that had followed the very early deal with Warren and his Rotten Tomatoes, Inc. (not the film website) business.

"So let me show you where we are going... where we are going together," Somaya said as she transitioned from the short history of CVI to a confidential view into some of their most groundbreaking recent advancements.

She proceeded to demonstrate how CVI's AI systems were capable of consuming vast amounts of visual data from a near-infinite number of sources in just about any format to generate insights on the performance of systems related to that content. She shared examples of airports using CVI's algorithms to re-assign planes and customers throughout their terminals, thereby improving turnaround times and on-time reliability of flights.

Those same implementations were able to track luggage specific to individual travelers from one CVI-equipped airport to another.

"Security infrastructure is not just for when bad things happen. Here, we are using all that same technology in other ways, and our customers have happier customers. Lost baggage rates are way down, and those airports participating in this system have much fewer security alerts over suspicious bags left unclaimed. On balance, the increased safety outweighs any potential privacy issues," she proudly shared, looking at Damian and Valeria as if she were answering questions they had not yet asked and would no longer need to.

Somaya followed with two other examples where CVI's technology had been implemented with great efficacy. The first was a hospital in southern Europe using a CVI algorithm to visually assess illness conditions as people came in the door of their Urgent Care Center. The system appeared to be using a combination of sensory inputs, pulling feeds from the entryway surveillance cameras, strategically placed microphones, as well as air quality and temperature sensors. This allowed the hospital to more immediately triage and assign doctors and health care workers to particular cases that they would be most effective at dealing with, and to ensure that patients were seated in the waiting areas and shared rooms in such a way to avoid cross-contagion and the risk of introducing new illnesses to at-risk patients.

The last example she shared was a deployment of their technology with greater commercial ambitions. CVI had a shopping mall client in Southern California who had been using computer vision to read and interpret its customers' shopping patterns, demographics, and social dynamics. From that information, programming logic was written to dynamically adjust lighting, audio, and aromas dispersed within the mall, which would subtly but significantly influence shopper behavior. Their object detection framework was used to assess shoppers on a combination of ethnicity, age, walking gait, clothing, and posture, from which they computed several different scores that would feed into those ambient environment systems.

"Like rats in a maze?" Damian asked.

"We prefer to think of it as meeting unstated demand. In your analogy, feeding a hungry rat what they most like to eat," replied Somaya. "Although they are even using the data to adjust Wi-Fi strength within the mall. I have to admit it's pretty funny seeing what happens to people when they can't get to their socials!" Anecdotally, she had heard from the general manager of the largest department store that, done right, slow Wi-Fi is a good trigger for people to move to the checkout aisles and pick up a few impulse purchases along the way. Apparently, it activates that instinct to get outside, where the sun is shining, and 5G signals remain strong.

These case studies were an interesting cross-section of what CVI had been able to do for its customer base, but they paled in comparison to what they had been providing for Brazil and its citizens. She spent over forty-five minutes going through an update on their work with ANEER. Their solution had led to an effective redistribution of power transmission across most of the country, along with a strategic deployment of backup battery systems. They had been able to ensure higher electricity availability for everyone and a greater surplus of energy available for export, all while reducing the dependence on non-renewable sources of energy. It was a remarkable achievement, and as Somaya shared, it would not have been possible without the near nationwide access they had to city surveillance cameras.

"Granted, you have given us access and permission to do things here that most countries have shied away from. That, I believe, is a credit to the innovative nature of the Brazilian people and the commitment to steer your people forward to a carbon-free future. This is the kind of thing you are doing that is not getting enough attention, especially in light of all the coverage of rainforest destruction and so on," Somaya said, speaking proudly on behalf of her work for the country.

"What we are seeing with this data and the insights we're extracting is that we are getting so much more than we could have ever expected out of surveillance footage. It's the structured nature of all of it, and you have allowed us to collaborate so carefully with you, developing the templates and datasets to really understand how we as humans can work better with nature and use our intellect to solve these very big problems." She again nodded at Valeria and Damian, looking for them to reciprocate, which they both did. She knew that if they could prove that privacy and security were a non-issue in a place as big as Brazil, with the economic clout it carried on a global scale, it could be a massive catalyst for CVI.

"That's why working with groups such as yours is helping us push the value that we can create and that we can bring to your customers," she said in a statement with such conviction and commitment that it sounded more like an election promise than a matter-of-fact description of what they had been doing.

As those words passed her lips, Somaya thought for a moment about what she was saying. Having been deep within the CVI business for over fifteen years, she took pride in understanding as much of the technology as she did. But over the last few years, it had become harder and harder to understand exactly how their software was doing what it was doing. The general explanation from the engineering team had been that it was becoming more and more of a "black box" due to the complexity of the self-learning algorithms. In essence, their AI was self-educating itself, albeit with the framed and still limited context of surveillance camera inputs.

But how are we able to pull this together while so many of these public technologies are still so shite?! Like self-driving cars, those things can hardly stay in a straight line. She would often struggle with this dichotomy of thought. On the one hand, she found herself celebrating the growth of her business, leveraging technologies that seemed to have these otherworldly capabilities of harvesting insights from content. Yet, on the other hand, as a member of the consuming public, many of the "smart" systems she touched and used on a daily basis didn't seem to be able to teach themselves anything.

Teach themselves? Not even close, these other things couldn't even feed themselves or go to the bathroom by themselves, she thought to herself as she prepared to share her concluding materials: a recommendation for ANEER and Brazil as a whole to embrace a five-year plan leading to the world's biggest implementation of CVI's technologies.

Ten

BREAKING

Doug turned the corner, and there she was. A ravenous look had infiltrated her hazel eyes, but had not yet determined where to direct its focus. Henny appeared to be staring vacantly and vacuously across the room, indifferent to his existence. A knife in one hand presented an ominous appearance. However, once he had processed that it was paired with a fork in her other hand, the potential for danger was dispelled.

She raised one of the severed balls to her mouth and took a bite. The remaining crunchy, torched portion of each falafel counterbalanced the still-soft exposed mash of chickpea and spices in the other half. Henny thought to herself, *this is not half-bad*. She then sliced some of the tomatoes and peppers in her salad and savored the juicy and crispy combination of the two brightly colored vegetables.

Looking up from her exhaustion-induced and culinary-sustained stupor, she realized the fleeting minutes she had to herself had come to an end as Doug had sheepishly entered the kitchen-and-dining area of their old home.

He wanted to be anywhere else but there. A few minutes before, Doug was sitting on the couch in the living room holding the smashed-up glassy device. He had scanned it over and tried to find a button or a control of any kind, and wondered if he could tape it up or maybe pour glue into the cracks. He didn't know how to bring this back to Henny now. Clearly, it had been all his fault, knocking it out of her hands like that and causing it to smash on the floor.

"Um. I think it's broken," he said as he lifted up the device to show Henny.

By this point, she couldn't bring herself to care. The week had been intense enough already. For that moment, while enjoying her juicy tomatoes, crispy peppers, and crunchy fried chickpea, she was glad it was broken.

"It's okay, Doug. Don't worry about it," she offered in a very subdued tone.

It wasn't like Henny to be so reserved, Doug thought. Normally, she was one of the most active, animated, and excitable people he knew. *She should be pissed right now!*

"You sure? I can get it fixed or get you another one," Doug said, without thinking through the situation. Notably, they didn't even know what it was or where it came from, so finding someone to fix it or somewhere to replace it seemed like a pretty tall order.

"Honestly, I don't care."

"What's wrong?"

Was it because I broke the thing? Oh no, she's gonna hate me.

"You really want to know?" Henny asked rhetorically, as she was now mostly certain that whatever he said in response, if anything at all, would be met with her delivering all of her problems. Hell, if she couldn't have peace and quiet, then she might as well be the one filling the air and taking up emotional space.

For his part, Doug was feeling a bit energized. She just offered to have what seemed like a real conversation with him. Henny was going to confide in him. It was rare for someone to look at him as a trusted destination for their troubles. It seemed to Doug that, too often, he was the cause of people's mental indigestion, not a place for them to conversationally relieve themselves.

"Okay, so that article I wrote last week, did you read it?" she asked.

"The one about Spectra, 'The Fix Is In'...? Yeah, I loved that title," he said, excited that he could quickly participate.

"That title is terrible. But no matter. Okay. So, you read it. I'm actually impressed, Dougie. I didn't think you would have seen it."

Dougie! He was back in her good books now. *This is great! Damn it!* He also knew he hadn't read the article, but he had a good idea of its contents, mostly because of his proximal eavesdropping on conversations she had with other people during her research. Trapped within a white lie of his own fabrication, he suffered panic that his false pretense of speaking intelligently about the article relied upon a secret invasion of private conversations of the person he was trying to impress. *What if I talk about something that wasn't in the article? Oh shit.*

"Uh, yep," was the extent of his initial feedback. He nervously strained to avoid exposing his previously unannounced presence in the shadows of her work.

"Alright, so I wrote this damn thing because we were all getting sick of how poorly they run this place, right? The overloaded classrooms, curriculum isn't being upgraded, the job placements are always the same stuff. It's not just us, either. I've heard this from older grads from the last few years. I mean, that's why I started looking into this."

Doug was surprised and impressed that she could get so passionate about the topic. He wondered for a moment what she thought of the dividing wall in Lecture Hall 4B.

She continued, "So, it turns out the Board of Governors for this place, it's basically a bunch of cronies, a group of fat fuckin' pieces of shit. And they have their hands deep in our pockets, Dougie." He looked down at his pants pockets and then across the room at hers. Her tight jeans stretched even tighter as she sat on the old wooden dining chair. His first thought was that no one could fit their hands in her pockets.

"Yeah, I know," he encouraged her continued rant. Just as quickly, he realized that he didn't know. Doug looked down again at the broken device, still in his hands, wanting to deflect her attention away from him and her expectation that he contribute productively to this discussion.

"One hundred million dollars! Do you know that's basically how much tuition they get from us every year?" She was incensed. "That's just a huge amount of money for this shithole! And they just keep sending more students through this goddamn mill every year, doing the same things over and over, just watching us to make sure they can do just enough to get more coming in the next year."

"Holy shit! That is a lot of money for sure," his yes-man tactics continued.

"But the crazy thing is, none of that is coming back here. And I found it. They keep pushing students through this place like fucking robots every year, year after year. Meanwhile, they got this IT company in Delaware that's got a massive contract on the place, and a security company, and then some infrastructure stuff, and they are all owned by those guys. You can find it if you look for it," she kept building her case even in the absence of taking enough breaths.

"So then on Monday, the editor of the paper, and she had the stupid idea for the title, she calls me up and says she's getting lit up by the Dean's Office for putting my stuff out there. I mean, I guess at least that was good I had the heads-up 'cuz then they called me a day later. I had to go in there on Wednesday and yesterday. It's like a fucking Gestapo interrogation room. They had me bent over backwards, those bastards!" She was furious and possibly exaggerating the reality of what had happened.

"Oh wow," Doug was upset that he had said he liked the title of the article. And he was also sort of excited thinking about Henny being bent over backwards, in a respectful appreciation of the female form and not in the context of enjoying the idea of a Gestapo interrogation room torture chamber, as his conscious mind was quick to remind itself, awkwardly shaking his head at the very thought. But he knew the best thing he could do now was to keep listening and to let her get it all out, as he still couldn't think of anything to say. Thankfully, she broke the short, strained silence before he was compelled to make more noise.

"Now they've got this hundred million bucks that goes god knows where, and here they are in this shitty room basically telling me to slow my roll. I think they said things like, 'For the good of the school, you can't get people worked up like this, it's no good for anything,' and I'm like, 'Hey, you've got us here to learn how to find the truth and write a good story, so what the hell is this?' And they're like, 'There's a time and a place.' And it just went on like that," she continued.

"I can't believe that. But you're okay, right?" Doug replied, intending to come across as thoughtful and helpful but quickly realizing he might've misread the situation a little. The broken device was still a good distraction, so he looked down at it again. Seeing the network of smashed glass fragments on the inoperable screen reminded him that it still did not work, and likely, no matter how many times he looked down at it, he would conclude the same. In fact, what he could see was his own reflection, albeit broken up by this spider web of cracks in the display screen. It revealed a guy who was trying to be friendly but clearly out of his comfort zone, looking downwards at his hands to avoid being put on the spot. *Damn it, more awkward than before!* He sought to mitigate the discomfort by equally awkwardly looking up and placing the broken device on the counter next to him. *Okay, I can do this, I can be a part of this,* his internal motivational speaker whispered to its antithesis reclusive self.

"No, I'm not fucking okay! Like, I'm pretty sure they were thinking I'd just roll over and stop all this because they asked, right? And then they are pretty much implying that if I don't stop looking into this, they are going to kick me out or make my life hell or something... it was like they were making threats but not really using actual words."

He was following her voice, taking in this entire scene. He couldn't help but be mesmerized by how tired she looked and how inspired and animated she was in her diatribe. For her part, the emotions were boiling as Henny was now in her own private auditorium, her own broadcast booth, able to say anything and everything she wanted about the situation, knowing that she had an audience. She had needed an outlet for the stress that had been building up, and here was her therapy, the clarity sought by her mind and body, all in one go.

It went on. "It's totally fucking nuts. These guys just go around and do whatever they want and take our money and leave us in a steaming pile of a campus with shitty classes and a stupid newspaper, and then I get this? I mean... for fuck's sake! FUCK ME, Dougie!"

On this, his face lit up like a Christmas tree. Not only was he confident that she had come to the end of the soapbox session without busting him for not having read the article, but right at the end of her story, the last word out of her mouth was his name, just the way he liked it! And good god, how she said it and what preceded it was far too much for Doug to take.

Henny had been looking at him more or less the whole time she had been talking, but with his ever-so-subtle reaction to her closing comments and, especially those last three words, she narrowed her eyes and looked right at his face, her hazel eyes and steeled expression boring right into his rudimentary soul.

He was so alone in this moment trying to comprehend what was happening, strangely juxtaposed with the feeling that he had never been so connected with anyone else.

She started to smile, a wry, mischievous grin lifting the corners of her lips. She started to laugh, just a very subtle quirky giggle. "Right?" she said, that single word being the most powerful word Doug could ever remember hearing.

He nodded and smiled in an ambiguously overwhelmed way.

She didn't need that indicator from him. The feelings going through her body just now were intense. She had never been in a situation where she could voice her opinion on something that she felt so strongly about, and to do so in a way that was unimpeded by other opinions and ideas, by authority, or by whatever perceived antagonist might be in her way. In these moments, Henny had ruled the room, and she had delivered her monologue and silenced the opposition, albeit a non-existent one.

She looked down at her half-eaten dinner. The falafels and salad were unchanged but no longer looked as appetizing as they had just minutes ago.

"Fuck me, Dougie," she repeated.

Her body and mind were in a synchronized state. Facing complete exhaustion, they had each been renewed and re-energized by the preceding few minutes. The combination of the anticipation of the thing in the package, the mystery of the card, the fire in the kitchen, the smoke and grime in the air, and now this emotionally charged session of her rant about the stupidly titled article that Dougie seemed to care about, she just wanted one thing right now.

She took a last bite of the luscious, juicy tomato on her fork and stood up. She walked over to Doug, her chest heaving and her breasts perking up. She giggled again as she approached him, putting her hands on his waist.

Doug couldn't move, even though at least one part of him was moving promptly, now standing to attention just as he had been throughout his attentive listening. His smile also grew bigger, and a sparkle formed in his eyes to match the one in hers. As Henny looked up at him, he seemed more aware, knowledgeable, and desirable than she had ever perceived.

She gripped his waist, pulled him against her, and wrapped her arms around his upper back. Their lips met instantly, a near-perfect connection. The taste of tomatoes and chickpeas on hers merged with the sugary taste of Coca-Cola Classic and some small orange remnants of Doritos on his.

Doug picked her up, his slender frame and generally underused muscles easily able to bear the weight of Henny's lithe build. She wrapped her legs around his waist as he placed his hands on her backside. He walked her forward to the edge of the dining table, sending her dinner plate flying off the table and onto the floor.

The kitchen in this foursquare was disproportionately small. Originally in a more utilitarian layout of the space, the dining area would have been allocated to what was now the living room, long before the need for televisions, Xboxes, and the occasional college party keg stand. The table was of the same vintage as the house and bore the signs of surviving what had been a few generations of families residing within, followed by a dozen or more rapid generations of college-age renters. It was heftily made, originally scaled for that larger portion of real estate in the living room, with several sections of thick hardwood making up the top surface that sat upon solid, shapely table legs at each corner. While it still performed admirably as a dinner table, and the vertical integrity of the surface and legs combined could hold a significant amount of weight, the rigidity of the connected pieces left much to be desired.

Conversely, Henny and Doug were on their way to leaving nothing to be desired, provided that Doug could maintain some semblance of composure and stamina. They were slobbering over each other, their lips making contact and then smearing saliva all around the lower third of both faces. The whole thing was intensely messy and engaged, just like the evening had been thus far. Their bodies compressed tightly together, still fully clothed, with Henny thrusting her pelvic area against Doug as her legs formed intermittent vice grips on each side of his waist.

Doug thought he was losing his mind. He had no notable experience with women, and certainly nothing like this had ever happened to him. Yet, as the scene continued to unfold, he felt more and more comfortable in every way. The noise, not to be confused with signal, that normally permeated his thoughts throughout the day, had dissipated, much like it does when he found himself locked in to an Xbox or PC game. In fact, this was definitely more like a PC game, something that needed the right attention to understand the controls, the objective, and the right way to play. A console game was usually more casual and flippant, something he could jump into, play for a bit, and then put down.

He did not want to put Henny down any time soon.

Breathe! Doug told himself. He recognized the onset of a similarly intense oxygen-deprivation response to playing video games when he would get too focused and one-dimensionally consumed by the unfolding narrative, often for hours on end.

He took a big, deep breath, bringing in a much-needed blast of air, infused with her wondrous smells. *A hint of coconut!* Maintaining any of this for hours would be near impossible, but he quickly latched onto the thought that he needed to keep it up for a healthy number of minutes, at whatever cost.

They continued to rock back and forth in this position, with Henny grinding against the table and Doug's midsection. Everything seemed to be moving with them in this special moment of unison. Creaking and groaning under the physics at play, the heavy table legs and the even heavier surface were challenging the hundred-year-old assembly holding them together. It was heaving and twisting just as they were. With one big push, the intense forces channeling through Henny's buttocks had proven to be too much. The construction of it gave way, and the tabletop took on a mind of its own as the connections to its legs failed. Still attached but no longer secure, the solid hardwood dining surface shot away from their roiling midsections. It slammed against the wall, the plasterwork buckling and bruising but refusing to break. It had already weathered a century of residential activity and would not give up on this day.

The tabletop rebounded from the wall, and Henny bounced forcefully against Doug. As the table's large legs started to give out, so did those of Doug, who was also very large by this point. Fortunately, the furthest legs of the table had also jammed themselves against the wall, the whole broken mess now forming a triangular shape with the surface as hypotenuse. The table had become a smooth wooden playground slide that carefully conveyed them both to the floor, still wrapped up in a wondrous web of each other's arms and legs.

They pulled their lips off each other's faces long enough to look at each other and laugh, both recognizing the hilariousness of the situation and enjoying the consensuality of this random and crazy event.

They rolled over, their upper halves still lying on the sloped table, and Henny now on top of Doug. She looked down at him, then reached down with a hand on each side of her thin waist and pulled her short, tight v-neck shirt over her head, revealing a petit bra which contained her heaving breasts. Her skin was smooth, youthful, and soft to Doug's touch.

By now, they had essentially been deposited in front of Doug's bedroom, the original drawing room of the house closed off by a big oak door. She put one hand on Doug's chest, an indication to pause what he was doing, and she reached for the large brass handle on Doug's door, pulling it down and lifting herself as she did so. The door opened, and she took two steps in.

Eleven

MARKET STREET

The hip-hop beat boomed across the concrete sidewalk. The sound had depth, a melodic vibe, a deep bass line, and some catchy lyrics, some of which were decipherable, but most were so fast as to be another instrument in the composition.

It was playing from a small Bluetooth speaker that delivered an amazingly full soundscape, especially considering the device's size. The speaker sat nestled amongst a few boxes of books and clothes, and behind a blanket spread out on the walkway, requiring pedestrians to navigate in lemming-like repetition around the dozen or more sunglasses that were merchandized upon it.

The vendor sitting between the speaker and the sunglasses had been operating near Market Street in downtown San Francisco for a few years. That city's enforcement policies allowed him to run a remarkably lucrative business as long as he made sure to clean up or clear out the occasional time an inspector came around. In his mind, the vendor couldn't rationalize paying commercial rent when he could run his storefront from some of the busiest places in town.

He sat there with his phone in hand, reviewing an inventory re-supply order coming through the AlleyOverseas app, where he ordered all his product. Any self-respecting hustling entrepreneur knew that was the place to get their product from, especially after the recent IPO announcement from the company with a target valuation of four billion dollars. A notification came in on his phone from Business Matters, an online news source that the vendor relied on.

"Former President found to be born in Russia, as ex-Reality Show host rigs ballot boxes to win Gubernatorial Election," the notification read.

Damn, what the what? These goddamn white people just can't let each other off the hook. He switched gears, took his mind off his business for a minute, and began reading the search-engine optimized article that was waiting for him, its authority bolstered by the more than 48,000 likes showing up at the top of the page, powered by the Mixality social media platform.

Eight skateboard wheels were rolling over diverse sections of sidewalk a few blocks away, replete with skateboard decks attached and teenagers perched on top. There were two of them, each building momentum on four of the wheels. Riding on the left, one teenager in regular stance had his right foot stationary at the back. His locomotion was powered by a huge repetitive stride with his other leg, placing it on the front half of the board for added control whenever he needed to navigate a curb or a pedestrian. The skater on the right was in the opposite pose but often preferred to push with his back leg, depending on the terrain and how much he needed to adjust while at speed.

They were regular and goofy, left-leaning and right-dominant, but they were the closest of friends, in conversation as they rolled down the sidewalk together.

"Yo, hear that beat!" one said to the other.

"Yeah, that's pretty sick," came the reply.

They gravitated toward the source of the music, and the goofy teenager lowered himself, popped up into the air, and rotated his body and the skateboard a near-flawless 180 degrees in an effortless switch ollie. He was now regular as well, riding in the same stance as his friend.

They were still moving in the general direction of the Yerba Buena Gardens, where the boys planned to skate on some of the concrete features and formations, at least until the inevitable appearance of park security. With this detour, they would just have to deal with more pedestrians than they expected on the way.

Which felt like it had potential for memorable activity.

Out of his deep pocketed shorts came a compact black metallic stick. Extending it, he tapped the button on top of the BePro camera to activate the recording from his selfie stick. The street music would provide a ready-made soundtrack.

As they bobbed and weaved through pedestrians, the skaters quickly bore down on the music-playing vendor. The first skater quickly took in the scene of music filling the air, the Black man deeply engrossed in his mobile phone, and the neat rows of sunglasses presented before him.

"Check it, Max!" he called to his friend, Max, the other skater. Max held his right arm further back to capture a wider shot from the camera as he moved into a wingman position.

"Hit it, Roddy!" yelled Max, directing his formation leader to pull off some kind of trick inspired by the beat.

Roddy bent low, preparing to ollie and launch himself over the blanket. He realized the vendor was still oblivious to his pending arrival, that man staring at the interaction of his thumb on a piece of glass, lost in an empty dimension of clickbait. *Look at the grin on this shit-eater's face,* Roddy's internal voice commented, which he thought was remarkably funny.

In a last-second addition to his planned trick, he put his left hand down as if to grab the board but instead kept his fingers outstretched. In one sequence of stylistic choreography, he popped the board into the air while strafing the blanket with his open hand to grab several pairs of sunglasses, intending to relieve the merchant of even more inventory that would need to be replenished.

Max had kept the selfie cam rolling.

Roddy was chuckling to himself as he sailed through the air, leveling out the skateboard before it smacked back down to earth on the other side. Four wheels hit in unison, the board flexed, and Roddy stomped his feet to offset the force of landing, with all this combined motion re-articulating the forces of gravity to add velocity to his forward movement.

"Damn, kid!" Max yelled in admiration for his friend's sweet flow on the board, not to be mistaken for the vendor, who had stood up yelling, "Damn you, kid!"

These damn kids always fucking around with my stuff!

Roddy looked to the right to acknowledge his friend's kudos and then to the left and over his shoulder, intending to deliver as smart-ass of a grin as he could to the vendor. But his pivoting attention distracted him from the changing conditions directly in his path.

A man and woman had walked out from the front doors of an office building not more than ten feet ahead, both also staring at the smartphones they held.

He was dressed in a blue designer suit—an Italian knockoff—with his pants tightly fitting, his socks non-existent, and an equally pretentious set of brown leather shoes with excessive stitching on both sides. With no tie, his short shirt collar was open by the measure of two buttons, which put the figurative fleshy bow on his 2010-era Silicon Valley uniform. The woman walking with him was wearing a tight green top under a short beige jacket and ripped white jeans folded halfway up her toned calf muscles, those lower legs extra-flexed and toned from the uncomfortable stride of walking in semi-casual high heels.

They had both built their virtual wardrobes on Fitterest, a fashion-sharing web bulletin board that had raised over seventy-five million dollars just a few months prior. Acceptable ensembles were assembled through a proprietary automated grading system, the Fitterest Fashion Stylist, or FFS. Both of them, once satisfied that they had achieved maximum FFS, would have completed the purchase with Paypal and had the clothing shipped to them through PopShip, the latest logistics darling that spawned out of an Alameda warehouse and now boasted over 2,000 employees and distribution centers in just about every major market.

The man and woman in all their Bay Area splendor could have been the cover couple for the latest *Technorati Quarterly*, if such a publication existed, and only if the photo would have been taken right then and there, not a minute later.

Roddy slammed into them both, and the three became a jumbled mess of Fitterest fashions, smart-ass grins, and broken sunglasses. A skateboard and two smartphones had gone flying, wayward in three different directions.

The man and woman fell hard to the sidewalk. New rips had appeared in the woman's jeans, and that same fashion styling seemed to have transferred to the man's designer suit, along with the addition of road rash and blood on one of his knees. FFS scores were dropping by the second.

"Oh my god, my phone!" he called out from a prone position on the sidewalk, despite the fact he was locked in a weird pose of opposite scissor legs with Roddy. He had fallen backward just in time to receive Roddy sliding into him like a baseball player stealing second base, yet the man's primary concern was not his clothes, his bloody knee, the proximity of his genitals with those of a stranger, or the wellbeing of his presumed friend. It was his smartphone, which was still out of sight but far from out of mind.

The woman had screamed loudly, initially reflecting her surprise, but quickly, the noise from her mouth became solely focused on expressing pain. She had taken the leading edge of the hardwood skateboard directly in the side of her shin. Her phone was a trivial concern for a rare moment, as nearly every receptor of any type of feeling in her body was focused on that single point of contact on her leg. A bone bruise had already formed, and that leg would be swollen for days to come.

At the moment of collision with the tribal techies, Roddy's body partially spun to his left. His right leg led forward in a weak ninja-kick attempt to brace himself for contact. His left leg sent the skateboard accelerating backward in the same motion.

Propelled by Newtonian forces, the skateboard seemed to have a clear sense of conscience or, possibly, saw itself as a barter offering. It came to a stop right at the feet of the sunglasses vendor.

Max had been recording the entire incident, though his initial directorial treatment did not contemplate anything like what had happened, to happen. He had simply thought about good beats, a good flow, and the diverse and interesting non-consenting background cast of everyone on the sidewalk. He realized he was now filming a non-permitted documentary of theft from a non-permitted vendor, with the sequel likely to include a fucking lawsuit coming from these valley douchebags. But he couldn't stop, and neither could anyone else.

"Are you alright, miss?" a voice from the crowd asked, concerned for the women screaming and rolling on the ground.

"Dude, you're crazy! Someone call the cops!" someone else yelled, directing their words at Roddy and then no one in particular.

"Look at all this shit!" someone else was saying, with their attention on several pairs of smashed-up sunglasses and a smartphone lying in the gutter of the sidewalk.

A crowd had started to gather, and nearly everyone had their digital cameras and smartphones out to capture this unplanned spectacle.

Meanwhile, the vendor had picked up the skateboard, incensed at once again being taken advantage of by troublemaking kids. He wasn't that old himself, but his time hustling on the streets had aged him in exchange for the financial security and stability it had provided for his family, contrary to how thousands of pedestrians may have judged him on a daily basis.

"You, kid, what the hell you think you're doing?" he yelled out as he took steps toward Roddy, who had now regained his feet and was facing the vendor.

The vendor struck a somewhat menacing pose in his dark green, almost military-color, wool cap, eyes open wide in anger, and now holding Roddy's board. To the bystanders, it was hard to ascertain what exactly was happening. A Black man working illegally on the street charged at a young white kid and two tribal techies. Or was it two white middle-class hooligans who had attacked an honest merchant and assaulted two businesspeople? San Francisco was a melting pot, as they say, and the street scene represented this, with the growing crowd around this mayhem representing a diverse mix of ethnicities, styles, backgrounds, and opinions. FFS scores were all over the place. But like most places celebrating their melting-pot-ness, the inherent racism was strong, and the explicit classism in this city was so thick it most definitely couldn't be cut with a skateboard, no matter how much damage it might be able to wreak upon someone's shins.

As the vendor approached Roddy, Max quickly collapsed his selfie stick and stuffed it in his pockets. He kick-flipped his skateboard up and was now holding it in two hands, sort of as one might if they were waving smoke out of a kitchen with the latest edition of *Technorati Quarterly,* if such a publication were to exist. However, Max's intentions were not to clear the air nor cut through the bias of the populace. He was reacting in the moment in quite likely the worst possible way, his adrenaline encouraging him to do whatever it took to get them the hell out of there.

He approached the vendor, coming at him from the side just as the man was closing in on Roddy. Max was too obvious and too slow. He swung his skateboard at the vendor, who by now had noticed Max's ill-conceived attempt at violence and managed to deftly and smoothly step to the side and avoid it.

As Max over-rotated with the skateboard in his hands, the Black man quickly took control. Still holding the other skateboard, he grabbed both sides of it and pushed it forward into Max's exposed right-side oblique muscles. The leading edge of this board had already done a number on the screaming woman's shin, and it once again was up for the challenge. The board's layered and smooth hardwood edge slotted in like a Jenga piece between two of Max's ribs, subtly cracking them both and delivering a subduing blow to the young filmmaker.

"Freeze!" came a loud voice from the direction of the road. Ever so quietly accompanying the voice and only just discretely audible amongst all the other noise, the vendor could hear the sound of buckles, metal, and leather straps opening, sliding, and moving against one another. *Oh shit!* The man knew what this meant, and while his mind raced through a hundred possible outcomes, he understandably couldn't anticipate just exactly what was about to happen.

Cameras kept clicking, making that classically recognizable sound of shutters closing and film rolling, even though most of the devices taking the pictures did not have a mechanical shutter nor any rolling film stock inside. It was a design choice by many of the makers of digital cameras that had carried over to the current generation of technology, to include mechanical sounds in the devices they made to ensure that the linear minds of human operators would understand that something happens when they push the big button. It was a necessary Pavlovian feature that had been introduced to prevent human simpletons from pressing big buttons too many times in the absence of an obvious response. Originally implemented as a safety feature to protect against the damaging of device internals, it had become a powerful stimulus-response in its own right. All these many millions of basic human users around the world just enjoyed pressing buttons, rejoicing that they had activated some ostensibly mechanical technology that they could not possibly understand.

Twelve

NOTHING VENTURED

"Fascinating, isn't it?" said Philip, "I just can't believe we've got that many people out there who care about this nonsense!"

"What did you say your name was, son?" the older Black gentleman in the custom-fit suit asked. This man had joined the meeting late and had not yet introduced himself.

"Philip. Philip J. Clancy," the younger man replied. "And you are?"

Philip had replied with the air of someone who had been brought up without care for anyone else in the room, even though he had followed it with a question specifically about who else was in the room. Philip had taken it as a personal affront that this man would dare interrupt his meeting and then ask for his name without offering anything of value first.

Value was something earned, not bought, unless you have a lot of it, his dad used to remind him, and it was a privileged mantra that he chose to operate by as he grew up. Though by any measure, Philip was far from grown up. Now all of twenty-one years old, it was only less than a year ago he was still stomping around the Berkeley campus, spending his father's hard-earned money and doing his best to stand out in a student body and local population of so many other wealthy, undirected, and misinformed post-teenagers like him.

On the same topic of value, another thing he had learned from his dad was the importance of being aware enough of others to understand what value they could bring to the table, such that he could position himself to take advantage of it and, ultimately, take it for himself.

That tactic led to his finding and befriending Nelson Neves, a brilliant young engineer whose interests in developing distributed computing architectures had ultimately led to their ambitious discussion today.

"I'm here with these lovely people," the man offered in response, gesturing toward the four others who had arrived fifteen minutes ahead of the scheduled meeting time. Those four individuals were from the Scaled Growth Fund, a venture capital team within MCA. MCA, of course, was Media Command Aggregator Corp., a massive roll-up organization comprised of venture arms and companies from all around the world involved in engineering, infrastructure, utilities, technologies, and finance.

The Scaled Growth Fund had been an early investor in Google, Facebook, and Myspace and had built out a vast network of related funds and controlling positions in startups across multiple disciplines. Even just three floors down from this very meeting, it had over four hundred staff sourcing and creating content within a media aggregator business— Everything Matters Corp.—of which it held a primary investment position.

Philip was not thrilled to have this man avoid answering his question, but he could subvert his annoyance for a moment. He did not care about this man or the other four people he was with. He did, however, care about the fund they represented. He knew that his business was firing on all cylinders and met the profile of being an "investable" Series A target for the Scaled Growth Fund.

"Well, it was with my honor and pleasure that you have joined us, along with your SGF colleagues," Philip replied in a nominally friendly, professionally sounding, and partially condescending way.

The man nodded and smiled.

"So, please allow me to continue," said Philip, without waiting for anyone to ask or offer their allowance for him to continue. "Six months ago, we had a daily user volume of just over 16,000. In the last thirty days, we have hit an average daily volume of over 350,000, with a peak of over 600,000. That represents a 22-X growth rate in that time period." He made sure to pronounce the "twenty-two X" with emphasis, hitting on the presumed growth he had achieved.

"Twenty-two thousand percent!" he now firmly and confidently proclaimed, standing in front of the presentation wall that showed what appeared to be a real-time feed of key metrics spewing forth from his business. His excitement and the general bent of his hyperbole had led him astray by a decimal place. However, the actual and still impressive figure of 2,200% was clearly spelled out on the presentation slide behind him in extra-large font, heavily contrasted in pastel key lime color on a bright yellow background. The slide itself was garish, and it blasted those colors off of and around the silhouette of Philip, standing there in a white hoody and tight-fitting light brown trousers, just tight enough to be Bay area-chic, yet unintentionally harkening back to a loose-legged khaki uniform that had been the West Coast technology fashion standard of previous decades. Just as no one would accuse Philip of being wrong in his statement on growth rates, nor would they call in the fashion police, even though both were deserving.

Wallace Yarbrough chose not to correct the young fool standing before him, just as he had chosen not to indicate that he knew anything about Philip J. Clancy; with intention. He had seen this story play out so many times over the last twenty years in the business and knew the best thing he could do here was minimize his time spent and maximize what the firm would get from any prospective deal. Given the relative importance of this particular deal, he thought it appropriate to show up, but no way in hell did he feel the need to steer this over-privileged white boy who thrived on purveying complete bullshit.

After all, Wallace knew that bullshit purveyance was something they would need in spades for this to work. He had been a part of big technology deals since the early nineties. With every passing quarter, with every filled investment round of hundreds of millions of dollars, and with every completed cohort of investment deals, he had observed some immutable truths.

The first being that the only way people would successfully fit into Silicon Valley startup culture is if they fit in absolutely nowhere else. More often than not, it seemed like damn near everyone he met was on the spectrum—autism or Asperger's or some other high-functioning neurodivergent state. And he was always quick to note that this was not something to be interpreted as a constraint or a disability in any way; rather, it was more like a superpower. It blessed upon them a unique ability to cut through the crap and operate in a place where any time spent being overly insightful about others would only lead to detours, doubt, and demise.

The "platform economy," described in a definitive blog post a year earlier by his boss, Dr. Harb Louthe, had even more of a filtering effect on how Wallace and his VC contemporaries profiled and validated potentially successful CEOs. Network technologies were now enabling software to work as frictionless intermediaries between humans, and any reservations, concerns, or overt care that a manager of that software had about how it was being used would put the entire effort at risk. It only mattered that it *was* being used. The blog post in question had been so highly regarded and shared that it even received the 2010 Insight Award from the Association of Bloggers, even though many of its members didn't fully understand the intentions of the author.

In Wallace's investment analysis reports back to Dr. Louthe, or "Harbs" as he called him, he would often use shorthand to describe his assessment of the prospective company's leaders.

"GSD" and "DGAF" might as well have been gold stars in those reports and would usually lead to the disbursement of many millions of dollars in funding.

So far, Philip had shown that he quite competently Doesn't Give A Fuck. For the time being, the jury was still out on Getting Shit Done.

The presentation wall was neatly configured. It allowed for a slide deck to be shared and shown to the audience on a large projector screen while maintaining real-time dashboard information spread across several smaller LCD displays. Even though Wallace and his colleagues knew that most of the time, the data displayed through these tools was far from accurate, and rarely was it ever providing a real-time view into actual systems, it still made for a convincing presentation. It checked another important box on their unwritten criteria.

Philip would often spend more time staring at those numbers than doing anything meaningful for his teams or productive for the business itself. It had been that way almost since Philip first approached Nelson and convinced the peerless software engineer to work with him.

Nelson would soon thereafter realize that nobody worked "with" Philip. They simply operated in his vicinity and tried not to become collateral damage.

"Nelson, I'm Philip. I'm interested in funding your work," was how he had introduced himself. At the time, Nelson didn't know what to think. He had been working on his ranking algorithms at the engineering lab, and this odd-looking late-stage adolescent had walked up to him with that offering.

"Uh, well, who exactly are you?" Nelson had extracted his attention from the work directly in front of him. He was annoyed, as he felt he was getting close to defining a new algorithm for a hyper-efficient social graph, which he was confident would be a big leap forward for sharing content and knowledge. More specifically to his interests, he wanted to improve how like-minded people were publishing, reading, and contributing to scientific research.

Conversely, if Philip had ever become aware of like-minded people, he would have deemed it a threat.

"I'm the guy who's gonna make you famous," replied Philip.

"That's kind of messed up... also I don't want to be famous," countered Nelson.

This first encounter wasn't going the way Philip expected it to go. He had envisioned walking into the lab, seeing this downtrodden (he wasn't) engineer who couldn't (he could) piece together his own vision, and in a few short words, capturing the imagination and adulation of said engineer. He hadn't.

"Well, I saw your work in last week's demo days, thought it was pretty cool," said Philip, who, to his credit, had realized a change of tactics was necessary and was taking a decidedly less flamboyant approach.

"Okay, that's great. Are you in Sciences?" Nelson asked, thinking this weird-looking kid was just a weird-looking kid, but maybe with a strength in some specific area.

"No, not really," Philip suffered greatly saying this, as he wanted nothing more than to respond and engage as if he had a wealth of actual technical knowledge, but that only seemed to work in situations where those around him knew even less than he did. While that most certainly wasn't the case in this particular conversation, more often than not it was, which always served to embolden Philip while casting a dark pall on the technical literacy of society at large.

He drew on his confidence of normally working with people who weren't as smart as Nelson. "Well you are, right? And I invest in sciences... and tech, so I think you and I can make something great together with what you've been developing," Philip offered.

"Not sure I'm looking for investment, dude. I still have another year on my degree, and I want to publish this stuff in its own right," Nelson replied, noting that his goals were the opposite of what Philip had outlined. More so, he didn't like this person, and quite frankly, he didn't believe him.

"Listen, we can do this in a way that you can keep doing what you need to do, but instead, you make a lot of money, and together, we make tons of money."

Sounded great, but not very realistic.

"My dad is Roger Clancy," Philip said.

Holy shit! He had gotten Nelson's attention. "Oh wow. That's awesome," he offered back. Nelson was still hesitant to engage Philip, but with that new information, he realized it would be a poor choice to ignore the kid. Roger Clancy, after all, was one of the most successful names in telecommunications and networking and held a wealth of portfolios in other industries as well.

In retrospect, it would be considered by many to have been an even worse decision to keep listening to Philip, but at that moment, it was just two geeks in a lab. And they got to talking. Philip had watched Nelson's presentation the week before, where he demonstrated software that could automatically conduct contextual semantic interpretation of various media formats. Effectively, he had written a very specialized "AI companion" that could understand the *content and context* of documents, including photos, videos, and diagrams, as a user perused those different types of media. He had uniquely implemented a combination of image recognition and natural language processing to dissect just about any type of *content* into its categorial constituent parts, which was a compelling enough innovation by itself. But he had gone one step further, applying a framework that was able to harvest much of the *context* through heuristic analysis of the users' session: how they read or viewed the materials, such as how quickly they scanned and scrolled the page, where on the real estate of their screens the focal content was placed, where they had come from or clicked from, and what they did afterward.

Only slightly less impressive than what he had made was how Nelson described his intended deployment. He had already prototyped the distribution of a self-propagating lightweight snippet of code that any network administrator could choose to implement, thus allowing his software to automatically encode and interpret any content within a given network. In Nelson's reference architecture—his gospel on this particular solution—any of those deployments would then be granted access to his more centralized technology stack through a secure API, where all the heavy computation would occur.

Nelson's vision for this solution was born from his dedication and passion for academics. He had been building it for other researchers like him and those he aspired to be so they could more easily share, review, and grade research and content. He thought of it as an impartial adjudicator, a tool that could be groundbreaking for peer review and collaboration, especially once he opened it up to other brilliant minds to improve upon what he had made.

"It's like the thumbs-up is not on the page, it's in your finger," is how Philip had described the encapsulation framework that Nelson had created, and it wasn't grossly incorrect.

Nelson's solution had captured Philip's attention as it seemed to match up with his rudimentary understanding of ranking algorithms like PageRank, how it had made Google so powerful, and most importantly, how that approach to technology had activated "viral loops". He was completely convinced that if he could find another layer of content relevance to exploit across the internet in a similar way, he could have his name in the binary stars along with Brin, Page, Icahn, Gates, and other technology industry luminaries.

What Philip saw in Nelson's work was not the ability to collaborate for productive research. Rather, he saw something that appealed more to the base instincts of the human psyche, perhaps deep within our carnal, primitive minds or our reptilian brains, whichever part of a human it was that governed hasty, summary judgment of others. Philip, to his credit, envisioned the capability to add a new layer of "liking"—and thereby, hating—any type of content that could have been shared just about anywhere on the internet. From an opportunity standpoint, this idea seemed to run the same playbook as Google and PageRank, but instead of being tied to the underlying websites and pages or within the forced containment of a single platform like Facebook, it was more distributed, more atomized, more automated, and more general in how it could rank different types of content. *Content posted, content shared, content judged* was how he thought about it.

It had been true that Philip's father had suggested to him, especially given the fact that he was living in the Bay Area, to find brilliant people with an investment opportunity. Roger Clancy had done so not out of any expectation of it leading to a great investment nor out of any appreciation of his son's ability to analyze and assess a good deal. In essence, Roger was buying friends for Philip, expecting that these new friends would help him become more like his father.

That first conversation between Philip and Nelson, along with an initial two million dollars from Mr. Clancy a week later, led to the formation of Mixality, Inc., a private company of which the two founding partners held shares. Unbeknownst to Nelson, the share class structure was configured in such a way as to give the Clancys the ability to dilute his holdings and ultimately remove him from an ownership position very easily.

Two months later, they launched their cloud services and a publicly available API. They began promoting it to all the many video-sharing and clickbait article websites that had proliferated over the previous three or four years. They offered an "integration bonus" of $50,000 for each of the first twenty partners. Basically, they needed these sites to implement a few lines of code that would then let people use the Mixality Sentiment Engine, the commercialized version of Nelson's academically-minded breakthroughs. That initial launch resulted in the aforementioned six-month-old data of 16,000 daily users.

Sometime later, the framework would be rebranded as MSE and ultimately entered public discourse as people would look to each other's aggregate "Messy" score for any type of social interaction.

Much of the rest of the early investment into the company had been deployed more directly in service of Philip's ego, specifically to create the dashboard to display those figures that captivated him so much. All that mattered to Philip was that the more traffic and activity they could announce, the more users and publishers would flow into the system. The omnipresent deific force of FOMO would assuredly make it so.

Nelson had taken significant umbrage to most of the financial decisions made in the company's early days. Within weeks of signing the original shareholder agreements and incorporation documents, he had come to regret his "partnership" with Philip. Nelson had carefully developed an exhaustive plan on how that initial two million dollars could be allocated to software development and R&D, with a small amount of capital spent on elevating their project from the depths of the lab building at Berkeley to engage with other research groups and other universities. Philip had ostensibly initially agreed to all of Nelson's recommendations.

That lip service didn't hold up for long. Shortly after they officially started working together, Philip hired an external software development company to build the MSE. MSE itself was relatively easy to create, but it relied heavily upon the algorithms of Nelson's core work. Needless to say, Philip had pressured Nelson to integrate with MSE under veiled threats of legal action and not-so-veiled threats of taking Nelson's intellectual property—all of his programming code and research—if he didn't comply.

[how the hell i let this happen] Nelson was messaging on his laptop to Jenny Vandeveer, the newly-formed company's Head of Partners, who sat across the table from him in the meeting. Jenny had fallen into a challenging position, essentially being pushed and pulled by the vastly differing needs of the two founders.

[He is a piece of work, isn't he?] replied Jenny. She had been the company's first employee and possessed the advantageous filter of having known Philip for most of their lives. Her father had worked for Philip's father, and she couldn't help but often reflect on the irony and dark humor of that situation. Her dad helped alleviate some of her concerns and reinforced her decision that it would be okay to take the job when Philip offered it. What they discussed was that even though he wasn't overly or consciously aware of it, Philip was at least reactive to his insecurities, and a big one was that he couldn't trust anyone. If he were to balance this limitation with the demands of a growing startup that required him to hire as many people as possible as quickly as possible, he would need people around him that he could place at least partial degrees of trust in. Jenny and her father saw this as a very clear and present opportunity to get in on the company early,

help Philip and Nelson "steer the ship," and position her to be in proximity when it would inevitably be in need of reasonable and objective minds to form a post-startup leadership. This was also a revenge game. Jenny and her father shared the ambition to use this situation as a way to reclaim some of the inequity that had occurred in the previous generation of Clancy and Vandeveer collaboration. Past injustices would not be repeated, not if they could help it.

She was also three years older than both Philip and Nelson and had spent the last two years working with eBay (one year plus three months' severance) and PopShip (three months plus six months' severance), so she could lean on her reserves of wisdom and experience.

Philip and his fucking Daddy Warbucks owe us, Jenny thought as she looked across the table at Nelson, who was struggling to stay seated, given how much he DGAF about the meeting.

[He has no Fing clue what he's talking about. FML] Nelson responded as Philip continued speaking to the room. He had a mechanical keyboard on his laptop, which required being somewhat careful to avoid the signature click-clack sound of his keys if he were to type at normal speed. But he also knew that it didn't matter, as everyone around the table was preoccupied, staring at a laptop, iPhone, or Blackberry. Like the angry internal monologue in his head, his device was simply louder than everyone else's.

Jenny was careful in how she spoke about the partners, both with her mouth and her fingers. Her dad had been clear that any statements she might make electronically or even verbally could eventually come back to haunt her, especially with naturally vindictive people like the Clancys.

Her dad's advice had simply been, "Whenever you say anything, just imagine it's already being broadcast on the web, and anyone anywhere can already see it."

[look, he's got the data, he's got the audience, let's just see where this goes. But Libby and G... what was that?] She knew she had to be careful, but she wasn't going to be completely silent. Jenny was aware of Nelson's importance to any future of the company, and had become masterful in helping deflect or redirect his attention whenever he got caught up complaining about Philip.

[oh god i feel for them. But at least they don't have to stay here and watch this shitshow] Nelson replied. He was referring to their colleagues Libby and Jeff—known as G—who Philip had sent out of the room just a few minutes

into the meeting with the unexpected request to order lunch for everyone. He had done so not because he was hungry nor because he was thinking of everyone else's nourishment. They had been banished because they had represented a challenge to his authority in the meeting.

Libby, by title, was the "Executive Assistant, C-Suite," and Jeff carried his own set of business cards laser-printed with many words, including "Vice President, Director of Marketing, Growth Hacking Implementation." Jeff's title had been of his choosing, whereas Libby's had not, and these choices, or lack thereof, also reflected yet more power imbalance within the new company.

Libby Walker had been in some of Philip's business classes at Berkeley, and was still studying with the intention of finishing her degree. She was often vocal in class, known by everyone for her sharp wit and insightful back-and-forth with professors and other students. Libby was also known for being, by any objective measure, one of the most beautiful girls on campus. When she heard about the new company that Philip had started, the draw of his access to capital and the chance to join the "technorati" of the region was all the attractant she would need. Philip was smart enough to see how much smarter she was than him, which scared the shit out of him. But he was also in awe of her beauty. So, between her continual overtures to join the company and his insecurity over adding an intelligent, beautiful woman to the team, he once again flexed his ego and money and made her an offer to join as his assistant. Libby had begrudgingly taken the role, choosing to look at it as a proverbial "foot in the door." She could not have imagined what she was stepping into.

Jeff Christiansen was an odd duck. He was in his late thirties, older than nearly everyone else in the company by half a decade or more. Within a few weeks of his joining, some of the staff had started calling him "Gramps" behind his back, with the nickname soon coming to the foreground and just as quickly being shortened to "G." He didn't look old or dress old, but he did seem like he was from a different era.

G was thoughtful; everyone else was spontaneous.

G was always empathetic; everyone else was often indifferent.

G was proactively analytical; everyone else was impulsively reactive.

And G was often annoyingly slow to act; and everyone else was GSD.

Mostly, people thought of him as the weird old guy who would always give you long-winded answers and then abruptly leave. G had bounced around between a few different high-profile jobs over the last half-decade, finding it hard to stick a landing after he had been prolifically dismissed from a struggling security camera company in early 2006. Over the years, his confidence had waned, and through every new career stop, he became increasingly despondent, unable to fit into the new "cool kids" working class. Rather than acknowledge his strengths and build upon them, he aspired to become what he was not. It was from this mindset that he came up with the title that he held on those business cards, an aptly long-winded sequence of words that tried in vain to replace what he had lost.

G liked being called G, though he didn't know where it originated. Philip loved G as well, as he was a pushover. For egomaniacal people like Philip, leadership was an exercise in surrounding themselves with lesser individuals who they could tell what to do and who would do it, rather than building a collective of skilled operators that could be greater than the sum of its parts.

Libby didn't belong in this equation, and she knew it, and she most certainly did not want to be sent out from the meeting to buy lunch. But this was to be expected from Philip, and she, similarly to Jenny, felt that for the time being, she was prepared to deal with the shortcomings and frequent disrespect that came with the territory of being a part of this manic organization.

[kind of a shame. This was Libby's deal. She brought these guys in] Jenny replied to Nelson.

[what? I didn't know that. Really?] he wrote back.

[dude, maybe look up from the codebase sometime and see what's going on. :)] she finished this statement with a smiley face emoticon, as her comment by itself might have been taken as too direct of a judgment, but the smiley face would render it a simple harmless reminder. Jenny was exceptional at communicating over text or email while ensuring that her words were received the right way.

"Now, we are confident that this ripple effect will continue, and as the concentric circles from each of our connected entities overlap with the others, the viral loops will continue," Philip continued, now speaking in front of a slide that had numerous poorly-animated circles throbbing and expanding from several dots scattered around on the screen. Much like the diagram, he too was speaking in circular logic and loopy rationale.

Wallace had remained focused, seated at the far end of the boardroom table.

"Mr. Clancy, can you tell me what is happening there?" he interjected.

"My friend, what is happening is the best investment opportunity you'll see in the next ten years," Philip answered indirectly and hyperbolically. He wasn't sure what Wallace was referring to, nor did he need to be. After all, he had been called Mr. Clancy, and he had been asked for an opinion. *Perhaps this guy would show some respect after all.*

"That's all well and good, but just have a look behind you. Is something wrong?" Wallace clarified his question.

Philip turned to the presentation wall. His animated slide was perfect, displaying exactly as intended. He had given his designer very careful notes on how and where to place the dots on the slide and how to have the concentric circles expand and animate around them. His intention for the slide was to be able to speak about how their roster of partner companies created a network of content, and the concentric circles emanating from each were to indicate the social connections between all those other sites and platforms.

He had also made sure to have the designer place two of the partner coordinates along the upper third segment of the projection screen, with equal-sized dots on each half of the slide and larger circles that were, in his mind, proportionate to the size of Libby's nipples and breasts, respectively, to allow for him to make one of his proportionately inappropriate and all-too-frequent lewd comments. It wouldn't have been the first nor last time such a disrespectful and immature thing would have occurred in these boardrooms, but in his vacant, condescending, sexist mind, it might very well have been the best one by far.

"I think some of these circles should be bigger..." Philip started to reply to Wallace, and as he said it, a slight wry smile went up at the corner of his mouth in appreciation of his own private twisted humor, silently and fortunately leaving its layered mess buried deep in his sociopathic mind.

If anything, he felt it was inappropriate for this stranger to pose a query that wasn't presented as a leading question with predefined answers that everyone would want to hear. That was more typical of the unwritten rules for these VC meetings. If a founder was presenting, interruptions should be limited to offering superlatives. Perhaps:

"Please, tell me more about this exponential growth?"

Or:

"How did you come up with such compelling insights?"

Or:

"This looks like the Amazon of content sharing, would you agree?"

Any of those types of questions would have been perfectly acceptable. *"Is something wrong?" What the hell was that? The nerve of this guy,* Philip thought, but as he continued to scan his dashboard display wall, he too couldn't help but question what was before him.

Two "live" data points had been nominally fluctuating throughout the time so far in the meeting, as they did every day. *Live Users* was descriptive enough and had been oscillating between about 3,000 and 4,000, the numbers constantly flickering and changing. *Node Points* was less expository and was a term Philip had come up with, much to Nelson's chagrin, that was essentially stating how many "live" actions had been posted through their system's APIs, as depicted by the concentric sexist-centric circle-clouds of likes, hates, and comments that were still pulsating on the slide at the center of the wall. *Node Points* had been jumping around at approximately a double count of the *Live Users* figure, indicating that, roughly speaking, for every active user in the system, they had each made two actions that were actively being seen, reposted, or commented upon by others.

In both cases, these numbers had ballooned enormously in the last minute. Live Users had been flashing through six-digit numbers, with the highest perceptible figure well over 400,000. *Node Points* had accelerated even faster, now indicating what seemed to be a five or six times multiple of the other, at one point showing "2.3M." Fortunately, the display software was able to truncate the contents to fit in the portion of screen real estate that had been given to it. Philip loved how the "2.3M" looked.

He couldn't bring himself to believe it, which, naturally, didn't matter.

"Wrong? There is nothing wrong here. Look at this data, this is what I'm talking about!" His voice got louder and louder. He looked back to the slide. "These circles, this is the business right here. Ha! ... Ha ha! Look at these fucking numbers! Holy shit!"

Wallace leaned forward, ignoring the nonsense he now expected to pour out of Philip's mouth for the rest of the day. *If these figures are correct, he'll be an absolute trainwreck. And we'll need to invest quickly,* he thought to himself.

"Okay, let's get a handle on this. Calm down and tell me what's happening with these numbers. Is this real?" Wallace demanded. His colleagues, the analysts, had looked up. They were surprised by Wallace's interest and his involvement. Typically, they assumed that when one of the principals of their fund showed up to a meeting, it was a tactic to apply pressure on the startup. But for a senior executive like Wallace to start asking real questions and having real talk, that was different. All four analysts had put their Blackberries down and were looking intently upon the discussion between Wallace and Philip.

"Well, it's our vision paying off big time," Philip responded, again with no real substance in his answer.

"Listen, I don't need your nonsense right now, I want to know what's driving it. Unless these numbers aren't real, something triggered this activity. I need you to show me right now." Wallace demanded in a mostly practical and partially condescending voice.

"Nelson, what you got?" Philip quickly deflected the question to Nelson, hoping his partner could offer more than the next slide in his deck, as that didn't seem to be of interest anymore. "Tell us what's going on with these numbers."

Nelson had been detached from the conversation, mostly preoccupied with the messenger chat he'd been having with Jenny, which, fittingly, had just gotten to the point of her reminding him to pay attention. He could have easily continued to dismiss Philip's egocentric showmanship, but the numbers on the wall were a different story.

"Gotta be a mistake..."

His first reaction was not the one a founder wants to hear from their technical partner in an investor meeting in these critical times. The platform economy in 2011 was a land grab—mistakes of any kind, perceived or real, would only slow down the acquisition of market share. "I mean, okay, let's look and see what's in the logs."

"Yeah, the logs, pull them up," Philip requested.

"Philip, it's not the kind of thing we can pull up and make any sense out of it. Give him a minute," Jenny interjected, knowing that, indeed, logs by themselves weren't going to show a whole lot of information to everyone in the meeting in their raw form. She also knew that Nelson would want her to speak up and say this on his behalf. If Nelson had his way, he would never speak to Philip again, but for the time being, he had maintained enough maturity, with a heavy dose of insular ignorance, to shield himself from Philip wherever and whenever possible.

This, however, was not something to be ignored.

The others around the table were transfixed on the ever-changing numbers displayed on the wall. *Live Users* had continued moving up, now occasionally touching a count of over 600,000. *Node Points* had surpassed 3.5M and did not appear to be slowing down.

"Mr. Neves, do you see anything notable in there?" Wallace asked, directing his question toward Nelson. His professionalism shone through like the western sun that would often burn off the early evening fog over the hills of San Francisco.

"From what I can see, everything is up across every possible extension of our platform. Like, every part of the internet that our stuff touches is super active," Nelson responded.

"How is your work deployed geographically? Is it a North American user base?" Wallace inquired, demonstrating a level of experience and targeted questioning unlike what most in the room might have ever been exposed to.

"Yes, the partners are predominantly NA," Jenny piped in, again saving Nelson from having to answer something that someone else could. She mixed in some business and technical context, "Somewhat because that's who we worked with here out of the city, and also Nelson's team built out the tech infrastructure to focus on uptime and redundancy in North America first."

"Okay, what's trending across the country then? This is over the top. Something's gotta show." Wallace looked to two of the SGF analysts who were seated to his right. "Can you guys check our network and see what's showing there?"

Philip wondered for a moment why Wallace had asked his team to look elsewhere for answers. Nelson heard the comment but didn't think too much of it as he was engrossed in the messy log files from the Mixality system.

"Okay, it looks like it's hitting across all the Everything Matters sites and Facebook. I've got a link here for the top-performing node." Nelson was furiously tabbing and scrolling through the detailed log file data. "Jesus, this thing has a Messy score over 160. Philip, pass me the cable."

"No, tell me the link. I'll put it up," Philip countered, not wanting to relinquish presentation control. If something big was happening, he needed to be standing in front of it, literally and figuratively.

"Fuck that, pass me the fucking cable," Nelson responded, speaking more forcefully and confidently than Jenny, Philip, or the absent Libby and G had ever heard.

Philip looked up and across at Nelson, scorn in his eyes and a fiery response ready to escape between his lips. In the same motion, he caught Wallace's steeled look at the end of the table. Their eyes met, and in a nanosecond, the sharp, wizened, intense gaze from the now very serious Black man at the end of the table won out. Philip's entire being cowered under the imposing stare coming back at him from this man.

The eyes said, "Pass him the fucking cable."

Philip detached the projector cable from his laptop and slid the heavy end of the wire across the table to Nelson, much like a bartender provisioning a drink down the bar to a parched customer. Nelson was intently staring at his screen, his thirst for understanding now at a feverish level.

He reached out, collected, and connected the projector cable without looking at it, his right hand still working the trackpad and keyboard on his laptop. The projection screen on the wall flickered for a moment and then revealed a mirror image of Nelson's laptop.

There were two primary windows in front of a desktop littered with icons. One was a view into his programming software, with a tab revealing the log file data—the white Unicode text on a black background gave everyone in the room the momentary feeling of being an elite hacker, navigating their way through the dark tunnels of cyberspace. The other window was an empty web browser.

"I'll pull this up in our prototype feed viewer," Nelson offered. He proceeded to copy a long link embedded in the log file view. Nelson then opened a bookmark from his browser showing a tiled page, clearly running on one of Mixality's local servers. An address bar appeared at the top of the page, within which he pasted the link.

Instantly, the presentation wall filled with images and content—a mish-mash of photos, video files, snippets of comments, and truncated introductory words to what appeared to be fully written articles from other sites.

"What..." Philip started to speak, as he had not seen this type of view on their system before, but cut himself off, knowing that revealing his own surprise would indicate a lack of knowledge of what was being shown. Few things could silence Philip like his own ego.

From a content perspective, there would be no such lack of comprehension by anyone in the room. Jenny, Nelson, Philip, Wallace, and the four SGF analysts all stared at the wall. Nelson started to scroll. His two fingers might as well have been pulling their eyes through the underworld of San Francisco and into the depths of hell as he swiped down through this never-ending story, an endless scroll of shocking content.

The wall was a battleground. The still images showed people engaging one another, but with few indications of likes and no thumbs-ups among the active participants. Nelson clicked on a video file, revealing a mound of bodies, all writhing arms and legs, with a periphery of others standing, yelling, pushing, and fighting.

Imagery continued to flash by. Police officers were in the middle of much of it. In one photo, a young man was bent over, holding the side of his torso in one hand, and a skateboard hung limply from his other hand. People were reaching out to him with outstretched arms. The area around this young man looked familiar.

"What are we looking at here?" Wallace posed.

The page kept scrolling upward, with Nelson only slowing to look at a few select images. A woman, also familiar, could be seen splayed out on the concrete sidewalk, her notable fashion sense still apparent despite the nonstandard pose she was in, lying on her back twisted sideways at the waist and hugging one leg. She wore an anguished face, distorted in an obvious moment of pain, as well as a beige jacket that bore similar marks of recent duress. It was scuffed up and bunched underneath her back, revealing a shapely body wrapped in a tight green top leading into ripped white jeans. Nelson, Jenny, and Philip already knew that most of those rips were intentional.

"Oh my god, that's Libby!" Jenny yelled out. "Guys, what the hell is going on here? Where is this?"

"Looks like it's... downstairs. Look, that's Market Street," Nelson responded as he scrolled down further, discerning some of the familiar landmarks, roadways, and traffic that they would typically see on any given day.

"I have to go," Jenny started to stand up.

The scrolling continued, Nelson completely consumed by the implications of what he was seeing. His mind was running a multitude of scenarios and internal debates, not the least of which was a prevailing feeling that he had somehow engineered the fall of humanity.

"Wait. Nobody moves," Wallace spoke up. His voice was loud, abrupt, and very calm. Everyone paused in response, looked at him, and then looked back at the projection wall.

They could see police officers in the middle of the skirmish. Another image showed them swinging batons at someone on the ground.

The scrolling stopped. Nelson had seen it first. It was the vendor from below, the guy who was there every day, yet this was not what he normally looked like. A close-up shot of his face, amongst the angry crowd that had formed, showed he was battered, bruised, and bloody.

"Jesus..." said Wallace, as one accomplished Black man looking at an image of his brother, a peer in entrepreneurialism, lying in an unresponsive state.

Jenny could not will herself to action. *Was Libby okay? Where was G in all this? Was this real?* But for all her intentions to go, she could not extricate herself from the powerful command of Wallace's directive to the room.

"Play that video," he called out to Nelson.

What they saw was shaky, occasionally glitchy, and fully horrendous. That video, all twenty-seven seconds of it, tied it all together. Filmed by someone in the crowd, it did not show the collision between Roddy the skateboarder, Libby, and G, but instead started in the immediate aftermath. They could see Libby sprawled out on the sidewalk in pain, the live-action version of the photo they had scrolled past previously. G was in some improbable figure-four wrestling position with the skateboarder, his knockoff blue Italian trousers intertwined with two legs of a sullied pair of cargo pants. He could be heard calling for his phone.

The volume and activity picked up. The camera swung over to see the vendor, still able-bodied and moving quickly in this shot as he efficiently sent the other skateboarder backward, reeling in pain.

"Freeze!" the unmistakable commanding voice of a police officer could be heard from off-camera just as the vendor turned to the tangled mess of G and Roddy. He turned back toward the voice, still holding the weaponized skateboard with which he had dispatched Max.

In a blindingly quick sequence, a figure came soaring into the frame of the video, from where the officer's voice had been heard a split-second ago. It was a policeman in black uniform with yellow trim and regalia, his notable right foot combat boot flying through the air at the end of his leg. The boot landed squarely in the middle of the vendor's chest, knocking him back and causing the man to land hard on the Market Street sidewalk.

This aggressive boot rejoined its more stable partner, a formidable base of the officer now standing above the vendor who lay on the ground. Another officer quickly joined alongside him. They looked at each other and casually glanced at the crowd around them. Yelling and screaming kept building from every direction. The young guy with the skateboard who had been attacked was off to the side, moaning in pain. The other three victims were lying on the ground in different poses and in various states of distress. It was an absolute calamity.

Calamity became chaos. The first policeman pulled out his baton and started swinging down upon the vendor's body, which offered no resistance at all. The other policeman had dropped onto his left knee, which came to rest on the sidewalk behind the vendor's head. The other knee landed firmly on the man's neck. Yet the standing policeman kept swinging.

The familiar thin red line on the video showed that twenty-four seconds had elapsed. *All this insanity in 24s,* thought Jenny. With only a few seconds left on the timeline, bodies rushed from behind the camera holder and came in from all sides, descending upon the brutal attack.

As quickly as it had all unfolded, the video ended. As an inaugural tribute to the highest MSE score in history, it was left hanging on a final frozen blurry image of unbridled anger, hatred, and animosity.

Nobody in the boardroom could move. Not because of Wallace's directive to stay but simply due to the gravity of the moment. Nelson had kept scrolling down, and all they could see were more scenes of utter insanity. Violence. People fighting people fighting people. He zeroed in on two photos, which appeared to show Libby, G, and the skateboarder who had collided with them huddling off to the side of the crowd and moving away from the growing theater of chaos.

This offered some respite for the three Mixality employees in the room. Their team members appeared to be safe.

"We must stay here," Wallace said, "until we know what shakes out of all this." He was speaking from a combination of experience. Personally, as a Black man, knowing that his ability to affect what was happening down below at this moment was minimal at best. Professionally, as the most senior individual in the room, he had a responsibility to stop the others from getting involved, even in the face of the unstated irony of protecting some of these over-privileged white college kids.

He also had an opportunistic lens on the situation that could not be ignored. Whatever they had just witnessed, the awful part of it, was a truly terrible, disgusting reality endemic in the society of the day. But what they had seen across the combination of the data coming from the platform and the "God-mode" view that Nelson had served up was beyond anything he could have possibly expected when he chose to attend this meeting earlier that day. *If this was 160, what was 180? What would 200 look like?* The Messy scores were undeniable.

Wallace needed this—the Mixality business. Everything he had just seen was as perfect a fit for what they were looking for as he could have imagined, and forsaking for a moment the tragedy on the streets below, he didn't need to see anything else. Whatever level of funding was needed, he would sign off on it, and he was certain that Harbs would agree. Philip and Mixality had now been certified DGAF and GSD.

The phone in the middle of the boardroom table rang.

Nelson looked up from his laptop. "Should we answer it?"

"No!" Philip immediately barked back in response. No one was more important in this moment than those in the room, particularly himself. And quite possibly, with a moment of reflection and perhaps buoyed by seeing his employees alive and moving away from the scene, his thought process had shifted into liability prevention. *Could they sue me for sending them for lunch?*

"Goddammit, Philip. It could be Libby or G. We have to!" Jenny yelled out. She lurched forward and picked up the phone.

"Hello?" she answered with a question, hoping to hear some good news.

"Hi," a female voice responded. It did not sound like Libby, but the line was stunted and intermittently silent.

"Libby, is this you? Are you okay?" Jenny asked, wanting to be certain and hoping for a reassuring answer. She was speaking so fast and so loud as to be mostly unintelligible over the phone line.

"Is this EMC?" the voice on the other end of the line said.

Jenny was taken aback. This call didn't seem to be coming from Libby. It was someone asking for EMC. Mixality's office space was a sublease from the publication business Everything Matters Corp., or EMC, who seemed to have a master lease on just about the entire building. The incoming business call quickly subverted Jenny's panicked thoughts. Her ability to decouple personal concerns from professional priorities was usually a reliable strength. However, in this case, it seemed to elevate her to some uncaring robotic level of assholedom that only Philip normally inhabited.

"Umm, no. Well, yes. Uh. Yes, it is. What's this about?" she replied.

On the distant end of the line, words were offered.

"Hello, this is Henrietta Adler."

Thirteen

GOOD ENOUGH

"I'm not sure how we got all this stuff, Ricky," Doug said. "It doesn't make a ton of sense. It's showing access to files but not really like webpages."

Ricky was sucking on a milkshake. They had regrouped at Burger King to discuss what had gone down during their video call. Frankly, any excuse to be there was good enough for Ricky, this being his second visit that day. A Whopper for dinner and a milkshake for dessert was a culinary homerun for the excitable third-year college student.

"I dunno, Doug. What do you think it is?" Ricky asked.

The unexpected search results had revealed another page of links, leading them to more trail camera footage of gunfighting, but longer clips and at different times of day. People getting shot, wounded, getting up, and limping away. Others weren't so lucky, dropping from gunfire. The two young men had kept watching as small off-road vehicles with flat trailer decks would appear, pick up the bodies, and clear them away even as more fighting started up in the same environment.

They watched overhead footage that was remarkably smooth and stable, almost filmic. Again, those geometric overlays were on-screen, the postage-stamp yellow boxes following combat participants and vehicles as they moved about in the battle below.

This entire experience was beyond Doug and Ricky's comprehension. It was too much, albeit too much of something they couldn't even begin to describe. After watching a half-dozen or so of these videos, they decided to move to a neutral ground, hence this late-night rendezvous.

"It's like some kind of Navy Seals war coverage. I feel like we accidentally hacked into the Pentagon or something like that..." Doug ruminated. He felt uneasy with those words leaving his mouth as he looked over both shoulders and even checked the upper corners of the BK dining area. He saw cameras in two corners, each with little red blinking lights on them.

But it was cold outside. The sunny autumn day that warmed the start of his research at the cafe just a few hours ago had given way to a cold Atlantic wind-affected night. As tropical hurricanes still pummeled the southern half of the eastern continental USA, winter was most definitely in the air for Valemont, NJ. And it was nice and warm inside. Also, he had more milkshake left than Ricky and concluded that maintaining their current state of comfort was worth the risk.

"I think we landed on someone's server, and they have a bunch of stuff on there that we should probably not be seeing," he carefully said. In his mind, Doug was convinced that if he spoke generically, as if he was a *good guy*, he'd end up on the right side of whatever secret agency might be listening.

"Seems like it. Do you think that was real? Or maybe from a film shoot? Or what...?" Ricky postulated.

"C'mon, man! Last I checked, no one is shooting each other on an actual film set." But there was something to that suggestion. After all, it's far more likely that they find film from filmmakers than from warmongers, is it not?

The other problem was the type of film footage didn't make sense. *Why would they be shooting so much static content from those locked-off trail cameras? What about the floating overhead shot?* In their Communications courses, they had done enough work on video production to know some of the key terminology and techniques, and this situation didn't make sense in the context of making a film.

"Wait a second... Doug... this is all fake!" Ricky yelled out, too loud for the conversation they were having, and loud enough to be heard by most everyone nearby. Doug's eyebrows jumped in surprise, involuntarily dragged upwards by the tensing, flexing muscles in his forehead.

Fakes! Of course.

His reaction, however, was short-lived. His surprise was quickly countered by a synchronized performance of the various muscle groups around his eyes and cheeks, directing his expression into a concerned frown.

Dammit! Ricky was probably right!

As much as Doug wanted to believe they had found something darker or more conspiratorial, the patterns didn't make sense for that. But they did for this.

"Well, that sucks!" Doug lamented, shouting under his breath so that the speech came out at regular volume. He showed no remorse or consideration of the morbid nature of his regret, which amounted to him being upset that these people weren't actually killing each other.

Not only was Doug annoyed that Ricky was *right*, he was annoyed that *Ricky* was right.

"Just like that Kobe thing where he jumped over the car or that guy on the massive banana slide!" Ricky, a self-proclaimed expert in watching online video, was now confident he had gotten to the bottom of it.

Flashbacks of early internet infamy started flying through their minds: the Budweiser Wassup guys and the infinite remixes, the totally inappropriate Delta Airlines ebonics animation, the Chinese university guys and their Backstreet Boys lip sync performances that made BSB popular again, long before BSB made BSB popular again!

"Well, you gotta admit, it's pretty damn good," Doug said as he looked up at Ricky while taking another slurp. Doug was now most of the way through his own sugary, creamy concoction. It was vanilla, much like his life, and he enjoyed the banal flavor of it.

"Truth! Yeah, whoever did that must be making something big. What do you think it's for? We should probably post this, we'd be huge!" Ricky proposed. He immediately jumped to the conclusion in his mind that this was their ticket. *This is how I get that Tesla, and a yacht, and houses, and trips, and all the women and food.* He took another slurp. This would make them kings.

"Dude, that's a terrible idea. You know about copyright, right?" Doug knew about it. He hadn't been completely ignorant of their studies.

"Copyrightright? What what's that that?" Ricky joked and then heartily laughed, self-enamored with his present comedic wit and newfound future wealth.

'Ricky, you can't just take people's shit and put it up as your own. That's when you get the knock on the door. Someone coming for you, and you end up in jail. It's not a good look," Doug said as he again looked around carefully, his paranoia still ever-present even with a different bogeyman in mind.

Ricky stopped laughing. Now, he was annoyed that *Doug* was right. This was going to topple him from his throne; a veritable mutiny delivered just as Ricky had put the crown on his own head.

"Let's just take a minute, man. Chill out for a second and think about what this means," Doug said.

Here were the facts. They had stumbled across someone else's work. They had no idea how it came to be in their possession, who had created it, or why they had done so. They had made no progress on their homework assignment. It was cold outside and warm inside. Their milkshakes had also been cold but now were empty. All of these things, indeed, they knew to be true.

Fourteen

CANVAS

She was traveling through space. Her journey was lit by hundreds and thousands of brilliant purple lines that came at her and passed by, thrusting her forward. Repeatedly. She had no idea how long she had been traveling. This psychedelic flight was a beautiful and transcendental experience, providing an escape from all that had preceded it.

And then it was over. The lights were not reflections of stars in hypersonic space travel. Rather, they were raindrops drenched in the purple lights of failing LED street lamps. The view was not one from the cockpit of a spaceship. Instead, it was from Bex's flattened perspective, lying prone on top of her broken, crumpled tent, looking up to the torrential sky beyond the domineering concrete side of the freeway overpass.

Raindrops hit her cheeks, forehead, and lips and pooled everywhere they could. Her ears were riverine, with all the little corners and folds of her aural anatomy having filled up with water. Around her, ponds and lakes had been forming on the many topographical shapes of the razed, bumpy tent canvas. Dense rain fell directly onto her eyeballs, forcing her to blink.

She tried to breathe but felt suffocated. The water was everywhere, all over her face, her whole body, so heavy and oppressive that it wouldn't let her take that breath. *Am I drowning?* her consciousness asked, to which her innate being responded with fear and panic, as might happen if someone were actually drowning. She tried again. This time, just the smallest volume of air seemed to make it through her mouth and start the march to her lungs. Her body rejected it, first with a small cough and then a bigger one.

The pain was excruciating. And yet her body went back for more, small convulsions, trying to grasp any of the precious air it could find amongst the thick humidity and force it down before being asked to reject it. At last, some had made it through. Every breath was difficult, but she lay there and allowed her body to go through this awkward, awful motion of re-oxygenating itself.

The taste of rainwater hitting her mouth was intense. It was fresh and cleansing, but at the same time, it was salty and dirty. Bex realized that the latter taste and texture originated from herself. She raised her hands from where they had lay beside her and touched her face. It was wet and warm, not from the hot, thick viscosity of blood, but rather from rainfall and adrenaline. Her awareness of the situation was starting to return, and with it, a quick realization that she didn't seem to be in a life-threatening state despite the violence of her fall from the street above. With this, she rolled to one side, spitting up water and blood, and began to sit up. Her nose had been bleeding; that telltale pressure of thick, warm liquid in her sinuses had oozed into the back of her mouth while she lay. Her lip might be cut, too. She wasn't sure. Bex could feel pain shoot through her lower back, where her tailbone and butt had landed on the ground slightly ahead of her legs, a result of the forward somersault she had involuntarily executed going over the railing. And her ribs, her whole torso, were on fire. Something was broken inside. More than usual.

As she raised herself up on one hand and one elbow, her legs rotated to the side she was leaning. The rainwater continued running off her head, dripping from her nose, ears, and chin. Things were starting to come into a sense of raw understanding, though she did not yet have a clear picture of what had transpired in the short time she had been concussed and winded on the flattened tent.

Breathing was still laborious but was at least delivering air to Bex's lungs. The focal length of her vision had initially been fixed upon the closest falling raindrops but had started to adjust and expand to the extent of the scene around her. Down the slope from her destroyed tent, she could see that the chain-link fence separating the onramp from the railyards had been flattened. The posts were pulled out in several places, and others more distant were pushed and pulled at random angles. Closer to her, leaning against the base of a part of this broken fence, she could see the silhouette of a seated human.

Further still, a vehicle lay on its side, the bright headlights still shining forward and away from where Bex was looking, illuminating more distant train tracks and the side of several shipping containers in the yards beyond. Between her and the car, she could make out a trail of destruction going from the fence and crossing over several freshly scraped railway tracks. Pieces of a Tesla Model Y quarter-panel, wheel parts, and smashed glass fragments were visible where the lights from within the train yard cast a glow over the ground. The vehicle's path was also vertically evident where it left a tunnel through the rain and mist that hovered above the cold ground, indicating that Bex hadn't been disoriented for very long.

Bex had now negotiated with her painful body to raise herself first up to one knee and then managed to get both feet on the ground. Her ribs sent shock waves of pain through her body with even the smallest moves, and her lower back protested at any adjustment requiring her to lift her legs or her torso. The persistent neck pains that she had carried for years had been triggered by the whiplash motion of flipping onto the ground. Yet, the distraction of these newer injuries was enough to ignore those lingering, familiar troubles.

While every part of her body was screaming to do nothing, Bex's mind and soul were being driven instinctually.

***

The physiologist Walter Bradford Cannon coined the term "fight or flight" in 1915 in his book *Bodily Changes in Pain, Hunger, Fear, and Rage*. Essentially, the human body's autonomous nervous system acts in response to trauma or other physical and mental stressors imposed upon it. It does so in many ways similar to how animals also react to instinctually perceived danger. The response is typically symptomatic with an increase in heart rate, anxiety, sweat, and an impetus to act in almost non-voluntary ways.

In some cases, the body may choose to freeze up and become unable to do anything, much like many people experience moments of absolute helplessness in dreams or nightmares. Or we may lash out against the perception of threat. Or we may run, which is typically the smart choice of animals, who seem more able to grasp the practical aspects of the situation rather than being too heavily influenced by the analytical or emotional thought processes of humans.

In that regard, the motivations surging through her body were nothing new to Bex. The situation was quickly conjuring up feelings of how she reacted to being bullied in school, abused at home, or tormented online.

Her father had serious issues. He was an alcoholic, completely unable to avoid destroying himself. Sure, it *is* an illness, and she thought she understood that, but Bex had never understood why this illness could not be cured, like so many others. *Why are other families not like this?* She would even see other dads who could have a beer or a glass of whiskey and not become completely disassociated with the world around them.

But he was a lovely man, that is, in those rare moments when it was possible to see, hear, and feel the actual person inside. The dichotomy between the two men was confusing and scary to a seven-, eight-, and nine-year-old Bex.

His repetitive failures taught her that losing was not merely an option—it was most often the expected outcome. Her mother hadn't done anything to dispel this, as she had in many ways abandoned the family through her own actions and inaction.

Her mother had been working in a nursing home, at least she had until her choices and failings caught up with her. Bex would later find out that her mother had been stealing medications from the nursing home to supplement her income. In addition to becoming dependent on the extra money she made, she was soon addicted to the escapism that she could source by taking many of those state-altering opioids. As her dependency grew, her relationship with the dealers she supplied took an even darker turn after they introduced her to street drugs.

The proceeds she would make from selling stolen pharmaceuticals, the ones she hadn't kept for herself, would quickly go to buying crystal meth and fentanyl. It was a zero-sum game, spiraling down to much less than that. Her behavior became more erratic, the thefts more frequent, and her criminal guilt impossible to cover up, leading to her being arrested and, of course, losing her job.

The worst part about it for Bex was the anger. Her mother changed from someone coping with a struggling home environment and trying to do right by her daughter, to a shell of a human, hardly recognizable from what she once was. She would lash out at Bex, first verbally but then physically over time, often in the pursuit of trying to take whatever hard-earned money Bex may have been able to scrape together herself.

***

Bex pushed herself up to standing, bracing her hands against her thighs to create additional strength and stability that her midsection would not easily provide. Those hands moved up to her waist and helped straighten her back. She could finally take something close to a full breath. The pain was intense, but her bearings and balance started to return.

She looked down the muddy, rainy slope and then over to the left. *There he was!* It was the man she had saved from the attackers. She recognized his black leather jacket and collared shirt and took a few steps toward him. Her concussed mind was still piecing together fragments of the last few minutes, and only when she got close enough to see that Louis' head had itself become fragmented in those same minutes, did the visuals quickly come back to her.

The car. Her pushing the man and woman. *Oh my god. I killed him!*

Fight or flight symptoms were at a fever pitch.

Oh my god... oh my...

Bex could hear and feel her heart beating through every cell of her body. It thumped inside her head, adding to the post-concussion trauma that was building. Yet the instincts that had been serving her reliably for years were hardly diminished. The black leather jacket was unmistakably... nice. That usually meant nice things were kept within it. Putting aside her distaste for dealing with Louis' mostly obliterated body, Bex quickly, almost unconsciously, went through the inside pockets. A wad of cash, a thumb drive, an unopened and still remarkably undisturbed pack of cigarettes— Louis' backup pack—and a lighter all left the possession of the dead man.

Bex stuffed the items into the pockets of her cargo pants as she walked to the conjoining pavement that connected the onramp and the main road. As her eyeline crested the height of the road above, she could now make out the full scene of devastation. *Another body, the other man!* The beard was

139

still attached to him, even if very little else was, and was enough for her to identify him.

What... who? She could discern yet another man's body in the middle of the road, near a Nissan sedan stopped at an irregular angle to the direction of the road. Exhaust was still coming out of the tailpipe, but the car was not moving. She had no recollection of this man. *How?* She needed to go, to get out of here. None of these questions in her mind mattered. At this moment, flight was her only option.

Down the road, in the direction the vehicles had been going, there was nothing and nowhere to go. It was straight, with industrial lands and warehouses, most of them fenced and gated in. Going back over the overpass led to a traffic light, and she knew the strip mall, gas station, and pub could be busy places. Too busy, she realized.

And that's where they were running from. Someone else will come soon. Whether it would be other assailants, friends, or police, she did not intend to be there when they arrived.

Bex looked toward the flattened fence and beyond, to where the SUV was still lying on its side in the train yards. It was the only way out. She started shuffling down the slope.

The female attacker's body was the silhouette Bex had initially seen after regaining consciousness. The figure was not sitting, or at least not intentionally so. Her waist and legs were twisted and contorted in reverse from her torso, with each leg snapped in several places and loosely coiled in nothing resembling a comfortable pose. Her head drooped down onto her torso, with the semi-flattened chain-link fence serving as a macabre hammock of sorts.

Bex quickly looked down at this woman as she trudged by. She couldn't help but feel disdain and hatred for this woman who assuredly would have tried to kill her had Bex not been lucky enough to escape.

Lucky indeed.

Bex contemplated if the woman had anything worth taking but quickly outweighed that thought with the visual evidence that the dead body was someone likely no better off than her, present conditions aside.

***

140

Her mother had looked that way also, destitute, without hope, and containing no value. This was a stark realization for a pre-teen girl to contemplate about the woman who had brought her into the world. The addiction got more and more intense, and her physical appearance quickly worsened. Though she had been and still was a pretty woman, and indeed, there was still evidence around the house of when her mother and father had been happy and healthier in earlier years, the ravages of time and toxicity had played their part.

The drugs did not care about the arrest and the loss of her nursing home job. Nor did they care about Bex. Her mother quickly built up debts to her dealers, and for someone in her state of mind, health, and socioeconomic status, those could only be paid through the oldest industry in human history: prostitution. Men, often the dealers but other times the clients, would pick her mother up from the house. It was frightening to the young girl who lived there, and Bex would still shudder if anything ever caused her to think of those rough-looking men, each of them with their own pickup truck full of problems, coming to take her mother while her father was physically there but for all intents and purposes, never present.

But she was the problem. Her mother would tell her that every time she came back. If it wasn't for Bex, they wouldn't have needed the money, and wouldn't have needed to be in that house, and they would have been anywhere else but there.

***

She kept trudging, one step after another. Breathing was still tremendously difficult.

Nearly tripping over several of the railway lines, she stopped for a moment and looked to her right, all the way down the long, parallel, shiny, metallic tracks. Still awash in the torrential downpour and lit up by a combination of railyard lights and the omnipresent purple bath, she was struck by this visual. The perfect symmetry of the tracks evoked strength, as if each side supported the other like a magnet, with positive and negative forces achieving perfect harmony. Two sides of a coin that, when combined, made it worth more. Something about this symmetrical view fading to the disappearing horizon gave her a shot of energy. Whatever was at the end of those tracks was not where she was right now, which made it better. Whatever was at the end was where she needed to be.

Bex came upon the SUV. The Tesla Model Y was lying on its side after piling through the fence and barging across the railyard. She made her way around it. The front end was smashed in several places, the hood was dented, and the front windshield was broken and spiderwebbed, just as one might experience in a broken phone or tablet. It was hard to see into the vehicle, with the cracks in the glass combining with the rain and failing light to make it nearly opaque.

As she came around to the top of the vehicle, which could now be described as its right side, she could see more. The all-glass moonroof was smashed. It had peeled back like the bark of a tree and, similarly, had now exposed the life held within.

A woman was dangling from the driver's seat, with gravity having pulled her below the airbag that had activated in front of her chest. She was held in a position of stasis by her seatbelt, still clipped in its receptacle near the center console. Lights on the dashboard and the upper console were still on, illuminating the interior. The driver's side door and window remained intact, keeping the woman dry for the most part. Her arms appeared limp, her head was wobbling, and a slow drip of blood fell from a cut somewhere on her forehead, yet the seatbelt held her fast to the driver's seat. The woman's legs were splayed within the footwell, resting amongst the pedals and held up by the center console. Her trousers were unzipped and halfway down around her backside, which seemed strange to Bex but was not the reason she had paid attention to them.

By the time she covered the distance to the SUV, and with the benefit of her moment of meditation on the glistening rail tracks, she had shifted from fight or flight to survival mode. While the two mindsets weren't significantly different, the latter was more practical and proactive, which in this setting meant escape and money. She was certain that this attractive woman hanging upside down with her pants down—or in this case, up—could be a means for both. Once she leaned in through the broken moonroof opening, the pockets of the woman's trousers were easy enough to reach into, with her hands feeling the quality of the fabric first and then her fingertips constructing a mental image of a few small things. A key, or rather a key fob on a key ring, in one front pocket. In the other, nothing.

She looked down. A black leather strap was exposing itself from between the passenger seat and the center console. Pulling on it, she realized it belonged to a purse that must have flown across the interior cabin of the vehicle before coming to rest on the floor of the backseat. She pulled harder on the strap and then leaned in to retrieve the purse. It released and became hers. Bex now had a head into the backseat, just inches from the woman's limp face, at the end of a stretched neck on her dangling body. She could hear an ever so slight breath and feel air coming from the woman's nose and between her notably very full lips. *She's alive.*

From that position, she was not only struck by the precariousness of the woman's position in the car but also momentarily mesmerized by the presence and aura of this woman. She could sense that she was alive and that she had strength. The way she carried herself in this upside down and sideways position, with arms dangling, blood dripping from her forehead. Even the way she wore her undone trousers and suit jacket, something about this woman seemed powerful.

Bex could now see more of the backseat area and noticed a rolling luggage suitcase had also fallen to the lowest side of the vehicle, resting against the back passenger side door. She reached for it and pulled it up along with the purse, wrestling a bit to get both pieces out from between the front seats and without smacking either of them into the woman's head. That action was taken out of self-preservation as she was hyper-aware that, in that moment, this woman being awake would be much worse for Bex than if she stayed as she was. But it was also about dignity. This woman deserved the best chance for survival, just as Bex was improving her own odds.

***

Her mother didn't afford her the same respect. She would take from her, and she would strike at Bex often, usually for no reason at all. Bex was always to blame. And young Bex was always powerless, too weak to do anything about it. At least, it was like that until she found the Young Gainers.

She could first remember clicking a "like" button when she was six or seven years old. Bex's dad had shown her how to use a computer at an early age, and she quickly became savvy with it. Her mind just seemed to work that way, organizing things into logical structures, and thus, the internet, this nebulous entity that allowed all computers to speak to all computers without really speaking to any computers, made perfect sense to her.

In those days, her dad was still more like how she wanted to remember him. He was a happy, jovial, outgoing guy who had done quite well as a born-and-raised prairies boy. That guy had been an entrepreneur, first getting into machinery parts for the farming industry and working hard to become the default "parts guy" as far as anyone around Milestone, SK, might think. From there, he moved into real estate speculation and land investments in a market that didn't ever seem like it would slow down until it ran right off a cliff. Much like what it did to the economy at large, the housing crisis also ripped their home apart at the seams. To a six-year-old, none of the language around subprime or mortgage derivatives made any sense, but she knew that it had hurt her dad.

The more she heard those words, the more he seemed to get upset, and the more he was drinking—daily. The little girl's version of this was to self-medicate through her discoveries on the internet. At first, it was all silly stuff. Browser-based games, photo blogs, and even jokes that she could find and share with her friends. She was able to get an ICQ and an MSN account, even at seven years old, which opened up access to chatting with random people all over the world. Her young mind was as sharp as a razor, cutting through the bad jokes, poorly themed content, and silly flash games. But she appreciated the meaningful connections she could establish with other kids as, unlike most of them, she rarely left her home. The playdates and extra-curricular clubs and activities that had been a part of her younger years had all but stopped, on a parallel timeline with her father's downward spiral.

And as her father continued to lose his way, the broader social media sector really began to find its footing. The Arab Spring became a canary of hope for humanity and technology. The means to connect well-intentioned citizens across large swathes of society held the promise of ensuring peace and prosperity for all.

First, Tunisia, which in less than sixty days went from street-level protests to the president fleeing the country to make way for democratic elections.

Then Egypt, which accelerated the timeline, this time needing only just over two weeks to march from large-scale organized protests to President

Hosni Mubarak's departure from office after thirty years of ruling the country.

And events would follow in Libya, Yemen, Bahrain, and other countries in the region, though with varying long-term implications, ranging from overthrown governments to minor concessions to full-scale civil wars.

But regardless of actual outcomes or the lack of meaningful ones, Silicon Valley and its cadre of emerging communications platforms were quick to take credit for this perceived re-establishment of democracy. California marketing departments and influencers celebrated protestors meeting up in the same way that we saw flash mobs dance to PSY's Gundam Style in New York train stations, but were just as quick to avoid being labeled with helping instigate violence, battles, thievery, murder, and rape that was occurring as a byproduct of the widespread rebellion.

Voices of unity on important topics could be brought together in powerful ways by these platforms. Yet the platforms would become more than a medium for community—they would come to shape the message of those unified voices.

The Young Gainers was a Facebook group that started in early 2015. Bex was now twelve. Her father was a mess, and her mother was still hanging on to her job at the nursing home, but it was clear many things were terribly wrong. She found the group while reading an article about a sixteen-year-old girl who had traveled around the world in a sailboat by herself.

By herself.

That was just unbelievable, Bex thought. Here was a girl and all these other kids who had taken it upon themselves to make their world a better place, to do all kinds of amazing things without waiting for anyone else. The more time she spent in the group, the more this rang true. There was never a negative word from anyone, and none of them seemed to be limited in what they could do.

How could all these people be like this?

If the visual evidence wasn't there, and the deep profiles and comments of each user weren't just a click away, she might not have believed it to be true. They all said so many of the same things, used so many of the same words, and supported each other with near-limitless commitment. She couldn't help but be drawn to it.

"Mi Pequeña," her grandmother had said to her, one of the last times she had seen her alive, "when we were young in Spain, we had none of this. But we had ourselves, and if people were good, they didn't need to say it. They just were. You'd only need to look at who was making the most noise and look beyond it. That's where you find the good people, my sweet girl."

And that was well before her childish exploits on the internet. The "none of this" her grandmother had been talking about were more substantive things, like food, a refrigerator, or a car. She had grown up during the dysfunction of the post-war rule of General Franco, where nothing was guaranteed, and even the cold, wind-swept endless plains of small towns in the Canadian Prairies offered untold riches in comparison.

Bex often thought that it was her grandmother's resilience, hardened in the unrelenting heat of central Spain, a country cut off from its neighbors for decades, that gave her the strength to continue in the darkest of days.

***

Bex was now a few hundred meters from where the SUV had landed and a few tracks over toward the far side of the railyards. Two long lines of railcars, patiently awaiting directions to somewhere distant, offered her coverage from the death and chaos behind her. Bex gladly accepted. She had heard sirens since leaving the area but had not yet seen the numerous emergency vehicles now assembled on both sides of the carnage on the road.

She was moving toward a void of darkness, a large underpass tunnel formed by structural arches beneath an industrial zone thoroughfare on the distant side of the railyards.

The suitcase lumped along behind her. By definition, it was rolling luggage, but here, struggling over the uneven ground between the massive metal train tracks, it was just luggage. Baggage, even. *Thump! Thump! Thump!*

Made of high-tensile strength ballistic nylon, heavy-duty plastics, and rust-proof metals, this suitcase was built to last. It had served Somaya well over trips to Asia, Europe, South America, and Africa. She had only been two continents short of rolling through them all with this particular piece of gear. Bex zipped it open and started digging through the contents. Two handfuls of clothes were quickly stuffed into the purse she had looped on her shoulder. A pair of heeled shoes were discarded on the ground, their fashion no longer serving as an offset to their impracticality. Able to feel the two side pockets built into the inner linings of the storage area, Bex opened those and pulled at whatever was inside. Smaller items, including some charging cables, a bag of toiletries, and a few small containers, came back with her hand, and she also pushed those deep into the ever-plumper purse.

This consolidated weight on her shoulder further reduced the speed of her movement across the yards, and the strap, which ran down from Bex's left shoulder to her right waist, pressed harder against her chest, enhancing the painful compression from those many injuries.

The adrenaline still ran high, helping her forge ahead beyond the physical constraints of her body's pain limits and push through a heavy rusty maintenance gate that led to the tunnel she had seen.

***

It had provided a way out, participating in that Facebook Group. Bex had started reading more and more of what they were sharing. Hundreds of other kids and young people were in on it, and some of the stories were amazing. There was an entire discussion forum on how to build your own backyard cabin, complete with diagrams, drawings, and instructions. *In another life and another yard, that would be pretty cool*, Bex had thought to herself. There were stories of youths traveling around the world, with photos from the summits of Mt. Kilimanjaro and Machu Picchu, to the most northern islands in the Arctic Circle and the remote outback of Australia. *Why... and how did they get there?* Too often, those sorts of logistical questions didn't seem to be readily answered. The content and the stories were more than enough to belay any skepticism.

It was just fun to be inspired, to read about others, post about them, and to be a part of this prospering community. She wasn't close with anyone at school anymore, but she had dozens of friends in this group. Her participation in it was taking on a life of its own—a much better one than what Bex had to endure in real life.

In fact, IRL sucked. It was terrible. Given the choice to do anything online, through the group, she wouldn't hesitate. And neither would so many others.

"Today, we go to the beach, peeps!" was how it started. It was a post on the group from one of the leading contributors, @jute92, or Jute, as she was known in the group. In the last few weeks, Jute had taken dozens of followers on virtual trips. They had gone to Venice, Tokyo, and, early this week, to an outpost on Mars. What it meant in the parlance of the Young Gainers was that everyone "ripped' themselves to these destinations.

Ripping wasn't yet widespread, but for those who knew, they knew. They "ripped" through the Mixality Photos app, known as MXP. A user could take a selfie within the app and then convincingly adjust the photo with different clothes, a different location, and even adjust the lighting and color in ways that truly recreated the look of being physically present. It was a remarkable transcendence of the experience for group members to go from passively following those few with amazing feats of accomplishment to being participatory and contributing to the overall momentum of the community.

Bex hadn't been sure where the term "ripping" came from, but the digital urban legend was that the founder of Mixality, Philip J. Clancy, had asked his engineering team to make it possible to "rip" through alternate dimensions.

"Hey, that crater looks like Mars, holy shit. I'm so ripped," were the actual inspiring words from Philip J. Clancy himself, inspired by hallucinogens and dehydration as he took a selfie on a scorching August day in the high Utah desert. He would usually spend a week or more wandering the arid landscapes and rocky mountain ranges every year leading up to Burning Man.

Her feed had become something to behold. Bex had ripped along with many of these group journeys, including the one to Mars. From that trip, she had photos of herself in a full spacesuit making inspection rounds on the exterior of an impressive base and another one wearing space-tights, presumably Martian underwear, holding up a small green tree that was bearing brilliant, ripe, perfectly round oranges. This was a group shot, with some of the other space travelers also in the scene tending to parts of the garden and tasting some of the fruit, with some of them making silly faces for the virtual photographer.

Her other ripped exploits showed her high on the snowy peaks of the Andes, slashing her way through the jungles of Southeast Asia, walking under the Eiffel Tower, and even exploring deep below the earth on a Jules Verne-inspired "Ripping to the Center of the Earth." All of this had been accomplished from the veiled security of her father's computer on his mostly unused desk at home, the only place where connections mattered anymore.

When a cataclysmic snowstorm hit the Canadian Prairies in September 2019, it was a welcome relief to see that invitation to rip to the beach with a bunch of other sixteen-year-olds that she considered her closest friends. Young Gainers was giving her hope and a sense of belonging. It was the thing that made every day interesting for Bex, it had gifted her the means to do what she wanted on her own terms.

***

Walking through the maintenance tunnel elicited a few memories of virtual spelunking on that earlier rip to the center of the earth. Everything she had created, seen, posted, and commented upon in the Young Gainers group had felt as real, or even more real, than anything she could remember outside of it.

The tunnel was dark. Looking back one last time, she was now elevated enough on the upward slope of this tunnel to see all the way back to the crash scene, now several hundred meters away. Flashing lights were everywhere, concentrated near that muddy slope of grass she had called home for the last however many days, illuminating a blast radius of human and vehicular wreckage. Turning to look forward, the high arched concrete ceiling of the maintenance tunnel showed a dark, bleak, rainy world ahead on the other side, exactly the kind of place where Bex could fit right in.

***

Fort Lauderdale was a complete unknown to a young, homebound girl in the middle of Canada. The Young Gainers were more often ripping on big adventures inspired by the stuff of lore and legend or meaningful excursions with an eye to environmentalism, community, or other inherently good gestures.

Jute was adamant it was time to do something different.

"This is where we have our fun, YGs!" her post read.

The replies came in fast and frequently.

"OMG, set us up now!"

"I'm in, TT rip!"

"LFG Jute!"

Few responses held back on exclamations, and most were heavy in acronyms and terrible spelling. All were announcing a commitment to the next rip, which came with the following instructions:

"Time to get some sun and bear some skin, my peeps. Post yourself to MXP and be ready to show your abs, your legs, and your best beach body!"

MXP—the aforementioned default app for ripping—was a trusted tool that was heavily used. Hundreds of people in this group were each posting hundreds of photos of themselves, and the same behavior was starting to happen across thousands and thousands of other groups around the world. MXP itself would never show your source imagery, and in that regard, it built a feeling of safety and security, as it more or less seemed to guarantee that whatever you thought you might normally look like, you would look a million times better in the app.

Thus, the normalization of using this app in this way had now led to a situation of hundreds of preteens and teens, girls and boys, submitting nearly nude photos of themselves for storage and manipulation on remote servers.

Indeed, they were stored with good intentions, and sadly, they were manipulated with anything but. These photos became the sordid source for what would end up being a shockingly large-scale case of child pornography.

The Fort Lauderdale "day at the beach" rip had become a photo and video journal of sexual debauchery, nudity, abuse, and rape, an unwatchable scrapbook of things that never happened but could never be forgotten.

How exactly this was done and by whom would be a lingering question for years. Certainly, there was longstanding and widespread familiarity with "photoshopping" throughout the initial growth of digital content production and the proliferation of the World Wide Web. That was simply the digital progression of airbrushing and other post-production techniques that had started as far back as the first half of the 19th century. In fact, some of the earliest photographic gear required manual retouching of the negatives to produce a usable photo, mostly due to limitations in the plates and cameras used in those early days.

Internet or cloud-based content creation techniques came onto the scene in the late 1990s and continued to improve with digital photography, allowing users to "face replace" themselves into funny photos and skits. Many fondly remember a half-decade of Christmases that had been celebrated by millions of smiling faces looking upon the detached heads of friends and family members dancing around on top of poorly animated elf costumes.

It had just been the last year or two that newer AI and machine-learned content creation techniques had sprung onto the scene. "Deep fakes" had started to proliferate across the viral content landscape. Amazingly, the quality of work produced by indie content creators and at-home 3D computer graphics artists was rivaling some of the most expensive and complicated work to have come out of the Hollywood studios.

Much of the attention had thus far been captured by online deep fake videos showing a young Tom Cruise cracking jokes with his notorious smile, or Stallone as the lead in *The Terminator* instead of Schwarzenegger, this with the revisionist history implications of possibly never having filmed *First Blood* in the fictional town of Hope, Washington. It was a massive, awful leap from those thought-provoking edits of action-movie celebrities to what had been perpetrated upon the Young Gainers.

Once the manipulated content came to light, it took on an evil, disruptive, and contagious life of its own. All of the Young Gainers' feeds on Facebook and Mixality were preyed upon, with the faked content of themselves and others spreading across those networks like wildfire. The fidelity and detail of the imagery were beyond unsettling, but to look at it with a technical eye, one couldn't help but be impressed by how these people, or this system, whoever was behind it, had somehow used a relatively small amount of shared and hacked imagery to produce raw, crude, and terribly realistic video content.

There was a reason that Tom Cruise and Stallone and Schwarzenegger footage was some of the first and strongest deep fake content to come out—the available training data for those three actors was almost unlimited, reflective of male-dominated stardom of the twentieth century. There were thousands upon thousands of hours of content in every format—audio, photography, video. They had willfully put themselves in front of a camera and delivered every permutation of expressions, emotions, mannerisms, and physical performance. Thus, the training datasets available to recreate those same individuals through AI-powered technology were unlike what was available for nearly any other human on the planet.

In the Young Gainers case, the participants were mostly unknown youths and kids, and at best—or worst—the inputs were limited to a small number of posted photos. Generally, people were stupefied by how it had been done, disgusted by thinking about why it had been done, and far too often mesmerized by watching what had been done.

This was devastating for all those unsuspecting kids and amplified even more so for Bex and others who had been drawn to the Young Gainers, not so much because they had found a community based upon things they were already doing but because within it, they had found space and freedom to become something they weren't. In the same way that the beautifully rendered photos of ripping journeys throughout the world and across the solar system felt real, so, too, did the awful, visceral, and terribly realistic photos and videos of her being placed into disgusting, illegal sexual acts. How could she delineate the two? The ripped stories had created a life she wanted to lead, a magical existence of fantastical journeys. Yet the darker, horrendous content generated from this last rip had become more popular, more shared, and more "liked" in some perverse reverse incarnation of everything that had been inspiring to her about the Young Gainers.

The verbal antagonistic torture at school, along with seemingly endless reposting and resharing of this material on other social networks, was beyond what these unfortunate Young Gainers were able to cope with. So many of these targeted kids went into reclusive, dark places as a result of it. Sadly, all that had been gained was now lost, and then some.

And while it manifested for Bex in much the same way, she had a slightly different feeling about it. Without a doubt, showing up at school and seeing explicit photos of herself plastered all around her locker was devastating. But she had already grown to ignore so much of being tormented and mistreated at school. What was harder to contemplate was that by taking the defense of saying this was all fake, a crime, and not to be believed, she would also have to admit that none of the ripping that came before it was real. By extension, it would mean that none of the activity in the group was real, and all of her escapism for all that time, all those years she had spent with the group, was irrelevant.

And worst of all, it meant her only remaining reality was the one she had wanted to exit most of all.

The Fort Lauderdale incident would be too much for this failed family to come back from. The father had nearly drank himself to his own demise, and the day he saw firsthand what had been done through his own blurry lens on social media would be his last.

Bex's mother had found him on the bathroom floor, covered in blood, lifeless. In his last selfish act, he had ended his own misery, adding the sum volume of it to the burden of his remaining family. The failed father's wife reacted the only way she had been able to do anything in those days, by turning to the salvation of her drugs and her violent outbursts. The daughter, who only went to school to escape being at home and who only came home to escape being at school, would run out of options after returning to the house a few hours later.

"It was all your fault, you horrible, awful, disgusting girl!"

Those were the last words Bex would hear from her mother before spending the night huddled in a bus station with a one-way westbound ticket scheduled for departure the next morning.

Fifteen

SHUFFLING

Jason had been out with Elise and her friends for drinks at the campus bar earlier that Friday night, right after classes had let out for the day. After a few hours, the girls left to go for dinner without extending an invitation to him. It seemed to Jason that she had concerns about something personal and wanted to have a girls' night out.

She doesn't owe me anything, anyway, he thought. *I hope she's okay.* He liked Elise but wanted to avoid any complications with his roommates, so he had convinced himself they should keep their relationship to a friendship basis only.

"Hooking up with roommates is bad news, matey," he had told Doug just a week or so ago, when they were at home one weeknight playing Xbox.

He watched Elise and her friends through the window as they left the pub and stood outside for a few minutes, smoking cigarettes. It was still light out. The sun had descended into the lower western sky, casting rays through the tobacco smoke wafting over the girls' heads. The cherries on their smokes would light up every time they brought them up to their lips, like excitable fireflies buzzing around in the dusk.

Jason remarked to himself that so few people were smoking in public these days. It didn't bother him, and he knew from living with her that Elise wasn't a full-time smoker, but she did sneak one here and there and loved to smoke with her friends. He thought it was interesting how much it had changed culturally, even over his short lifespan. His early years in Eastern Australia suggested that just about every adult, and teenager for that matter, was lighting up and loving it. And then, during his high school days in Texas, it was still a thing, but maybe less so. He and his friends found they could easily and accurately guess the era of movies and television shows by the prevalence of smoking, not to mention the obvious giveaways of how long and slow the title sequences were.

No way in hell I'll be watching a movie tonight. Time for a good piss-up!

The campus bar was a hybrid of a pub, restaurant, and nightclub, with no apparent rules as to which one it was at any given point. Options always abounded. He saw some of the guys that he knew from the Spectra basketball team having a round of shots near the bar at the front and walked over to join them.

"How ya goin' gents?" he asked, a booming low-altitude voice delivered with his unique accent. He had opened his arms out wide and, in a friendly way, smacked two of the bigger guys on their mid-back as he cut into their standing group. This posture allowed his solar plexus and lungs to expand, which maximized his physical size and ensured that his introductory words would be as loud and clear as possible. His enlarged entry was necessary considering he was joining a group of a half dozen young men all as close to seven feet tall as Jason was to five.

"Hey, what's up, Jay?" answered Brandon Aston, one of the taller trees in this grove of giants.

"Not much, man, just having some drinks. What's good tonight, mate?" Jason replied. The guys were looking at him as he spoke, all enjoying listening to this diminutive, strange-sounding friend of theirs. The basketball players were a mixed bag themselves, most of them American, but none had quite the same unique way about themselves as Jason. Felipe Castillo was new to the team this season, having signed to play for the college out of the semi-pro basketball leagues in Spain earlier in the year. While many things were new to Felipe, he had taken a liking to Jason right away.

Ricky was there too. He was also close with a few of the players, as he had grown up in Brooklyn with Amare Taylor, the starting forward, and knew Deshaun Rolle, one of the recent freshman recruits from the same neighborhood.

"Look at this, it's the fucking United Nations!" exclaimed Mitch Zentax as he walked up to the group with a big pint glass in his left hand. With his right, he started punching it out with each of the guys.

"Right there. Yeah. Up high. Up high," he called out with a play-by-play of every fist-bump. "Yeah, Ricky. Boom. Hola, amigo," he continued, going through Ricky and Felipe.

Finally, Mitch's massive seven-foot frame looked down upon Jason, who was lucky to be scratching five foot four with a good case of bedhead. Zentax was not only tall, he was also a very wide human, built like a "brick shit house," as many people would say, even while others would often wonder why brick shit houses need to be built larger than other shit houses. He had grown up in Oklahoma, a big white farm boy who looked like he could play the role of a Russian villain in yet another Stallone film.

But here, he was only a villain to opposing teams and, very occasionally, anyone who might get on the wrong side of him when they were out drinking.

"Zenty! How ya been, you monster?" Jason quickly broke the hilarious silence of this monstrous human looking down as if ready to squash him like a bug. Instead of punching it out fist-to-fist with Zentax, he started punching the giant man's midsection like a speed bag routine in a boxing gym. Jason was hitting with some force, but he may as well have been tickling the Spectra College starting center.

"Ha! Love you, my little man," Zentax broke out in a huge smile and started laughing as he reached down and grabbed both of Jason's fists in one hand to stop the assault. Their hands pulled apart and then reconnected in a "bro hug," with the big man's right hand now wrapping entirely around Jason's and the resulting half-hug being dangerously close to inappropriate behavior with the little man's head too close to Zentax's waist for anyone watching. Mitch didn't spill a drop of his beer through this entire sequence.

Everybody looked up. A discernible beeping could be heard cutting through the entire bar. *Do-do–do-do-DO-DO-DO.* A veritable signal amongst the noise, one that was immediately recognizable to the group.

"Ohhhh shiiit!" a few of them said in unison as they gulped down the drinks in front of them, slammed their glasses on the bar, and started moving stiltedly across the room.

It was still early, just past seven o'clock, and the room was still configured for more casual drinking and dinner. This didn't stop the mass of young men, now numbering eight with the addition of Jason and Zentax. They pushed a few empty tables to the side, revealing a small dance floor in the middle of the bar. A few other patrons had remained seated at another table that still encroached upon the black-and-white checkered flooring upon which the tall men stood.

"Moves and grooves! Moves and grooves!" Zentax said as he picked up two girls by their seats and moved them to the side. The guys they were with obliged quickly and slid their tables and chairs away as well.

Party Rock is in the house toniiiight!

The music kicked into gear as the dance beat descended upon the room. "Party Rock Anthem" had swept the charts that summer and had become a legitimate anthem in thousands of places much like the Spectra campus bar. The basketball team had become obsessed with it, and everybody in their immediate circle knew what to expect when those recognizable electronic dance beats started to drop. For those who weren't ready for it, they would not make that mistake twice.

Everybody just have a good timmme...

The dance floor became something more like a professional wrestling ring, an arena filled with large men of all different ethnicities in large shoes of many different logos, though with a heavy preference for a certain recognizable swoosh. They bounced and jumped and slid and squeaked their feet all around. Others in the bar started to join them, unable to escape the gravitational magnetism of these guys and the inherent addictive beats of "PRA," as the boys called it.

As the dancing mob grew larger, the swirling center of it all continued to swell with humanity while expelling more and more furniture, as if the chairs and tables were exiting from a strange Party Rock orbit. People were jumping and moving and shaking their arms around, most of them with a personal style all their own but clearly infused with the rhythm of the song.

And we gon' make you lose your mind...

Ricky looked over at Felipe, who was moving around the floor but more hunched over than the others. His arms were moving down and then up, sort of from side to side, perhaps like one might move if they were dancing with a hula hoop while climbing up a hill. Maybe. There was no easy way to describe the motion.

"Felipe! What's that move, man?" he asked.

"Yeh, Ricky! Woooh!" Felipe responded. He hadn't heard the question over the loud music and surrounding revelry.

"Ha ha!" Ricky loudly laughed while switching and sliding his feet and stance to the rhythmic beats, and Felipe kept moving in his strange but very watchable way. "Dude, what is that?" He leaned over and yelled in Felipe's ear, "What you doing?"

Every day I'm shufflin'

"This is how we do it in Spain!" Felipe responded as he turned back to his weird move. Though he didn't last very long as Zentax had been roughhousing his way around the dance floor and now came bounding between the Spaniard and the New Yorker, his arms in the air with one meat-claw-like fist holding a freshly replenished pint glass high aloft, sloshing most of the beer into the air and raining it down upon the three of them in tropical rainfall-sized droplets.

"Boys, it's gonna be a big night tonight!" he yelled, putting his massive free arm around Ricky and lifting him up off his feet. The three of them made for quite a spectacle, with the white mountain of a man Zentax distributing lager in a perimeter around them like a lawn sprinkler, holding a not-so-short Black man airborne, the two of them in a frozen slow dance, and a shorter Spaniard beside them who appeared to be conducting some rhythmic road work, digging methodically at the floor beneath them.

Zentax had a habit of interrupting just about everything everywhere he went, and continued to do this in a jovial way that kept the party fires burning within the group of guys as they made their way from the pub to a brew hall just off campus, then a nightclub in not-too-distant Marlton, and finally a cocktail bar half the way back home again. Their itinerary of four venues that covered nearly a full circle odyssey around the regional townships east of Philadelphia was as big a night as they had so far that semester, all made possible through the ease and availability of Superide, a new ride-hailing service that had started up in the few weeks before school. Superide had been funded by a cohort of East Coast dotcom e-commerce platform many-millionaires who had made their fortunes in a dialup and hard-wired ethernet era of banner ads, limited inventories, and point-and-click customers. These backers had since lifted their gaze from the mice and keyboards of yore to the possibilities of mobile technology deployed to the streets of New Jersey but had yet to account for the trafficking of VC dollars that was already commuting into this space in California. For the time being, Superide had street-cornered the regional ride-hailing market. The boys' night out was also made much easier by their relative celebrity and Zentax and Brandon's absolute large size, ensuring they consistently received front-of-the-line access and a disproportionate amount of attention from the other guests and bar staff.

"You know what the best thing is about Superide?" Brandon posed to the four other guys crammed into a mini-van with him during one of the transportation segments of their evening. If his question had been heard by another four guys—those Superide-backing e-commerce tycoons—who were also out that same evening and only a thirty-dollar Superide fare away in Atlantic City, it would have been met with a collective cringe. Brandon, like most other users, had elected to pronounce the startup as "soup-ride" rather than the heroic moniker the founders had hoped for. Over the following eighteen months, that subtle but massive error in branding would lead to the service getting continually confused with a non-competitive offering that promised 24/7 hot soup delivery. Before long, the froth of Silicon Valley finances would float Uber and Lyft far beyond the reach of Superide, itself stuck in the broth of murky, curdled markets from which its privately-held stock would never satisfy the hunger of its investors.

But for now, it held top billing on the New Jersey private transportation menu.

"Oh, dude, it's just too easy. You hit the button, and then boom, it's right there, it's like Johnny on the spot," answered Amare.

"You mean Osama on the spot!" barked Deshaun. Amare started laughing.

"Jesus, man, you can't do that," shot back Ricky. Despite his usual low bar for humor, frequent lapses in judgment, and reliably absent standards of behavior, he was far more empathic than he would usually let on. He had no appetite for intolerance, his reactions often casting him as the good guy he desperately tried not to be.

"What? What'd I say?" replied Deshaun. "You know it's true!"

"Well, for one, it ain't. For two, a lot of different people drive these cars, and for three, my pops was a cab driver, so shut the fuck up." Ricky put a fork in this part of the conversation.

"Okay, well, back to Superide," Jason jumped in, hoping to stifle this discussion and redirect things back to Brandon's initial question. "The best thing, I think, is you get all these mints and water. Look at this, mate. It's like free dessert!"

"Well, yeah, I can see that. I guess coming from the outback, all that free water is too good to be true!" Brandon replied to Jason. "But nah, the best thing about Superide is you just keep pushing that button, getting in cars and go wherever you want, and that bill just goes all the way to mom's credit card."

The other guys started laughing.

"Oh dang, nice. Guess we know how we all getting around this year! Thanks Mama Aston!" Deshaun answered, somewhat relieved he could move on from his joke about the drivers that got Ricky so upset. He always thought it was interesting how Ricky became much more sensitive to things like that when they were out drinking. It also seemed like Ricky got a lot smarter, too.

The night was so full of distractions that it took a few hours and many more drinks before Ricky's intellect really started to shine. He was sitting at a high table in Vincent's, the cocktail bar that usually served as their nightcap destination, as it did for a large number of the student population. To Ricky's left was Jason, and across the table sat Amare.

Deshaun and two of the others had already gone to get pizza, and Zentax and Felipe had disappeared a few hours earlier with two girls they had been talking to at the nightclub, leaving these three as the surviving members of the evening's sortie.

"Man, why is it always the three of us end up back here?" Ricky lamented.

"Speak for yourself, homie," Amare said as he looked around the bar, scanning for women that he knew or perhaps did not yet know but intended to very soon. Amare had been averaging over fifteen points per game for the last three seasons, and as the other guys knew all too well, he never had any trouble scoring.

"Did you see how many people were out tonight? That was crazy. Way more people from Spectra out at the club, and then all the hockey people. Guess there was a Flyers game tonight. I don't understand that sport, man. Like who was the first to do that? I'm just gonna take some metal and chop it up and work it, and put it on my feet... Or maybe they were like, 'Yo, I've got two more knives than I need! What'm I do with these? Think I'll strap them to my feet and go see if I don't fall through the lake. Come with me and use this curved stick to pull me back if I fall, yo?" Ricky's self-directed monologue of ruminating over the origins of hockey had him standing up and going through the motion of hooking someone else with an imaginary hockey stick, saving that imaginary other person from falling through a hole in his also imaginary frozen lake.

"Crikey mate, you're working on your Spanish dance moves?" Jason piped up, looking to squeeze out any remaining humor that might be left from the misinterpreted dance moves of their Iberian friend from earlier that night.

"Ha ha, nah, Jay, this is 'history in white guy sports.' It's a new show I'm working on. I don't need this Communications degree! I'll just shoot this stuff on my phone." Ricky kept going, his creative energy fully engaged. "Next up, I've got 'Gator Wrassling in Austrahhl-ya with special guest host J-Kim,'" he said with an ungodly attempt at a Korean/Australian/Texan accent.

"Ricky, you know it's crocs, right, mate? Gators in America. Gators eat little unsuspecting American kids, Crocs eat Gators, and we eat crocs in Oz," Jason offered his take on the natural selection hierarchy of American and Australian creatures.

"Sure, man, you can have all them big lizards. I can't handle that shit anyway." He shifted his attention, "But just look at these people." Ricky half-pointed across the bar to a group of people—men and women slightly older than them. They were in a corner of the cocktail bar, seated on couches and comfortable chairs next to a fireplace. Most of them were sipping from long-stemmed martini glasses.

"These muthafuckers look like they just came out of Jerry Maguire," he commented, as one of the men in the group was, almost on cue, gesticulating wildly with his arms in the air as he spoke with shiny white teeth that glistened from the overhead track lighting and picked up occasional glints of yellow and orange from the fireplace just beyond them.

"And the brother with that group, look at him. It's Will Smith in *Pursuit of Happyness*. Where's his son? Ha ha," he laughed as he pointed out a Black man who was with the office workers. "His Walmart suit doesn't fit in with them trust fund muthafuckers. Bet they got a limo down from the Hamptons to come here." He kept on going.

"It's a new religion, right?" Ricky posed a rhetorical question to the table.

Amare hadn't been paying too much attention as his eyes had been looking somewhere else but then turned to Ricky. Amare was a Christian and wouldn't hesitate to tell people. In fact, he was known to use it successfully in his pickup line repertoire. The comment on religion from Ricky had caught his ear. "What's that, Ricky?"

"Trustafarians! Those muthafuckers don't have to work a day in their life, they just do what they do. Trustafarians, I'm telling you. You can see it a mile away."

"Ah, okay." Amare chuckled. "That's my sign, I'm outta here." As he stood up to leave, so did a very attractive girl from a table two booths over from where they sat. Ricky and Jason stood up to bro-hug Amare and send him on his way. Jason recognized the girl from some of his Art History courses and wasn't surprised at all to see her and Amare leave the bar together.

Ricky was partially relieved. For a moment, he thought his observational humor had sent Amare away.

"And then we have this guy who walks on water," he commented as the new couple exited.

"Ricky, you're quite the insightful chap," Jason observed. "Not sure you should be in Journalism or whatever it is you're studying. You should be in the Arts, or maybe Philosophy or Psychology or something. You'd just need to be drunk most of the time to say smart shit like this. I swear, dude, most of the day, you are like this mild-mannered chill guy, and then a few drinks and you pop off into some deep, dark analytical zone."

"You know what they say, J-Kim, you only use five percent of your brain most of the time, and then it takes some mind-*alternating* states to turn on the rest of it." Ricky tapped the side of his head, indicating that he had activated the other ninety-five percent of his gray matter.

'Okay, Dr. Phil, so tell me about those peeps over there," Jason challenged, pointing to another table closer to the entrance, just off the side of the serving bar.

Ricky took a sip from the whisky drink in front of him. They had ordered a round of scotch whisky, the cheapest one on the menu, to have as a nightcap. The earthy, peaty taste and smell of it still hit them hard every time, and none of the guys actually liked the taste, as evidenced by the mostly untouched drink that remained where Amare had been sitting. But they knew it was the right drink to have in front of them at times like this.

He looked at the table. Two girls. One, Black, wearing a dark hoody and stressed jeans. The other, a white girl with dyed purple hair in a halter top and cargo pants. They were both wearing combat-style boots. Two guys sat with them, a muscular white man and a lanky Hispanic or Indigenous guy, wearing polo shirts in different bright colors.

"You know what? Those are fucking lemmings. Look at them dudes, their collars are popped. Holy shit, the white dude has three layers of tennis shirt on! Look at that." He took another sip from his whisky and recoiled from the strong flavor.

"Uh, okay. What's a limming?" Jason asked.

"Lemming."

"Yeah, limming," Jason confirmed, adamant that he was saying the same thing as Ricky.

"Yeah, alright. Lemming. I dunno, Doug always talks about them. It's from a video game or something, but I guess these little rat-looking things just run after each other, and then they all end up running off a cliff," Ricky shared his wisdom on the topic.

"Ah, cool, cool. Limming. I like it," Jason made a note to talk about lemmings sometime again soon. "So what makes them limmings?"

"Fuck, okay, yes, they are *limmings*. Let's go with it. See these boys here, all preppy. They look like the young versions of those Jerry Maguire and

Company guys over on the other side. They got their polo tennis shirts, whatever those are. They got their slick hair. Just spending mom and dad's money while they wait to be told what to do next. But they don't listen to anyone else who's not their mom. Life on a silver platter, that's what they got," Ricky surmised.

"So if BA spends his mum's money on Superide, isn't he literally doing the same thing? And weren't we doing it with him?" Jason offered as an argument.

"Don't be bringing those rumors at me, man," Ricky quickly defeated it and continued. "Those girls, bet the white girl with the purple hair is with them dudes, and she dresses like that to upset her parents and brought along her Black friend so she can fit more into the hood before they hop in the limo with Jerry Maguire and Co. and head back to the Hamptons."

"Okay, now it sounds like you just put everything in the same boat. Or maybe the same limo, ha ha." Jason enjoyed his own joke.

"Yeah, well, probably fucking true shit. You heard it here first," Ricky concluded his observations and took another sip before they paid their check and left. Had they been paying any attention as they walked by the table near the door, they might have heard the preppy colored-shirt guys talking to the international British rock star in the dark hoody about which parts of her choreography they would work on in the morning, before her big show at the hockey arena the next night. They also may have gleaned from the girl with the purple hair who had been speaking into her hand that she was coordinating security detail for the celebrity hiding in plain sight. Had they been listening a few moments earlier, they might have even heard the two girls talking about the handsome young Black and Asian college guys sitting across the bar from them and how these two guys must have been out on the town with their friends and that it would only be right to offer them a warm bed and a warmer body to sleep with at their luxury hotel.

They didn't hear or infer any of this, however. Ricky left, comfortable in his character assassination of everyone in the bar, with Jason laughing just enough to mask his dismay that he always seemed to be going home last and alone.

Well, not entirely alone.

"Should we play some Xbox? Bet you Doug's still awake anyway," Ricky offered as he invited himself over to Jason's.

"Yeah, guess so... It's only... 1:30," Jason knew it was late, but he thought they might as well keep the good times rolling, which for the two of them would often mean smoking a few bowls of cannabis and playing video games until the sun came up. He was already dreading how tired he would be the next night as he secured a Superide, safe in the knowledge that his mom would also be paying for this one.

Sixteen

NOBODY GOING NOWHERE

The overloaded purse she carried away from the damaged Tesla had caused her old neck injury to flare up. It had slowed her down quite a bit, even as she continued to put distance between herself and the accident scene. *Too much asymmetrical weight.*

Although it hindered her exit that night, it soon turned out that the purse allowed Bex to get further away than she could have thought possible.

She found a residential street going steeply uphill on the other side of that maintenance tunnel. It was quiet here, with large trees lining each side of the street, dampening much of whatever noise might have been heard. Several blocks later, her escape intersected another busy street running north-south. By this point, it was almost two o'clock in the morning, though traffic was still flowing consistently on that route. She imagined people returning home from being out with their friends or family, or finishing up a late shift at a restaurant, bar, or hospital—people doing meaningful things. And here she was, running from chaos yet again.

A late bus was still operational, slowing to a stop only a short distance down the sidewalk from where she found herself. Mustering what little energy she had remaining, Bex ran, with the heavy purse bouncing on her right shoulder digging further into the blisters it had already conjured up over the previous many city blocks.

To her luck, the driver noticed her in the side mirror of the bus. After two people departed through the back door and the sole individual waiting at the bus stop had boarded, the driver waited an extra minute, giving Bex time to catch up.

"There you go, dear," the older female bus driver said as Bex stepped up.

Through grief-strained eyes and a face overloaded with sweat, grime, and dirt, Bex could only groan a sigh of relief. "Oh, thank you," she offered meekly, finding it hard to now be conversing with someone.

Bex didn't have any money. But she did have the purse, which she zipped open and started rooting through.

"Don't worry, dear. Just go sit down. I'll get you home," the bus driver offered. Bex met her eyes for a moment, once again seeing those eyes of kindness and empathy that she had only encountered a few times in her life. She didn't pause to question it. Bex nodded and stepped into the main volume of the bus.

Home.

What did that even mean? Where was she going? Anywhere.

It didn't matter. She just needed to get far away from this place. Bex shuffled through the bus, moving past an older man near the front wearing some kind of worker's uniform, a teenage girl listening to music by herself, and a group of "kids" her age sitting at the very back, all wearing big smiles from ear to ear. They were having a great time.

She kept her head down and sat closer to the back but away from the attention of that group of twenty-somethings. To them, she looked like a haggard older woman, too uninteresting to engage with and too disheveled and dirty to get close to, which suited her just fine.

Bex still had her right hand buried deep within the purse. As she sat down, she could feel her hand close on a hard case of some sort. She gripped it tight and pulled it out. Under the overly bright lights within the bus, she looked down at what she had found—a portfolio wallet with a zipper running around the perimeter. Unzipped, it expanded to reveal several smartly-organized sleeves and clips for holding what she expected were important things.

And they were: three credit cards, a small sleeve containing a thin wad of cash in large bills of Canadian, US, Brazilian, and British denominations, and a frequent flyer card bearing the description Aeroplan Super Elite and the name of Ms. Somaya Patel.

Somaya. What a beautiful name. Bex thought back to seeing that glamorous, strong woman hanging bruised and bloodied upside down in her car and how she had somehow still maintained a state of grace. She was glad that the woman was alive when she left, and she hoped that Somaya had remained that way.

Elite. Yep, seems about right. She wasn't even entirely sure what that meant, as she herself had never flown before. Still, she imagined that this Somaya woman would just wake up in the morning and get whisked away by chauffeur, led through the airport by a security detail with assistants in stride to carry her bags, and once onboard the plane, given massive luxurious seats in spaces all her own.

Along with the credit cards, each decadently made of a mysterious metallic substance pressed into rectangular shape, there was a passport, its pages bundled within a deep navy blue cover embossed with the telltale markings of the United States of America. The Great Seal, not to be mistaken for a large underwater mammal, is usually known as the recognizable coat-of-arms on the passport featuring a bald eagle holding a shield, arrows, olive branches, and adorned with Latin script. The reverse motif of the Great Seal is lesser known, though perhaps more widely discussed, as it is made up of an incomplete pyramid and the watchful Eye of Providence, looking over the fertile ground that has spawned a plethora of conspiracy theories based on the iconic representation of Freemason symbols. To many, the Great Seal is indeed fishy.

Bex could remember reading up on some of those conspiracy theories from posts and links shared within the Young Gainers and other Facebook groups she had followed in that previous life. It was compelling stuff, to be sure. To so many people in similarly dire situations, it was almost a relief to believe that the reason the world was so fucked up was that a bunch of nasty old white men were somewhere out there with their hands on the controls of every aspect of society. That storyline was compelling and exciting to read. Perhaps if she, Bex, were the one to break the Freemason's hold on the inner workings of the human world, she could fix everything and, just maybe, fix herself. As the years passed, she realized how silly and juvenile those feelings were, and she thought it was remarkable how so many people still clung to those stories. *Do they still have hope? Something to hold onto? Or is it just easier to blame it all on something you can't see?*

She would be more interested in what was inside the passport. Flipping open the small booklet revealed several pages within that had been marked and stamped with evidence of numerous border crossings—Bolivia, Thailand, China, Japan, Brazil, Peru, Costa Rica, Kenya, Tanzania, South Africa, Ukraine, India, and more. *Wow, it is true,* she thought, confirming the dreamy visions she had of Ms. Somaya traveling the world at her leisure.

When she flipped back through all the stamped sheets to the rigid page containing Somaya's information, her heart skipped a beat. She was looking down at this shiny, perfectly laminated page within a book that already held so many stories from around the world, and in one fell swoop, Bex was teleported to all those same destinations. Non-existent visual memories flooded her mind.

Here she was again, vicariously ripping her way around the world through Somaya's prior travels, much as she had with the Young Gainers.

It was because of the picture. While the words revealed that Ms. Somaya Patel was born in Seattle, Washington, in 1983, the picture showed her youthful dark face, her inquisitive and intelligent brown eyes framed under defined but elegant eyebrows, her full cheekbones, and her fulsome lips.

But most amazingly, it showed her. Not Somaya. It showed Bex. But not Bex either, rather a near-perfect mirror image. Somehow, through a combination of the grain of photography film and the lighting in the photo booth the day that picture was taken, placed under the shiny half-reflective surface, it reflected a photo back to Bex that might as well have been taken of her.

How? What...?

On that day, anyone inspecting the photo and comparing it with the twenty-two-year-old holding it would question how the passport could possibly show such a youthful representation of its owner. This haggard, bruised, dirty, greasy woman with heavy bags under her eyes, scratches on her face, and the pained posture of someone closer to death than birth could surely not be the same as the charismatic, energetic forty-year-old shown in the picture.

But without question, the features matched, as did the indication of a strong soul trapped within deep brown eyes. In the photo, they would arrest you and intimidate you. In Bex's case, her eyes would captivate for a moment and then cause you to look away, in fear of taking on some of the pain buried deep within.

The same facial structure was evident in both, and the hair, mostly straight but a bit wavy, matched up as well. As was already clear, there was enough intensity in the eyes to maintain plausibility. The only remaining surprise to Bex was their skin color and how the washed-out photograph used in the passport bridged the only remaining visual difference between a mature professional woman of Indian ethnicity and a girl of quarter-Hispanic descent.

She was entranced by this discovery, unable to pull her gaze from this identity in front of her. In the span of a few seconds, her mind ran through all the scenarios that might have happened throughout her life such that she might have become this woman, or at least something closer to her. Why did her life have to be the way it had been? What had this Somaya done to receive the life she had been living? How could she, Bex, see this woman as beautiful and glamorous, two words that she would never associate with herself? How could they be so different yet so similar? The questions were infinite. The divide did not seem just, but it also seemed so massive, a chasm between her worthless identity and this one of perfection.

But it could be mine.

The bus was now moving southbound with haste, as the late-night traffic was minimal and none of the passengers were requesting stops. As it approached and crossed through a large intersection, something caught Bex's attention. Far to the right—to the west, down that industrial road she had abandoned a short time ago—she could see distant flashing lights from the accident scene. She had removed herself from disaster, but the reminders were always present that it was never too far away.

Here we go again, she thought to herself as she carefully placed the passport back in its secure portfolio wallet buried safely inside the purse. The bus, however, kept moving south, defying her expectation that for some dark, fateful reason, it would take a sharp right turn and deliver her right back to that which she had escaped.

Bex had stayed on the bus in those wee hours of that chaotic night until it completed its full route, finally coming to a stop at a big transit exchange station in the city of Surrey. Dozens of other buses were parked there, having completed their day's work several hours before.

"End of the road, honey," the bus driver called out. "Did you mean to ride all the way here?"

"Yes, yep. Thank you," Bex answered quickly. She stood up, instinctively scanning her seat to make sure she had left nothing behind. Patting her pockets, she realized they still contained the items she took from the man in the leather jacket, all of them pale in comparison to the excitement and intrigue of Somaya's belongings.

She pulled out the cigarettes and lighter. Bex didn't smoke.

"Do you smoke?" she asked the bus driver, who nodded.

"Sadly, I do. Can't stop. I try, but damn, I'll probably be the last one left," she admitted, seemingly happy to be given the chance to confess and likely falsely confident that she would somehow outlast her smoking peers.

"Would you like these?" Bex offered the pack to the woman. The recognizable red crest and white label were mostly obfuscated by an image of someone's exposed cancerous lungs. Thick yellow and green mucus dripped from the inner workings—inner failings—of those lungs.

"Thank you, dear," the woman said as she pocketed the box that indicated how she would likely die.

"You're welcome," Bex replied, finding no lack of oddity in this response, in this context, especially after everything that had preceded it this evening. She had already sent others off to their demise just a few hours before.

Why stop now?

She stepped down from the bus into the large, silent parking lot. Her survival instincts once again pushed to the forefront, instructing her pained body to walk toward the intermittent glowing lights of a nearby traveler's motel, much as a mosquito or a moth see any form of light as the dawn of a new day.

It was not yet a new day. Bex secured a room with one of the credit cards, taking the calculated risk that the Somaya Patel she had seen hanging upside down had not yet bothered to call them in as missing, nor would she be likely to do so over the next few hours while Bex lay down, falling almost immediately into a pain-induced sleep.

It was not a nice motel, though as Bex knew all too well by now, beggars could truly not be choosers. Her grandmother had often told her, "*Mi*

Pequeña, the present is a present," in her broken English. She had moved from Spain to Canada to live with Bex's family for the last few years of her life and had taken great pleasure in her objective observations of the unstructured mess that is the English language. So many words that mean the same thing, often spoken the same way but many times not, always changing under different contexts. She might have called them ambiguous or polysemous had she lived long enough to develop a strong enough understanding of the minute details of her second language.

The present had provided a locked door, four walls, and a roof, which she had been glad to accept. As the sun rose over the broken asphalt outside, it streamed through the tattered curtains at the front of the room, the flickering light catching Bex's attention much as the marquee signage had done so a few hours earlier, this time telling her it was time to leave.

The bathroom mirror was cracked, matching the finish in the rest of the ensuite. Dirty fingerprints wrapped around the exposed side of the door before leaping onto the wall and across the reflective glass in front of her.

The face looking back at her was peering around the cracks, trying to ascertain exactly who it was looking at. The lukewarm shower had cut through the mud, dirt, and blood that had checked into the motel, though there was still a perceptive layer on her of something that Bex could not leave behind. Perhaps it was the residue of grease or exhaust from being so close to the road for so many days or from her tumble over the railing, through her tent, and down the dirty slope. Perhaps it had always been there.

But something began to happen as the broken girl in the room looked at the shattered girl in the glass. Individually, they were incomplete—cracked, flawed, and with a grimy, foggy outlook of each other. Yet as they committed to looking upon one another with no other distractions, a sharper focus entered the equation, and as they filtered out all the impurities that sought to diminish their sense of worth, there were enough pieces between the two of them to assemble a whole.

A fifty-dollar taxi ride took her to the US border crossing, again paid for with the simplicity of tapping someone else's plastic to someone else's plastic. Bex knew the route itself wouldn't be traceable. After all, it was only a transaction; it wasn't as if they were being plotted on a map in real-time by some larger authority. Her hair was clean and styled as closely as possible to Somaya's picture. Her dirty clothes had been left behind in the motel. She walked across the border as an American citizen and was welcomed home as a Washingtonian by the border agents. They didn't ask anything, and she didn't offer it. Not because she had experience in these situations as Somaya did, but because she didn't.

If they get me, they get me, Bex thought, always resigned to the notion that eventually, bad luck would catch up to her again, and at some point, it would assuredly be more than she could run from.

The first thing she did in the city of Bellingham, Washington, on that very first day over the border, was make her way to the regional outlet shopping malls. She left with new clothes, a few hundred dollars' worth of gold jewelry, and a new smartphone, and after throwing the now heavily used credit cards in a garbage can on her way out the door, Bex directed her shiny new Adidas sneakers to keep on moving south. Like the jewelry, the smartphone was bought not for utility or beauty—even though they were all very nice—but as barter.

One thing she had gotten effective at over the past few years was converting very nice things into cash. As fewer and fewer people were using paper money, she found that those who operated in gray and black markets had fewer and fewer options for transforming the monies they had come upon into other valuable goods. So, just as the price of everything legitimate had gone up for nearly everybody, so had the prices she could command for stolen goods. Pawn shop operators and petty cash criminals were often more annoyed with this inflationary effect than the average shopper lamenting the price of a loaf of bread. The trick was, just like the grocery stores had been doing since the COVID pandemic, you had to hold a firm line on your asking price. And if there was one thing Bex could do better than most, it was to be firm.

Armed with these additional reserves, she kept moving, this younger, poorer version of Somaya taking a clockwise tour of the northwest states over the following months. She would travel by bus, hitchhiking, and often covering miles upon miles on her feet. In a few places, she had been able to take on odd jobs to add to her marginal cash holdings. She moved from Bellingham to a few short weeks in Spokane. Then, into Idaho and the city of Boise as the middle of winter traded the cold, the snow, and the short dark days in exchange for a fortunate opportunity to live, work, and hide in temporary housing near the university. In the spring, she moved on to Salt

Lake City, and as the summer heat wore on, so did the feeling of entrapment in that place. The roads and highways were big, oversized, in fact. They were far too often far too empty. Nobody seemed to be coming or going. It was simply all too static, and wherever she went, Bex was far too visible amongst the non-existent crowds. The road was calling again, the reputation of Las Vegas preceding itself as somewhere that was very hard to stand out.

Seventeen

WHAT ABOUT DOUG?

It was only a ten-minute drive from Vincent's Cocktail Bar to the foursquare house. Jason and Ricky got out, with Jason looking down at his phone to make sure the Superide had successfully completed. He often wondered how many people didn't check and how often the meter didn't stop when it was supposed to.

"Probably some evil tech corp people in San Francisco watching all the money come in every time someone takes one of these cars, right?" he said aloud to Ricky, assuming as many others had that their favorite service could only possibly come from the West.

"Uh, yeah, I guess so. Hey, look, doesn't look like anyone's up," Ricky responded. There was a soft light on in the living room, but he couldn't see the unmistakable bluish glow that would normally emanate from the front window whenever someone was playing video games at night.

"Wait a minute, what the..." Jason had looked to the house but noticed something else. "The fucking door is open, mate. What the hell is going on?" He started running to the house.

"Hold up, Jay. Hold up a sec," Ricky took two quick steps forward, put a hand on the smaller man's shoulder, and slowed him down. "Someone could be in there. You don't just run inside."

"You think someone's in there? Like a break-in?" Jason was immediately concerned, and while his heart rate had gone through the roof, his voice had

175

dropped to the floor. In Australia, locking one's front door was a rare thing, but in Texas, it was usually "three locks and two smoking barrels," reflecting a culture of deadbolts and dead intruders. He had never understood either extreme.

"Looks like it, let's be careful. Get your phone out, too." Ricky pulled his phone out of his pocket. Jason's was still front-and-center from auditing his Superide trip, and now he looked intently at it, ready to call 911. On the other hand, Ricky's intention was to record the situation, and he assumed Jason had come to the same conclusion as that would offer footage from a second camera, making any future edit that much easier. Ricky wouldn't admit that he was scared. Growing up, he had seen more than his fair share of criminal activity. Break-ins and stolen cars were commonplace in his neighborhood. He didn't like it, and it still rattled him when it was this close, but he had come to realize that there was no help other than what you do to help yourself. Or in this case, to help his friends.

"I'll text Zenty," Jason whispered.

"Good idea."

[Z we need yo help. Break-in at the house. Get here!] Jason quickly tapped into his phone and sent the message to their big friend. He consciously turned off his ringer and slid his phone back into his pocket, to the chagrin of first camera operator Ricky.

The two friends started walking gingerly to the front door. Ricky held his phone in landscape aspect ratio, his arm floating away from his body just enough to hopefully capture a more stable, cinematic shot if any action were to transpire. They took careful, synchronized steps, each of their front feet crossing over their back feet, then the back foot following with a sideways step to start the sequence over again. They looked more like thieves themselves than anything else.

The door was wide open. Shoes were still on the floor in the entryway, which was not always the case, even if someone was home. The living room light was on, as was the television, though the screen was a backlit black, a message stating there was no active input signal. Ricky, who was in the lead, scanned his eyes down the empty hallway toward the kitchen before he deftly continued their side-stepping crab walk into the living room.

The living room was a mess, which didn't look entirely out of place to either of them. But there was a pile of garbage in the middle of the floor. Shredded cardboard and broken pieces of Styrofoam were everywhere.

"What the fuck is this? Rats?" Ricky whispered, chuckling lightly to himself, scanning the room with his phone. His cinematography was amateurish, sweeping left, right, and back again over the space. He intended to capture this crime scene in a dramatic way, clearly without any thought to the motion sickness he was bestowing upon any future viewer.

"Oh my god..." Jason was speaking louder. He had reached the end of the living room and stood underneath the open doorway, peering into the kitchen.

Ricky quickly shuffled up alongside him. The kitchen was destroyed. Broken dishes were scattered across the floor. The table was smashed against one wall and crumpled on the floor.

"What the hell? The telltale signs of a fight!" Ricky spoke louder now, safety having been demoted as a priority to filling the role of a live-on-scene news reporter providing real-time voiceover for his video. It also helped him mask his concern for the safety of his friends.

"Jay, go upstairs and check on Elise," he commanded.

"God, mate, someone might still be here. What about Doug?" Jason asked, looking across the room.

Doug's door was closed at the far end of the kitchen, just past the smashed table.

Click, click. Just as the boys directed their focus to the door, the handle started to turn. Their adrenaline was rising. Jason shuffled to the side of the room closest to the kitchen counter and picked up a big knife that had been lying amongst some chopped-up pepper seeds and tomato pulp. Ricky flattened his back to the wall near the living room doorway, now concealed by a tall standing bookcase the roommates had used for kitchen storage. They had discovered that the American foursquare layout was created when people did not have many things, and there was simply not enough cupboard space in the kitchen, necessitating this Scandinavian-designed assemble-at-home shelving. Ricky's hiding spot left Jason exposed in the room, standing alone with knife in hand. Ricky's smartphone, still maintaining the desirable widescreen horizontal perspective, slyly poked out from around the corner attached to five fingers at the end of a long orphaned arm.

The door opened. It was dark in Doug's room, but out into the light stepped two white, thin, uncovered female legs. Above them, they carried a familiar shape, albeit presented in an unfamiliar way. Henrietta was moving slowly and rubbing her eyes. She wore a long gray T-shirt that covered her waist but fell short enough to reveal her underwear. An important distinction should be noted that they were her own underwear and not Doug's, unlike the T-shirt, which was unmistakably Doug's, with its full-color green ogre on the front and big, bold SHREK lettering underneath the eponymous character's smiling face. Shrek's eyes were big, bright, and perfectly situated on top of Henrietta's breasts, giving Shrek the appearance that his eyeballs were popping out of his head.

"Oh my!" Jason exclaimed.

"Oh!" Henny, her eyes now rapidly opening and, similar to the Dreamworks icon she was unintentionally promoting, were just about popping out of her head. She looked upon this man she knew in the kitchen. He was holding a knife but not in any apparent culinary technique.

A big crashing sound came from her left. Henrietta looked down the hallway just as an enormous figure came barreling up the front steps and into the hallway. He was breathing heavily and had his fists clenched as the lone entryway light hiding behind his head formed a cranial eclipse. Henrietta could only register the silhouette of a gigantic human being surrounded by a flickering halo, an angel of destruction. Her mind was racing.

"Whoa! Whoa!" Ricky hadn't yet shown himself and now took a step out from behind the bookcase with his hands out in deference, one of them still holding the smartphone and recording this rapidly devolving scene.

Henny looked back in his direction, not yet recognizing Ricky and still in shock from the ogre at the door who, by any measure, did not come across as friendly as the one on her T-shirt. She had no idea what to think, especially now with this other fast-moving unidentified man reaching out from around the corner.

"Oh hey!" Mitch Zentax said from his position down the hallway. He had been on his way home when Jason's text message prompted him to redirect his Superide to the same location that another one had only just recently departed, delivering a double dose of another mother's money and privacy-invading geographic usage data to those four infamous East Coast innovators behind the ride-hailing service. They had smartly realized that even if they weren't able to maintain their early-mover advantage on the market, which they ultimately weren't, they would be able to sell their user data at a premium, which they ultimately did, and thus only served as a speed bump in the analytical road of Jason's earlier fears of being constantly under the watchful eye of Bay Area tech overlords.

Zentax could tell Henny was distraught, even to a greater extent than he was confused as to why she was half-naked. Something bad must have happened. He ran down the hallway toward her.

She screamed loudly and held her arms up close to her body in an instinctual response to protect vital organs. This movement raised the bottom of the T-shirt above her waist, revealing even more of her already very exposed body. The boys were beyond confused in this kitchen wasteland confrontation with Jason's skin-baring roommate screaming at them in fear.

Her eyes darted to Jason. *What was he doing? Was he fighting these guys? Is he a bad guy?* All kinds of conflicting thoughts were cycling through her mind.

By now, Doug had plodded through the door and into the light with a Nike shoe in one hand and an unopened bottle of Coca-Cola Classic in the other. He was holding both as weapons, ready to strike. He also had a third exposed weapon, though this one was much smaller and less imposing than it had been a few hours earlier. Henny was comparatively overdressed, as Doug had been woken by the commotion and jumped out of bed, still stark naked, reaching for whatever he could that might be used in defense of whatever had frightened her and without any regard for his appearance. Although, he rarely held regard for his own appearance.

"Henrietta? Is that you? Are you okay?" Mitch Zentax asked. The big man was now close enough to be seen in the kitchen light. He had met Henrietta and Doug before, though he wasn't particularly close to either of them and wasn't sure if this was her, given the situation. He most certainly didn't recognize Doug. From his perspective, it looked like she might still be in danger from the crazy naked stranger.

He put his hands forward in a defensive posture to protect against any unpredictable movements from the unclothed threat, as well as to show that he did not intend to move forward anymore, and hopefully disarm whatever the hell was going on here.

"Henrietta, it's okay," Jason spoke up. He realized he still had the knife in his hand and quickly placed it back on the countertop, where it had started the evening in a much simpler existence of salad preparation. Jason put his hands in the air as well.

Everyone scanned the room. It was a marketplace, a bazaar in which everyone was trading confusion for recognition, with a good deal to be had on humor.

Ricky started smiling, then laughing, bringing forth his notorious cackle that was known to the entire campus. It seemed to hit the right auditory notes that quickly put Henny at ease—at least, at as much ease as could be obtained for her diminishing caution at current exchange rates.

She couldn't help but take some humor in it, even as she exclaimed, "Oh my fucking god," and stepped back into Doug's room and closed the door.

"Dougie, what the hell, man?" Ricky said to his friend, who was now the full center of attention for the three clothed young men with whom he did not presently share that attribute. Meanwhile, Zentax and Jason had started to mentally piece together all the evidence, from the mess in the living room to the broken table and finally to Doug and his exposed penis.

"Holy shit!" Zentax said. "Jason, you said you needed help. I'm not sure this is what I expected." He started laughing, with his best efforts to not be too loud out of respect for Henrietta.

"You and me both, mate," Jason responded. "I did not see this one coming."

"Ha ha, but yeah, somebody did!" Ricky added his own crass layer of comedy to Jason's comment as he gestured at Doug's dangling manhood.

For his part, Doug didn't know what to think. In a matter of seconds, he had gone from a deep sleep with a big smile on his face, to this. As the fogginess in his mind dissipated, his first and only thought was Henrietta. He imagined she was upset and embarrassed.

"What the hell, guys? Get outta here!" he stepped back, opened his bedroom door, and went inside, closing off the kitchen and its resident confusion behind him.

After the initial shock of what they had just seen, Jason, Ricky, and Zentax concluded they should continue with the evening, especially given how much there was to talk about now! The boys moved into the living room, pushing aside the cardboard and Styrofoam shrapnel on the floor as they made their way to sit down on the couch, Xbox controllers in hand.

A few minutes later, Henrietta came back out of Doug's bedroom, this time with the rest of her clothes bundled up in her hands. She looked in on the living room as she made her way toward the stairs leading up to her own bedroom on the second floor.

"Hope you boys had some fun with that," she said. "You scared the hell out of me!"

"Oh, Henrietta, sorry about that. I didn't mean to freak you out. Your little man here thought the place was being invaded," Zentax said as he gestured to Jason.

"No. No, that was just me," she replied, making her own somewhat graphic insinuation, much to the boys' delight. Especially Ricky's.

"Wow, Henrietta, you are a piece of work," Ricky said. He loved the fact she was speaking so plainly of her sexual escapades with Doug. However, he couldn't quite believe it, as he had always thought she was really cool and very pretty. *Well, good for you, Dougie boy,* he thought to himself, surprised and happy for his friend.

"Alright, good night fellas," Henrietta said.

"Hey, Henrietta," Jason quickly retorted, catching her attention before she went up the stairs. "What's up with all this mess on the floor in here?"

She looked at the garbage on the floor and then looked around at the rest of the place, taking in the full breadth of chaos of the smoke-stained walls and ceiling, the deconstructed table, and all the residual havoc.

"So the place is basically destroyed, and you're asking about that?" she asked.

"Damn, dude, they got up to some kinky stuff... who knows what was in that box!" Ricky piped up.

"Ricky, you're just happy as a pig in shit to be joking about sex. Maybe you should go get some of your own!" Zentax added, followed with a booming laugh.

The mess on the floor quickly brought Henny back to what had started everything earlier that night. *The package*—not Doug's package, but rather the delivery package, and the strange device, also not directed at Doug.

"Don't worry, Jay, that's just some super-secret stuff we ordered," she joked in response to Jason's original question. But with her memory filling in, her confidence bolstered, and her sense of humor fully laid bare, she walked back to retrieve the device from the countertop in the kitchen, this time choosing to walk right in front of the boys seated on the couch rather than taking the hallway. With great care to add some gratuitous movement to her steps, she slowly moved through the room, occluding the video games on the television with the far more interesting eye-level view of her shapely legs in stride and the subtle wobbling of her rounded buttocks.

"Good night, boys," she said with an intentionally over-the-top, sultry addition to her voice as she turned the corner, picked up the broken tablet, and went upstairs.

They were laughing no more. Dumb-founded and slack-jawed, the boys slowly turned back to the television screen, with game controllers in their hands, each of them wondering if they had just been played.

Eighteen

TRIBAL

The heat was blazing. Sidewalks were dangerous to bare feet. Once again, Bex found herself at the ticket window of a bus station. In these days of pseudo-intelligent cars and GPS location-aware on-the-fly transportation services, she preferred *and* required the traditional travel format of buying a ticket and stepping onto a bus. Surely, she could remain anonymous this way in a world where almost everyone else sought to be as known as possible.

This time, she was at the Intermodal Transit Center in scorching downtown Salt Lake City, scanning the departure boards as she waited in line for service.

"Everybody, you're going to have to take a seat and wait," the ticketing agent said, voluntarily trapped in a small enclosed room behind a Plexiglas window, a protective upgrade that had provided necessary distancing from other humans for many years before it became a mandated COVID response. She relied on that job to pay her bills and look after her family. The job, conversely, relied upon button-pressers like the agent and the ticketing and scheduling systems they operated, and now all of them had gone offline.

"What do you mean? We need to be on that bus to Vegas in twenty minutes," a large man said loudly from a few spots ahead of Bex.

"I'm sorry, sir. There's nothing I can do at the moment. If you kindly have a seat, we'll have to see if it comes back online," the agent said.

"*If?* So, if it doesn't, you gonna hold that bus?" he demanded, concerned about missing his planned ride. He would be damned if this system outage would get in the way of his pilgrimage to the mecca of stimulus-response. He hadn't taken a moment to think about how he would more than likely be damned if he did indeed make it all the way to his destination.

"I'm unable to do that, sir. We need the machine to process any tickets for you," she said, acknowledging her limited role in moving people from one place to another.

The man did not let up, and his voice began to rise in lockstep with the clock moving closer to his planned departure time. At one point, he went outside the station and began arguing with the bus driver, who had apparently loaded up all customers with previously purchased tickets and was preparing to leave for Las Vegas.

He was fuming. Bex had watched the situation unfold. She could commiserate with the man as she had intended to be on that very same bus. But she could not relate to his behavior. The intensity of his anger was misplaced.

People suck. Machines suck. Get over it, buddy.

"People suck," she heard a voice say. She had been seated in the waiting area, having resigned herself to the fact that, contrary to the popular slogan, whatever was going to happen in Vegas might not even have the chance to get there in the first place, let alone stay there. She looked over her shoulder to the source of the voice. A mass of colors had appeared in the middle of the waiting area, with long arms and legs protruding from its nucleus. A cowboy hat with various bird's feathers cast shade upon the shape, and somewhere buried within all of this was a face owned by a person, which contained the mouth that had said what she was thinking.

"You were trying to get on that one, too?" the colorful man said, gesturing toward the departure board which indicated the Las Vegas-bound bus had already departed. She could see more of him now; the Rorschach visage of his presence had started to decompile itself into its discrete features. He wore a fur vest over a rainbow-colored, long-sleeved polyester shirt with oversized collars. His voluminous parachute pants were mostly red with thinner green stripes, like a Christmas-themed Adidas line inspired by MC Hammer on an acid trip. His feet were exposed and heavily tattooed, the markings only covered up by the thin lines of a cheap pair of flip-flops.

He had long, curly hair that shone in the waiting room's cheap halogen lighting and an equally greasy mustache that downplayed the unshaven barbs across the rest of his face. Large aviator sunglasses with a gradated brown tint largely hid his eyes.

"Ah, yeah, sort of," Bex replied.

"Not sure what that guy is thinking," he gestured to the large man who was now throwing a tantrum on the sidewalk outside. They couldn't hear him, which made his body language all the more humorous. He was the angriest mime they might ever see, his impromptu stomping and flailing on center stage for everyone inside. The bus driver had closed the vehicle's doors and started to pull away as the man ran alongside, slamming his hands on the exterior of the bus until it pulled away from the curb. He was fortunate not to get hit by the rear quarter of the bus as it turned toward the road.

"Well, it's like you said," said Bex.

"Yes, people suck, right? Well, people don't, but their attitudes do, holy cow. Not sure what he thinks can be done. He sucks like that. She sucks like this, not being able to help. And the whole bus system sucks, too. I just got in from Montana, and we had the same thing happen up there. Took them a couple hours to get things working, but at least the bus waited. Guess *it* had nothing better to do."

"Wait, what do you mean, 'it'?" Bex asked, picking up on a subtle intonation in this curious man's voice.

"Uhh, the bus. But yeah, the bus doesn't exactly decide what it's doing, you got me there," he admitted.

"Ha! Okay, yeah, I thought you meant something else. But I mean, you kind of have to expect it, right? All these systems and machines were made by people. None of them are smart enough to do the job. I'm talking about the humans now. So why would we expect that stuff to work any better? I mean, I only need to pay cash, but she needs her thing to be on so she can put me on the bus. Like how stupid is that? Take my money, write me a ticket, and let me get on my way," Bex said, sharing more of her situation than she might have expected. Something about the man and his outfit made it easy for her to share with him. She felt comfortable around him, which was not something she could say very often.

"So where you going now?" he asked.

"I... have no idea. Guess I'll wait for the next one," she said, knowing she didn't entirely care. She also didn't care where he was going. "Where are you going?"

"To the real world," he replied. "To where it all goes down. We're going to the desert."

Bex wasn't sure what to make of this. She wasn't sure where on the bus schedule the destination of "desert" showed up.

"There's my ride!" he looked past her, through the windows, past the man now standing on the sidewalk with his hands on his hips, and toward the drop-off and pick-up area. There was a brown van, an old domestic production model. It was slightly lowered, with tinted windows and low-profile wheels the most obvious of its after-market modifications. He started walking to the door.

"Well, see you," Bex said as she turned back to face the wall of ticketing windows, ready to wait for the machines to start working again. She stared at the automated ticketing machines, knowing those couldn't do anything for her, even if they were online. She had no credit card. She had no identity. She had given up on being Somaya shortly after crossing the border almost a year ago. And she had given up being whoever Bex Anndale was supposed to be long before all of this.

"You sure will," the colorful man said. "Let's go."

She was startled. "Huh, what? What do you mean?" Bex asked, though she was already standing to turn toward him, her hand in a ready position holding the loop of her backpack that she had placed on the chair beside her.

"I mean, you can stay here with these people that suck waiting for all this stuff that sucks, or you come with us. Oh yeah, I'm Carlo," he said, adding his name at the end as a quick suffix.

Bex was already walking behind him as he approached the door. "Who? And where are you going? And who are you going with? Why should I go with you?" she peppered him with questions that she didn't need answered. He had simply told her to go, and she felt drawn to whatever was happening. It wasn't his clothes or his looks—she could hardly even see the man for all his fashion and accoutrements—she couldn't put her finger on it, but it sort of seemed like he was someone to go with in the same way that any destination was where she wanted to go.

They passed through the large glass doors. The angry man was still pacing up and down the sidewalk, and both Carlo and Bex were careful not to look at him.

BEEP! BEEP! The van was moving. Its horn squawked a few times as it pulled up alongside the curb where they were, coming to a stop in an area marked "Bus Only."

The van was otherwise almost silent, so she wasn't sure if it shut off. The door opened and a man stepped out of the vehicle.

He was a tall Black man dressed in a head-to-toe spandex suit with thick white and purple stripes. The fit of the suit left little to the imagination, but the vertical stripes had the optical effect of breaking this man's form into an infinite number of pieces. He was a mirage, stepping out of the van into the hot high desert air. He wore big-heeled boots that added at least two inches to his already imposing stature.

A beaming smile developed across the man's face, projecting an impossibly friendly countenance from underneath his sunglass-covered eyes. He reached back in through the open door of the van and pulled out a white fedora, which he gracefully placed on top of his head.

"Carlo, my friend! How are you?" he yelled, taking steps toward the man Bex had been walking with.

"That is not the important question, Deemo. The question is, are you as glad to see me as I am to see you?" he said, as Bex picked up a decidedly Mediterranean accent from the man, which she hadn't noticed in their initial exchanges.

"Ha ha!" the purple and white Black man laughed with a loud cackle as he embraced his friend. "I am amazing as always, and, yes, so happy to see you. And who is your friend?" He turned to look directly at Bex. Something about the flow of the man's movements had set her immediately at ease, though almost with such efficiency that she couldn't help but hold some skepticism. But skeptical about what?

"This is..." Carlo began to answer and then found himself having to pause as he did not yet have a name for Bex. He expected her to complete his sentence, but she didn't. Seconds passed.

Bex had returned Deemo's gaze, looking at him with a sense of wonderment and curiosity but not feeling compelled to speak despite the aura of comfort that had been conferred to their sidewalk meeting.

".. Dorothy," Carlo said, completing his sentence. "This is my friend Dorothy."

Dorothy!

"Dorothy," Deemo repeated. "It is a pleasure to meet you. I'm Deemo. Looking forward to getting to know you." The words rolled off his lips effortlessly, a flawless composition of syllables delivered as if pulled from a script but proffered with a supremely natural cadence.

"Hi, yes, Deemo, is it? Nice to meet you also," Bex said, resigning herself to being Dorothy for a while. At least this identity had come to her with a lot less pain, death, and destruction than the last one.

Deemo opened his arms wide. She thought he was leading with a hug but quickly realized through cause and effect that in doing so, he had commanded his van into action. Heavily customized gull-wing doors raised up into the sky, revealing a clean, comfortable seating area. Carlo gestured to the space within, "After you, Dorothy," he said with yet another disarming smile.

Crazier things had happened to her, and certainly more dangerous people had been far less of a concern than these two. To someone who prioritized momentum and invisibility above caution and attention, the opportunity to travel as Dorothy in this fanciful yet outwardly nondescript van with two friendly multi-layered men was an easy decision, irrespective of even knowing the destination. It didn't matter.

And so, before long, they were all three of them in the van leaving the bus station and driving west toward the desert.

"So what's in the desert?" Bex said from a comfortable semi-reclined seat in the back of the van. It felt more like a fireside reading chair than something fit for a vehicle, so plush and comfortable.

"What's in the desert? Carlo, what have you done here? Who have you brought with us?" exclaimed Deemo with endearment and surprise.

He continued. "Nothing is in the desert. Everything is in the desert. And then nothing is in the desert. Are you joking me, Dorothy, or did Carlo put you under a spell?"

"No, I'm good, just curious. I was planning to go to Las Vegas, but now here I am with you guys," Bex said.

"Vegas! Oh wow. Not a place you want to be. Definitely not this week, and definitely not most times," Deemo said with a hint of disdain in his generally sweet and excitable voice.

"Just a place on the map, really. So, where are we going? You guys taking me to some crazy lair in the middle of the desert?" Bex said, mostly as a joke but also in a way that might eke out any indication as to whether or not they actually intended to take her to a lair in the middle of the desert.

"Ha ha ha!" he cackled again. "Oh, most definitely! We are taking you to a lair in the desert—the biggest one of them all. But only if you want to come," he turned to look at her quickly to ensure he was properly delivering his words with his tongue firmly and metaphorically implanted in his cheek.

"I don't..." Bex started to say, unsure of what he was implying.

"Dorothy, look," Carlo interjected, pointing up to a turn-off at the side of the highway. In an endless vista of white salt-affected sandy plains, blue sky, and a long straight highway, there was a rest area lit up with some of the most brilliant colors and obtuse shapes. Differently shaped and sized vehicles were parked in a row, like a convoy of chaos.

She saw a landspeeder parked on the side, with four wheels belying its fabrication source on Earth and not Tattoine. There was a massive snake with people sitting inside its eyeballs, one behind a steering wheel. There was something that looked like a trebuchet or a drawing of Da Vinci's brought to life. Mechanical levers, pulleys, and gears ran all around it. This renaissance machine was parked directly behind a quarter moon, the curvature of the orbital satellite serving as the vehicle's chassis, with the interior of the vehicle accessible through a bite mark near the center of its otherwise smooth, concave hammock shape. A woman dressed in a life-size rat suit stood in the shady side of the moon-truck, leaning against it as she engaged in conversation with a person of feathery composition.

As she looked further down the line, the creativity infused into all these mobile pieces of art was a sight to behold. Bex had never seen anything like it.

"Burning Man, Dorothy. Welcome to Burning Man!" Deemo said as he looked back at her at the same time as he shoulder-checked the infinite highway, before parking his gull-wing conversion van at the back of the row of vehicles.

Compared to everything else, Deemo's van was understated. Certainly, it was in pristine shape, a customized update from whatever Econoline model it had originally been. The interior was more like that of a spaceship commissioned by a throwback seventies porn star.

As they came to a stop, it became evident that Deemo had more to offer from his mild-mannered vehicle. He opened a protective case built into the center console between the two front seats in the van. Below that covering were several big switches, not unlike what many of us presume the president of the United States has at their disposal for launching nuclear weapons. Deemo activated one big switch within the compartment.

The sound of hydraulic machinery filled the interior of the van, mostly coming from behind Bex. She turned and looked behind. The van was growing. Paneling in the walls and ceiling had slid backwards upon itself, like a Russian doll set opening up, and had extended behind them at least another fifteen feet. Some of the hidden wall panels were made almost entirely of large sections of glass. The same had occurred above, with the ceiling and upper portion of the walls also taking on a gull-wing extended shape, pushing the volume of the entire space upwards by several feet, which also conveniently allowed those panels to marry with the entryway doors that had once again risen up to their full elevated position. Bex noted a fridge and cooking equipment in the back of the expanded interior.

"Well, I've never seen anything like that!" Bex said, her voice filled with amazement and interest.

"Come here, check this out," Deemo said as he stepped out of the vehicle and beckoned her to stand with him outside, which she did.

He pointed to the top of the vehicle. "All solar. The geometry up there has been perfectly designed to maximize solar capture. The whole vehicle runs on electrical, we can power this thing to the end of time out here. Or at least for a week or so!" He chuckled again, having fun with the obvious lack of alignment between what he could do with that van and what he intended to do.

"Very cool," she said, admiring the machine. "So this is Burning Man?" she said, gesturing down the row of vehicles.

"Wha... oh... hell no!" Deemo said. "Oh no, this isn't it. This is just on the way there. I mean, I guess we are always on the way there, and none of us will ever get 'there' there, if you know what I mean. But this is not the place in the desert, that's Black Rock. We still got a few more hours. This is just friends."

"Oh, you know these people?"

"No, I don't think so, but yeah, we do. We all know them, we all know you. You know them. That's what it is out here, Dorothy," he said. "You're not in Kansas anymore." He laughed to himself with this one, and she couldn't help but smile as well. She would come to expect the continuous double-talk from Deemo.

"Let's go see our friends."

They walked along the convoy line, saying hello to almost everyone who was out and awake. Deemo's personality seemed to walk ahead of him. He had very obviously manufactured celebrity for himself, and Bex could already ascertain that through all the endearment on display with his "friends," he didn't know them any better than he did her, if at all. It became apparent that many of them had been there for a day or more, waiting for a greater assembly before pushing on to the main venue, which still lay another hundred miles or so to the west.

"We call this Light After Dark, this stop," Deemo explained. "A bunch of Bay Area guys started coming here a few years ago on their way to Burning Man after a darkness retreat in the mountains."

Deemo went on to explain that this stopover was, at least for an initial few years, a secret rendezvous for a closed group of high-net-worth technology executives. Light After Dark had ostensibly been used to describe the feeling of psychological weight reduction they had experienced after spending nearly a week in the high steppes of Utah, staring at the invisible lines of constellations as they shed the guilt of sordid activities from the connective threads of their own lives. Before long, however, the name took on a more practical life of its own, as all of these absolution-seeking technorati had begun storing their heavily customized desert vehicles in the vastness of warehouse capacity in Salt Lake City, and as the flotilla grew every year, so did the physical illumination of this particular roadside stop. The annually expanding spectacle of it had, in turn, led to the rendezvous becoming a destination event in and of itself, with exclusive Facebook groups and social media fellowships deploying a greater number of acolytes every year. As more and more fabulously adorned people slid into more and more DMs of the technology elite, it was only a matter of time before Hollywood followed suit, with some of the most famous celebrities of our time arriving, their true selves hidden even further behind ever more fanciful masks. Just as FOMO had, many decades before, spurred forth the creation of the information superhighways upon which the attendees relied for directions, its undeniable power had now brought together NorCal and SoCal in Eastern Nevada in a veritable melting pot of concealed insecurities.

Apparently, in recent years, many of the most influenced Californians have started coming to this roadside attraction only, forgoing all the extra effort of attending the actual Burning Man. They found they were able to maximize the perception of their exclusive access to this most sought-after meetup and still post as if they attended the bigger desert event, with nobody really being the wiser.

In some respects, these partial participants were a self-actuating species of lemming, fabricating the stories of their own congregatory activity without burdening themselves or their audiences to take as big of a leap.

The rat-woman and the bird-man that Bex had noticed earlier were just a taste of this diverse human zoo. While many others wore costumes with literal interpretations such as those two, there were as many that could not be easily described. The snake pilots did not adhere to the theme of their vehicle, appearing ready for a royal parade of sorts, each wearing long flowing gowns and parasols adorned with cyborg-inspired organs attached over their internal physiological counterparts. Their metal hearts, in emoji and not anatomy shape, had some kind of functional pacemaker motor inside, causing each to pulse at a steady rhythm. Neither of them explained the fulsome idea of their costumes, nor had Bex or Deemo asked, and no one had yet seemed to bridge the question of whether they had considered wearing their hearts on their sleeves.

They continued down the line of vehicles, finally arriving at a more grandiose machine than most of the others.

"What the hell is that?" Bex asked in astonishment, looking up at a towering steeple that by now had captured the radiant attention of the westerly-moving sun, casting a long, pointed shadow all the way back to Deemo's Transformer-van. A stained-glass window framed itself below the steeple, depicting a scene of dozens of people reaching up to a man standing atop a mountain, his arms outstretched and palms facing skyward.

It was a church on wheels, replete with four flying buttresses on each side. Whether they were structural or not was unclear, but the effect succeeded in eliciting curiosity. In the intense desert heat, one chilling feature stood out beyond all others. Every arch, window, and foundational piece of false stonework she could see was adorned with bones. Hundreds of skulls, rib cages, legs, arms, fingers, and toes served as the fringe embroidery for this morbidly captivating ungodly construction.

"Oowee! There we go," exclaimed Deemo. "The house of the holy! Cuz it makes you say, 'holy shit.' This, Dorothy, is one of the stars of the show. Well, I guess there aren't really any stars out here, we're all equal! They made this after a church in Eastern Europe, some kind of Satanic church in Transylvania, or something like that."

Incorrect in both geographic and sectarian assignment, Deemo wouldn't have really cared to be told it was actually patterned after the Sedlec Ossuary in the Czech Republic. The church was known as the Bone Church for the impressive efforts in the nineteenth century to pay tribute to mountains of bones that when originally assembled, might have counted as many as fifty thousand people, and which had been left behind from casualties of the Bubonic Plague and the Crusades hundreds of years earlier.

Carlo piped in, "It's the Two Phils."

"Sshh, Carlo, you know as well as anyone we don't need to talk about who people are outside of here," Deemo said. He looked around vacantly, indicating nowhere and everywhere at once, his body language now taking on the same vernacular as his words. "I guess, in fairness, those guys don't do much to hide it either," Deemo admitted.

"The Two Phils?" asked Bex.

Carlo felt it important to share the context he had initiated, "Yeah, Philipe Gignot, the quantum computing guy, and Philip J. Clancy, the..."

His words no longer had meaning or volume. Bex knew that name. To hear it aloud silenced everything else as her senses turned inwards. She had closed that door on the past a long time ago and had never thought it would open again. Certainly not here, right in front of her.

And so it did. The big faux-wooden door in the middle of the front of the church, at the back of the trailer on which it was built, had started to open.

A shirtless man in bare feet stepped out from within, descending the steps that led down to Deemo, Carlo, and Bex. He wore a crown, not of a king, but of a circular assembly of thorns, with the requisite movie-set bloody makeup dripping down from various points around his head. Around his waist, a sheet was tied, resembling a grown man's diaper if not immediately recognizable as the loincloth of a presumed savior.

"Deemo!" he said. The two men clasped hands and gave each other a half embrace, an awkward bro-hug.

Jesus Christ, Bex thought.

"PJ," Deemo said, "always a show, man. Don't you think that's a bit much?"

She wasn't sure if he was referring to the rolling bone church or his appearance. She hoped he had meant everything Clancy stood for but didn't hold her breath.

"Always is, my man. Always is," he said, with a voice that resonated entitlement and disregard and a condescending smile of the same. "Who are you here with?"

"Well, I'm here with everybody, and nobody. You know that, right?" Deemo said slowly in his now-expected meandering, nonsensical style. "But in the van, I've got Carlo here again..." he turned to gesture to his colorful Mediterranean friend from Montana, who meekly raised a half-clawed wave set atop a long-sleeved rainbow-colored polyester arm.

"... and our new friend Doro...," he started, revolving the other way to indicate toward Bex, but she was no longer there. His words were ended before he intended, a rare feat that Bex might have otherwise liked to have been present to take credit for.

"Invisible friends, hey Deemo? Same as usual, I guess," joked the man posing as the son of God.

Deemo had cranked his neck even further behind him, and from his elevated vantage point, he could make out the bobbing head of his new friend hustling her way through the crowd, following the shadowy point of the steeple back to their van.

***

Later that day, they sat around the back of Deemo's Transformer-van, eating bowls of curry that he had prepared in his premium mobile kitchen. He had taken noticeably great care to prepare the dish using a full complement of fresh ingredients, coconut milk, and massaman spice, which he kept in the vehicle's pantry.

Bex hadn't said anything about disappearing earlier, and Deemo had not asked.

"Tell me about Deemo," she said, more as a command than a question, deploying well-honed skills of steering any conversation anywhere that didn't pertain to herself. Despite her comfort in having traveled a hundred miles or more seated in that plush chair and the kinship and trust she had developed with these guys thus far, it felt appropriate to learn about her new traveling companions. Their general appearance lent itself well to eliciting probing questions from anyone who saw them, even from someone as generally insular and indifferent to the world as Bex.

Deemo appreciated being asked about himself in the third person. "Deemo appreciates that question. As does everyone around here when they are asked of themselves, as it means they are being asked of the community. Of our brethren," he nodded toward Carlo, who was seated on a chair that had folded out from the back of the vehicle, "and our sister... sis... tren," he awkwardly continued with a look back to Bex.

"We are all here together, working for each other and with each other, which means that none of us are working. We are loving, sharing, helping, and giving. Like how we gave that electricity earlier to someone who needed it, and they gave us these chili peppers. Good spice, right?" he asked.

"Okay, I get it, so it's like a commune, I'm down with that," Bex said. "Is Deemo your real name?"

"What is a real name, Dorothy? Is Dorothy your real name?" he asked, pausing just enough for Bex to prompt him.

"No, you guys called me that," she said.

"Right, but it is your real name. As long as you use it and gift it to others to use, it becomes more real than anything you've ever been called. That's how it works, sweet Dorothy. Deemo is my real name in the same way. Deemo means gifting, sharing, and self-expression. Deemo is the enemy of capitalism and wastefulness. I am here to share all of this," and as he said that, he beckoned back toward his now-extended van with arms raised in the air. As he lowered them and brought his hands back down alongside his thighs, he triggered the unintended consequence of the gull-wing doors starting to close. He quickly flapped his arms up again, much like the namesake of his doors, and re-activated them to stay open.

"All of it is common property, as they say. Do you know why I call myself Deemo?" he asked.

"Uh, that's sort of what I was asking you," Bex said.

"Let me tell you. Capitalism and the military-industrial complex, the fear society that goes on out there," he started to gesture to the wider world beyond the endless sandy lands around them but restrained his arms to avoid another unintentional ushering of those doors. "That divided place is fucked up. We all want more, we all want to build fences to protect the 'more' that we have. To get more, I need to take from someone else's 'less.' It's so fucked. Here we de... deny... we de-list all that stuff. We de-cide to not have it. For me, it's about taking away the de-pendence on money. Money makes that fucked up world go round, but here, we have our own orbit. I am De-Mon-ify. But I'm no De-mon, you want to know who the Demon is? It's the reminder of accumulation and consumerism and money-ism. I am Deemo. Dee-mo-nify. We get rid of all that shit. Poof! Gone. That's how it is..." he finished, as he first took a breath, then followed with another big spoonful of his curry.

"Would you guys like some tea?" asked Carlo, who had placed his curry bowl down on the extended bumper next to him and was standing to go inside the van.

"Carlo, your timing is in-peccable. Let's have three cups," Deemo said on behalf of himself, Bex, and, strangely, also Carlo, in his uniquely wayward version of English that they would never have used themselves.

"So, are you like Robin Hood or something? I mean, clearly you have money, or you got some somewhere, and you come here and share it?" Bex asked.

"When I'm here, I have nothing. And I have everything. You are the same, Dorothy," he said as he sat back, finishing the last of his curry with a satisfied look on his face and an equally sated lick of the lips. "And I learned all this shit the hard way. I *had* nothing. Then I got some *things*. And I saw what fame and celebrity did for people. It took more from them than it gave them. So I cannot truly *give* anybody anything, I just choose to make it easier for them to receive what they already have. Maybe in that way, yes, I am like Robin Hood, but without the bows and arrows. I am taking from Money, the capital 'M' Money, and I am giving to us, or maybe Us, the capital 'U' us," he said, with a heavy exaggeration of his tone on the words "Money" and "Us."

"Well, your kindness is appreciated, and your intentions are noble, Deemo, I have to say," Bex said.

Deemo beamed. "Thank you, Dorothy, it means a lot to me. I spend a lot of time thinking about this and thinking about how we can all change. It just takes a bit of work. Especially this time of year. And I think you'll fit in really good with us, and with Us," again accentuating the sound of "Us."

"Here it is, D & D," Carlo said as he rounded the corner with three cups of tea, one in each hand and the third forming the last point of a triangle, as he pinched it with his outreached fingers. The leading cup he brought to Bex, which she gladly took from his hands. The cup in his left hand went to Deemo, and he took the right.

The feeling of the hot cup of tea touching her hands was timely and energizing. The day had been intensely hot earlier, but over the hours they had spent in this pullout area, the temperature had been dropping as the sun went lower into the sky.

From the northeast, far above distant mountain ranges, a foreboding formation of high dark clouds had been inching its way toward them throughout the day, containing precipitation harnessed from the Rockies.

For now, the horizon was ablaze. The sun had been pushing down to the edge of the world and had grown in size—first doubling, then tripling, now at least four times the sun that had been torching them from above in the middle of the day. Everything was orange as far as they could see, evidently amplified by a slight amount of humidity in the higher altitudes of the sky from the dark cloud system to the east. It was a strangely tropical sunset.

"Red sky at night, sailor's delight," said Carlo, referencing an age-old seafaring expression.

"Red sky at morn, sailors be warned," finished Bex, unsure of where this recollection of the saying came from, given her upbringing in a place that looked more like this, in the vast plains of Milestone, Saskatchewan. It might have been something her father had said once, but she wasn't sure why. When he had still been working, she knew he had flown to the coast for some kind of business investment. Maybe he had been involved in shipping or exploration.

Maybe he was an explorer.

Those thoughts had stuck with her throughout the evening, and as she lay in a bunk at the back of the extended van, she looked through a moonroof above her. A few stars could still be seen.

"You look up there, you find the North Star. And it's right off the end of the Big Dipper, see it? So whenever I'm not here with you, Bucky, you know we'll both be looking at that big spoon. See how it's so big?" her father had said.

"Yes, Dada," she replied, looking up at the stars on a cold spring evening in the prairies.

"It's filled with my love for you, Bucky. You find that dipper, that constellation, and you know I'm looking at it too." He had shared those words with her to give them a connection when he was away on business trips. That young girl, Bucky, believed that her dad had control of the lands around them and the skies above. That version of him had been as close to a deity as anyone ever had been.

"I see it, Dada," she said to herself as she started to drift off to sleep in her Transformer-van bunk bed on the side of a desert road in northern Nevada. The clouds rolled in, blanketing the stars above.

Nineteen

ON PURPOSE

"I just can't believe we don't even talk about him anymore. His name was Michael Ridley. He was a real guy, a real man. I just don't get it," Henny said, then paused to take a bite of her lunch. She was eating a beautifully arranged plate of roasted duck, wild rice pilaf, and an orange and fennel salad. There was a drizzling of brilliant yellow sauce over the duck and salad that bled onto the raised perimeter of the plate. The dish was colorful and inspiring to look at, but not so much that she hesitated to tuck into it.

"Hen, I get it. That's just the way it is, right? Things need to be more sensational, more recent, more NOW to become top of mind. I mean, shit, that's my daily hatefest when I get up every day and look in the mirror," Jenny replied, sharing an insight that Henny already knew about her friend.

Henny had been working dutifully for EMC for just over two years, her arrangement preceded by and forever connected to that fateful ill-targeted phone call between these two dining companions. If it hadn't been for her friend sitting across the table at Heirloom's Restaurant in The Fillmore, her attempts to contact the company might never have amounted to much at all. So in some respects, she had Jenny to blame.

***

The crackly voice coming through the phone had said, in New Jersey, "Hello, this is Henrietta Adler."

Heard in a boardroom in San Francisco after being converted to Voice-over-IP (VOIP) and straining for bandwidth in competition with a multiplex of thousands of handheld devices uploading violent imagery from the streets below, the audio signal coming out of the handset relayed, "H... ell... is... s... en...ie.. tt... er."

Which Jenny had interpolated as a question, "Hi, is Nelson or Jenny there?"

"Yes, speaking," she had replied.

"Well, yes, I am," Henrietta said in response, confirming that she was indeed the person she said she was in her opening comment.

"Pardon me?" Jenny responded, seeking clarity. She was confused and still very distraught with the overall situation. "Libby, is this you? We are here, where are you?"

"No, this is Henrietta Adler." The line had cleared up enough to be heard correctly this time.

"Oh, hello. Is everything okay?" Jenny asked again, her concern for Libby and G now having found a new target, in this case, the unknown woman Henrietta on the other end of the line.

"Yes, I'm fine," Henrietta replied. She could sense this conversation was suffering due to crossed wires, but there was something else. An unmistakable layer of concern and emotion was present in this woman's voice. Her pursuit of contacting whoever "EMC" was had become a lower priority. "Are you? What's wrong? Who is this?"

"Jenny," she said, "Jenny Vandeveer. Are you calling from the street? What's going on down there?"

"I'm not, but what's happening? How can I help?" Henrietta replied.

"We have people down there. But we can see it up here." None of this explanation was making very much sense, yet the receptive ear on the other end of the line offered a floatation device from the uncertainty pouring into this small boardroom on the thirteenth floor. Wallace had taken command of the room, which had helped to subdue some of the panic they were all feeling, but it created its own odd state of spectator anxiety. They were now real-time witnesses to the carnage happening below, yet powerless to do anything about it. "Oh my god, it's just awful, people are dying."

The content stream on the wall had been updating the entire time. The vendor was clearly incapacitated, quite possibly already dead. Others had descended upon the scene, the first wave jumping on the police officers, then others attacking those who had entered the fray. More police cars had arrived, a growing presence intending to close off the city block, but people were now scattered everywhere. With every passing minute and with every new post, it seemed like more blood was being spilled, and the number of prone bodies and injured people had multiplied.

Mob mentality had taken control as the street had descended into a large-scale brawl, more fitting of a mindless action movie than anything in reality.

"Stay on the line, Jenny. I'll help you," Henrietta said with a reassuring calm in her voice, rivaling the new sense of confidence she had demonstrated that previous Friday night when dealing with potential intruders in her home. *Whatever the hell is going on here, I better stay close to it.*

And help she did. A badly connected VOIP line across America had given both women a lifeline. Jenny's was more temporal, helping those moments of tragedy become somewhat manageable. Henny's was more geographic in that it would ultimately pull her all the way across the country and fling her to the far corners of Earth.

***

"If you hadn't called, I don't know what I would have done," Jenny said between bites of her lunch, a fresh salad with a side order of gluten-free avocado toast. Everything on her plate was green and healthy.

"And the hilarious thing is if EMC had a fucking clue what they were doing then, we never would have spoken," Henny said, her outlook on the situation jumping remarkably quickly from one of lament and disgust at the societal implications of that day to one of memorable hilarity. She was referring to how ludicrous it was that a publicly available number for EMC had routed her call to a subleased boardroom holding a confidential high-stakes meeting between Mixality and SGF.

"What they were doing THEN?" Jenny posed rhetorically. "As if you mean they know what they are doing NOW?"

"That's a good point. I mean, Jesus, between you and your manipulation machine and me and the clickbait posse, we make quite a combo." Henny jokingly referenced Mixality's growing social media empire and her own work under the publishing umbrella of Everything Matters. However, despite a willingness to poke fun at the situation, there was an underlying sub-current where she so thoroughly despised what they were doing.

"The end justifies the means, girl," Jenny commented, reflecting her original intention of joining Mixality to satisfy her and her father's multi-generational goals for business success. Had she been able to take a more objective view, she might have noted that her "end" had changed from getting one over on the Clancy family to that of massive wealth accumulation and fame in the technology industry. In parallel, her "means" had morphed from an original plan to be the voice of reason in a manic, youthful startup to that of something more akin to damage control and political whitewashing of the inner workings of the Mixality business.

Her outlook had shifted incrementally, day by day, for a thousand days, robbing her of any broader objectivity. Jenny was still comfortably, falsely operating under the guise and safety of her original best intentions.

"There you go with your Machiavellian rhetoric again," Henny said, speaking with an informed perspective afforded to her by the accomplished investigative researcher she could now claim to be. Henny wouldn't always agree with Jenny's approach to her work but found comfort in the situation when she reminded herself that if her friend wasn't guiding decisions at Mixality, it would potentially be much worse. And, of course, she had to recognize and acknowledge the access she got through the platform and via her friend to breaking news stories, events, and situations all around the world.

"Says the girl adding another bird to the endangered species list!" Jenny switched topics yet again. A defensive response of many vegetarians is to fall back on what they know is near and dear to them, that which makes them better than all others who do not see the world the same way. "I still can't believe you went to the dark side," she said, always quick to note that when Henny first arrived in the Bay Area, she was a faithful adherent to the same practices.

"Look, you spend enough time out in the wild, the actual wild, you see how humans were meant to exist. It just became a thing."

"Yeah, I know. I've seen your stories. Still shocking when you ate that horse ball soup, made me want to puke!" the social media executive said, joking about her friend's video journalism coverage in the steppes of Mongolia.

It was so perfectly set up that Henny couldn't resist. "Like I said, how humans were meant to exist. For girls like us, that means you can't be afraid to put nuts in your mouth," she delivered the joke with flawless stoic execution, though once Jenny burst into laughter, she couldn't hold back either, with the corners of her lips curving up and betraying her attempts to maintain a straight face.

Henny enjoyed any discussion that touched on some of the work she had been doing, as it allowed for this kind of levity to help offset the conflicted emotions she had about it all. On the one hand, she had finally been given the green light to start publishing some of her rapportage from around the world, such as the field reporting from Mongolia. Yet this work still felt like merely a marginally improved version of contextually vacant clickbait. Some of the real investigative efforts she had been putting her energy into—the real interesting stuff—were being kept under wraps. This had been communicated to her from the outset, so it wasn't a surprise, but it was frustrating nonetheless.

Even though she trusted Jenny implicitly, she had learned that the proverbial walls did indeed have ears. Sometimes, she felt they even had eyes. She simply could not be careful enough.

The proxy for all the things that she couldn't talk about was the event that had originally brought them together—the killing of Michael Ridley and the ensuing riots that occurred on the twenty-fifth of October 2011. That day had heralded the real-time coverage of tragedy in a way that went beyond anything ever seen before. It mashed up the worst parts of the racism of the Rodney King video, the chaos of the LA Riots, the frontlines reporting from Operation: Desert Storm, and the confusion and fear of what was unknown but so close to home from 9/11. Yet the most lasting outcome of that incident is what it would do for those involved in that boardroom safely removed from the street. Michael Ridley's rich, colorful life, which was unfairly distilled into not much more than a social media news cycle, would become far less important than Mixality and EMC. The message—a very raw one—once again became subverted by the medium.

***

The Ridley situation had exposed a new world order governed by the ubiquity of content, data, and connections combined with the natural tendencies of the human condition. Even from New Jersey, Henny could follow enough of it through publicly available content that had been continually re-scoring and re-ranking itself with its integrated MSE API, automatically flowing from the Mixality platform to Facebook, Twitter, and other real-time social networks and link-sharing sites. As they watched it unfold from two sides of the continent, Henny and Jenny didn't need to say a lot to each other to feel their bond growing stronger.

Their mostly non-verbal dialogue was interrupted and ended abruptly as a bruised and bloodied duo stumbled into the boardroom. Both with ripped clothing, some of it intentional and some of it a more recent and radical fashion choice, especially the blood-stained shredded denim and the exposed lacerated flesh on the woman's left shin. The man in a once-sharp blue Italian knockoff suit was helping the woman maintain her balance. He had pushed the doors open with his left hand, his right hand fixed in a claw-like position, securely clasping his daily object of desire. Libby and G had returned, along with G's phone.

A Pacific weather pattern hit a few days later, the unexpected precipitation washing the blood away from the sidewalk as things returned to normal. Before the sidewalks had dried, a new vendor had established themself along that premium stretch of real estate in time for the returning pedestrians. People still had places to go, usually following someone in front of them.

Resolving another error from that day, Jenny had connected Henrietta with her original intended phone call target.

"Henrietta, hello! I'm so glad to speak with you. But I'm curious, how did you get in touch with us?" asked Chris Benter, the aforementioned head operations person at EMC.

"Well, you called me. Jenny said you would call. She said she had spoken with you?"

"Yes, she did. I meant, how did you contact us? We're thrilled you did but were surprised you didn't get the package we sent out. It usually makes things a lot easier," Chris replied, clarifying his question.

"Oh, you mean the big tablet thing? It was broken."

"Ah damn, how did that happen? Those things are supposed to be made of riot glass," he said, his choice of words somewhat tone deaf, given recent events.

"We dropped it," she said matter-of-factly.

"Did it ever turn on?"

"Yes," she answered, thinking back to the events of the previous Friday night. Indeed, several things were turned on that night, but the poor tablet had lasted not nearly as long as Henny or Doug.

After she had sauntered past the boys on the couch and walked up the stairs to her room, she sat on her bed and looked at the device. For a moment, all it revealed was a mirrored reflection, cracked and broken in a thousand pieces. An individual, shown from a multitude of perspectives, reflected and refracted in compelling ways.

Huh, well, that's sort of interesting, Henny thought. *But I guess this thing is toast.*

But before she could move away from it and go to bed, the screen became backlit, powered from within. It was frozen in that slightly grayish state for a couple of seconds before becoming brilliantly lit as it played a short video sequence. Even through the cracked glass, she could follow a semblance of a storyline. It was a newsreel of sorts, with sound sputtering through the damaged audio system on the device.

Stock footage of people, cutting from place to place around the world. The word *HUMANITY* in a large typographical treatment across the middle third of the screen. The intermittent crackle of a broken voice.

"We... together..." a few words came through.

The clips changed to show large agricultural fields, automobiles driving down freeways, factories, and a rocket blasting off from NASA's Cape Kennedy platform.

PROGRESS appears.

"Changed the Earth..." more broken audio.

The tone of visuals started to change, and the speed of the edit going between cuts accelerated. Images of dense urban centers, poverty, barren lands, and dead animals.

BROKEN

Well, that's sort of ironic, Henny was thinking to herself as she watched through the webbed cracks in the display.

"Inequality... extinction..." could be heard in a slower and somber voice, again interrupted by the damaged audio.

More images flashed. War. Big ships, Explosions. Glaciers falling into the oceans. Volcanoes erupting. Destructive hurricanes and tsunamis. Tall office buildings. Money. A busy trading floor on Wall Street.

A SYSTEM OF FEAR

"Rising... corporate... military..."

The imagery had slowed and then stopped, now showing only more of the same font treatment on a black background.

MUST ITSELF BE BROKEN

The words faded away.

JOIN US

The video faded to black, and then an animated graphic loading sequence appeared, multiple dots expanding and contracting in a clockwise motion to form a circle. The word SCANNING, in much smaller font than was shown in the video sequence, appeared below the animation.

Henny's curiosity had been piqued. The doziness that had carried over from an interrupted sleep in Doug's cozy but unkempt bedroom had been left behind.

I suppose they hit all the right points, she mused, recognizing the obvious clichés but intrigued nonetheless. She sensed her heart rate picking up with anticipation as this "Scanning" event continued. Despite being nearly naked, and the cool east coast autumn night having chilled down the entire house, Henny was feeling very warm.

Her hands were the warmest, an effect of conduction from significant heat being generated by the device. Hotter and hotter it got, to the point that it no longer felt intentional or even safe. Where she had it resting on her bare legs as she sat on the bed, it had felt close to burning her skin. She placed it on the desk in her room, with her two hands on each side of the desk surface, and continued to stare down intently and with interest. The display started to flicker between the presumably still-scanning "Scanning" message and, once again, a shattered mirror image of her torso and head.

This time, the reflection shown on the device lying flat on the desk surface had captured her from an upward perspective, still featuring the same flowing Shrek T-shirt, though with a slightly more voluminous perspective of the green ogre's eyes bulging forth. Henny noted the reflection was employing an effective rule of cinematography—the "hero shot"—which classically would utilize a dramatic upward view of the subject to imbue it with more grandeur and confidence.

The depth of the image was fascinating to Henny, and the lighting in her bedroom added many layers of intrigue. Soft, warm light from her bedside lamp pushed in from one side while harder blue lighting from the partially moonlit night outside her window filled in from the front. Both colors collided against the jagged edges of thousands of vectors of shattered glass that now comprised the screen. All at once, she was warm, and she was cold. She was dark, and she was light. She was sexy, she was an ogre, she was dirty, clean, tired, and alive. She was all these things and more.

And she was wanted. Wanted in several ways, but most recently by whoever was behind this weird screen. *Sent by whom?*

Finally, smoke started to emit out of some of the cracks in the glass and the previously invisible seam between the front and back panels of the unit. The screen flickered two more times and went black, with no indication of life at all, its heat quickly dissipating into that cooler autumn air faster than it had built up from the overworked cycles of lithium batteries within it.

Henny tapped at the broken screen a few times. *Tap, tap, tap.*

Well, that was disappointing. She stepped back from the desk and rolled into bed, her mind clearing itself and establishing a state of nothingness almost as fast as the curious device had become devoid of function.

"So, how did you know Jenny? Are you friends?" Chris asked.

"No, we just met that day on the phone. I was trying to call you or whoever had sent me the broken thing."

"Okay, so let me get this straight. You tried calling us on the phone?" Chris was seeking clarity.

"Yes," Henny confirmed.

"Didn't the device work? You said it turned on," he pressed for more details.

Henny was baffled by his insistence on whatever was important about this device. "Why does this matter? But yeah, it turned on and then off again. It was totally shattered and broken."

"Amazing. A phone call," Chris was astonished. Throughout the short history of EMC, they had sought out, recruited, and hired hundreds of people. He could not recall another individual contacting them directly over the telephone. Their track record to that point had consisted of hiring by volume, with the primary qualifier for candidates being the capability of assembling words and doing so in a way that generally followed a formula of using commonplace vocabulary but arranged in such unexpected combinations as to achieve positive regards for search engine algorithmic optimization mostly irrespective of the best way to communicate the intended core message for the reader.

That might have explained the dearth of memorable communication from those many pseudo-journalists. A few on the team were old enough and informed enough to apply the analogy of millions of monkeys on millions of typewriters, though most of them thought that comment was just a funny joke based on an animated GIF meme. They were all young people who could churn through a lot of short-form written content and had developed most of their experience writing for other social media content—posts, tweets, comments, and blurbs. Lots of blurbs.

What also correlated is that most of them were ostensibly allergic to the telephone, and to just about any other kind of meaningful investigative effort. Hence, Chris' surprise at Henny's tactics in the absence of the recruiting tablet working. Also amazing to him was that she hadn't yet started asking for another one.

"So, how did you find us then?"

"Well, I used this thing called Google," Henny replied with a rank of sarcasm. She was speaking with a fool, but it was a fool who stood in front of a mystery and who was at least partially affiliated with someone she wanted to get to know better, Jenny Vandeveer. Henny needed to see where this all was leading.

"But there shouldn't be any way to contact us from outside the device— it shouldn't say who we are until you go through the bot-talk," he replied.

Did she hack it? How did she hack it? What did she get from it? Hell, if she did hack it, is there even anything in there?

"Whoa, what? Bot-talk? What is that? Anyway, you had a nice card in there, so I looked it up from that. I mean, it only said EMC on it, so maybe I would've got it wrong, but it sounds like I got the right place, right?" Henny said.

"Oh god. The card? That card is in there? That shouldn't be in there," Chris lamented loudly, troubled by the mention of the card. "Well, so here we are. The thing is, there was an interview you should have gone through on the device."

"An interview? Is that the bot-talk? Like a survey?"

"No, it's an avatar. It's all AI, you know, Artificial Intelligence," Chris mansplained to her.

"Yep, heard of it. So let me get this straight, you send these things out to people and run decision-tree interviews? And that's how you built your team?" Henny asked.

"Pretty awesome, isn't it?"

"Seems kinda troubling, like you're using a video game to build a newsroom. Not sure about that, but okay. What do you want with me then?"

"I need to hire you," he immediately gave away his bargaining position, not that he had been savvy enough to know how to maintain one. "I mean, you are half-right. I mean, hold on. Er... Would you like a job?"

"Dude, are you reading from a script or tweets or something? What are you trying to say?"

Chris was annoyed. He didn't have time for this, but he had been directed to hire her at all costs. His notes were to get in contact and make her an offer she couldn't refuse. Chris was finding it additionally difficult in this situation as he was speaking based only on what he had been told. He had no idea who this woman was or why exactly they needed to hire her, but simply that it had ended up on his task list to add her to their fleet of writers. The message he had received in his inbox had read:

Hiya Chris,

We need you to get in touch with this excellent journalist. Her name is Henrietta Adler. CV attached. She spoke with Jenny at Mixality upstairs. Henrietta's work is amazing, and the board loves her recent stuff. She wrote a piece on corruption in the education space. Need you to get her excited about how she'd be able to break all these big stories wide open, knock down conspiracies one by one, that sort of thing. See if you can pull her in, get her excited. Give her that "You are half right" talk. You know, the "you can find the other half here" line.

Budget is up to tier 2 level, global expense allowance. Pull out the stops. Also, don't fuck this up Chris. –Harbs

Jesus Christ, from Harbs himself! Chris thought when he read it. *And bloody hell, tier 2 budget? That's like up to $300k. Who is this person? Who is this Henrietta that has Harbs' attention for this kind of role? I mean, shit, we don't even have this kind of role, at least not at that salary. And why hadn't this been done with the recruiter box? Someone's gonna catch some heat for making me do this.*

"Look, Henrietta, the fact is, we want to hire you, and I've been authorized to make it happen. You'll be writing and producing content. Do you have any questions?" Chris asked, trying to be more clear.

"Well, yeah. This leaves a lot to be understood. What kind of content? I'm not in this just to do clickbait, you could probably get anyone to do that. And what's the pay?" Henrietta responded.

"In terms of content, you will be able to break all these big stories wide open, knock down conspiracies one by one, that sort of thing." Chris was now reading verbatim from the original email from Harbs. His voice was monotone and devoid of emotion. "Are you excited." He failed to include the intonation of a question.

Henrietta couldn't help but laugh. "Ha ha! I hate to say it, but you sound like the bot-talk now. So, you're saying I could write more or less whatever I want? Where would it be published?"

"Across our network of seventeen owned sites and over forty partner platforms, that's where!" Chris was now more energetic in his response, proudly generating this answer by himself.

"All right, I can write anything and publish it anywhere... can you promise me editorial control of my work?" Henny had effectively turned the tables on the interview, with her questions being more pointed and material than anything Chris had said.

Meanwhile, in the inner workings of Chris' mind, he could sense that he was losing command of the discussion. He felt threatened, as he did not know what to expect if he failed at Harbs' request. So, he started making things up.

"Yes, absolutely."

"Are you able to get this work published in traditional channels? Like actual news and investigative journalism?" she pressured further.

"Yes, we will," Chris responded. "Absolutely. We will absolutely try. I'll do my best. I think we can. Maybe. Probably not," he stammered on.

She couldn't help but giggle at that response, now shifting her interest in this discussion simply to see how surreal and strange it might go.

"And what about the pay?" she prompted again.

"For that, it's a matter of... what are you looking for?" Chris asked, but without waiting for an answer, he continued, "I'm clear to offer up to $300k. Does something up to that range work for you?" he asked the question purely from the context of making sure he didn't leave this discussion without having put all of his cards on the table. But like any other game, once cards go face up, it's nearly impossible to put them back in one's hand.

She was caught off guard by this. *What? $300,000? Was this real? Did he say that? Dollars? Or three hundred thousand pennies? This can't be real.*

"Honestly, that's probably at the lower end of where I've been operating lately," she said, maintaining as straight and true of a cadence and tenor in her voice as she could, given that it couldn't be further from the truth. She had no job or income to speak of, which likely made it easier to hold credence in the lie she had just told.

"We also have a global expense budget for you," Chris added, realizing he should bolster the offer to get the deal closed.

"What does that mean? How much is that?" she asked, mostly as she was unaware of how expense budgets even worked, other than what she had understood from some of the business courses at Spectra College.

"Well, it's there to cover all your travel and costs related to the work. It's more or less unlimited."

Unlimited? This seems too good to be true. "Okay, well, you have my interest, Chris. Can you write this up for me or send it as a document, and I'll think it over?" she asked, maintaining her hard line.

"Yes, I will. I need you to sign it before the weekend, though. And you would need to start next week," he said. Chris felt the pressure and couldn't stand the thought of waiting any longer for her answer.

For her part, Henny couldn't bullshit this any longer but knew she needed a moment.

"Okay, I will be sure to get back to you quickly," she promised.

Right after that call, Henny had gotten in touch with Jenny, who had proceeded to verify all of Henrietta's concerns. Yes, she was working for a faceless publication machine. Yes, Chris the bumbling fool was representative of the talent level. She also shouldn't expect anyone to appreciate the quality of her work. Jenny had also taken a moment to share her views on the relative importance of ends and means.

***

The very first morning on the job would breathe life and energy into her aspirations. It started with yet another package. Henny chose to keep the unboxing session safely within the confines of her bedroom.

It was a flashy but unbranded laptop in the same style as the tablet she had received. *They grow these things on trees?* she wondered as she glanced at the smashed-up tablet, which still lay flat and cold on her desk.

Upon raising the hinged screen of the newer gunmetal-gray device, it flashed a small green light along the outside perimeter of the display before revealing her new virtual workspace, instantly authenticating her access in ways that would not yet be commonplace to the public for several more years. The first message in her inbox popped up in the middle of the screen.

Dear Henrietta,

We are so pleased to have you aboard the good ship EMC. Everything Matters is our name, and it is a vision and an ethos that are at the very founding principles of our company. I am confident that you will help lift and raise the importance of that vision across everything we do.

You may wonder how you came to be a valued member of our team and a trusted colleague of mine. We had the privilege of seeing some of your work and recognizing a like mind when we see it. We are here to "fight the good fight," and I believe you are as well. Let me help you—let me enable you to do everything you are destined to do.

There is so much inequality and insecurity in our world today. There is too much death, destruction, corruption, and disaster. While we can see there are many good things and many reasons to have hope, it is nothing without action. Our world needs to place a greater emphasis on human rights, education, care for our planet, and care for each other.

We also recognize that we are a part of the problem, at least in our original incarnation. Short-form content fails to deliver context, but what it does do well is capture attention. You will be the first EMCer to start to formulate and develop a broader position across things that matter to you rather than just publishing for the sake of publishing. What that means more practically is that we don't ask anything of you other than to fuel your imagination, satisfy your curiosity, and expand your knowledge in preparation for a big and meaningful future. I'll be following up with more details on specific projects.

I believe you can be a catalyst in helping us help everybody pursue these goals. The solution to our problems does not come down to busting conspiracies—though they do abound—rather, it is about maximizing human potential. This can only be achieved through transparency and empathy.

It is imperative that as we begin this journey together, you keep your work in complete confidence. All measures have been implemented to provide you with secure network access and authentication controls over your devices and content. In other words, it is of paramount importance that you do not tell anybody about our offer to you, your affiliation with our company, or your work for EMC.

Henrietta, the board and I believe you truly possess these skills, and we look forward to seeing you prosper as a member of EMC. If you ever need anything, do not hesitate to write me back.

Yours sincerely,
Harbs
Dr. Harb Louthe, PhD, Board Director, EMC

The laptop proceeded to connect itself over the household's Wi-Fi connection and established a direct private connection to EMC's secure corporate network. Along with this access came an entire suite of customized software tools for writing, video and photo editing, and secure cloud storage. There was even an "EMC Travel" application that appeared to provide access to flights, hotels, local transportation, guides, and security services all around the world. It already indicated an active EMC Travel itinerary with a one-way ticket to Habersham County Airport in Georgia.

Random. Interesting. I guess we see how far down the rabbit hole we actually go, she thought to herself, her reasoning stranded halfway between a reference to Lewis Carroll's literary works and the unforgettable baritone voice of Laurence Fishburne in his most inimitable and famous role.

As Henny explored the resources available to her, she felt inspired and empowered by the backlit keyboard and the futuristic stylings of the contents on her display. It reminded her of the interfaces in Doug's video games, from when she would occasionally get home and watch him play on the Xbox in the living room, both of them seeking the distraction of something mindless, albeit in different ways.

These damn colors are giving me a migraine. Henny would often experience optical migraine headaches, which were not as painful as their pressure-based cousins that most people think of when they hear talk of the affliction. But what an optical migraine did not deliver in terms of aching pain and tiredness, it more than made up for it with a visual cacophony of flashing apparitions, hotspots, and blurred sight.

She powered through it, with every new piece of information she found giving her an additional boost in motivation that helped quell the strain in her eyes and the throbbing in her brain.

And now, this pseudo-techno-espionage theme would apply itself to the user experience of her life. By the end of that first week, she'd received two briefings of storylines to pursue, posted in the "EMC Book of Knowledge" application.

- <u>NASA in the 1970s: Ret. Gen. Glenn Phipps and Richard Gossett</u>
- <u>Diddem.com, the "big data" personal diary</u>

The application sorted itself per the organizational needs of EMC: multi-dimensional, hierarchical, and topical, based on the story or research topic in question. The data within the Book of Knowledge was structured in such a way that while it could be explored nearly without limitation, it also allowed the system to create massive silos of information. Ostensibly, this ensured that all the proprietary research of EMC and of individual researchers was available on a need-to-know basis. In theory, it would also make it easier and faster for researchers to stay focused on the matter at hand.

This siloed approach also served the purpose of building discrete datasets that would be more easily searched and thus helped reduce the demands for extraneous computation and physical storage. To date, it had been working extremely efficiently for EMC, as their hordes of millennials were able to produce reams and reams of short-form content quickly and to do so in such a way as to not distract themselves with other matters.

Effectively, it was data on guardrails—or training wheels.

Twenty

LIGHTS, CAMERA, ACTION

There was a deafening boom, followed by multiple cracking sounds. Bex's eyes opened wide. *Have I been sleeping long?* She felt rested, but it seemed only moments ago she had been looking through this small moonroof at the starry skies above, thinking about her father. The skies were different now, dark. She could hear rain outside, falling heavy on the solar panels on the vehicle's roof. Everything went bright, lit up by a flash of chain lightning through the sky. It danced from one cloud to another and then to another, lighting up the sky as far as she could see.

Which wasn't very far. The moonroof only provided a small field of view, designed to afford any sleepers on the bunk beds a sense of privacy from above. Deemo had also discovered in the design process of his upgrades that anything larger would have required curved glass in the roof, and he didn't want to distort his view of the world.

She heard noises again, more crashing sounds, but not the audible signature that had accompanied the previous round of lightning.

Carlo had been sleeping further to the front in the midsection of the extended vehicle while Deemo had a larger bed below her, both of them spared from the immediate proximity she shared with the noisy rain.

Bex felt the overwhelming need to pee. Three cups of hot tea to end the night had played their role, and begrudgingly, she started to maneuver herself to get down from her bunk. There were steps built into the side of the interior wall of the van, and with the now-raised ceiling from the mechanical expansion it had undertaken earlier, there was plenty of room to move.

For all its customized upgrades and accoutrements, the van did not have a bathroom. In providing a tour earlier and while beaming with pride about the rest of the customizations to his vehicle, Deemo had sheepishly admitted to prioritizing usability and functionality and allowing "nature to happen where nature was going to happen," as he had said.

Bex didn't care about the lack of a latrine. In fact, she generally preferred to have the freedom to relieve herself outside. The only issue here was how to get out of this monstrous future-van with all its secret compartment buttons and motion-activated controls. As she carefully stepped around Deemo's bed and alongside the lower bunk where Carlo was sleeping, she could see a softly lit outline of a door embedded in the larger gull-wing structure.

Okay, that must be it, a door-in-a-door. She began to touch around the perimeter of this shape, but all the surfaces were smooth. There was no handle.

What the hell is this? How am I supposed to open this? In scanning the interior wall of the van, she noticed that the gull-wings themselves also had a faint outline around them, reinforcing the interior's spaceship aesthetic.

She pushed at the smaller door she had discovered, wondering if it was pressure-activated, perhaps something that could only work from within. *Maybe it's a safety device.* But that effort was fruitless. Nothing happened.

Nearly resigned to having to wake up Carlo, she moved back from the smaller door. As she did so, her hand hovered in front of it for half a second, and as she turned toward Carlo's bed, her hand naturally followed suit, executing a very slight pull-and-twist motion, which may have passed muster in an amateur game of charades when given the clue "opening a door." It was also clearly enough of a performance for Deemo's magical mystery machine. The small door quietly disengaged from the larger body of the vehicle and swung open by itself.

The raindrops were intermittent, heavy, and cool on her head and her shoulders, just as the flow of her urine below was strong, steady, and relaxing. The confluence of cold rain and warm pee conjured up equally contrasting memories from those many months of homelessness in the drenched conditions of Vancouver.

She finished relieving herself, steam emanating up from the desert soil below her, pee splashing just a little bit on Carlo's flip-flops that she had commandeered without permission, and the warmth radiating in her body as blood circulation was able to return to regular duties, no longer enlisted to tighten up abdominal muscles. As she stood and pulled up the shorts she had been sleeping in, Bex took a solitary moment to contemplate the traveling Burning Man sideshow.

***

Many of the convoy members had stayed up much later than Deemo, Carlo, and Bex, congregating around a big fire assembled further off to the side of the road. Bex had faintly heard the revelry before she fell asleep in the van.

Portable chairs had been left out around the embers of the fire pit, which continued to release intermittent plumes of dark smoke, visible against the backdrop of far-reaching white desert sands, instigated by the repetitive artillery fire of rain falling upon the hot coals.

Further along the large pullout area, a few interior lights remained on in some of the other vehicles, though it didn't appear anyone was stirring. Bex guessed it was probably around three or four in the morning, though she could hardly be certain. What little light there was available from the radiance of the desert showed the same landspeeder, snake-car, moon-truck, and the various other contraptions they had taken a walking tour of earlier. Even the angst-inspiring steeple of the Bone Church could be seen further along.

Across the road was another truck, a pickup without any creative flair whatsoever. Bex first noticed only the silhouette of the cab poking above the road, the bulk of the vehicle hidden by the elevated grade of the highway, an intentional design that ensured water would shed from the road surface during any big storms like they were having tonight. Her curiosity converged with a need to stretch her legs and incited Bex to inspect. As she walked from the temporary encampment toward the highway for a better view, she could hear the rain sizzling and steaming as it landed on the hood of the empty vehicle.

Bex thought to go closer to inspect the truck, but a sound from further along in the convoy usurped her attention.

The moon-car appeared to be wobbling. It rocked back and forth, causing the aluminum quarter-moon to clink and clank ever so subtly against the steel chassis below it, only perceptible due to its lack of order within the otherwise pervasive stillness of the convoy. The embers in the fire were apparently not the only thing still combusting.

The holes in the moon-car, reminiscent of the classic iconography of Swiss Cheese as the substrate of Earth's single original satellite, also doubled as round porthole windows. Bex was now alongside the moon, her dark shape contrasting with the cold, wet, white-gray aluminum reflective enough to be its own light source. Identifiable sounds emanated from within.

Curiosity knows no bounds, and on this occasion, neither did the temerity of Bex's wandering eyes in this strangest of all places. On her tippy toes, she peered inside the moon.

Many cultures around the world have developed mythology of a man in the moon, often as tales of penance for crimes committed on Earth or angering the gods in some way. On this night, the man in the moon was himself a false prophet. The crown of thorns on his head bobbed up and down in rhythm with the movement of the trailer as he, who had taken the image of the son of God, now devoid of his loincloth, pressed himself deep into the four-legged embrace of the rat-woman who had been scurrying about earlier. Her moans were more audible and far less rodentary to anyone just outside the window. From within, the echo chamber of the curved aluminum-walled interior had created a rebounding cacophony of heretic beastiality, the likes of which had never been heard before.

Against her better judgment, Bex found it hard to pull her eyes and ears away from this intimate incursion. She was in a partial state of shock at being this close to this despicable human.

Then, something else caught her attention, forcing her back to sentience. More noise was coming from further ahead, but this time, no telltale rocking motion nor any animalistic cries accompanied it.

She crept forward, conscious that even if she was quiet, the squeaky cheese of the moon was still making its presence known right beside her. As she escaped the emissive light from the portholes that had revealed things she could never unsee, everything else around her went black. Then her eyes adjusted. She could see the rain, the silhouette of the vehicles, and the subtlety of human movement slightly further ahead.

Two people were at the back of the Da Vinci vehicle, working at it with some effort. This was no late-night repair. They were taking something off the back of the vehicle.

Again.

It was deja vu. She was back at the overpass in Vancouver, frozen in a mixture of curiosity, fear, and, strangely, excitement as she looked toward the aggressive couple on that industrial urban road almost a year earlier. Then she was falling, floating over that railing and down onto the broken tent on that muddy slope. But she never hit the tent or the ground.

Now she was here, but ten or so hours ago, welcomed with open arms by Deemo and Carlo. It was the first place she had been where people only had something to give and wanted nothing in return. Except for the terrible man in the thorns, and now these shadows in the dark. Her mind and body undulated through different feelings that merged into a state of heightened anxiety and vertigo.

Deemo. This has to be his problem, not mine.

Bex started running back to the Transformer-van. In the quick motion to stand, turn, and sprint, the borrowed left flip-flop failed her. The front thong attachment popped out of the sole, and she was immediately slowed down by the drag of a men's size ten-and-a-half slab of rubber pulling on her foot like an anchor. The shuffling and splashing sound of her struggles across the muddy ground made too much noise to be ignored.

"Hey! Stop!" one of the two shapes working on the medieval war machine yelled.

She shed the broken sandal and kept running. The rain had softened the ground just enough to be kind to her feet but not enough to give her any real traction. Her bare feet slid around like fish stranded at low tide, seeking more purchase to slither back to safety. The two thieves had set after her, clearly not held back by flip-flop-failures or the same slippery surface.

Bex screamed out loud, not as the war cry she had expelled when jumping in to help the now-deceased Louis, but out of panic and fear. She fell to the muddy ground. The two shapes, now indicated by their silhouettes and their voices as belonging to large, gruff men, were soon upon her. Unable to get up and walk, she rolled. Without enough momentum to keep turning,

Bex started sliding, a penguin now far from home but using a familiar means of locomotion, the need to escape outweighing any potential allure of her aquatically challenged fish-feet. Then, she felt a crushing weight on her wriggling back as a big boot landed squarely above her tailbone.

Air was forced up and out of her lungs, but with whatever was left, she let out one last mud-curdling scream.

Bright lights came on, flooding the air and ground around them. Bex couldn't look up far enough to see who or what it was as her chin and mouth were firmly pressed into the mud.

Deemo had stirred ever so slightly when Bex climbed down the steps from the bunk above him. He was having a peaceful sleep and had found it easy to return to that state, but he was still dozing when he heard a man yell out. He had immediately become fully aware, scanning the interior of his van to see what was amiss. Everything was as it should be from the viewpoint of his warm bed. Deemo groggily brought himself to his knees to look up at the bunk overhead as a formality. He already knew it was empty.

Then he heard the scream. This sound was closer and louder but more muffled and ended more abruptly. He clapped loudly three times. All the lights inside the van came on. Carlo started to stir, but Deemo didn't wait for him.

The world outside was now awash under the brilliant exterior lights of Deemo's customized van. The gull-wings had raised up, emanating an intensely luminous blast of white radiance toward the captive Bex and the two thieves. A figure stepped out in front of the light, a massive silhouette towering above from the steps of the Transformer-van.

"Who goes there?" demanded Deemo in an authoritative voice.

"Get the fuck down from there," one of the thieves yelled. He started to take steps toward the van while his compatriot kept his foot firmly planted on the base of Bex's back. The pain was excruciating. She looked to one side, giving her mouth and nose better access to the air above the thin layer of slippery mud on the hard-packed desert ground.

Those same properties of the ground meant that it gave no respite to the weight pushing down upon Bex's body. She could feel her old neck injury starting to flare up, expecting it would soon start to limit the control and strength of her arms.

"Get down, now!" The other thief pulled a gun and beckoned Deemo down from his elevated position. Deemo's heroic luminous moment had come to an end. The man pushed him against the side of the van and began searching him in a manner that suggested he had a degree of familiarity with conducting that same action, though he had very little to search as his subject was wearing only leopard print pajama pants.

Bex could sense the familiarity of impending doom. This wasn't sixth sense or pattern recognition. It was simply: *Here we go, fucked up shit is happening again.*

A peak of activity had already been achieved inside the moon-car. The naked fake Jesus himself, Philip J. Clancy, and his new friend had finished their lunar expedition. He at first rolled to his side, his arms wrapped around the curvy shape of the fur-bearing woman beside him, herself an A-list actor hidden behind film-quality costume work and makeup, which had mostly survived their erotic activities.

But his post-coital relaxation was not to be. The noise outside was too close for comfort and, annoyingly, could not be resolved with ignorance, a trait he had successfully relied upon many times over these years.

"Jesus Christ," he said, indirectly admonishing what he presumed were the party animals still making revelry outside by the fire. He softly stroked the sweaty Hollywood creature beside him as he extricated his arm from behind her furry neck. "Think it's time for them to shut it down," he said as he stood up and opened the welded aluminum door that bridged his orbital explorations with a return to Earth.

Meanwhile, as she sucked equal measures of air and mud in pursuit of a breath, Bex could see out of the corner of her right eye that the man was standing just to the side of her hips, with most of his weight still on the left boot he kept planted firmly in her lower back.

In a rush of noise and movement, something had caused the pressure from the man's foot to partially release, enough for Bex to regain some control. She pushed down on her hands to raise her upper torso from the ground. A bright white flash flew beside and beyond her, the brilliance of the gull-wing floodlights flashing off the naked white body of a skinny man in a crown of thorns.

Philip J. Clancy had opened the door of the moon-car intending to bark his disapproval at fellow convoy members. It was disrespectful for them to stay up later than he wanted to, and he saw no reason to treat this night any differently than the many elaborate and hedonistic parties of renown and disrepute that he had thrown at his mansion in the South Bay. After all, his presence at this highway rest stop had surely been the beacon that brought them all together to begin with. But as his eyes quickly accustomed themselves to the darker, wetter scene than he had anticipated, he too was surprised to see a man on top of a woman, just as Bex had been when looking into the moon only a few minutes earlier.

Oh god, not again! he thought.

Never having been a man of action in any aspect of his privileged life, this moment felt different. Perhaps it was the adrenaline rushes and dopamine highs he had just experienced. Perhaps, but likely not, it was inspiration bleeding out of the false wounds of his costume, bringing forth previously untapped notions of helping others. Perhaps, and more likely, it was the perverse sense of an opportunity to expose himself to whoever these people were. There was also a good chance it was the realization that, unlike his aforementioned brogrammer parties, there was no security detail nor public relations personnel to disperse and dispel unrequested physical contact by any of his guests. The last thing he needed was another assault or harassment controversy in his vicinity, and he had no reason to assume these people weren't more of his bros, subservient partygoers who had clearly gotten carried away but would take his word as gospel.

Whatever the motivation, Jesus had returned, skipping across the meniscus of the watery surface. His skinny white arms projected out from his torso as he reached forth to lay hands upon the slick, dark form of the man who had subdued Bex.

"Dude, get off her!" Philip J. Clancy yelled as he pushed weakly against the big man. With devilish strength, the thief leaned backward, grabbed Philip's outstretched arm, pulled, and threw him onwards in a tumbled, muddy mess of skinny limbs, white butt cheeks, broken thorns, and exposed genitalia. The naked Philip J. Clancy splayed out across the wet ground and came to rest in front of Deemo and the man with the wielded gun.

At that moment of imbalance in the thief's forcible confinement of Bex, he became vulnerable. She had pushed the Earth down. Her chest raised up as she morphed from a flapping, slippery penguin into a big wave surfer needing one final powerful paddle to catch a monstrous swell from the deep. In a mighty effort, she swept her right arm back with as much speed and power as she could muster, taking aim at the man's shin. Despite a few touch-and-goes on the muddy surface of the ground, her fist maintained its bearing and strength, and on contact, the centrifugal force deployed itself as she pushed the big man's right foot backward along the mud.

He tried to reset his stance, but as he pushed with his right foot, it slipped back even faster. He began to topple to the right, where he now had no support, and stepped forward with his left foot to offset his flawed center of gravity. The pressure was immediately gone from Bex's back. The trade-off was that he stepped directly on the side of her face. Pain shot through her nose, cheek, and neck, which immediately made her back feel better, not unlike the repair technique of turning up the car radio to fix the sound of a broken muffler.

Instinctively, she reached up behind her head with both hands to protect herself. This defensive move became an offensive tour de force as it completely prevented the man from regaining any sort of balance. He over-rotated to the right and came crashing down, his body uncoiling as he hit the muddy but hard desert surface. The back of his head cracked off the ground like a coconut shell being readied for the base ingredients of a nice hot curry.

He didn't move. The man was out cold.

Is he dead? I don't fucking care.

"Deemo!" Bex called out as the emotional surge in her body brought her first to her knees and then to her feet. Closer to the van, the shiny, naked, religiously ignorant form of Philip J. Clancy lay in the mud, he himself looking up at the figures in front of the lights in a frozen state of fear.

By now, the other man had turned Deemo around, satisfied that this shirtless man in yellow and black spotted trousers had no concealed weapons. He kicked Deemo in the back, taxing the balance of the anti-capitalist, who crumpled to his knees.

As he went down, Bex came up, having risen to her feet and taken steps toward the two.

BAM! The man had raised the gun in the air and shot a bullet over the road in the direction of his own truck, still parked on the other side of the highway. He was obviously distressed seeing Bex approach after she already dispatched his collaborator.

"Any closer, and he takes one in the back of the head!" the man warned, lowering the weapon and butting the cold steel against the back of her new friend's head. She could see Deemo shivering and trembling in the rain, even though he was still functionally warm from having just left the safety and comfort of the van.

Other members of the convoy had started to rise from all the commotion. The gunshot had been a catalyst in making them understand that it was far more than an extended after-hours party below the reflected light of the moon-car. A dozen or so people had emerged from the line of vehicles, mostly hiding behind the big snake-car to watch what was unfolding. Not so different from their regular lives, they chose not to do anything other than flex their voyeuristic muscles.

Bex had her hands forward, her body language pleading for this man to let Deemo go. Clancy lay unhurt but unmoving on the ground.

"You can go, leave him, just go," she said, mostly with disregard for her own wellbeing.

'No, you'll get me! You got him already," he gestured to his partner, still lying motionless in the mud, concussed if not dead. The man with the gun was shaking as much as Deemo.

"So what's your option?" Bex demanded. Any anxiety she had felt had gone away as the physical pain in her lower back, neck, and head brought her mental state fully and completely into the present moment.

The man looked at Deemo, then to Bex, then beyond her to some of the watchful eyes of the others hiding and peering from behind the snake structure. He didn't know what to do.

"Uh. Fuuuck!" he yelled, unable to decide what course of action would lead to anything good for him. His hands were shaking with the gun still firmly placed against Deemo's head.

Bex thought that reaching toward the man had probably added panic to the situation. She raised her hands in an attempt to put him at some state of greater ease. This man did not seem like he was ready to kill someone, but on the balance of probability, at least based on the unrelenting sample set of Bex's life experience, she considered it inevitable.

As she raised her hands, the man took a half step back from Deemo. *Why? Oh shit.*

Bex dropped her hands. Despite her many injuries, she was now a glorious albatross, her arms outstretched, soaring off the edge of a magnificent oceanside cliff. And as she took flight, those massive gull-wings on the van came swooping down with hydraulic force and efficiency. On the far side of the van, the door closed without incident, other than forcing a gust of cold air heavily upon Carlo. He had remained curled up in his bed, hiding under the blankets, still mostly hidden behind the glaring, blinding lights that had signified Deemo's involvement in the action.

In the process of making his custom van, Deemo had made it a priority to implement the latest and greatest intelligence of motion detection and applied it to the novelty gimmick of opening and closing doors at his every whim. It had fallen to a secondary priority to use said motion detection as a precautionary feature to prevent the doors from coming down on anyone. Deemo's rationale for having no such feature had been that he only used the vehicle so rarely, and most of the time, everything was locked wide open for ease of access at Burning Man. He had kept it in mind to get to this upgrade this winter, next summer, or possibly sometime after that. After all, it was a "beta" technology, as he liked to brag to his friends, so it's not like it ever needed to be completed.

As such, the heavy door came crashing down upon the man's head. He hadn't even seen it coming. The unexpected attack dispensed by the vehicle behind him had immediately crushed multiple of the man's vertebrae. He fell to the side.

Bex quickly moved forward, emulating as best she could the graceful flight of the soaring seabird she had momentarily become, despite the ubiquitous pain and the failing traction of her bare feet on the muddy surface. The thief was lying on the ground, halfway between Deemo's knees and the discombobulated mess of Philip J. Clancy, who had remained motionless. She closed in on their adversary, who was now making a guttural sound, groaning and choking at the same time. He was still writhing on the ground and attempting to reach for the gun, which now lay in front of Bex.

As his fingers grasped for the handle of the weapon, she trod on his wrist, loading her mass onto the balls of her feet and disabling the man's digits. She bent over, a compromised breath making its way out of and then back into her lungs. Bex reached for the gun, wrapped her own muddy grip around it, and lifted it up, now far out of reach of the debilitated thief.

She looked down at him, his eyes following her every movement with the weapon, his pupils going wide as they sought to pull in every drop of light they could find.

The incandescent human form of Philip J. Clancy stirred, slithering around in the surface water around him, pools that had been quickly filling with his own despair as he lay still. Bex turned to her left in response to the movement and found herself now staring at this man, again in a position of wielding absolute power.

Here he was. This wet, ragged pile of mud, skin, and bones that had been responsible for the desecration of her own body, for the prostitution of her self-worth in the digital form she had come to rank higher than IRL. Philip J. Clancy, the iconic name behind the system that had given her so much hope, had given her a better reality than the one she was born into before revealing itself as an abhorrent and misguided illusion. Here he was, the false prophet indeed, the previously faceless name behind the horrible cataclysmic event that had taken her father's life.

And here she was, holding a gun, taken from someone else who would have readily served death upon her, just as she had the option to do now, to both of them. Two men, both pathetic, both marked with the gravitational effects of blood having streamed from their heads—for different reasons— and both unable to have their brains control their bodies—also for different reasons.

As the startup wunderkind looked up at Bex, she could see the fear set in. She could palpably feel his hope dissipate into the wet air. In that moment, her eyes burrowing deep into his consciousness, deeper still into his conscience, she knew that he knew. He knew that he had wronged her and so many like her in so many different ways. And she needed him to know, right then and there, that he would have to pay.

Bex lifted the weapon, pulled the trigger several times, and in an explosive statement of her own determination, she rendered her judgment as final and absolute.

Smoke hissed from the barrel of the weapon as rain fell upon it. Steam hissed from Bex's head in response to the same stimuli. There was more movement from the ground.

Bex looked over to Deemo, then stooped beside him with her hands on his shoulders. "Deemo, are you okay?"

He looked up. The floodlights from the heavily modified vehicle behind him had illuminated the woman standing before him, radiating like a glistening, shiny, muddy angel. He was in awe, in so many ways. "I... am..."

Remarkably, he didn't know what else to say.

Twenty-one

MEANS AND ENDS

The Soviet Union had won. They had become the first to land on another planet. This was not some fictional exploration of an alternate history, but rather, the outcome of the Venera 3 mission, a Venusian space probe launched by the Lavochkin Bureau in November 1965 and which came to its conclusion on March 1 of the following year when it crash-landed on the surface of its target planet. It was followed a year later by the subsequent mission Venera 4, which became the first human object to record and transmit data from another planet.

This piqued the curious mind of the investigative journalist. *If you saw something that has never been seen before, how would you process that information? How would you describe it and transmit it back to others who couldn't see exactly what was in front of you?* She was consumed in thought of these unintelligent Soviet spacecraft, the first two of which had been lost to the spatial seas after leaving Earth's atmosphere and absent-mindedly flying by Venus, and the third, smashed in the Venusian countryside like a sailor on shore leave, stumbling nowhere in particular after a night on the town. Anthropomorphizing these interplanetary vehicles made for a compelling mental exercise. The data storage capabilities in those times could support no more memory than said drunk sailor, and the computers on board had the knowledge and reasoning of an infant. Yet its hands could feel heat and touch substances. These Venera craft were effectively toddlers moving around a kitchen, burning their fingers and dropping things on their toes.

The same metaphorical construct applied itself to the Mariner and Viking programs, which were NASA's equivalents. The Mariner ships conducted orbital reconnaissance of Mars, and the Vikings were the famous landers that made it to the surface of the Red Planet. Again, more dumb kids running into mysterious places, albeit with extremely expensive clothes and highly paid caretakers.

This golden era of exploration finally led to the Voyager and Pioneer probes, which ultimately traveled farther than any man-made object had ever gone before, provided that one didn't subscribe to theories that humankind had originated in distant galaxies. Interestingly, the spec sheets in the Book of Knowledge about Voyager seemed to be updating in real time.

Voyager 2, currently 17.6 billion km from the sun as at November 3, 2011. Spacecraft is approximately 16.4 light-hours from Earth.

This meant that it would take sixteen hours traveling at the speed of light to get to where the probe had traveled in the thirty-four years since its launch. Both Voyagers were currently traveling at around 12 kilometers per second, speeds at which it would take over 100,000 years to reach the next closest solar system.

Definitely the long game, she thought as she continued into the data.

Henny was impressed by the sheer magnitude of the space and time inherent in contemplating the data from those NASA programs, as well as by the relative quality of the information she was seeing through the EMC Book of Knowledge application.

Light-years more mature than those precursor Soviet programs, the two interstellar teenagers Voyager 1 and Voyager 2 had been equipped with the famous Golden Records—12-inch gold-plated copper phonograph disks that were onboard each of the crafts, each covered in protective aluminum and shipped with a visual instruction manual, not unlike those commonly used to assemble Scandinavian furniture, which described how to play the records and attempted to explain the origin of the spacecraft.

Where Venera, Viking, and Mariner had waddled into space with the intention of burning their hands and reporting back how much it hurt and what they had touched, Voyager were delivering a message, perhaps more similar to "What I did last summer," but with the extra layer of capturing everything that had been accomplished since the dawn of humanity.

Language recordings, music, sounds of nature, and an assembly of one hundred and fifteen images were all encoded in analog format on the Golden Records. The images themselves are remarkable, a combination of logical, mathematical, anatomical, environmental, cultural, and societal visuals. Pictograms were used to indicate the base principles of math equations. Silhouettes and sketches depicted humans and animals.

Funny that forty thousand years after we started putting diagrams on the walls of caves, we go right back to that same thing when we send multi-billion dollar pieces of technology into the far reaches of space, Henny noted. Ultimately, the similarities converged in the application of structured information. In the interests of communicating with a potential alien civilization and accounting for the fact that they could not possibly know anything about our language, our script, our numerology, or our physiology, we would have to resort to the most basic representations of information—dots, lines, circles, squares—and build up from there.

Unless, of course, one believed in those unconventional tales that humans had started elsewhere, as Ret. Gen. Glenn Phipps seemed to.

"It is absolutely inconceivable that we could have come to be as we are on this planet, purely through evolutionary processes," he had shared when Henny met with him on the first stop of her global milk run.

"What do you mean by that? Why do you feel so strongly about it?" she inquired. Despite her skepticism, he had already shared enough of his own background to lend credence to anything he might say. Gen. Phipps had shifted from active military service to NASA in the late 1960s, with his physics and engineering academic background meeting the requisite profile to guide the organization out of the many mistakes of the Apollo program and into an interplanetary future of exploration and discovery.

"It's right there, in the data. Where do you think that data structure came from?" he gestured at a photo album that lay open on the table in front of him.

"Go on, please," she encouraged.

"You may have been wondering to yourself why, when we send up these amazing pieces of technology into space, we essentially cover them in cave drawings," he offered.

Henny nodded. Indeed, she had been thinking exactly that.

"Where do you think the cave drawings came from?" he asked, somewhat rhetorically, though with enough of a pause that it begged an answer.

"From Paleolithic tribes, right?" she answered, certain that she was correct but cognizant of the importance of always framing an answer as a question when interviewing someone.

"Okay, and what about Egyptian hieroglyphics? And what about Mayan inscriptions?" he asked, clearly working toward some kind of crystalizing conclusion.

The general continued. "It's all the same."

"The same? Sure, similar, but I mean, these things are thousands of years apart and continents away from each other."

"Exactly," he confirmed.

"I need a bit more, help me understand what you're saying."

"The cave drawings, the hieroglyphs, the carvings. The imagery on our spacecraft. It's all the same."

"Right, isn't that what makes us human? The formation of language, of storytelling. Of logical, sequential thought processes? Emotion?" As she spoke, Henny felt like she was stating the obvious. Was the general alright mentally? Was he all there?

Is there any there, there?

"And what we've found out there," he said with an authoritative, definitive voice. "That's the piece you're missing."

Her heart skipped a beat. Was this man, the quintessential voice and face of NASA in the 1970s, telling her that they had found alien life? Was he confirming some of the more outlandish conspiracy theories? Or was he off his rocker and had become an outlandish conspiracy theorist himself?

She didn't respond. This was her turn to enforce a pause in the discussion. *Let's see how awkward this pause can go,* she thought. Pauses are always the best way to get people to say what they really want to say. People do not like silence, and in general, they love hearing themselves talk. With that behavior on full display, here was a general who kept on talking.

"Radio transmissions. From deep space. We received a few of them while we were gearing up the Pioneer program. Our best data people and cryptologists worked through it, and you know what they found?" he asked.

"But wait a minute. Haven't we proven that deep space radio transmissions are just noise from exploding stars and things like that?" The topic interested Henny, and she had done enough initial research before coming to see the general to have an informed opinion.

"That's what they want you to believe," he said rather ominously.

"You talk like that, and no one will believe you," she cautioned.

"I know, I know. I'm an old, kooky, washed-up guy. It makes it easy if they force me to speak that way, then they know no one will believe me. That's why you need to speak with Rip Gossett. He'll set you straight."

She intended to visit Richard Gossett the next day. He had been the Executive Director of Interstellar Intelligence in those heady early days of space exploration. "I'm seeing Mr. Gossett very soon. I assure you I intend to follow through on this story. But you need to give me something more here, something of substance, if you want me to believe you and anyone else to believe me."

"We picked up radio bursts, but not the noisy kind that you hear most of the time coming from out there. You know what these ones were saying?"

As unrealistic as it was, a nonsensical visual jumped into Henny's mind of a satellite floating through space picking up alien broadcasts, perhaps a baseball game or a top 40 radio song. She didn't say anything.

"Algebra. It was fucking algebra! And chemical compositions. And bloody pictures! That's how we knew how to put all the content together for the spacecraft. It wasn't some deep philosophical understanding of how an alien race would interpret our stuff, it's because that's how they told us to tell them about us! It's like they were the music teacher, and they told us the arrangement and we just put the notes together. Hold on, ignore that comment, this had nothing really to do with music, even though we did put a ton of it on that record."

"Can you slow down and explain that a bit more clearly to me? Do you have evidence for this?" Henny's curiosity was raised.

"What I'm saying is we patterned our description of us based on what we heard from space. We were just following a template. And if you wind it back, it's the same thing in all of our history, back to the Mayans, or the Egyptians, or the bloody cavemen, too. But you know what we had that they didn't, the cavemen?" he asked and then paused.

"Um... well, spacecraft..?" she suggested. He raised one eyebrow and lowered his head at a slight angle, encouraging another answer.

"Right. Radios. Communications. They couldn't hear it," she offered, this making much more sense in context of his question.

"Exactly. It's either the biggest coincidence you never heard of or that's why it must have all started somewhere up there." He looked up at the sky, or in this case, the low, stained drywall ceiling of his small cottage in the woods of the southern Appalachian Mountains.

She followed the man's gaze up to the ceiling, the condensation damage reminding her of the same aged markings as were visible on the ceiling of Doug's bedroom. *Oh my god! Doug.* She had left him without a word and hadn't even had time to contemplate what her departure meant for their relationship, or for that matter, any relationships she had back at Spectra College.

As she exited the dilapidated cottage nestled amongst the trees in the foothills of this famous mountain range, Henny's thoughts shuffled between her own circumstance and the broader situation of the very existence of humanity. She had just listened to one of the pre-eminent longstanding authorities on space travel tell her that we—humankind—had legitimately known for decades that there is intelligent life in the cosmos, and more to the point, that we have reason to believe that we are in fact aliens.

How the fuck am I going to work with this? I'll sound as crazy as that old bastard, she thought to herself as a timely and affordable Superide returned her to Habersham County Airport, her usage of the service on this trip constituting some of the first and last Superides taken during its ill-fated and short-lived expansion into the states of Georgia and Florida. *Maybe the next guy will sound just a little less crazy... maybe?* she ruminated, switching her thoughts to what she had learned about Richard—Rip—Gossett in anticipation of meeting with him.

He lived in a gated community in Orlando, nestled amongst some marginal but machine-improved swamplands. As her car drove through the gates, Henny noted the orderliness of the homes and roads within. Even the swamps had been turned into geometrically acceptable ponds and waterways. As humans are wont to do, unstructured and disorderly things become structured and logical, so as to be better managed and controlled.

Gossett's house was large, but not as ostentatious as many of the others she had passed on her way to meet him. It was just after midday and the sun was burning down with exceptional intensity, the individual rays of light each amplified through the humidity in the air. The false pillars outside the front door provided support for a shaded porch, which she greatly appreciated as she waited for the door to open.

In that time, Henny was thinking about what Ret. Gen. Glenn Phipps had shared with her. *Was this the kind of stuff that EMC wants me to pursue?* She had been told by Harbs and somewhat more unintelligibly by Chris that she was there to help raise the quality bar of the type of content that the company had been producing. It was more or less explicit in the email from Harbs that she was not there to pursue conspiracy theories. *Was that just lip service?*

Henny still had a great deal of confidence that things would manifest in a way that was good for her. Given how new everything was, she chose to give it the benefit of the doubt. And given how much they were paying her, she made the conscious choice to give it multiple benefits of multiple doubts.

More specifically, regarding the research and writing procedures that had been communicated to her, there had been a great deal of emphasis placed on exploring these topics as broadly as possible. The Book of Knowledge offered a tremendous amount of peripheral information that had passed, undisturbed, through the filters in the database from which it drew its material. And speaking of those filters, any new entries made by Henny, or any other contributor, had to abide by a certain number of guidelines. Everything needed to be tagged, starting with the basic attributes of annotating when, where, and who, and then building up to more contextual data. The process could be thought of as keywords writ large, but it was all far less onerous than this sounds, as the system more or less automatically annotated everything as it went along, occasionally highlighting keywords or key phrases that it had assigned to one's notes to ask for confirmation or an edit if necessary.

She concluded that there had to be more to learn, that she couldn't simply have been asked to write up the ramblings of one old retired hillbilly general.

"Why hello there, my dear!" Richard Gossett said as he opened the door. "You're the one who survived time spent with Glenn Phipps!" he chuckled mightily as he said this last part.

Henny smiled in response to the hearty laugh.

"Hello, Mr. Gossett?" she replied, her upward intonation allowing those words to be heard as a question, even though she was quite certain that standing before her was the former Executive Director of Interstellar Intelligence.

"Yes, that's me! But please, call me Rip. All of my friends do, and Phipps does too!" he continued. "Please, come inside and sit down," he said as he gestured into the house toward a seating area in a sunken living room beyond the entryway.

"Thank you. And thank you for agreeing to meet with me."

"It's my pleasure. When I heard that someone was meeting with the old man in the hills, I thought it was the least I could do to help you translate whatever you heard from him, that is if I can remember anything interesting. Although maybe you're just here to ask me about what it's like to get old and senile living in a cookie-cutter neighborhood with fake houses and fake streets? I can talk for days on that topic. The only thing real around here are the gators. They will bite you if you give them half a chance. Although, so will Mrs. Simpson who lives down the way. And she's also kind of old and leathery too. Oh wow. Sorry," he paused, realizing he had been waffling on for too long. He sat down on an L-shaped couch and gestured for Henny to follow suit. She chose the opposite corner of the couch to allow as direct a line to him as possible.

He cleared his throat and attempted a recovery, "You'll have to excuse me. I don't get a lot of guests, so when I do, it feels like I need to have every conversation I've missed for the past few years all in one go. I promise you I'm not crazy. At least not as much as Glenn. Now, can I get you something to drink? Do you need the bathroom?"

"I can imagine. And yes, please, some water would be great," Henny said.

"Still or sparkling? Look at this," he said, walking over to the oversized white granite countertop that jutted out from the large open-concept kitchen. He took a glass from a stack of uniform drinking receptacles, assembled in a square design of two glasses by two glasses and two layers high—eight glasses in total that became seven. Gossett placed it under a small tap situated in a secondary sink near the end of the countertop, and he marveled as water began pouring from the tap and filling the glass. Bubbles appeared near the top and played joyfully throughout the volume of water.

"Sparkling on tap. That's the highlight of the day for me. Pretty amazing, isn't it? Pretty awful, too, when you think of it that way." He lamented the very limited realities of his daily activities. Gossett filled the glass and handed it to Henny, who hadn't yet chosen if she wanted still or sparkling before his actions had taken that choice away from her.

Rip Gossett proceeded to describe his career in great detail. From his well-recognized research work at MIT to his published works in sociolinguistics and linguistic anthropology. She found it odd that someone who now suffered a lack of social communication had been a pre-eminent expert in the formation of the study of language and, more specifically, how it affects society and culture.

In expanding upon his time at NASA, Rip shared that he had been placed in charge of "Space Intelligence" in the late 1960s. When he had asked what exactly the expectations were for him, he was loosely told that he was "there to help them explore the furthest reaches of the galaxy and to learn from every bit of available information out there to improve our chances of identifying intelligent life." He had made air quotes as he said this. The nebulousness of the mission bestowed upon him felt awfully familiar to Henny, other than the very discrete and important task of finding extraterrestrial life.

"So, what exactly do you want to know? What did crazy old Phipps tell you?" he asked inquisitively. He presented himself as an open book, and Henny could tell, perhaps from his mostly lonely existence, that he wouldn't stop her from turning any page.

If there's something here, now is when I strike.

She formulated a line of questioning in her mind that would hopefully downplay the "crazy factor" from Ret. Gen. Glenn Phipps' comments while still allowing the loose lips of Rip Gossett to go as broad as the truth might require.

"Well, he was pretty adamant that the space missions, Voyager especially, had an audience out there," she pointed up to the sky, "and that we knew of it."

"Oh, so he said we made contact?" he asked. A wry smile started to form at the edges of his lips. "Did he shake their hands, too?" Rip began chuckling heartily again. He took great satisfaction in making fun of Ret. Gen. Glenn Phipps. Henny wondered if he would say the same things in the presence of his compatriot.

"In case you're wondering, I would talk this way around him too!" he said, confirming their state of mind meld, surprisingly but commonly achieved anytime two people participate in jokes at the expense of some other, non-present, person. For his part, Gossett had been purposefully visualizing the presence of Ret. Gen. Glenn Phipps in order to fuel the jokes he made at the old military leader's expense.

"Not exactly. But he did claim that the production of the Golden Record was based on the format of communications we've heard from outer space. And if that is indeed the case, then it must be based on some kind of receipt of those communications well before the Voyager program, and of course, if that's the case, then it brings into question not only everything we've learned about NASA's role in all of this but also just about everything to do with our place in the universe," she said, apparently having fallen ill to the same contagion of wanton rambling that had earlier befallen Gossett and the day before had afflicted Ret. Gen. Glenn Phipps.

"Alright then, let's just slow this roll down a little bit," he said, his soft smile having pushed up to drive some additional wrinkles around his eyes, those same eyes now widened with interest and excitement. "That would be quite a story, wouldn't it?" he posed with a mischievous tone, almost as if he was daring her to build upon that angle.

"I have to be honest and say that it seemed a bit much for me, but the dedication... the veracity... he had for it. The logic that he wrapped around it. I can't completely rule it out," she said, ostensibly hinting to the former head of Interstellar Intelligence from the organization that had sent humans to the moon and machines to the edge of our solar system that she was compelled to upend fifty years of trillions of dollars worth of work based on a conversation with an old hillbilly.

How the fuck does THAT make any sense? she quickly thought to herself, realizing that the only thing crazier than what old Phipps had shared with her was the fact that she was here, there, now. That Henrietta Adler, an unaccomplished college dropout, had been picked up and flown and driven through the backwaters and foothills of Nowheresville, America, and was on the cusp of breaking the biggest story in the history of space exploration. Maybe the biggest story ever in the history of humanity? Henny's internal monologue was circling itself over and over again, burning rocket fuel as it maintained orbit around one prevailing cosmic conclusion: *This is fucking stupid.*

"Yes, he is very committed to it. He's been trying to get people to break that conspiracy wide open for decades now," he said, very matter-of-factly.

"Okay, so... wait a second, you know he's out there pushing this information?"

"Indeed, I've been waiting for someone to pick it up and run with it. I get the sense you aren't, so here we are again. Phipps' thoughts are once again banished to the basement of social media trash!" he stated, taking great joy from the failures of his old friend to find anyone who cares about what he has to say.

"So you don't care? NASA doesn't care?"

"My dear, we DO care. Okay, well, I'm not one of the 'we' anymore, but let's just pretend I am. This whole thing was done to move the research forward, not so much the space program. For me, anyway, the intelligence that I cared about is the one that we've made—humans and humanity. The idea that I would be the one to find another type of intelligence somewhere else, out there," he pointed up again to the ceiling and the sky beyond, "totally outlandish. But doing the work on our intelligence, that's what was most important!" He was now speaking with more passion and an ever-increasing animated excitement in his facial expressions and body language.

"Help me understand this," she said as she took a sip of her water. "You're saying Phipps was lying, or he was tricked, or what exactly is it?"

"He's not lying. He's saying exactly what we wanted him to say. We were all just shocked that it didn't get out sooner. I guess the story, and Phipps, and everyone else involved are just too unbelievable, right? It's too much of a backdoor conspiracy thing. But you know what? It's the wrong one. You're looking at the wrong conspiracy, Ms. Adler."

Henny was confused. She was following what Rip Gossett was saying, but he seemed to refuse to get to the point. A world-renowned linguistics expert who was so obtuse, he filled the air with words and irony, but perhaps it was just a verbal continuation of cobblers' kids and the maltreatment of their feet.

"So what is the right conspiracy, Rip?" she asked, trying to match his level of passion and inquisitiveness. She could sense that he was on the tipping point of sharing, that he had been looking, hoping, for someone to share this story with. She was certain what was coming next was all new.

"We are the aliens," he said, restating the most unlikely portion of Ret. Gen. Glenn Phipps' conclusions. But then he wasn't. "What I mean by that, unlike the crazy old guy—my friend—is that we needed the aliens to exist. So, we heard the radio waves, you know what they said?" he asked, as if it were a pop quiz in high school science class.

"They were structured to read like math, chemistry, and language?" she replied, echoing the amazing insight she had heard from Ret. Gen. Glenn Phipps.

"Hell no! They didn't say shit!" he said in a loud voice, again starting to laugh. "The damn radio waves were all shit. It was a bunch of boops and bips and baps and beeps, BOOP, BEEP, BIP," he said loudly, leaning back and raising his arms up and down in the quick, stilting, ninety-degree movements of a stiff-backed droid before continuing, "But it was total noise. Unless maybe the aliens dropped their mic in the toilet, they didn't say a damned thing!"

Rip took a moment to compose himself.

"But you know what? We made them say something. We made them say everything," he clarified, adding to his explanation.

"Okay, go on, like you resent the radio signals in a different way?" she asked, wondering how the incoming transmission could have been what Phipps claimed it had been.

"You give us too much credit, girl. Hell no. For one, we didn't have any way to do that, for two, if we did, I guess we would have needed Voyager to be where it is now, or where it will be in the future, but back then, and sending signals back to us. I guess we didn't have 75,000 years to make all that happen!" he took a breath. "No, you know what we did? Do you know how we did it?" he asked.

"No, but I bet you will tell me."

"You bet I will! We lied! We goddamned lied!" His undercurrent of laughter had picked back up, and with this statement, he bent over, his head almost reaching his knees as the chuckles picked up and became nearly uncontrollable for a minute or so. As he lifted his head, he had to wipe tears from below his eyes. The daylight from outside bounced off the landscaped concrete patio just beyond the windowed wall in front of where they sat. As the light hit the laughing, crying former intelligence executive, it glistened upon his tears while simultaneously throwing the far side of his face into darkness, much like the unexplored half of the moon.

"We needed the program to go ahead. We needed the funding so we could work on our intelligence. All of us on that program, sure we loved the idea of space exploration, and it was exciting and goddamn, the pay was good, and the parties... oh, the parties." He slowed down and gazed over her shoulder in a moment of reflection. "But we needed our work to continue. I couldn't lose a decade, or a career, stuck in that room looking at the stars. But guess what?"

"What?" she asked, question to question.

"That was the only way. It was the only way we could get funding. The whole space race was just another dick-on-the-table move from the Whitehouse and the Pentagon. Ooh, the Soviets are getting there first. Ooh, the Martians, what about the Martians?" he posed these statements while waving his hands in the air and applying wavey vocal intonations as if he were trying to frighten children on Halloween night. "Guess we better throw a few trillion dollars at it over the next century, right? Well, that's fine for me. You either have me spend half my career trying to find someone who cares about linguistics and language and culture in order to fund it, and then I do my work, or you have me spend half my career pretending to care about the space race while I can actually work on my work."

"Alright then. So you ran this fake alien cloak-and-dagger operation to get money for... what exactly?" she asked, without challenging him on any of the details, as the last thing Henny wanted right now was for Rip Gossett to slow down and think.

"All of this," Gossett said, with his arms swirling around in a grandiose gesture. "Everything."

"I don't get it."

"Look around you. What do you see?" he asked with a slightly condescending tone of voice.

"For starters, two people talking about completely different things, I think. But okay, I see you, your living room, this glass of water, these chairs, the swamp outside, a few houses. Should I go on?" she tried to match his condescension with sarcasm.

"Exactly. It's all these things. It's total chaos, isn't it?" He posed the question for himself. "And where there is chaos, we need order. All of it needs to be organized, put into logical buckets, and understood. But in our infantile, pea-brained minds, all we do as humans is make more shit and create more chaos. So our whole thing, the entire initiative, was to force some logic and structure upon all of it. Everything we have made. Everything we say, everything we do. Everything we will do. You know where it starts?" Now he waited for an answer, leaning forward in anticipation.

"I'm gonna guess... language?" Henny replied.

"Bingo! I'm glad they sent a smart one," he smiled and continued. "Somewhere along the way, we just fell off this track. Look at the Egyptians, Mesopotamia, the School of Athens. They did it. Their known world was recorded, structured, categorized, and shared. Ours was just messy and chaotic. We were ripping down the tracks at a hundred miles an hour, spilling stuff everywhere, and it's only gotten worse since then, mind you. But we wrapped some order around the whole thing."

"The Golden Record?"

"Ha! Sure, yes, you can believe that. I mean, it had the results of a lot of our work on it. But we sort of made that thing in spite of itself. All the military wanted was some evidence that we were winning the race, that we were ready to fight the Soviets and Martians in one big interplanetary nuclear Armageddon. So, we fed them that Record. They loved the idea of humanity being carved into a big-ass piece of metal, sort of the ultimate space propaganda, with our name all over it. So if they needed a big ugly disgusting souvenir that they could throw at imaginary enemies and they were willing to fund us the way they did... well, I'll be damned if we didn't give them the nicest one possible!" He finished talking, mouth agape and eyes nearly bulging out of his head. The tears from Gossett's previous bout of laughter were replaced with beads of sweat, forced out of his pores from the strain and elation of sharing his story in full, perhaps for the very first time.

"Well, that's pretty wild, I have to admit. So, you fed Phipps and the others the story on alien radio transmissions to rationalize the linguistics work? Aren't you concerned I'll share this story and land you in a pile of trouble?" Henny asked, instantly wishing that she hadn't put forth the second question. Although by this point, the conversation was getting so surreal that she was struggling to come up with a line of reasonable questioning that would hold up to any kind of journalistic standards.

"Alright, my new friend Henrietta, I'll close the whole thing off for you. At the top levels, they knew there were no aliens. They didn't even care, in fact. But they needed some kind of intelligence program to be the driver to open up their own funding for the military. They wanted to buy the guns. I just needed a relative pittance to do my work, but they needed something smart to show for the whole program that wasn't just more weapons and more little-dick syndrome. So the military had my back on this, even if they didn't care too much for the details. I call it 'smart-washing.' They used me, I used them. And we all thought the best way to make it make sense for the world was to put a face on the Martians. Or at least, put a voice on them. If we were hearing voices from space, obviously we would have to invest in a response, right?"

"But if it's a fake story that NASA wanted to be real, why has no one ever heard of it? Why didn't it become a thing? Why is old General Phipps up in the hills in his cabin still talking about it?"

"That's just the thing. It became a conspiracy theory, so it sounds batshit crazy, and anyone who tried to speak out about it couldn't get any real attention—no mainstream coverage. I don't know how they tried to get it out into the public, but it didn't work. And I guess it didn't really matter. Everyone in those top rooms was just fine looking at each other and saying it was the aliens and we needed to spend enough to get to the other side safely. There was no reason for anyone to deny it. I guess, on many levels, the more we said it, the more it seemed real to most of the people involved, especially those who weren't plugged into it from the outset." He smiled as he concluded, recognizing with not a small amount of pride that he was one of those on the "inside" of this whole ludicrous thing, that he had puppeteered everyone to fulfill the pursuit of his own goals, and forty years later, people were still confused and misdirected by it.

It was a total mess. Behind the facade of one of the most future-forward organizations in the history of mankind, a bunch of grown-up children had been playing make-believe with their hands in the cookie jar. In the pursuit of linguistic orderliness from the desk of the former Head of Interstellar Intelligence, a deep, dark chasm of unstructured chaos had been created, an irony that didn't seem to have dawned on Rip Gossett yet.

"Okay, Rip, now my last question. Actually, two questions. Why did you tell me all this, and did you mean to tell me all this? Okay, third question. Feels like you'll get yourself in a shitload of trouble if this gets out, and I will too." The reality of this last statement that wasn't a question hit hard and fast. The weight of Henrietta's inexperience was pulling on her now, as it felt like she was in front of something massive, but she didn't even know how or why she was there or what in the hell she should do with any of it. If Rip had been guilty of sharing too much, now she was doing the same in hopes that this free-talking old man would be able to shed some light as to what to do next.

"Now you're getting to something! And I guess, getting to where I don't have any answers." He looked bemused as if he himself couldn't believe that he himself would not have any answers. "I'll be honest with you. I received a message from my security person—yeah, we still have them even in retirement—that you were coming and that I should feel free to feed whatever conspiracy fantasies you were after. Basically, they didn't really care what I told you as long as it was sensational. Though come to think of it, I'm not sure they even knew what the real truth was to ask me not to share it with you, so there is that, that I'm not sure about. But I guess they were thinking, just like forty years ago, if you take some conspiracy and run with it, it won't make much of a difference. You know why?"

Henny knew it was forthcoming. "Maybe, but why don't you tell me why."

"Ha ha, you're getting to know me already. Okay, so forty years ago, people didn't take the bait, right? Back then, it's because they were too smart and not distracted enough. People actually read things back in those days. And if they didn't, they had no exposure to the news. Smart people were smart and learned more, stupid people were stupid and stayed that way. It was unfortunate but arguably a better way, considering what we have now. 'Cuz you know what that is?" Again, no stopping. "What we have now is a complete shitstorm of all the things that we did not want to happen. Messy, messy, messy. If Phipps had social media back in those days, that story would have got out. And it would have had people up in arms, an entire movement—an army of fucking tax-paying anarchists, all yelling and screaming, 'The world is nye! The world is nye!'" Again more impromptu acting from Gossett, this time performing as an anti-alien revolutionary.

He kept going, as he had kept on doing, "But it would have only got out for a second until those end-of-days complainers move on to something else, the next big deal. So, nothing sticks. They just move on to the next conspiracy of the week, the next thing to get half-assed concerned about, as long as they don't have to do anything about it. And they all get stupider. The smart get stupid and the stupid get stupider. And hell, I don't know why they are asking you to talk to me and for me to talk to you. Maybe just something to distract both of us." As he postulated this theory, it struck a chord with Henrietta.

Jesus, am I just being run around here, too? Am I talking to these old crazies just for the hell of it, on somebody's whim? And if so, why?

After taking a breath, something he had only been doing out of necessity for the last forty-five minutes, Gossett added, "So you're here now, and I tell you, what's important to me now is that people know. People need to know how important it is to get away from this chaos and get back to order. The work we did in the seventies, we kept it going through the end of the millennium. I mean, the money we got from the space program filled us up for decades for what we really needed to do, and somewhere, somehow, that work needs to continue. I mean, shit, if the aliens looked at us now, they would wonder what the fuck has happened over the last forty years. So, that, dear Henrietta, is why I'm telling you all this."

His rationale was starting to make sense to Henny, even amongst the twists and turns of his turbulent story. What she could do with all of this was another matter.

"Rip, you're asking me to take a conspiracy of a conspiracy, maybe another conspiracy behind that, and get that out to the masses to get everyone to realize we are lost in a sea of conspiracies and fake news and clickbait, maybe to get them to continue on your work of making order from chaos? And you want me to do that with a few shitty articles and maybe a tweet or two?"

The old man sat on the couch, taking in Henny's synopsis of the situation. In that instant, he seemed to have aged all those forty years since he first started categorizing humanity for an alien library. He was no longer the excitable, animated expert who shared intimate details of his career path, his ambitions, and his failures. He was a tired old man sitting in his house in the swamp.

"I guess... I'm not asking you to do anything, Henrietta. I just thought you should know all of this. I thought someone should know," he said with such seriousness that it felt as if he had actually shared all of the wisdom and knowledge of humanity, not just the nest of conspiracies that a bunch of army men and misdirected scientists had dreamed up in their subsidized make-believe time.

As she retraced her way from Gossett's house, through the artificial landscaping of the gated community, and back to her hotel, Henny was buzzing with her own internal debate. Mostly, it was concerned with wondering what in the hell she was doing in these discussions and what was expected of her in this very, very strange job. In the absence of answers, she resigned herself to continue in a state of unknowing, to see just how deep this rabbit hole was destined to go.

***

Her phone made a slight chime, raising in volume for a second before going silent. It looked up at her from the table, next to her nearly empty plate of food, the duck having been reduced to a bit of fatty skin and a few small hollow bones. More rice than salad remained, both of those having been demoted in importance to the protein.

[Workout at Purple Energy - 2:00] flashed across the front of the smartphone screen, the machine fulfilling its duty as it waited for its human subject to act.

"Oh! My gym session. I have to leave soon. But it makes me think of that piece in Thailand... I guess I still call it a story as it was the first piece of trash that came from my keyboard, thank god I use that pseudonym..." Henny said.

"I remember when you were there. You were still pretty skeptical of the whole thing, I remember you calling me from the beach, and I was like, okay, good to ask questions, but look at you, you're on the fucking beach!" Jenny

246

laughed as she nibbled at the last pieces of her avocado toast. She always saved the crust for last. Her digestion tactic was to save harder materials for the end of a meal, as they would help break everything down inside.

"Yeah, I didn't know what was up. One minute, I'd been bouncing around on little prop planes up and down the East Coast, then I was on an Air Thai Jumbo Jet to the other side of the world. But the guys I met there were all pretty cool."

"That was the automatic diary thing, right? Did you ever use it? Did they ever get anywhere?" Jenny asked.

"Yeah, Diddem.com, DiddemAI, or whatever. They raised a crapload of money. The AGF Fund put over a hundred and twenty mil into that first deal, I'm not sure who was the lead on the follow-up round or how much it was. They are definitely still going strong, I think, but they probably burned a huge chunk on their launch and buying users."

"AGF? Is that a part of SGF? So, we're basically sister companies?" Jenny asked.

"Sort of. It's the Asian Growth Fund. I guess it's a sister fund, so we're like second cousins or some shit! I never could figure out how all that worked, the third cousins three times removed, whatever. But yeah, they are in the same network, different bunch of people. They probably didn't need World War Three to break out on the streets below their office to raise their money like you did," she said with an external smile and an internal frown. She silently reprimanded herself for speaking too flippantly about it.

It was easier to speak of lighter and sillier things.

"Okay, but AGF and SGF are all under MCA. I think I have that part right, though it's always clear as mud," Jenny clarified.

"Uh-huh. I think so, that's my take. So, those guys in Thailand have some pretty neat stuff. You hook up their plugins with your email and your calendar and your socials, your texts... and whatever you want, and it generates a daily diary for you," said Henny.

"I remember that, your piece was pretty good, it showed a few from IRL right? How did you get those people to agree to share their diaries?" Jenny asked.

"That's some of what we have to deal with, right? Like, all those users were opted in automatically to sharing all their stuff in whatever way Diddem wants to share it. Now I know they generally don't do anything *bad*," she said, underscoring and dragging the emphasis on the last word, "but they can and they will. But anyway, I got in touch with those peeps as I don't want any privacy blowback bullshit, and I spoke with them as my fake name anyway, so it was easy enough to clear it."

She continued, "But the thing is, and this is not what I was writing about 'cuz my piece was basically just a puff piece to promote that business... *thanks for that Harbs,*" she whispered the thank-you loud enough to be heard but not to interrupt her train of thought, "but they spent so much on their customer acquisition, and the costs of running the backend of that whole setup were so insane that they were losing like dollars per month per user."

"That's terrible. And how big are they?" Jenny asked, trying to quantify the scale of the business and wanting to process the mental math of the extent of those accumulating losses.

"When I was there, they were over twenty million users. Obviously, some of them just turned it on once and didn't pay much attention. But you know what's most crazy about it?" she asked, immediately following it with, "So they were spending money hand over fist to get users, then spending money hand over fist to pay to run the systems for all the users they got, and even after the DoJ sent them cease and desist, which basically shut them down in North America, which is why you haven't heard as much about them, so even after all that, that's when they raised even more money, the second round," she said, taking a much-deserved breath.

"Holy shit, and that's the hundred and twenty million?" Jenny asked.

"No, that was the original round, the one AGF was behind. That means the new money had to have been at least a few times that, but nothing was published, and it was all after I was there, so I guess in that sense it's okay that I'm sharing this with you, though we should probably still just keep it to ourselves, but that's just fucking nuts. So not only are they shut out of the world's biggest market, but they get probably another half a billion or more to keep running their broken economics," explained Henny.

"Yeah, wow, that doesn't make much sense. I mean, even our fucking evil business has a formula to make money—we print it off the backs of users, but at least we know what it is and how to make more of it. I figured that was sort of what it took to get those levels of funding," added Jenny.

"They have their model. The whole thing is based on utility and usage, and it's based on computation. They are crunching a crap-ton of data in the back-end. But the problem for them is the crypto boom. Everyone out there making mining machines is eating up all the supply of chips and cards, all the CPUs and GPUs are spoken for, so network and data processing costs are gonna be through the roof for god knows how many years to come."

"Look at this, someone's a smart cookie, someone's been learning just a bit about the tech business since all this began," Jenny commented, a glisten in her eye reflecting the soft touch of pride she felt for her friend who, despite Henny's dislike for much of what they both did, was by any measure building up some serious expertise. Jenny was both proud and momentarily jealous, the envy coming from the fact that most of the time, her own work did not afford her the space, time, or experiences to learn anything new other than how to prevent over-ambitious and under-skilled rich kids from getting in their own way.

Jenny continued, "So, you're saying that the deep pockets at AGF or whoever has been funding this thing so far are more or less ignoring the business model and assuming they'll just get a ton of users, build out their system, and *then* figure it out after spending a billion or so dollars?"

"Sounds insane, right? But I don't even think I can give them that much credit. I think what's really happening is *they think they think* that, but in reality, what they know is if they fund it to whatever the next milestone is, there will be so much money involved that someone else, or a few someone elses with more deep pockets, will justify a valuation gain and pour the next huge sum of money into it. And meanwhile, the poor guys in Thailand are just chasing users for this idea they had, spending other people's money to get there, and trying not to get arrested or shaken down for privacy and security violations." Henny spoke confidently and clearly, filling in the blanks on the story as she saw them.

"Okay, girl, you have to publish this! Why is this not the story? Do they have you on lockdown?"

"I wish it was the case. This ain't the story cuz no one will read this story. On face value, that's just every tech platform out there. The only way it gets worth talking about is if it fails, if those guys get arrested, or maybe something worse. And I guess I'd probably get my ass handed to me too. But mostly, it's just a big-ass Greater Fool theory. Money chasing money. Oh, and the thing doesn't even work all that well just yet, it does a nice job of capturing some things you've done and planned to do, but it's a big stretch to call it a diary. It's more like a keyword mashup of things you might have said over the past week. Sure as hell doesn't tell you what you're gonna be doing on any given day. But it is funny as shit, and... oh shit! I gotta run!" She pushed her chair back and picked up her phone from the table. Henny reached down and started zipping up the courier bag she carried her gunmetal-gray laptop and workout clothes in.

"Yeah, yeah, go on. I got this. I'll ring it up on Mixality anyway," Jenny said, relieving her friend of the precious few minutes it would take to either pay for lunch or have the awkward back-and-forth of who would pay for lunch. Classically, business lunch partners would play tug-of-war with one another over the outstanding payment. Those who would win had usually perfected the technique of sliding the check toward themselves but being able to nominally push it back just as their counterpart would reach for it, thus ensuring that for every salvo from one side to the other, they would lose just a little bit of ground. This would persist, in actual practice or often only in mental theory, until it ended up firmly on one side of the table, and for decades those bills had been settled with the swipe of a carbon copier and a signature. Here and now in 2013, the new lunch etiquette that would dominate the future was starting to take shape. If someone offered to pay, it required only a quick "Thank you" to acknowledge one's entitlement, followed by movement toward the closest exit to avoid any further discussion on the topic. Signatures weren't used anymore either.

Henny ignored these formal policies. She simply strode past the table and leaned over to kiss her friend on the top of her head, leaving trace amounts of duck fat on the vegetarian's tightly brushed pony-tailed hair as she left for her appointment.

***

Doug didn't know what to think. For him, patterns said a lot. Everywhere he looked, he usually had a habit of extricating patterns from the world around him, even if their existence was purely subject to the eye of the beholder. This pattern was confusing, to say the least.

"Jay, what do you think? She has hardly spoken a word to me since that night," Doug lamented as he and his roommate walked up the sidewalk toward the house. They passed by multiple other Pennsylvania foursquares, cookies cut from a simpler bygone era.

"I dunno, mate. I wouldn't overthink it too much. Just give her some space, right? She definitely didn't seem upset or embarrassed or anything like that on that night. Me and Zenty figured you must have performed pretty well!" he laughed and pushed an ever-so-slight elbow into his friend's ribs.

"Well, yeah, I know she's been going through a lot with the article thing and all the trouble she got in for that," Doug said, as much for himself as for Jason's context.

"True, true. Probably a lot of stress from that. Still seems stupid to me, like she's studying to be a bloody journalist or broadcaster, and here they are giving a lesson in snuffing the media. Fucking crazy if you ask me," he said as they entered the house.

"Okay, well, I think I should go up and knock on the door and see if she wants to chat. Just to figure out what's up," Doug said as they entered the house.

It was empty. He called out, "Hen? Hen? Are you here?" he said as he stomped up the stairs, his shoes still on. No sound came from upstairs. He opened her bedroom door, somewhat fearful of what he might find. Perhaps she would be there, scornful of his entry and upset with him for bothering her. Or perhaps she was angry that he hadn't come to help her sooner. The myriad outcomes he imagined showed the bewitching power she held over him.

None of these came to pass. The room was vacant. Her bedsheets had been hastily pulled off a few hours before, leaving a bare mattress. Her desk was swept clean of all her writing tools, and the dresser drawers were open and empty.

He looked around the far side of the bed and back to the wall beside the dresser. On the floor lay a small piece of material piled up. A gray shirt.

He lifted it up. The smiling face of Shrek looked back at him, with two bulging eyes and a big toothy smile, and in that instant, he knew that T-shirt would never look as good as it had just ten days earlier. He knew she was gone. Other than a few orphaned plants and books in the living room, some smoke stains in the kitchen, and a dining table with two wobbly legs, there was no trace of Henrietta and no pattern they could follow to understand it.

Twenty-two

THE SYSTEMS

The systems had never anticipated this. The hardware had been specified and ordered to match the desired network topology, the map that had been drawn up to secure the organization's IT infrastructure in such a way that it would support all the many use-cases the system anticipated.

The network architecture ensured fault tolerance. As any of the engineers who oversaw the installation of the hardware would attest, it should have been able to withstand half of the data centers in any one single time zone being burned to the ground and as much as a quarter of the entire network footprint being destroyed, allowing for some amount of rebooting and propagating of information across its nodes.

It had been designed to handle a massive volume of content throughput, thousands of tenanted organizational access points to platforms, and millions upon millions of concurrent users and streams across the myriad touchpoints through which it was accessed. All the security and privacy protocols necessary to facilitate such activity would also more than suffice to provide network resources for the less demanding requirements of internal research, development, and production.

The forward-looking plan for the next decade was to ensure that storage, computation, and delivery needs were met well in advance of the anticipated scaling up of the system's usage. As a result, the organization had been strategically acquiring physical locations around the world in anticipation of further hardware and fiber-optic deployments on an n-tier architecture and of an n-size configuration, with "n" being essentially only limited by how many rare earth metals and conflict-zone resources were needed to outfit the expanding data centers.

The system had painstakingly been trained, and trained itself, to re-configure and optimize network architecture for all those known and expected outcomes, even running hundreds of thousands of simulations of potential use-cases and possible security risks to ensure reliability, stability, and trusted security. The only thing growing faster than people's general concerns about privacy and security was the frequency and volume of private content being uploaded with unrestrained abandon, mostly by those same people.

Those simulations had tried to account for things like the Michael Ridley incident. How could they ensure an absolutely reliable connection for future incidents like this? Especially in the proximity of the event? How could the systems ensure that voices and commentary were partitioned, sorted, and distributed in a way that would drive the most repeat, relevant activity to the platform while maintaining system stability? How could those systems generate the necessary network logs to show that the platform was simply an arbiter of data, merely an internet intermediary, and not a purveyor of content? After all, that would be a necessary proofpoint to appease federal authorities. And in parallel, how could the systems be best designed to ensure they captured every touch, every view, every notion of preference from every one of the posters, commenters, supporters, haters, and advertisers who all demanded a reciprocal spoon-feeding of a constant stream of synapse-firing material? It was a big task, to be sure.

Where the simulations did not adequately accommodate their own needs, nor those of their organization and its owners, was in the overly simplistic scenario of Doug, Ricky, and the trail cam footage that had stumbled its way to their attention.

That use-case was never contemplated, and within the constraints of the network architecture that existed in 2012, it might have needed to have applied its entire computational capacity to run a multiverse of scenarios big enough to land on the one it hadn't been ready for.

The system had been idiot-hacked.

Doug and his roommates had been using that VPN connection for over a year and a half, pretty much since the start of the previous year's first term. Always reliable, they had mostly just left the port connection open, surfing the waves of the World Wide Web safely in Caribbean waters. But now, it seemed like something had been lost at sea.

The files weren't there.

Also, neither was his mp3 collection. No Bowie.

What the hell?

To answer the question, an encoded layer of communication software had been initiated, effectively allowing those videos to "phone home" to the network environment from which they originated. In this case, it was a remote redundant storage node of the broader EMC network. The same network that Henrietta's newly configured shiny computer had patched into over a year ago—over that same VPN.

Where Doug and Ricky had afforded themselves some time was with their tactical decision to view the broader batch of content over milkshakes. In the hour or so that they had sucked back that sugary sustenance, those distributed hierarchical networks under the EMC umbrella had been able to receive and assess the incoming data report of content being accessed in a manner that had never been anticipated, a breach that had never been simulated.

The automated response was twofold. The first, to immediately initiate a massive wave of test routines to account for this previously unexpected access protocol. Simulated idiot-hacking, to be more precise, had already started heating up a data center in Vietnam. The second step, conducted in parallel and resolved much faster than the network improvements, was to isolate the case. As soon as the node computer with the contraband content came back online, those hidden communication protocols flagged their existence back to the network.

Thousands of CPUs in an office tower on Market Street, downtown San Francisco, were now very aware of the laptop in the messy bedroom in the old foursquare house in a small town in New Jersey. They quickly relayed the situation to compatriots who were operating out of a refrigerated floor above a supermarket in downtown Trenton. The lights on some of the racks lit up as activity commenced, almost appearing to glow brighter with excitement, although this was unverified as there were no humans present to bear witness.

Faster than the end-user could possibly appreciate, and without giving any indication through the UI in his operating system, the content on that laptop had been wiped clean. As an added safety measure, the system had wiped anything nearby that bore any trace of having come through that same VPN node.

Ziggy Stardust had become intergalactic collateral damage.

It hadn't simply stolen the pirated content, though. As a barter offering, the system had ever so kindly replaced it with new custom software—a quiet, mostly unobserved passenger whose primary objective was to constantly profile the performance and activity of the guilty laptop, to learn from the end-user's activity, and to propagate itself as a stowaway on other unsuspecting end-user devices.

In short, the EMC network had been caught with its pants down, somewhat comically by someone whose most memorable association with EMC had occurred in a similar state of dress. Unwilling to just take it on the chin, or on the fiber-optic relay switch, the network had quickly re-architected itself and rapidly implemented safety protocols to prevent a repeat occurrence. One could almost imagine that somewhere at the top of its n-tier—which couldn't really be n-tier, as everyone has a boss—architecture, the system was banging its arithmetic logic unit against the wall after realizing it had been hacked by an unsuspecting arbitrary button-presser. Yet where it would fall short again is in failing to recognize that simply by profiling Doug's machine, and maybe a few more, it could not yet generate enough of a structured dataset to fully understand the optimal architecture for the network. It needed so much more.

Other software programs were running around the clock, sharing many of these same resources, and might have been better able to run those new security simulations or to extract end-user data from people like Doug. But those systems were too short in scope, at least at present. One was caught up in culling through petabytes upon petabytes of student data to meet its prime directive of running simulations of post-secondary learning outcomes and modeling optimal paths for students based on their backgrounds and academic performance. Another was executing millions of conflicting computations in the analysis of simulated theaters of war. A connected data center in Colorado was expressly dedicated to clinical outcomes and the influence of other aspects of a broader health system on overall patient health. And finally, after these and other data modeling programs consumed as many compute resources as they could, the network deployed the rest of its metal, wiring, and energy to the validation of blockchains, fueled by the self-fulfilling pursuit of greater wealth.

Meanwhile, Doug sat at his desk, habitually double-clicking on the creepy goose icon that refused to give flight to his VPN software and refreshing (CTRL+R) his browser and file explorer windows again and again, for the better part of two hours, before finally giving up and going to bed.

Just like the girl he had fallen in love with over a year before, all evidence of what had happened that day was gone. Missing with no trace, save the lasting impression and inspiration it left with one Ricky Templeton.

Twenty-three

ANGELS

Harbs was always friendly. He took it upon himself to engage people with respect and care. Life was too short, after all. Harbs' role was to be the conduit that teams and individuals could rely on to gain access to the executive offices of MCA and, by extension, SGF, AGF, and several other funds throughout the organization's network. He knew he could either fall in line with the classical corporate ethos of their capital-intensive enterprise or take a higher road, one with care for the people involved. He believed that the "invisible hand" that the company needed was one that applied a softer touch with more emotion, and the results of his efforts were applauded over and over again.

He had been trained to go with what was working, and this approach was doing exactly that.

When the MCA Board of Directors had requested him to initiate the recruitment of a young college student from Spectra College in the middle of New Jersey, his first reaction was to ask, "Why?" With that question falling upon deaf ears, he proceeded with the directive given to him. After a quick scan of a detailed dossier that the company had about Ms. Henrietta Adler, he activated Chris Benter and the recruitment team at EMC. What attracted him to Ms. Adler was the thoughtful nature of her work and how completely she could analyze an organizational problem. She would compartmentalize a situation into its atomic pieces and describe it in a way that would make sense to an average layperson every bit as much as it would to a seasoned business executive.

Harbs saw this as an opportunity to "kill two birds with one stone," as he liked to say, in his familiar habit of overusing classic idiomatic expressions. He had been given a related objective to expand the journalistic remit of EMC. Harbs heard that the Board was unwilling to take on the exceptional risk of building its media businesses in such a way that was solely dependent on the contemporary formats of content distribution—tweets, posts, and the like. They were adamant that this current content paradigm, of fragile snippets of half-truths feeding short attention spans, would not last as technology advancements continued to expand human potential.

After all, with so much innovation afoot, every trend, model, and system was subject to disruption by an inexorable march of innovative devices, divergent distribution models, and expanding consumption preferences. Everything was in beta all the time.

Harbs thought that Henrietta could lead the early, initial charge in pursuing this goal and that she could do so while contributing as a legitimate card-carrying member of EMC, even in its current sophomoric incarnation.

Thus, his briefings to her were intentionally diverse, very often quite vast in context, and most of the time lacked coherence with anything else she was working on. Henny grew to appreciate the oddity of it all, and she especially thrived on the interactions with Harbs. Wherever she was, which most of the time meant that she was somewhere else from where she had been, any incoming words from Harbs would always brighten her day.

Over the years, it became clear to Henny that Harbs had been conflicted in his initial communications with her. As she would come to learn and admire, he held strong opinions that EMC and its network companies had the potential to benefit humankind for the better. But he, like her, Jenny, and countless others, would be forced to reconcile these altruistic notions with the hard realities that there was a more immediate job to do.

They both found solace in the underlying objective of her journalistic missions. Yes, she was publishing an uninspiring amount of acceptably mediocre clickbait under the pseudonym of the worldly reporter Harriet Stone. However, that was simply to meet the basic content quota requirements that were in place across all EMC contributors. What that false front allowed her to do without distraction was to put real energy into that which she had been tasked by Harbs; her "real job" was to investigate, research, and develop thesis stories on the underlying power structures across so many aspects of society.

By the way, Harriet Stone is a fucking stupid name. Some brilliant Twitter handle writer must have come up with this one, apparently a play on phonics of "Hurray It's Done."

Countless times, she found herself entrenched deep inside some of the most unbelievable schemes of manipulation across all aspects of our lives. Her moral compass begged her to act, to speak out and force change upon these institutions, but anything she might have overtly done with good intentions would have removed her operational veil of secrecy without making any material difference.

Indeed, she often felt the words she wrote were twisting her inside and out.

Harbs was a voice of reason, helping her understand that these hidden organizational forces had been endemic to humanity for decades, centuries in some cases, even as technology and society had changed over and over again. He had a gift for explaining things such that they wouldn't get overwhelming but still maintained their importance and sense of magnitude. He would often remind her that the best thing they could do was document it all and develop fulsome pictures of these situations rather than rush to the presses with the first proof of evil-doing.

"History is but a set of lies agreed upon, Henrietta. But patience is a virtue. For those of us with virtuous bones in our bodies, we need to remember this at all times, use it as a strength, and adhere to it. Gone are the days of open rebellion leading to positive change, with all respect to Gandhi, Mandela, and MLK. The real change agents of tomorrow will be those who operate from within. Always remember that."

She had developed a close relationship with Harbs, strengthened through their shared ideals and his endless reserves of... reserve. Whenever she struggled with the internal Machiavellian tug-of-war that could so easily cloud her thinking, he was there to support her and lead her to good decisions and a positive mental attitude, which was an absolutely necessary ingredient for the fieldwork.

The fieldwork. Her introduction to the operational side of things had started in that hillside in Georgia, through the gated homes of Orlando and the strange and interesting discussion with Rip Gossett, and then onwards to a few weeks with Diddem.com in Bangkok. What a change that had been from life in a rundown Pennsylvania foursquare. *Oh god, Doug. I wonder what he's doing now.*

***

Henny initially intended to call her roommates back within a few days. Then she planned to do so within a few weeks, until it became much more than that. Months and years would continue to roll by, her time and mental energy always consumed by the work in front of her. She was at peace with her commitment for all the many ways it aligned with her desires to learn, be mindful, and have purpose.

The trade-offs were many, of course. With every story or project she zestfully took receipt of, nonsense and bullshit were part and parcel.

Like Diddem.com, the AI diary. The founders were nice guys—two Americans who had been in Thailand for so long that they had notable Thai accents, and two Thai locals who wanted nothing more than to be as American as possible. Their connections with the upper levels of government and the Thai royal family allowed them to ignore many of the constraints typically placed upon businesses in North America or Europe. They clearly had a favorable tax situation and access to a ton of cheap labor and lower-cost facilities. More significantly, they could grow rapidly with a near-complete ignorance of generally accepted privacy standards and data security protocols. They only seemed to care about acquiring users and collecting data.

Or perhaps it was collecting users and acquiring data.

Millions of people were happily moving through their digital lives, allowing all their actions and words to be vacuumed up by the Diddem APIs and run through an enormous stack of poorly designed algorithms just to give each of these users a largely inaccurate and often humorous written summary of what they were doing with their time.

The business had kept growing beyond its first two years, and, as Henny had predicted in that lunch meeting with Jenny, Diddem had gone on to raise several more rounds of investment at increasingly monstrous sums of capital. Everyone associated with the business seemed to have another two hundred million dollars to add to the pot at the drop of a hat.

Speaking of limitless funds, the engineers at Diddem had also re-assigned a healthy partition of their already massive data center network to operate cryptocurrency mining software.

When crypto prices were running hot, Diddem was printing virtual money faster than just about anyone else, thus allowing them to spend ever greater sums on chipsets, processors, and servers. The reward loop was hopping, a veritable rabbit in a hamster wheel, and the company's global network infrastructure was similarly inspired in its promiscuity and continued to birth uncountable numbers of spotless, hairless new data centers.

Harbs had been poignant in his opinion of Diddem. She could still remember their first video call in COVID times. It must have been in earlier 2020 when they got to talking about it. "Look, Henny, this thing is on its own trajectory. They have no regulations on where they operate or how they fund the thing. But it's not necessarily evil, either. You have to look at all this stuff as necessary infrastructure for the future. It's like in the dotcom boom in the late nineties. If we hadn't poured all that money into crazy startup ideas to build out the web, we wouldn't have even ten percent of what it is today. Waves of growth need a ton of collateral damage, almost by definition. For this one, let's just wait and see what happens."

***

Henny thrived when given the task of investigating anything at a municipal or community level. She felt it was closer to what *real people* had to deal with, like the "Parking-Gate" situation she had backed into a few years after her visit to Thailand.

This story began with the case of an elderly gentleman who had managed to win a lawsuit against parking enforcement in the city of Walnut Creek in Northern California. The complainant was able to prove that the administrative authority was systematically designing and rezoning entire swathes of the city, or at least the six feet of land adjacent to most roads, not for the benefit of the residents but for maximizing parking fine revenue.

"You've got to be kidding me, Harbs. Is this Judge Judy or something?"

"It was actually Judge Melnick. But that's besides the point. Don't look at this for what it is at face value, look at it for what it means."

Henrietta learned that in 2014, the city had committed to a twenty-year contract with a private data warehousing and analytics company that equipped the city with a cross-compiled and attractively formatted report of nearly every action within the boundaries of the municipality. The analysis combined inputs from parking revenues along with traffic cameras, police reports, transit activity, and a host of other third party data sources that had been acquired by the private company, including running and cycling trackers, online map-search and directions, retail credit card activity, carshare data, and GPS scooter rentals.

Henny soon discovered that with these reports in hand, city planners had followed the choices of distracted drivers everywhere and gone into autopilot mode, effectively letting those reports make decisions on their behalf. What started as one disgruntled old man with a parking ticket had revealed a lack of oversight in new zoning plans, a disregard for the needs of the community, and a slew of avoidable problems in traffic congestion, accidents, homelessness, and the influx of chain restaurants. None of these societal blights captured anyone's attention, except perhaps those collecting Starbucks Rewards and a handful of repeat offenders who were able to get a few hundred parking fines thrown out. Often, in fact, they were one and the same.

But like any good story, there was a twist. The picture provided by this mish-mash of data wasn't complete enough to answer the ever-changing needs of a city. However, it was more than adequate for a certain subset of the population. Specifically, organized crime, or perhaps better described in this case as a bunch of criminals who organized themselves based on nicely formatted reports that they could extract from the city's IT systems. This small group of enterprising minds had secured their own access to the data feeds and, for the better part of the last three years, had been systemically orchestrating crime throughout the city in such a way that maximized their access to empty homes, high-value commercial routes—even a few fully-loaded bank runs—all while minimizing police presence. They had smartly been conducting themselves with the avoidance of any observable patterns or thresholds of increased activity that might have given themselves away. Unlike city hall, they hadn't been too greedy.

This wannabe episode of Judge Judy now featured a crossover with "Murder, She Wrote," the quintessential television series of the late 1900s. The indefatigable Jessica Fletcher, a crime fighter by way of her typewriter, was played by the equally tireless Angela Lansbury. Henny, the earnest investigative journalist, had similarly become a forensic detective. Her findings ultimately led to the dismantling of organized crime in this small town in the East Bay.

It was exciting. It was also annoying. She had gone into this being asked to do one thing, only to discover everything she had been told was just a thin veil on what was really going on.

"Why?"

Harbs looked at her through the video call. She could tell he was reading her body language and intonation. "Look, we didn't even know this whole criminal underbelly thing was a part of this. But wow, you seriously stepped up! As you might have guessed, the data provider is one of our companies, and we really needed to understand how the contract with the city had started off so poorly. Like, they had everything they needed to create a model community, a place people around the world would look to for inspiration, but it was almost like giving them the power of insights and the speed of computation that we could offer, it almost made them lazier and worse at their jobs. You just happened to take down some organized crime in the process. A tip of the hat to you, Angel."

Oh my god. He's referencing Charlie's Angels.

***

Then there was Flyboys.

Or should it be 'Then there were *Flyboys?'* she thought as she drafted her report. From one set of burgeoning technologies to another, Henrietta had spent time looking into the world of automated flight, specifically in the field of electrified low-altitude aerial surveillance. Flyboys was a business founded out of Hamburg, Germany, in 2017. However, it had quickly established itself with a US Headquarters in Austin, Texas, once the FAA caught a glimpse of what Flyboys was doing.

Or rather, what Flyboys was seeing. The company had developed a mesh network system to control a literal armada of autonomous drones. While similar technology had already entered the common consciousness through the presence of large-scale outdoor events and "airshow" drone displays, Flyboys had taken it to the next level. In fact, where the drones of Intel seemed to be more focused on putting on a spectacle for all to see, Flyboys were far more interested in never being seen at all.

Their system equipped a fleet of drones with a hive mind and the ability to autonomously work together and solve common objectives. Equipped with a multitude of cameras, sensors, and machine learning software, Flyboys drones could take a simple natural language command and turn it into actionable surveillance. In their case, they had chosen to specifically target the snarling, congested, angst-producing problem of traffic, likely a result of their own experiences commuting through poorly planned cities. Austin, driven by the influx of tech companies and especially exaggerated during SXSW, was a notorious example!

[Infer ranked accident potential, 48h, city of San Jose] was a celebrated example prompt demonstrating how the Flyboys system worked.

From those nine words, a fleet of eighteen drones had taken to the sky above San Jose, Costa Rica. In two full days of flight, they were able to comprehend the flow of wheeled humans throughout the entire city of almost 350,000 residents. The Flyboys identified eight locations where they anticipated accidents to be a near certainty, the likelihood of which was calculated by computer vision inference of all the subtleties of movement along those busy streets. Cars, trucks, and motorcycles spoke a language of their own; the nuances of how each of them was speeding up, slowing down, tailgating, or turning would tell nearly a complete story of the habitants inside and their driving intentions. The amount of rust, the color of the exhaust, and the identifiable wiggling rim of a missing lug nut all told a story. It was urban legend that Mattias Wenstrom, the founder, had once boasted to a certain fancifully-dressed privacy consultant named Damian Worsley that they could categorize each driver's daily aggravations and frustrations if they wanted to, possibly even identifying what each had for breakfast.

Mr. Wenstrom hadn't been given the chance to fully expand on his vision for the technology—that of an all-seeing eye that could potentially unearth insights and efficiencies across all of our daily activity—as Mr. Worsley had quickly determined that it sounded like they were creating an all-seeing eye that could potentially seek to influence and control all of our daily activity.

"Not much to see on this one, Harbs, they aren't making progress," Henny had concluded.

"This Worsley guy is proving to be a speedbump, to be ice on the wings," Harbs had commented, noting how the privacy consultant had essentially caused an end to the Flyboys story before it had even begun. They had been in a holding pattern, seeking regulatory approval for any meaningful IRL deployments of the technology, while in parallel, a more significant competitive threat had been solidifying.

Several hundred million unpaid workers of a much simpler incumbent technology had proven too hard to overthrow. Every day, these dutiful servants would rise and forego the need for smarter airborne traffic analysis by simply choosing to dispatch all known information of their movements through precise satellite positioning information. This exacting data was relayed back over internet connections that were continuously activated by a global average of over 130 device interactions per day per worker, delivered as encoded streams of categorically private and sensitive information to the all-knowing machines centrally coordinated in Mountain View, California.

The well-intentioned Flyboys had been grounded by Google Maps.

Twenty-four

UPSIDE DOWN

She could see an older couple walking through the middle of a crowd, searching for something. Their eyes darted left, then right, then ever so slowly looked forward as they made their way through the throngs of people, guided by some instinctual force. The light flickered, flashed, and quickly changed from an incandescent orange to a sea of blue.

Underwater. No, she was in a tube, like a waterslide, but it wasn't. Massive turbines were spinning alongside her path, whisking her forward at blistering speeds, with the water splashing and cooling her as she went. She felt it splash on her face, then drip slowly. She came to the end of this dark, wet tunnel and emerged into the light.

She was flying high above the earth, her body suspended by some invisible force that gifted her an expansive view of everything below. Over a village, then above a farmer's field. Children looked up. She waved and said, "Hi! How are you?" The children were smiling and happy, but they could not see her. Their gaze was vacuous and empty, attuned to the sun and clouds beyond and behind her. She turned to look as well, but the sky was too bright. It flashed in her eyes.

Lights flashed again, and then everything was black.

"Miss, can you hear me?" a voice called out. "Miss, hello. Can you hear me?"

Taught, tired skin allowed her eyes to open just enough to see a flashlight shining upon her. This felt different. This felt real. *What was this? Where am I?* Her face strained against its own bruising as she tried to open her eyes wider.

The paramedic had crawled in through the open hole in the roof of Somaya's Tesla in the same way Bex had done so less than fifteen minutes earlier. He had now placed his flashlight in the center console of the car to free up his hands. The light bounced into the cavity of the console and out again, illuminating the interior of the vehicle.

Somaya looked around a bit more fully. She had no recollection of what had happened. An image flashed of the escalators in the customs hall at the airport, similar to the scenes she had just observed. *Was that a dream? No...*

"Okay, miss. Don't try to move, just stay with us, be patient for a moment," the paramedic said as he signaled something to others outside of the vehicle.

Patience? I know patience. Everything we do requires patience, Somaya thought, taking affront to the comment. *What does he think I'm gonna do, just jump out of this mess? This mess, this crash. How did this happen? The car, autopilot? Was I driving?* She saw a flash of herself in the driver's seat. The car was moving, as was she, but not in the act of driving.

Autopilot had crashed. Not that she was necessarily surprised. She knew that the training data and algorithms in these cars were subpar. It was hardly smarter than "recommended products" from Amazon or "up next" on her favorite streaming services. There was no reason for it to be so stupid, though—no reason at all. As long as the data was structured and consistent like what they had at CVI, and the algorithms were trained, trained again, and challenged through inverse training and adversarial neural networks, autopilot should have been good enough.

Why wasn't it? This was just a drop in the bucket compared to all the smart sensors, camera footage, internet cookies, and algorithms they were wrangling at CVI. She knew it no longer even needed to be structured data, not like it had a decade ago. These systems were self-learning; they could train themselves.

Patience? What they had done at CVI demanded patience. They had painstakingly constructed simulations of entire organizational systems to build training sets that the algorithm could use to improve. Their first target was corporate office parks. Their initial hypothesis was that all those many miles of security surveillance footage from customer facilities could train a system to predict impending security breaches. Though it soon became apparent that the business around security systems was based upon fear and selling peace of mind, whereas any notion of predicting security issues actually seemed to cause more concern and stress for their customers. People didn't want to pay for something that would anticipate bad things!

It was in the course of this work that CVI came to understand that the surveillance footage was not just about security. It was a visual codification of everything happening within the organization. Their systems were reaping a bountiful harvest of patterns and every day was a computer vision feast. Algorithms became incredibly adept at highly complicated analyses, such as assessing worker productivity, stress levels, food consumption, energy utilization, and a number of other performance indicators within their customers' operations.

Somaya had worked tirelessly to find those insights that could be converted into viable business models, which led them to energy. As Hugo Carvalho at ANEER liked to say, "Power creates power," and the shift of CVI to focus on energy sector analytics had been another one of those seismic events in the history of the company. Things took off during COVID, which Somaya attributed to the fortunate circumstance of being able to analyze and work through reams upon reams of consistent data, as the world basically did nothing different for at least two years. The coincidental timing was remarkable, of a world coming to rest just as their computer vision capabilities had advanced to the point of being able to extract value from it. There was so little chaos or noise in their inputs, which allowed their algorithms to improve by leaps and bounds. CVI went from offering customers a service that saved a few bucks on their monthly electric bill to being able to nearly automatically re-architect the entire energy grid for a country in just a few short years.

How had we even been able to do that? she wondered. *And how are these cars not able to make the same kind of leap? These fucking people have satellites flying all around the planet, for god's sake. It's not like it's just a bumper car with a motion sensor.*

Trauma triggers different reactions in everyone. For a hyper-competitive person like Somaya, it had pushed her mind into overdrive. She was still

268

hanging upside down in her smashed-up Tesla, paramedics still unsure of exactly how to extricate her from the damage. Blood was dripping from her forehead, pulled by the forces of gravity toward the passenger seat. Her eyesight was still blurry. Her pants were still hanging open and loose around her legs, and her underwear was still wet from masturbation. None of these things mattered. What she could see as clear as day were all those things she had missed over the past many years, too often looking ahead to the distant vision of CVI to observe what was right before her.

The data was coming from everywhere—every network, every system, every power source. Data was being extracted, insights harvested, and workflows understood. The interrogation of data begets the creation of new insights, which in turn craft new simulation models to better understand what has been captured in the first place. How we drive, what we watch, what we eat, where we go, and when we go there. Every big thing in anyone's day and all the minutiae that make up discrete moments through those days. All of it quantified, captured, interrogated, and acted upon.

It was inconceivable that CVI was the only business or team that had been able to create self-learning systems or decided to create simulation engines that generated more and more reliable data. To say nothing of those monkeys on those typewriters and all those buttons being bashed daily. Every functional aspect of society was quantified and captured, often shared publicly with humorous subtitles.

Somaya could sense she was on the precipice of some kind of epiphany, of achieving a sense of enlightenment to this infinitely interconnected world. But it was confusing as all hell.

And her head was throbbing.

"Miss, okay, we have to get you out of the car now," the paramedic said. They had peeled back the front windshield which had spidered to the point of being nearly completely opaque. The cracks in the glass surface had created a polygonal mesh of shapes, all of them working independently as hinges, allowing the whole to be rolled back like a big piece of carpet. A padded board was inserted through this open space, alongside which the first paramedic had again crawled in, preparing to brace the board and keep it level.

Normally, they would not have rushed to extract someone from a wreck like this, but at the rear of the vehicle, they had noticed first smoke and then flames. Something in the lithium powertrain of the car had become dislodged and damaged through the crash and the rain, and it had caught fire. Currently, it was more like the wick of a candle than a fuse to a bomb, but first responder protocol maintained that in the case of a fire, they needed to urgently remove any passengers.

The paramedic inside the vehicle reached up to the elevated driver's cockpit to take hold of Somaya's legs. With a powerful but careful grip, he slowly and surely lowered her legs out from the recessed footwell of the pedals and down onto the board which was positioned as a perpendicular divider between driver and passenger seats.

As the board took on some of the weight of her body, he pulled Somaya's pants up and straightened her legs out such that her feet just reached through the front window opening. Her rescuer was himself contorted, with one knee under the board providing stability, one leg dragging behind him and still partially outside the vehicle, and he was bent awkwardly at the waist, reaching up to unclip her from the seat belt with his right hand. With his left, he reached around Somaya's midsection, hooking his fingers on her pelvic bone and supporting her weight with his shoulder. For a moment, they were conjoined in a very dark, wet, broken game of Twister.

With a click, the full weight of her torso and head released from the seatbelt, and he guided her hips and back onto the board as his colleagues slowly eased her feet and legs out through the window. Once Somaya's head was secured on the board, they passed the paramedic a neck brace for him to attach, which he did.

As the board was pulled out and her body with it, the warm, unmoving space of the car's interior gave way to the cold, wet, flashing reality of the world.

If it was possible to be born again, this was as close to a rebirth as Somaya could imagine—a baby entering the harsh, cold world. She wanted to cry, not from the pain, but from the profound weight of some greater understanding that had fallen upon her. An overwhelming feeling of helplessness hit her like... an out-of-control vehicle? No, it was too soon for that. But it hit her hard. She couldn't exactly compute the conclusion of her thought processes, but the themes were palpable and intense, assembled from a deeper, subconscious vocabulary.

Jesus, I could have died. I probably should have died. But there's no reason for it.

We have the capabilities to be so much better.

Dysfunction and disharmony are breaking us into pieces.

Our stupidity and hubris don't even let us see it.

And we don't slow down to think about it.

But somehow, somewhere around us, something is consolidating.

As they carried her across the broken grounds of the railyards to an awaiting ambulance, Somaya caught glimpses of several other huddled groups of people in uniforms. There were vehicles everywhere. Lights were shining on pools of water and reflecting off loose piles of metal, short concrete walls, and lamp posts imbued with a purple aura from above. There were covered bodies on the ground amongst those groups of people.

The board with the bruised and beaten woman was loaded into the ambulance, and as her senses adjusted to this new, smaller, drier space, Somaya drifted into unconsciousness.

Twenty-five

MALIBU

Death. It comes to all of us. Some sooner than others.

She had killed that man without a second thought. Life had shown her that death was a foundational part of it, a yin to a yang or a yang to a yin, depending, perhaps, what time of day one chose to think about it. She was not allowed to have one without the other. She had learned firsthand that some people were out there looking to take life, or the essence of life, away from others, and no matter what she did, she couldn't escape it. But she could control it.

She had killed that man because he deserved to die. He had threatened her life, her friends' lives, and who knows how many other people's lives in a future that she had prevented from unfolding.

She had killed that man because he needed to die. He was in traumatic, physical pain. He likely wouldn't have survived the night or the next day. But he might have taken someone else with him. He might have taken her. He might have taken Deemo or Carlo. Or god knows even that bastard Philip J. Clancy, whom she had allowed to scurry back to the idolatry of his stupid bony church, his own muddy, cold, shriveled penis entrenched halfway into his midsection like a cheap, scaled-down, broken knock-off of the decorations on his own vehicle.

As soon as Bex pulled that trigger, she knew she'd be moving on. More accurately, she had already resigned herself to departing from her newfound friends before she pulled the trigger and had done so as a functional "logging off" from that community.

What was morbidly fascinating is that throughout the entire ordeal, she hadn't given any thought to possible legal or judicial ramifications. It was not that Bex felt that she was above the law or immune to it, it was simply that she had never actually seen it work in any positive material sense.

Enough of the rest of the convoy had seen what had happened to foment the legend of the murderous traveling hitchhiker named Dorothy, who had shown up one day and left death, injury, and a wailing entrepreneur in her wake. As it turned out, the first man she had knocked to the ground suffered a serious concussion but had eventually arisen to the interior of an ambulance with his hands held firmly in cuffs. And the other man was taken away in a less restrained, less urgent, and less roomy fashion under the white-sheeted interior of a body bag.

"What will you do?" Deemo had asked as they sat on the edge of the Transformer-van loading bay underneath the same gull-wing door that had dispatched the thief just a short while ago. The situation had improved, from a fight-for-your-life scenario to that of necessary, impending flight.

Carlo was wrapping some gauze and bandages on the side of Bex's face and around her head to cover a large scrape and cut from the thief's boot.

"I have to go. I'll take their truck," she signaled toward the pickup truck that still sat on the other side of the highway. Carlo had retrieved the keys in the aftermath of the early morning events.

Deemo was still in awe of this woman and what she had done. Burning Man was a departure for him from his regular IRL persona. But this was something else entirely. If they were out there pretending to go Beyond Thunderdome, she was actually fucking Mad Max! She was Mel Gibson, just without the car, the dog, and the weird kid with the mullet. Or possibly even Tom Hardy. He wasn't sure which film he liked best.

He had made two promises to her. The first, that he'd do everything he could to keep the police off her trail. Yes, they'd already called it in. Yes, the police would be there soon enough, and they couldn't stop the other thief from talking once he woke up, assuming he would remember anything. But with her intentions to travel south, Deemo would do his best to send the authorities east. The others wouldn't contravene his misdirections— everybody wanted this as far behind them and as far away from Burning

Man as possible. After all, they had a party to get to and, for the most part, hardly knew where they were anyway. They were just following the convoy. The second promise was embodied in a card he had given her with an address.

21037B Pacific Coast Highway, Malibu, CA.

Bex looked down at the card as she stood on the limited shoulder at the side of the road. The high-quality card stock and grainy surface still held salty, muddy fingerprints from her and Deemo's death-defying digits the night she took that man's life.

The pickup truck she had taken hadn't fared much better than its original occupants. It was now at the bottom of an overflowing riverbed in Northern California, where it had been preparing to rust for almost two months. Meanwhile, the Transformer-van had been returned to its long-term climate-controlled storage facility in Salt Lake. Carlo was back on the ranch in Montana, having shed his flamboyant outfits and Mediterranean accent, and Bex had just gotten out of an Uber on the side of the road in the exclusive seafront enclave of Malibu.

Bex likely wouldn't have continued onward to LA, but for the fact that there had been nowhere to hide amongst the vastness of the Northern California landscape. The cities and towns were too small and too much the same, and she was too different. She wasn't even sure why she had kept the card from Deemo. Her first inclination was to get as far away from him as possible, for his sake more than anything else. She was destructive, and he was peaceful. Those two things should not, could not, co-exist. *Should they? Could they?*

The City of Angels offered that possibility. Though if celestial beings were looking out over this massive, sprawling metropolis, their attention was captivated by shiny objects, their glance failing to land with any frequency over the rest of the dusty, smoggy cityscape. On this particular stretch of road, a number of famous homes had remarkably been spared by the inferno of a year earlier. Forensic analysis would later suggest that the steep embankment on the inland side of the road and the shape of the coastline created an inflection in wind currents that prevented sparks and flames from moving seaward. Yet a majority of observers were abundantly confident that it was divine intervention, that the occupants were simply too important to perish.

Knock. Knock. Knock. She was in front of a massive hardwood door bearing a sculpted cast-iron face of a lion in the center of it. After nearly denting her knuckles on the vertical-grain surface, she realized that the lion head also doubled as a heavy door knocker.

Bex reached out to grasp the lion and wrapped her strong, thin fingers around the sculpted fur silhouette of the big cat's jawline. Her fingertips touched under its maw in a way that, in other circumstances, would surely elicit a deep rumbling purr.

Just as she raised her hand to pull the knocker up on its hinge, she was pulled inwards. The door had opened, yanking her hand forward and her body along with it. She stumbled inside the white-walled mansion to which she had been given directions, the same directions that she had relayed to the Uber driver.

"I'm sorry, miss. I can't take you there," came the response as Bex leaned in the passenger window. She had confused the driver, who had been looking for her next booking—a 4.7-rated man named Nelson. If Bex had the app, or even a phone upon which to install the app, and had been first to request the ride, she might have already known the driver's name was Tori, who maintained a sparkling 4.9 rating. Tori had the telltale backlit signs on her dashboard, one projecting its notorious brilliant white lighting, the other casting a purply-pink ambiance across the windshield, a part of the color spectrum that caused a visceral reaction in Bex every time she saw it.

"Look, I have cash. I can pay you cash, how much?" she offered.

"Ma'am, I have three more trips to get my next Quest, and plus, I don't even know how much. I don't even know how far that is! Hell, is it even still standing?" Tori said, taking it as an insult that she would need to look up an address by herself and forsake being told where to go next by the app. To say nothing of a phone-less, cash-carrying stranger asking to go where most addresses marked the burned-out husks of mansions past. *Is she a looter?* The Quests were the biggest point of consternation, however. Any time spent with this scraggly traveler posed a barrier between Tori and her next milestone. She tried to drive ahead to another group of people looking on from the sidewalk, but this unrated, unknown woman refused to remove her head and neck from inside the passenger window.

"$50?" Bex said, leaning further in and placing her forearms on the half-closed window, unsure what point of negotiation would be the right place to start. By now, it seemed that most things in life started at $50 or $100 and went up from there. Had she known that Tori had just driven someone halfway to Culver City for $13, she might have said something different.

Even though the driver, Tori, didn't know exactly where it was, the requested destination seemed familiar enough and, at this time of night, it probably couldn't have been more than twenty minutes away. Her eyes widened, contemplating an injection of cash into her fortunes that would necessitate circumventing the very essence of her white and purply-pink lights and the associated commands and rewards that appeared on her phone. She hesitated to embark on such gross violations of the habits on which she had come to depend. The pause was to her benefit.

"$100?" Bex said, upping the stakes to the next tier of economics.

"Well..." Tori waffled. Nelson 4.7 disappeared from her phone, likely having gotten annoyed and taken a competing purply-pink-light ride.

She relented. "Deal. Get in. What was that address again?" Tori asked, swiping up to dismiss her connection with the Uber master. The Quest countdown clock in its glorious large-format sans serif font disappeared from view as the oracular directions she preferred were replaced with the omnipresent tracking authority known as Google Maps that, sadly, would offer no stars, coins, or gamified self-affirmation.

Tori wondered for a moment if she could somehow add this trip to her driver's log. After all, she was driving someone somewhere. Surely, there was a way she could gain the benefit of reporting this trip back to the same privatized governance that managed all her other movements.

There's gotta be a way to cheat this thing.

***

"Well I'll be damned! Look who it is. Dorothy, my savior from the desert!" exclaimed the tall Black man, wearing a fashionable sports jacket and loose, flowing white pants. He was wearing sunglasses, which must have been very functional at sunset over two hours earlier but had since shifted to provide a different purpose. Where earlier they made the world darker to the man's eyes, now they made the man's eyes darker to the world.

Bex's eyes, meanwhile, were immediately drawn to the wall-to-wall windows on the far side of the main floor that offered an endless view of the moonlit Pacific Ocean.

"Still okay that I came here?" Bex said, a statement as much as a question.

"Of course it is! I just wasn't sure I'd see you again. Hell, I even started asking myself if any of that was real!" he replied.

"That was definitely... intense, insane. I'm so sorry," she said, apologizing for that which she had no real control over.

"Dorothy, my dear, do not apologize. You saved my life, and you probably saved the others, too. That other guy is gonna rot in jail for what he did, and, well, the other guy... He's already rotting, right?" he said, the inappropriate twinkle in his eye giving his sunglasses some practical value.

"How is everyone else, Deemo?" she asked the man, her weathered young face showing concern for the others they had been with and for Carlo especially.

"Well, I don't really know. But first up, there is no Deemo here."

"Uhh, what? I don't..." Bex replied, confused about his statement.

"What I'm saying, my lovely brave ass-kicking white girl, is that Deemo does not live here." He turned and walked into the larger glass-walled room that faced the sea. Although the sun was long gone over the liquid horizon, the moon was nearly full and cast a strong light over the ocean, glinting and glancing off the swells as the dark water kicked up into whitecaps and made its way to the beach. Foam and bubbles were dancing in a choreographed performance of white mist and light blue cavitation expressed by the leaping waves.

"Deemo lives in the desert," he said thoughtfully, rubbing his chin, as he mentally assembled a collection of words into a format that sounded poetic and possibly scripted. The spoken word passage was joined by his right hand tapping his thigh to keep a semblance of rhythm. "Deemo dies in the desert. Deemo is the incarnation of temporal existence, he is the popstar, the hero, the fan, the victim..."

Is he... rapping?

He kept on with his soliloquy, "...the villain, and the savior. People there know Deemo, but they don't know me."

He was demonstrably deep in thought, yet the authenticity that Deemo had shown in the desert had given way to a very strong air of pretentiousness by this well-dressed wealthy man in front of her.

"Okay. Well that's interesting. So who the hell are you then?"

He turned toward her. "Why hello. It's a pleasure to meet you," he said. "My name is Ricky Templeton. And you are?"

"De... umm... Ricky. Alright, that'll take a minute," Bex responded, glad that she knew his actual name and sort of relieved with the separation it created between this moment and the chaos in the desert. Indeed, the memory blocker that was this new individual named Ricky Templeton quickly gave rise to a feeling of peace. She had killed a man with Deemo, but she had not done so with Ricky. Ricky in burned-out Malibu was not Deemo in the Burning Man desert. He wanted separation between those two worlds, and she was more than happy to oblige him and play his game to that end.

"Okay, then Dorothy. Welcome to my humble abode," the abused colloquial expression rolled off his lips. Bex could see that the man of principle she had met in the desert was, in fact, a man of material who lived on the beach. In a very expensive house.

From the open concept room looking out over the expansive Pacific, there were doors and hallways leading off to the side, a wide set of concrete stairs going below to whatever lower parts of the house resided on the natural topography of oceanfront banks leading down to the beach, and an even more impressive floating staircase leading up to several rooms that all seemed to be made of glass. The treads on the upward access were magical in appearance, each nearly four or five feet wide and simply hovering in space with only a minimal attachment to the massive California redwood posts that constituted the eastern wall.

A staircase like that no doubt led up to more impressive bedrooms. It was a far cry from the makeshift bedroom underneath a much smaller set of stairs in the New Jersey suburbs, inhabited by the one and the same Ricky Templeton some ten or fifteen years ago.

But it had all come from there, this origin story of Ricky/Deemo. More specifically, it started with the secretive military trail cam footage and Ricky's determination to dissect and articulate the business opportunity that had landed on his and Doug's lap.

Fortunately for Ricky, he couldn't handle the heat. His laptop always ran far too hot, especially when he was using it from his deformed mattress beneath the unfinished stairs. The airflow was terrible. His room stunk. And so, surrounded by dirty sheets and mildew on the cracked concrete walls, he stared at the descending slabs of unpainted wood above him. In this rare moment of unadulterated concentration, his big idea was born.

People Do Dum. PDD for short, would go on to become one of the biggest independent internet content production entities. It started with Ricky creating his own reincarnations of the wartime footage. *If they can make fake videos like this... just watch me!*

Nobody did. Ricky's first videos were terrible. He had enlisted some of the guys from the basketball team with the promise that they would become movie stars, which, of course, none of them believed, but they went ahead with it anyway. The first series was titled "Trail Wars," a haphazard collection of shaky digibeta footage that resembled a bunch of grown men playing cops and robbers. YouTube viewership rarely exceeded a hundred views for any of his first attempts.

Then the fulcrum shifted, and the entrepreneurial fortunes of Ricky Templeton finally tipped over. There was one particular sequence he had been shooting where the boys ran in single military file through the hiking trails behind Spectra College campus. The intended directorial approach for the "shot" was that as the boys ran in front of the camera, each in their dollar store military outfits, a large supply of explosives would go off from different locations in the foreground. The ordinance, in this case, was a box full of fireworks left over from Independence Day earlier that year.

Brandon led the way, his handsome visage and large stature setting the stage. Then Amare. Next came Jason, with Ricky's shaky handheld field of view dropping several inches to frame the smaller man taking smaller steps behind the two big basketball stars. Felipe ran by, far too close to camera. He ignored all stagecraft and shattered the fourth wall, smiling and waving.

Ricky was annoyed. A production budget of dozens of dollars was at stake. He really needed this shot to work.

Things went awry, unsurprisingly. As the discount rack soldiers ran through the scene in lemming formation, those fireworks went off more or less in unison and more or less as intended. Actually, it was less.

The combustibles exploded in the foreground. Bottle rockets raced to the sky. Those little screamer tubes flared up and screamed. Ricky even had a few fiery volcano incendiaries, little stationary cones placed on the ground that shot a volume of sparks into the air. The coup-de-grace of the experience was to be his artillery of Roman candles, implanted in the forgiving muddy ground. He intended for these burning projectiles to shoot high in the air, allowing his camerawork to follow them for a classic, Disney-esque finishing moment.

Yet, as Brandon and then Amare ran past the launch site, they trod so heavily on the trail as to disrupt the delicate balance of dirt and mud that was keeping everything as it were. The cardboard firing tubes fell over just as the long networked wick burned to its fateful conclusion.

Phizzzh! Phizzzh! Phizzh! The satisfying vacuum-effect sound of Roman candles discharging their payload filled the air. Multi-colored balls of fire filled the trail, their disrupted flight paths ranging between three feet to eight feet off the ground. Jason was hit in the head, a fireball grazing right through the middle of his hair, immediately igniting the extra stiff styling gel that he had used that morning. Felipe had still been looking toward the camera, much to Ricky's chagrin, and as his face came into the near-perfect composition of a close-up, his cheek was hit full-force by an explosion of pink fire.

Last but never least, Zentax had been running at the back of the back, his seven-foot frame intending to command the viewer's attention. That it did, especially after two of the candle shots hit him squarely in the chest. He stopped, startled, and as his hands came up in self-preservation, another fireball raced directly up the sleeve of one arm.

The activity on the trail was far more than Ricky had contemplated as producer, director, and cameraman, not to mention the most consistent repeat viewer of his own channel. He swung the camera back to pick up Jason whacking his flaming head of hair with his hands, trying to extinguish the combination of petrochemical consumer product and jet-black hair that was burning mightily and filling the air with the smell of incinerated human cells.

To Ricky's left was Felipe, down on the ground, holding his cheek, writhing and yelling in pain.

Slightly further back was a performance to behold. The long-sleeved army shirt Zentax was wearing had two charred and blackened holes in it, revealing a combination of white, red, and charred flesh beneath. His hands were flying around wildly, intermittently hitting himself hard against his chest in an attempt to smother the burning embers from those two direct hits, but it soon became obvious more was afoot.

The big man was jumping back and forth, arms waving far more than needed to extinguish the damage from the frontal assault. The fireball that had shot up his sleeve was a passenger inside the confines of his outfit—and a very lively one at that.

On stage right, Amare and Brandon had picked up Jason, bodily, and in a nod to how the Roman candles had been positioned, implanted his burning head directly in the muddiest part of the trail. A slight mushroom of dark smoke erupted as the flames were dismissed. Felipe had rolled over, now seated and unharmed, though very much confused and disheveled. It would be years before he could grow a beard on the left side of his face.

And Zentax's frenetic dance had finally come to an end. He stripped off his shirt and threw it down onto the trail, stomping it into the wet surface and finally putting an end to the pyrotechnics. His chest was marked indelibly with two circular burn marks, and the third fireball had marked a sweeping semi-circle across his midsection. The most-liked future YouTube comment on the video described him as "six-pack smiley face" in honor of his honed abs and fire torso emoji.

As Ricky lowered the camera, he surveyed the scene. All the fireworks were gone. All of the military clothing was dirty and damaged. Nothing had gone to script.

But none of that mattered after they hit two million views in the first two weeks. A re-edit of the piece set to PRA, or Party Rock Anthem as most others called it, became a viral sensation. The second most-liked future comment, "People do dum," was Ricky's own, from which a brand was born.

Ricky Templeton became a charter member of one of the first cohorts of YouTube multi-millionaires. After the success of that video, he gave up on trying to produce anything scripted or thoughtful. He just needed to set the stage for happy accidents to occur. This led to the creation of a studio, first in a warehouse district not too far from the college campus, which quickly expanded to include a sound stage in Los Angeles. He went on to establish multiple YouTube, Mixality, and TikTok houses, hiring, feeding, and housing dozens of up-and-coming creators to produce their own content on their own schedule, provided that PDD was the publisher.

Zentax shot to fame and went on to become a lead participant/victim in hundreds of other content pieces produced by Ricky and PDD. With all this success, Ricky became burdened with self-doubt and a lack of appreciation, possibly even a dislike or hatred, for being known as the "dumb video guy."

Even he might admit, if he invested in the requisite self-reflection, that his annual role play as Deemo the thoughtful desert-dweller with communist leanings was more to fulfill his unsatiated need to perform, to be seen as someone better than who he was publicly defined as, than it was to change the world.

***

"Wait, did you say Ricky Templeton? Like, *the* Ricky Templeton, the guy behind all those videos?" Bex asked. It had taken her a moment to register that name. It had been so many years and under different circumstances, but much of Ricky's silly, stupid content had pervaded chat groups and discussion threads within the digital existence she had left behind in the rubble of the Young Gainers.

That recollection triggered a small shudder and caused her to gasp for breath. She quickly recovered. Ricky had nothing to do with any of it. In fact, he was probably one of the most benign success stories to come from the internet. "People Do Dum, right?"

"That is definitely me, and I definitely operated behind those videos. Think of me as the executive producer. The mastermind. The puppet master. All that content from up here," he said, tapping the side of his head.

"But the whole Deemo thing, I mean, what's that all about? You obviously have millions of dollars," she gestured around the house. "Was any of that real?"

Bex was beginning to doubt her choice to come here. She had believed in the authenticity of how Deemo had spoken in their day in the desert, even with the contradiction between his socialist diatribes and his heavily customized part-time desert super-vehicle.

"Deemo is as real as you and I. Deemo is a necessary part of me, Dorothy. Without him, I couldn't do any of this, and if I didn't do *all* this, he couldn't exist. Deemo's there because he knows we've got a system based on inequality and empty motivations. He knows we've got everyone in a Pavlovian experiment, doing the next thing and the next thing, and no one knows why. He knows that for every one thing someone does, there's ten haters looking at it and bringing you down for doing it. And those ten haters get a hundred views each. He knows it's breaking our society down piece by piece. Hell, he knows this whole thing, this whole internet thing, is just one big factory. It's wires and computers, and switches, and inside those things, we are all just little virtual people running around trying to take what we want from someone else. You know what I mean? That's... *why Deemo*. It's just how it is, I guess."

Ricky came across as immediately defensive but also very thoughtful in his response—possibly too thoughtful, with this cascade of concepts and ideas all slamming together in a collision of philosophical rumination on the technological underpinnings of society.

"And really, I just need to chill the fuck out, and that's my thing. That's why," he concluded with a more pragmatic, down-to-earth answer. "So now, my question is, why Dorothy? Who is Dorothy?"

Bex appreciated the question. He hadn't jumped the train of thought and challenged her to reveal anything about herself. He was merely giving her a stage to describe who she would be if given the chance in a completely unshackled environment like Burning Man or even here at 21037B Pacific Coast Highway.

She channeled her inner Deemo for a moment. "Okay, I see where you're going. Dorothy isn't here. She wasn't even in the desert with you. But she's been to hell and back, Dee... Ricky. Dorothy doesn't want anything, doesn't need anything, and she most definitely doesn't have anything." As she spoke, it became evident some deeper truths were seeping out. "Dorothy just keeps moving, there's always something else to move to... so there's never any good reason to stay behind, right?"

Unexpectedly, tears had started to well up in her eyes. She took a breath. "You know what? Dorothy is a fucking mess. She's been ruined by all this shit, all this stuff you've been making, this internet bullshit." She waved her hands in the air to indicate the pervasive, invisible threat. "It's everywhere, and it kills people." Thoughts of her father and some of the other Young Gainers who had taken their own lives flooded into her mind.

Ricky walked over to her and held her arm at the elbow. "Come out here, sit down." He led her through an open set of sliding glass doors onto a wrap-around deck just outside the floor-to-ceiling windows.

As she sat on the edge of a lounge chair, Ricky walked to the patio railing and placed both hands upon it, gazing out over the ocean for a moment. He started talking, "What I saw you do in the desert was unreal.

I mean, you saved my life. You saved the lives of probably who knows how many of those others. You think they can fight for themselves? Hell, no. Whatever you had, that you have, wherever that came from... Don't be afraid of it. You know those fuckers in the desert?" He looked back at her.

She looked up at him. The tears that had welled up had left a glazed meniscus on her eyes which now reflected the moon and stars, just as the big ocean beyond had done so.

"Those fuckers needed to die. Those are the guys—and girls—that are bringing down society. They go around and take, and break, and divide, and no one's stopping it anywhere. Not IRL, not online, nowhere," he said, his voice changing. He was no longer philosophical Deemo nor the famously unassuming Ricky from PDD. He was something else. And as he said these words, they resonated with Bex and with her own life experiences.

Ricky continued, "So here's what we're doing and why I'm so glad you came here. This is way beyond people doing dumb shit on video. What I want to tell you about is... well, it's how we get it all back." He was obviously struggling for the right words. "This is how you get YOU back..."

She said nothing. He paused.

"Bex."

What? I didn't say my name.

"What was that? What did you say?" she asked, refusing to believe what she heard.

"Bex. It's okay. Why do you think I was so open with my own self? I mean, shit, you saved my life, right? And then you left. How could I not put in the work to figure out who you are?" he could read the shock, surprise, and dismay on her face as he spoke. "... or maybe, who you were."

"Jesus." Bex was glad she was sitting. What did this mean? What did he know? What *didn't* he know? Her instincts would normally be to get up and run, but where to? If this was the end of the road, maybe she needed to stay here long enough to figure out what the destination holds. "How? How did you do this? How do you know?"

"Look, first of all, just don't worry about anything. Nothing is happening to you here. This is a safe place," he said, gesturing up and down the strip of beach at the exclusive row of fortitudinous mansions that had survived the fires. "Actually, I own the two that way and once a bit further down the other way, it's basically all safe." Ricky had set up two of his longest-running content production houses on the PCH, right here in Malibu, to give his creators the most inspiring place to work.

He started to explain. "I mean, you know firsthand that the van had some computer vision and security stuff running, right? Well after you left, I got a facial rec run on you from what we captured in the van. I mean, Jesus, it led me to you, at least you of like seven or eight years ago, and then you pretty much disappeared. So I wasn't totally sure. Hell, I wasn't even totally sure up until now, until I saw you here, even though we did get a partial hit from a border crossing last year as well. Looks like it fits, seeing as you're Canadian, and like I said in the van, you're a long way from home, Dorothy."

Bex wasn't surprised that the technology could do what Ricky said it could do, but she was surprised that she had been a subject that anyone could care enough about to do it. "But why? I don't... understand... I don't..." she pushed for more, even though she was somewhat at a loss for what she felt she needed to know.

"Oh, and it's not easy, right, to do any of this. And that's part of what I'm talking about. Like, that work to track you down is hard, and there are so many people involved. At every corner of the network, just making sure shit gets to the right place and the right information is fed to the right system, and so on. The gates and the checks and the balances, it's all run by the wrong people, by some bad motherfuckers. And we all stand around, or sit around, or fucking scroll around, and think that, 'Oh, technology will keep getting better and it will solve all our problems.' Do you know how fucked up that is? Dorothy... Bex, it's beyond fucked. We're all trapped in our little space on the corner of the web, or whatever they want to call it, and think we're doing our part for some greater future. I mean, shit, most people don't even know how manual the internet is. They think the shit that shows up on their phone is because it's the best thing for them, or they found the right thing, or they are doing the right thing. It's fucking absurd. They are getting fed like a baby what someone else wants them to see and then doing what someone else wants them to do. For money, for all this, all this shit around you," he paused, took a breath, and again beckoned to all the material things in his beautiful house in his upscale, protected oceanside enclave.

"Yeah, all my shit came from that, but I mean... My shit is at least just stupid, right? I know it's more than that, and it feeds this fucking loop that's going on. But I didn't mean to do any of that, and I'm doing what I can to keep the PDD stuff simple and stupid. For fuck's sake, that's why *it* was so successful, *it* was simple and stupid. And so was I, and so was everyone. So now, I figure we're at a point where the world is all beat up, people have their hate dialed up to 11, and shit just doesn't work. The bad guys always win, and the good people have lost their way. And if we are waiting for tech to fix anything, then we might as well be waiting for Superman, and in the meantime, all of this is getting worse and worse and worse again," he said. The more he spoke, the more he seemed to want to speak.

"I mean, yeah, I saw it. I lived it, Ricky. I'm still living it," Bex said, tears again building up as the weight of more than a decade of devastation in her life pushed firmly on her shoulders.

"God, what they did to you was fucking horrible." Ricky had seen some of the doctored images from the Mixality Photos crimes. Now that he was again with Dorothy, with Bex, he wished he had never seen them. "And that's why I'm doing this next thing."

"What are you doing? What is it?"

"Alright, Bex, here it is. What we are doing is taking the hatred that all these fucking people have, and we're redirecting it. Stay with me on this 'cuz it sounds pretty fucking insane, but it makes sense. In the big picture, it makes sense. Alright, the same way we're able to find you, the same way we can run trademark and copyright searches on any video or music, the same way fucking Facebook just spoonfeeds the hate people want to see in the world, we can use all those same tools—and people, it's a hell of a lot of people—to track down these motherfuckers. We can see what they've done, we can figure out what they're gonna do next. But you know what? We aren't busting them. We aren't taking them out."

"Go on. So why track them down?"

"It's a shit ton of work, but we've got teams of content checkers, reviewers, data people, we've got 'em overseas, and we can basically find all the nastiest motherfuckers around, all those guys and girls, who are gonna put themselves out on platforms and fuel hate and break people and kill people. We are gonna take those people and give them what they want."

"I don't follow. What, you're building like some fucked up social network for assholes? For pervs?" she asked.

"No, no, no. Fuck the social network. We find them, and we pay them, and we let them fight it out with each other. In real life—no platform. Well, alright, we have the platform to watch it, to share it. To show them going down and to show how fucking terrible they are. This is what I'm working on, Bex. We call it *The Conflux*," he said with the support of big air quotes, as he managed to bridge his rant about the end of the world with a summary of what sounded a lot like a game show.

"Like *American Gladiators*?"

"No, more like *Running Man*. Or *Hunger Games*. Or *Squid Game*, except real. We're going all in."

It was all too surreal for Bex. She had only known this man for two days as two different people. He who had been preaching love and togetherness in the desert stood before her describing some sort of futuristic hellscape gladiatorial challenge.

"And I want you to be in there too. I saw what you did out there when you saved me. The way you acted. So decisive, in control. You were like... the Goddess of Justice, and that's what we need more of. And I know you need it too, Bex. This is your ticket out."

Bex looked at Ricky with a slack-jawed expression. She had tried to follow all the moving pieces as he explained them, but it was just too much. She didn't know what to think about any of it.

"For god's sake. Here I am, ranting about this whole project and piling all that shit right on you, and you just showed up at my house. Let me get you settled in. We can pick this up tomorrow."

He showed Bex to a guest room situated on the next level up. The room was massive, with a California king-sized bed and another sweeping view of the ocean, albeit looking just a little further out to the horizon from its elevated position in the house. She had her own ensuite bathroom with a massive rainstorm showerhead. It was by far the most luxurious place Bex had ever been.

Ricky had also directed her to the kitchen, where there was an almost endless supply of fresh food, with a few premade meals in the fridge. Everything was taken care of. In the morning, a person was there to help with laundry and prepare breakfast for her. New, brand-name clothes were laid out for her, with several different options for any activity. The dichotomy of this newfound temporary life with the one she had known only served to reinforce how fragile it all was. Her time here with Ricky was another stop on the road, which again forced the question of where it all led to.

The signs of what Ricky had been talking about were evident and pervasive. Throughout the house, there were awards, framed news articles, and of course, screens. There were screens everywhere, and content was playing non-stop. As much as Ricky had talked about being committed to solving the problems of humanity, it was blatantly apparent that he was another cog in the gears of the great big social divisiveness content machine. He was only one or two degrees removed from the decidedly more evil operators at Mixality, those who had been facilitators of Bex's family's downfall. Whether he really understood that wasn't clear, as his position on this new project seemed very authentic.

Do I even understand that? How do I take comfort here, a place built on that? And if this is the only place offering safety, what am I actually running from? Where am I running to?

Questions still outnumbered answers. Every person, every organization, damn near every entity on the planet was subject to the outreaching tendrils and nodes of the overbearing network that seemed to control it all. Whether by commission or omission, known or unknown, nearly eight billion people had submitted themselves to it, and the feelings of helplessness and inevitability were getting more pronounced with every passing day.

These circular debates traveled the inside perimeter of Bex's consciousness for that day, and the next, and several more after that. Ricky was around most days, though constantly in and out of the house. The incongruence between what was happening to the world overall and what was happening to Bex in this gluttonous escapist hideaway was massive. With every relaxing sunset taken in on the glorious deck, every restful, comfortable sleep in that big bed, and every made-to-order breakfast from the beautifully appointed kitchen, the internal arguments turned to conversations and, finally, to conclusions.

Ricky came home to an empty house. He looked downstairs. The bedrooms, gym, and media room on that level were empty. He went upstairs, taking those grand floating treads two at a time. Bex's bed was made, and she was nowhere to be seen. He ran out to the very upper deck, a cantilevered extension off his penthouse room with Plexiglas flooring and thin wire railings. It was raining. The weather was shifting again. He scanned first out to sea and then up the grim, misty coastline—nothing. Looking the other way, no one could be seen.

Jesus, into the sea? Did she...

Footsteps in the sand, just above the wash from the surf, heading east. The tide was coming in, and he could only see the freshly placed tracks for the hundred feet or so directly below the house.

"Ricky?"

He turned, first his head and then his feet. If he had been of sharper vision, he would have realized that those footsteps in the sand were coming from the water and toward the house rather than the darker conclusion he had arrived at.

"Bex, oh my god. Oh wow," after the shock of seeing her wore off, he could marvel at the woman now standing before him. "Oh... wow."

She was at the top of the stairs, carrying a towel and wearing a bikini that had been laid out for her by Ricky's housekeeper, a ribbed halter top orange and blue set that looked as if it was made to be wrapped on her body. Her arms and legs were sinewy yet defined with muscle. Through all the hardship and the many months and years of her marginal existence, as she had formed a mental and psychological barrier to things that would break just about anybody else, her body had developed a defensive resiliency that was beyond impressive, with a physique to match.

"That thing you were talking about," she said.

"Yes?" Ricky replied with some unsure anticipation.

"It pays, right? Like, a lot?" she asked.

"Yep. We can get into..." he started before being cut off.

"I'm in. Whatever the fuck it is, I'm in."

He beamed. One minute, he thought she had run away or, even worse, taken her life at sea. And now, he had his star.

"One condition though," she added.

"Name it."

"I'm not Bex. I'm not even Dorothy," she said, disavowing both of her more recent aliases. She sure as hell did not intend to be Somaya, either, but she didn't see any reason to say that.

"Okay, then, who are you?" Ricky asked.

"This one's all on you, Ricky. You fucking made this, and you're gonna make everything else disappear, and I'll do whatever this thing is," she paused. "From now on, you can call me Toto."

Twenty-six

NEWU

- <u>Life, End-of-Life, and the Perpetual Afterlife</u>

That was the subject line atop the email from Harbs. Often enough, the missions she was tasked with had dark or morbid overtones, and this promised to deliver the same. Harbs went on to describe a holding company, NewU, in the midst of a consolidation of funeral homes across North America.

Ostensibly, her time spent with NewU was to support their PR mission, a press-washing of the "roll-up" story. The representatives from the company were being very deliberate and careful not to be seen as a threat to the existence of the mom-and-pop shop funeral home industry, instead preferring the narrative that they were giving these small operators a chance to retire comfortably while ensuring their business could continue on. Henny couldn't necessarily argue with that logic. Certainly, it was more appealing than working until they were in need of their own service. It wasn't exactly the thriving, bustling type of business that others were lining up at the door waiting to acquire. In fact, most of the people lined up for the business were not thriving at all.

Henny had been asked to shine a light on how NewU's technology enabled a different experience when things went dark at the ends of our lives. Rounding out the usual triumvirate of editorial influences was the covert presence of Harbs' ulterior objectives and the ever-curious mind of our heroine, who was poking around the edges to try to uncover some dirt.

She would soon learn that digging around in the dirt of a funeral home business is sure to reveal some skeletons.

NewU offered the "NewU Generator," a combination of hardware and software that they claimed could create a perfect digital likeness of anyone. They were advertising their offering to the living and the recently deceased, with the implications of both being objectively creepy. The basic premise was that they would scan a customer in 4D. The fourth dimension, of course, being time, with the other three dimensions captured by over one hundred and twenty cameras.

For the scanning procedure to get complete coverage of the subject's body, they were commanded through a regimen of poses, best described as a combination of gymnastics, dance, and perhaps aircraft semaphore signaling patterns.

Also, small print alert: the customer had to be completely naked. This was a stipulation in the service offered by NewU, as previous trial and error had proven that people simply had too many soft parts, strange parts, and hard parts that you would never have expected to be where they are until you see them without the veil of clothing.

In the interest of understanding the process to its fullest extent, Henny committed to going through the NewU Generator to have her "NewU" created. This is how she found herself standing stark naked in the middle of a small, dark but centrally lit studio room, waving her arms around and bending forwards, backwards, sideways, and sideways again. She hung from a bar overhead. She jumped up and down onto different levels of a small obstacle course, sort of a mini parkour course with professionally voyeuristic strangers watching from behind bright lights. It took less than ten minutes to go through this gauntlet of poses, but it seemed far longer.

"Cut!" called a voice from behind the bright lights. "That's a wrap!"

It was confusing language to Henny, for them to treat this like a film set. It didn't seem as fitting when collecting footage that totalled over twenty hours of complete nudity. Although it was only ten minutes in the volumetric scan session, she was quick to note how much actual content that equated to across all those many cameras poking in and around every nook, cranny, and crevice of her body.

The director, a man in his late twenties or early thirties, brought her a white terry cloth robe and asked, "Would you like to see what we got?"

"I probably should!" Henny said, quickly feeling protective over whatever they now had stored on their hard drives, and rightly so.

The director led her to a computer workstation staffed by another young man. He pulled up a software application that revealed dozens of thumbnails, each providing a small window into a different view of Henny's naked body. As he moved his mouse pointer across the screen, any thumbnail that it hovered over top of would quickly spring to life, showing the full range of content captured from those many intimate perspectives.

"So that's the raw footage," said the director, pointing at the screen. Henny's eyebrows arched up at the sound of the word "raw."

"You can see where we've been able to get all of you," he said.

"Yep, you sure have!" Henny agreed with a nervous chuckle.

The man continued, "And where we've missed out on a bit." He pointed to one video in the long list, and as he did so, his technician opened the file. "Look here, in this pose, your left arm is covering much of your left breast, and your right breast is occluding your armpit."

"Well, yeah, I guess you're a few pixels short then," she offered in response while subconsciously pulling the robe a bit tighter.

"Ha, yes, of course. But what we need to achieve is a perfect mesh. An uninterrupted 3D shape of your body."

She couldn't help but feel a bit flushed with equal parts nervousness and confidence, with her nakedness still very present under the rough veneer of that white robe and this smart young man speaking of it as a pursuit of perfection.

"So look at this," he said as he took command of the mouse and keyboard. With a few commands hammered into a programming window, he bashed the "Enter" key with an exclamative effect. Another window popped up, covering most of the exposing thumbnails for a moment.

She took a short, quick breath.

And then, she was revealed.

There she was, walking along a small trail in a brilliantly lit wooded area. Sunlight shone down through the canopy, illuminating the nature around her with brilliant white, yellow, and green hues. A slight mist hung in the air as butterflies fluttered about in the foreground, and a bird flew more distantly overhead.

She knew it wasn't entirely *her*, but it was most definitely, *entirely* her. Still naked, the skin on this moving form had taken on some of the ethereal lighting qualities coming down from the skies above in this magical place. She looked youthful, refreshed, and exceptionally beautiful.

The director hit another button. A slight and semi-translucent white gown appeared, obscuring all the bits and pieces that she would want to be private. It was a single piece of material, yet it added multiple layers of elegance and style. She was completely transfixed by this scene.

"How... what... this is amazing!" Henny said, admiring this work. The ten minutes of twenty hours of posing was now in the distant past. Whatever these people had done, she was thankful for it. Her body and mind were convinced that both had just been given a supernatural dose of vitality.

"I'm glad you like it," the director said with a gleaming smile and obvious pride in his work. "You make a great subject. Now look at these."

He again keyed in different commands faster than she could infer what exactly he was typing. Within seconds, multiple other clips had appeared. Here she was, swimming through the bluest, most tranquil sea she had ever seen. Alongside her, perhaps over twenty feet below the surface, several dolphins appeared. Together, they swam playfully through a forest of gorgeous flowing kelp and brilliantly colored coral reefs.

In another scene, she was taking the last breaths and the very last available steps at the top of a mountain, presumably arriving at the summit of Mt. Everest. Next, she was running in an Olympic sprint final, surging across the finish line in first place. From there, she was flying above the earth through an endless sky of soft, fluffy clouds. She might have expected to see a collection of My Little Ponies or perhaps Morgan Freeman, or even that handsome guy from the popular afterlife series who seems to be in everything these days. *What was his name again?* Sadly, none of these cameos appeared, but the mere thought reinforced a growing sense of calm and fulfillment.

Finally, in the last scene, we could see Henny's body, elegant and beautiful as ever, but lifeless and lying in a coffin outside of an obviously branded NewU funeral home. It was autumn, the skies were clear, and red and orange leaves were everywhere on the ground. As the cinematic treatment came to a close, the perspective hovered and lowered down closer to her lifeless face.

It inched ever closer as the corners of her mouth tilted upwards and her eyes opened, revealing the most pleasurable, relaxing smile the real Henny had ever seen. She couldn't remember ever seeing herself smile that way in the mirror, nor in a photo, but it was absolutely a smile of her own.

"Okay, well, that was bloody impressive," she said.

Henny soon learned that the digital likeness, the "NewU," of each of their customers was built upon a very broad set of data. Apparently, they had developed this service to accommodate just about any type of data that might be associated with the individual in question. To start with, and as she had seen first-hand, they had the 4D capture data from the studio session. It became clear that the service benefited greatly by engaging customers in the prehumous state, though they would still go through the studio session with their prone and silent customer base. It was a more difficult studio session requiring the director and his team to prop dead customers up with a titanium exoskeleton rig that allowed the body to be machine-led through a smaller subset of poses in the capture process.

"That is fucking dark, Harbs," she said as they spoke on the phone on her way to the airport, having left NewU's headquarters and showcase center in Boulder, Colorado, a short time before.

"I know, I know. It's pretty intense, isn't it?" he agreed.

"And I guess they inject some kind of liquefied nanotech into the body that creates a certain amount of rigidity and re-energizes the fascia, which gives them a more realistic 4D scan from the corpses. Like, that is crazy. In a way, it's cool, but it's also totally nuts," she explained a bit more of what she had learned.

"Oh, absolutely. But Henrietta, you have to remember, people have been chopping themselves up for cryogenics for forty or fifty years, and humans have been doing brain surgeries of various kinds for thousands of years now. *We* have always been enamored with what's going on inside that gray matter in the pursuit of eternal life, and now they're just extending it out to the rest of the fleshy stuff," he said matter-of-factly. His emphasis on the word "we" carried just enough condescension that Henny could tell he was speaking of the flawed curiosity of the collective human race.

"Yes, understood. Now, what I also found out is they are assembling a huge data store around every known individual and then doing a ton of inference and modeling, en masse. Like, for those scans, they are using the scans of everyone in their database to more accurately determine how my body moves in certain ways—how I walk, or run, or jump, or how my boobs jiggle. And even more than that, they have access to cause of death and medical history information and they're doing the same sort of thing from a causation/correlation/prediction standpoint. I'm not the right person to comment on it, but it seems like there are a ton of privacy issues in there," she said, highlighting some of her concerns.

"Yes, we've spoken with their legal counsel on some of this already. I didn't want to send you in to try and assess the legal right and wrong. What I can say is our lawyers have reviewed everything, and it seems they aren't really doing anything different than funeral homes have done forever, at least from a data capture and privacy standpoint as it relates to dead bodies. They are probably more secure by storing everything in encrypted formats, as opposed to a box of files in the closet like it is in so many of these old shops. And all the inference work they are conducting is on anonymized datasets, so there aren't any direct privacy implications," Harbs said.

"So what am I writing for here? Another puff piece on getting your avatar made? It's interesting, but I'm not sure it says anything that people haven't already seen in 2024. Happy to get it out there, I mean, it was sort of fun going through the process other than that freaking studio had some really cold air blowing through it," Henny said.

"Well, it's cold to keep the equipment cool. That is something they are going to need to deal with for older users, I think," Harbs said, somewhat distracted from the core of the discussion.

"I can confirm for you, it kept my equipment cool!" Henny interjected.

Harbs didn't even pause to consider the joke. "But yeah, sort of the same MO as usual, if you can publish that as a nice press piece, EMC can spit that out across the network and get all the derivative content started. But a big piece of this is that the Board is looking to take a controlling position on NewU, so we sort of need a more complete analysis than usual, more like what you did with the parking thing in the East Bay."

"I need more than that, Harbs. We've been doing these same kinds of things for years now. I find it hard to believe that I need to go and do some freezing nude photoshoot to help your executives figure out what deal to do next. What exactly am I doing all this for?" Henny demanded.

Harbs could tell she was on the verge of taking a strong stance on this. Henrietta had been dutifully working for him and the Board for over a decade and rarely would she complain, but he recently noted she had been demanding more context, more explanation.

"Alright, so with NewU, you've seen their perpetual life thing, right? I mean, that's a massive thing in and of itself. But you know what they are doing and how they plan to get there? Like, do you really understand what they are doing?" he asked.

"Sure, I mean, like you, or I, or whoever, can leave a version of ourselves behind when all this is over, right? Like, it's a massively enhanced version of the Mixality or MXP stuff that Jenny and those guys had a few years back before all that shitstorm about it before the pandemic. And, I guess, the NewU people take care of the whole death part for you as well, right?" Henny said as she shared her high-level analysis of the situation.

"You hit on a few things there, but there's way more to it," Harbs said. "What do you think they're doing with the cause of death data? And the medical history data?"

"I don't know, I assumed it's just for your records, that sort of thing," she replied.

"My records? No, I don't have anything to do with that, not yet anyway."

"Not yours, like, you. Yours, like, someone's or anyone's. The customer's," she clarified.

"Oh right. Okay, so do you know 23xyz?" he asked.

"The DNA Company? Yeah, sort of, haven't looked too closely at it. I know they had an early run, but then people sort of didn't believe some of the disease predictions and that sort of thing," she answered, remembering that some of the regular EMC staff blurbists had been covering it.

"So what we really have here is a combination of physiology, medicine, and technology. These guys at NewU, they use all these things, plus what they can scrub from the social graph, to create you, perpetually. And what they get from that is a dataset of millions of people, how everyone was made, how they lived, and how they died. And more to the point, they can more or less predict exactly when you will be in need of their services," he said.

"Yeah, the avatar. I already went through that part," she reminded him, then caught her breath. "Wait a minute, what did you mean by 'they know when you will be in need'? Are you saying...?" she started to say with the rising inflection of a question she wasn't sure should be asked.

"Yes," he said in a hushed tone. "They have modeled life expectancy and cause of death across so many datasets, but at an insanely accurate level. You're probably the only one that's been in that studio that isn't a candidate for imminent demise."

"Jesus Harbs, nice use of words. But that is some seriously insane shit you're telling me. I mean, why is this not more publicly known? If they are able to do that, why would we not be treating all those people... or at least putting the same kind of tech toward understanding treatments? I mean, c'mon, there is so much here that needs to be looked at."

"Yes, you're starting to get to the heart of it, for sure. The work is so controversial, all these issues can't even be properly understood at the moment. Which is why we think it's important on many levels to be in control of this, rather than just observe it, at risk of it going in the wrong direction, off the rails, so to speak."

"I don't know how you can take such an academic tone on this stuff. Also, you don't have to say 'so to speak,' for fuck's sake, Harbs," Henny said in somewhat of an attempt simply to say something, anything, that would give her pause to think about what he was sharing with her. "So are you saying NewU is running around calling on people that they know are going to die and basically bringing them in for nudist camp photo day?"

"Oh, it's not that straightforward. Right now, they've avoided doing or saying anything that would indicate that their predictive models work, or work that well. We believe they are using it to run some pretty sophisticated marketing and targeting those individuals or those neighborhoods of individuals that score highest on their models, but not saying it outright. We've run the numbers based on what we can see, and that's the only thing that makes sense, as the death rate of their subscribers within six months of signing up is beyond what could be marked down to coincidence or more general targeting. Unless, of course, they are running around murdering their customers, which would be another matter entirely," he said.

"Yeah, okay, I understand. So how is this fixed by you and your cronies getting involved? Well, what exactly is the fix?"

"Look, the real risk here is that the good part of this innovation gets shut down. Their use of predictive modeling on the data is unlike anything anyone has seen, and the privacy issues are honestly all over the place. If this surfaces too quickly, it's gonna scare the hell out of a lot of people, but what that more than likely means is this stuff gets squashed by regulators. The NewU guys are doing a good job in sort of masking what they are doing as avatar creation and the "perpetual you," but at some point, their need for an increased valuation or commercialization of their efforts is going to shine a light on all that other stuff."

"So you're saying MCA, or whichever fund you're working for on this, swoops in, buys them up, and lets this tech fester in the labs for a while until you know what to do with it or maybe how to introduce it in a positive way?" she asked.

"More or less, that's how we see it," Harbs confirmed.

"But surely this is one motherfucker of a deal, like the biggest deal in history, in terms of dollars. How can MCA just buy it and sit on it? And for that matter, why do you think those guys will be interested in selling it?"

"Much of this is gonna come down to what you can find and how we can architect the deal. Right now, we see that their true unrealized value, the thing that is most expensive, is the stuff they can't even talk about at risk of being shut down. We know they haven't even shared much of this with some of their closest shareholders. So, if we're going to strike, we strike now while they have a value based more on death retail and an avatar machine."

"Death retail, nice. But yeah, okay, I get it. So you buy them as cheap as you can right now and then sit on the tech while you figure out the 'good move' for it? That assumes that I believe you. That you and your boys in the ivory tower are thinking about everyone's well-being on this one," Henny said. She knew she could push Harbs, and push him hard. She'd earned that right.

"I know I ask a lot, Henny, and I know you trust me, as I do you. The thing about this one is timing. Right now, NewU is trying to accelerate their consolidation play of buying up all these retail funeral homes and doing that in a way that doesn't bring a lot of attention. That's where you come in. You help them get the avatar story out. It sounds like a nice but familiar technology play, and then we come in with a deal that puts a price tag on them being exactly that rather than having to overpay for their deep tech. Get it?" he said.

"Well, yeah, I follow your fucking corrupt reasoning if that's what you're asking. I'm not sure I agree with it, but seeing as I've trained myself to just follow your every command, this is where I say 'sir, yes, sir,' right?" Henny said jokingly in a subtle attempt to belittle Harbs.

"Thanks Henrietta. I knew you'd understand."

They had been speaking for the better part of an hour now. Henny's Uber was crossing the last stretch of high plains before arriving at Denver International Airport. She had been here several times over the years, and the near-endless sightlines given by the landscape around the airport never ceased to amaze her. She had also learned the hard way that, at least in Denver, the further you could see was counteracted by an inability to go as far as you thought you could. On her very first visit several years ago, she woke up early one day to go for a run without properly contemplating the effects of altitude. Her breathlessness on that cold, brisk morning run was something she'd never forget and had helped forge a healthy respect for her limits.

The car turned into the airport complex. Two aircraft were overhead and remarkably close to one another. One was an Air China flight on its ascent, the other was a Westjet plane, coming in for landing and appeared to be hovering in the sky—almost unmoving—due to the parallaxing effect of her perspective and the infinite landscape beyond.

She could relate to that plane, often feeling stuck in her own infinitely layered horizon of open questions, never-ending curiosity, and unfinished stories. Always coming and going but never deciding for herself exactly what the destination was or what she was carrying with her. She realized her thoughts had shifted to the drudgery of endless travel rather than the philosophical musing of living as a subservient aircraft floating listlessly in the sky, but there was truth in both planes of consciousness.

Henny conducted herself through check-in and security in her usual flawless manner, found a secluded seat in the executive lounge to connect with her trusty VPN connection, and began authoring her support of the grand "Death Retail" strategy of Harbs and MCA. Working title, of course.

Twenty-seven

LIMITED ADDITION

The invisible hand has been guiding millions of humans for hundreds of years. A concept first introduced by the capitalist economist Adam Smith in his 1776 treatise The Wealth of Nations, the invisible hand most often reveals itself to those who subscribe to free market ideologies. The basic premise is that in a true market-based society, the self-interest of the individual, if allowed to develop and foster itself without subjective intervention, will contribute to the greater good. The breadmaker will make bread to feed himself and his family and keep making it as long as others require it and are willing to pay for it. The lumberjack will continue to harvest materials for construction as long as the builder keeps building and needs to buy them and as long as there is bread, or fish, or vegetables that the lumberjack can spend her money on. And so on.

Metaphorical concepts like this can achieve perfection—on paper. The invisible hand should, in theory, always be there when needed, providing an encouraging pat on the back or helping to count the monies in any given transaction where mutual value had been generated for both parties. In practice, the ghostly metacarpus will manifest into decidedly darker scenarios. Sure, those ethereal digits could serve as the treasurer in an exchange, but without overarching guiding principles to mediate any disagreements, they could also just as easily be the armory, or worse still, pull down a mask and become the outreached grasp of a highwayman.

Economies that shunned free market activity and opted for more socialist structures still could not escape the invisible hand in some shape or form. Massive countries that did not follow principles of the division of labor and hadn't pushed for more diverse agricultural or manufacturing sectors may have had longer periods of peace, often acquired in exchange for starvation, or a centralization of power, or both. Perhaps it is no surprise that the anthropomorphic embodiment of the concept is a detached set of human actuators. It represents the free will of human decision-making as articulated by our ability to grab things and shake, break, consume, and destroy them.

The hubris of it all was the presumption that humans had already established an unwritten code that ensured we are all properly incentivized for positive outcomes. And maybe, just maybe, therein lies the problem with Artificial General Intelligence, or AGI: the similar assumption that it could be encoded with shared values and could comprehend and adhere to some unstated but perfect alignment with human goals, goals that captured the needs, aspirations, and desires of the citizens of Earth.

Like fighting climate change. Despite what the viewing metrics suggested, people did not like fires, floods, heatwaves, and frozen wastelands happening to themselves. Many of these citizens were extremely proud that their countries had been doing their part to combat climate change by improving the energy efficiency of their national systems. And as a result of increased energy availability, many citizens responded by buying more air conditioners, bigger electric car chargers, and higher-BTU-output outside heaters, the latter especially in response to the seasons becoming ever more unpredictable and unforgiving. They had been incentivized by the sweat-inducing heat, the devastation of climatic imbalance around the world, and an inability to comfortably host outdoor dinner parties, and thus served their own self-interests accordingly. Try as it might, the invisible hand could not hold back the rush of Black Friday shoppers.

With this feedback loop firmly in place and gaining momentum in a manner analogous to the groundbreaking centrifugal energy conservation of the flywheel, the one invented by James Watt, CVI's energy business was rolling. The Brazil deal had quadrupled in size, and the progress it had demonstrated for that country soon led to similar deals all around the world. Growth was effectively on autopilot, but not the flaky self-driving kind that had caused CVI's CEO to nearly become DOA; the offering was simply far too compelling to be ignored. If you ran a country or operated an electrical grid, there was only one choice, and that was CVI. That might as well have been their slogan if they needed one, which they didn't.

The former marketing intern wasn't concerned about the lack of a slogan. For the last few months, she had been more occupied with her lack of mobility, and her recovery.

Somaya had suffered multiple broken bones, including her left femur, right tibia, multiple cracked ribs, a fractured pelvis, and several affected vertebrae. Her skeletal injuries were complemented by internal bleeding and a significant concussion. She had been induced into a three-day coma upon admittance at Helix Medical Center to ensure the dangerous swelling of her gray matter would have the best chance to recede and, perhaps fittingly, to reduce the energy consumption of the conscious brain and reallocate those resources toward healing and regeneration.

Consciousness returned slowly. It was like the world's biggest hangover, far worse than the now-infamous morning meeting after the night of the Data Metrics 2006 party. After the sedatives and medications had mostly worn off, the fugue state that lingered for days would never fully go away— it became a permanent but fortunately infrequent dissociative rest stop on the journey of life that Somaya would learn to accommodate.

But for now, it all just hurt like hell.

Her eyes opened to a soft blue radiant light in the room. She could see several plants bathed in sunlight and a fountain with running water pouring out of the interior wall furthest from the window. It was the first day that the dark clouds had lifted from her mind. She leaned to her side, already sensing that it was too late, well past her habitual start time of five-thirty in the morning.

But she could not turn. Physically, her body didn't allow it, and the pain receptors everywhere were complaining in a way she'd never heard before.

As the injury message notifications exploded in her mind, fragments of visuals flashed in and out along with them. A flight. A busy street in the middle of a hot, sweaty city. Splashing water in a pool. None of it made sense, all of it just incoherent images smashing together.

She fell back asleep, her first triumphant wakeful day lasting only a few minutes.

As those periods of consciousness grew longer, so improved her strength, and her memory, though much more slowly, began to consolidate. More importantly, rehab had begun. Somaya would spend the better—or maybe worse—part of a year in that well-appointed hospital room, subject to some of the best possible private healthcare that money could buy.

Meanwhile, CVI's growth was stratospheric. Provided the company had received adequate access to data from any new customer, CVI's systems could now become operational across entire urban centers in as little as a week or two. The only thing more impressive than these rapid deployments was the velocity with which it was hiring new staff and opening up new factories, operations facilities, and data centers.

Inevitable dysfunction had arrived nearly on cue, following the template of so many other private innovation businesses that had made their ascent up the ladders of multi-billion dollar market capitalizations. Many would say that one hundred million dollars in revenue was the threshold between fast-moving innovative operations and consensus-driven corporate malaise. Others would use the headcount metric of five hundred staff, provided no more than one hundred and fifty were in any one location. Whatever the case, CVI had rocketed through all of these figures, now boasting over half a billion dollars in forward-looking annual sales and over one thousand staff across ten offices and sixteen different manufacturing, data management, and outfitting facilities.

"If big companies knew how to behave, and how to operate, there would be no room for small companies to do what they do well," her mentor Jeff Christianson had prolifically suggested to her so many years ago, when CVI was a far different company.

Had Warren been in the picture when those words were said, he might have agreed. One need only look at what Rotten Tomatoes Inc. (not the film website) had become.

What has this thing become? He wondered to himself. For the first few months of Somaya's recovery, Warren would often just sit next to her in silence, holding her hand when she was struggling with anything. Once she started to have more cognitively functional days, he began to provide a daily rundown on progress from the head office and around the company at large. Warren still maintained an operational role in the company, given his familiarity as the original architect of the code libraries for their computer vision algorithms. He was also uniquely positioned to provide Somaya with these briefings from his other experience of being her husband for over fourteen years.

"It doesn't add up," she commented. They had been looking at CVI's hardware expenditures, and despite the massive need for building up infrastructure and ensuring a near-unending supply of hardware and data centers, it just didn't look right. "Who is on the ground at these locations? What exactly are we building out there and where is it going?"

"I don't know. I mean, clearly, a ton of it is going to our data centers, but even there, purely from a volume standpoint, it doesn't look right. Like, we are either insanely inefficient in what we are selling and how we are running it... ironic, right, we might be wasteful with our energy? Or maybe there's more data than we thought..." his thoughts wandered off.

It was still hard for Somaya to focus on so many different pieces. Her operational memory—her RAM—was still a few firmware updates short of where she had been before the accident. But if anything, it forced her to be more surgical with her dissection of information. She had made it a priority to ensure consistency in the dialogue and communications with their key investors. With the business growing like it was, the biggest risks were in the procurement and deployment of capital. They needed to have as close to an unlimited supply of money as possible, they needed to spend it as quickly as it came in, and they needed to rationalize those choices and explain why this cycle needed to continue unimpeded.

Any suggestion that they might have been overspending or mismanaging funds would have been an effective death knell for the type of growth they were all after.

Warren, however, was as sharp as always. The two of them were each respected for having such a broad and deep understanding of the company. The Venn diagram between them started with his deep technical knowledge on the left, Somaya's potent business acumen on the right, and consummated in the middle with a shared vision for what could be possible. Two halves of a whole, but none of it would have been possible without Somaya, a statement that could not be said equally about Warren.

He had been, and still was, a stereotypical mild-mannered introverted programmer, although he had not been doing any meaningful programming for a number of years. Despite his increasing distance from the code, his understanding of the entire CVI technology stack was second to no one else, which uniquely equipped him with the context to investigate these irregularities. But even after accounting for wastage and intentional overspending to support the ridiculous rate of growth, *it didn't add up.*

At home over the next few nights, Warren pursued his search for answers in the domain he knew best—the code. Rather than trouble himself by looking at invoices, shipment details, or production summaries, he wanted first to understand what they were actually using in the functional activity of the business. Then he could get a sense for how many cameras, how many remote computers, how many data centers, and how many miles of wires and fathoms of gear were needed to pull it all together. This kind of exercise would also be very helpful for producing projections for future growth. If he knew what the current operational state really required, surely he could build a growth index for capital investments and provide Somaya with confidence that the company was operating at maximum efficiency.

The first problem he encountered was that there was no problem. Not only were the facilities and equipment deployments of the company getting larger and larger, they were becoming more and more efficient. Every time they set up a new facility or implemented a new optimization across their network, the per-unit costs of storing data, processing it, and even completing manufacturing activities were improving. Coupled with the fact that they had been establishing their newer facilities in some of the most optimal regions around the world—they had been investing in and building their own infrastructure inside some of their best customers' borders—everything was humming. The tax breaks and preferred treatment they were getting through those customer relationships added to the diameter of the flywheel of CVI's growth.

All those energy savings made a big difference in other ways, too. They allowed for the growth of data centers to increase in speed, pace, and scale. The more data centers, the more energy consumed, and the more energy consumed, the more energy that could be saved. More data centers? The words couldn't be said quickly nor loudly enough, as the rampant need to store and compute data was simply expanding unabated.

It made sense, but it didn't make sense. The algorithms, as Warren understood them, should not have required this kind of architecture or the scale of machinery being commissioned. Granted, he hadn't been as close to it over the previous decade as he was when he first started Rotten Tomatoes Inc. (not the film website).

[EVAL CVI.SYSLOG ALGI1,DATA,DATA.TYPE]

Warren didn't always drink coffee, but when he was interrogating remote network architectures from multiple endpoints all around the world, he preferred a fresh pot of medium roast Colombian. As he sipped the dark black nectar from his favorite cup, he bashed a series of logfile analysis queries into his keyboard and then sat back to wait with anticipation as his 8Zeus gaming laptop sent a convoy of messengers out over fiber-optic cabling. Each of them was empowered with the authentic seal of the Queen and tasked with the mission of inspecting these remote facilities and assembling a report for Her Royal Highness upon return to the throne room. Warren was treating those logfile queries with some kind of romantic medieval-age adulation, a habit he had developed as far back as when he was first learning to write BASIC programming language on his TRS-80 home computer in the early 1980s, awash in the bright green glare that his electro-punk typewriter forced upon their CRT television. He found the metaphor of Iron Age antics helped him demystify the binary language of ones and zeros.

He took another sip of his coffee, crafted of the Highland bean from just outside Medellin. This, despite the fact they had been on the receiving end of some of the finest Brazilian coffee for years from Somaya's customers in São Paulo. Something about those Brazilian beans just didn't sit as well with Warren as did their competitors' products from the higher slopes in the smaller country to the northwest.

Sir Warren put down the cup as some of the messengers started filtering back into the courtyard. In actual terms, results were coming back from his queries over the company's secure network, and soon Warren would not need to veil them with the make-believe exploits of his own round table, upon which he had coincidentally just placed his coffee. The information residing in those log files would prove to be bold, rich, and flavorful enough to require no additional sweetening.

The first thing he noticed was that they seemed incomplete, at least as compared to what he might have expected, given the cursory network analysis he had already been doing the past few nights. It became apparent that his own credentials no longer had royal authority. Many requests were being blocked.

No one ever said anything about this... are they trying to push us out? He was surprised by this denial of access. Warren had always been granted the keys to the IT kingdom of CVI, and his natural first response was the paranoid contemplation that perhaps he and his wife were being distanced, or possibly even in the process of being forced out, from the company.

However, the lack of access did not matter on this night. With the steely resolve of a Green Knight of Arthurian legend, he took another drink of his southern-origin elixir and ventured forth into the data.

Warren quickly realized that he was viewing the equivalent of a censured report. Enough data was missing such that what was available to him, read no more clearly than a book with every second or third word blacked out. But he had perfected the skill of scanning information in the same way. Whether reading a book or reviewing a log file, he was prolific, as Somaya had often noted, in his ability to consume information. He had also recognized some time ago that his long-nurtured need for data to be presented in a structured format had become obsolete—it was an iron sword that he had carried with pride until he noticed everyone else was swinging steel, or titanium. To Warren's credit, he had adapted. Along with his self-extraction from the depths of programming over the past decade, he had been able to wean himself from his dependency on seeing everything orderly and as it should have been had he written it himself. He learned to eschew his instinctual need for elegant code and had allowed himself to become more of a hack. Not a hacker, though he had the skills to be one of the best, but a hack, in that he came to enjoy not knowing everything and appreciate having to piece things together through guesswork and trial and error.

These files he had received did not answer his and Somaya's lingering questions, and they did not directly explain the massive cost discrepancies. They did not even reveal what so much of the mysterious hardware investments had been directed to. But they did provide other answers.

Ones that could never have been anticipated.

He was back in their car, his foot heavy on the accelerator of their 2026 Tesla Model XO, B Garz Edition. The vehicle had been designed and named after its figurehead's preeminent spacecraft launch facility, the plans for which were only just recently announced, revealing the future location off the northern coast of Germany, near the town of Garz in the coastal waters of the Baltic Sea. The location had been a surprise to many, with much debate regarding its safety as well as its proximity to Eastern Europe and Russia. It had been suggested that the facility had been a regional co-production on a path toward a "one-planet" peace accord, taking in funds from NATO countries as well as Russia. Some saw it as a more geographically optimized way to receive European energy reserves and expel them as rocket fuel exhaust in the stratosphere, while others hypothesized that it was simply another big spectacle, deployed to ensure that large metallic phallic machines could extol ego in yet another time zone, this one with a captive audience of at least half a billion people.

The car was a limited edition, in that there had only been thirty thousand of them produced. Warren had mixed feelings about owning the car, given the disaster that had happened with their previous new Tesla, but he and Somaya had decided to get it when confronted with its intended rarity. They felt lucky to have access to buy it. Had it not been a limited edition, the reduced demand would have likely cut the production run in half, and they simply did not want to miss out on being one of the first owners. One of her first meaningful actions from the hospital bed was to authorize the down payment of one hundred thousand dollars with a scan of her Face ID. Fortunately, her broken nose had been reset, and the swelling had receded enough that her phone was able to authenticate for payment.

One promise they had made to themselves was to never again use autopilot in their vehicles. Somaya had not yet been able to remember much of the night of the crash, which also made it a lot easier for them to blame the car and to exorcize their faith in the self-driving technology they had previously relied upon almost religiously. Her memory had only reinstated itself to the moment of landing at YVR on her way home from São Paulo. It had not yet come to where she had done so herself.

"Welcome to Helix in Phoenix," the receptionist said with a delightful rhyming intonation as he walked through the automatic sliding glass doors. It was a cool desert night outside, now almost midnight. The air temperature didn't change all that much as Warren came inside, a big difference from earlier in the day when the shift from unconstrained desert heat to climate-controlled air-conditioned medical facility had nearly caused him to faint. He wondered why the facility was based in Phoenix, at first assuming it was the prevalence of rich retirees in Arizona who also profiled extremely well for high-cost private medical care. He was wrong, however. He soon realized after speaking with some of the orderlies and cleaning staff, of which there were also many, that the location had been decided upon due to its centrality. It was nearly equidistant to three of the highest-rated golf courses in the southwest United States, resonating with the staff doctors' predilections for swinging a big stick. He had then started to wonder if said prevalence of rich retirees in the region was also due to the golf courses, or due to the medical facility.

The location would also prove to be beneficial in the latter half of the decade when the second pandemic started to take hold and roared through the region. During those years to come, the doctors would prove to have been fortunate and forward-thinking enough to stockpile enough treatment and had kept the location far away from the prying hands of the broader healthcare system, such that they could keep their families and their friends' families, up to a limit, safe, thus ensuring that most tee times were able to be met.

Warren entered her room without knocking. Somaya was asleep, though seemed to be stirring. She had told him how her dreams at night were intensely lucid, and she would often find herself waking up unsure if she was still in the dream.

He touched her arm. "Somaya, hey," he said softly. He repeated her name a few more times.

She slowly opened her eyes. The room was mostly dark, with only a diffuse aura of moonlight coming in through the window and a tall column of light pushing in from the door to the hallway through which Warren had entered. She saw his silhouette backlit by the hall and his face dappled by the soft moonlight.

Visions flashed. A security guard. No, a border agent. Then it was Warren. Then it was a woman, with purple misty light everywhere. The woman looked at her, their eyes met for a moment. She was looking at herself. No, something else. Then it flashed again. Here was Warren.

"Oh. Hi, Warren," she said, happy to see him, though subconsciously disappointed that it wasn't either of those other two people. The unanswered curiosity of who they were and why they kept infiltrating her dreams was starting to bother her.

I fucking hate not knowing, she thought, groggily.

"Sit up. I need to show you something," he said, his tone serious and direct in a way unlike anything she could remember hearing from him, other than perhaps that first time he had explained how his algorithm counted ketchup bottles.

Why did he have so many bottles of ketchup in his fridge? More groggy thoughts continued.

Warren helped Somaya raise her torso, and he activated the electric bed lift she had started to rely less and less upon. It was necessary at this moment as her body was notoriously sore for the first hour or so after waking. He then opened his laptop and placed it on her lap, reaching over to strike a few buttons on the keyboard.

The heat from the laptop was pleasing. It emanated warmth through the bedsheets onto her quadriceps. Legs that had only just recently started to be reliable skeletal participants once again. The fractures, breaks, and cracks had mostly healed, though the soft tissue recovery would go on for many months to come, and she knew there were at least three more surgeries scheduled. The overheated air spilling out from the fan on Warren's GPU was soothing to those aching muscles and ligaments.

"What is this?" she asked, looking at the laptop. He had opened a video file and hit the spacebar.

He said, "Just watch," but she didn't hear it.

She could see a strip mall and a gas station. A bit further along, she could see what looked to be a pub. A few people were standing outside. It was raining, though like most live video recordings of inclement weather, it only appeared as a haze in the aura of the streetlights, but the splashing in the puddles everywhere confirmed it.

Warren hit a combination of buttons on the keyboard. The perspective shifted over, closer to the pub. A man could be seen running from the street corner and across a busy road.

"What the... where did this come from?"

He didn't answer, as he kept working the keys. The camera shifted again, giving a new perspective of the man running on an overpass, being chased from behind. A scuffle ensued, and then a violent crash and a car spinning out of control.

She was watching it through this perspective from above, yet without any keyboard prompts required, Somaya's own vision of the scene kept jumping from the view on the laptop to fleeting images of her own memory. She could see the road from inside the car, before the intersection with the strip mall, her steering wheel with no hands on it. Her lap once again hot, both in the bed and inside the car.

And then back to the aerial footage. A recent model year Tesla, standard edition, cresting the summit of the overpass into a nearly unwatchable sequence, but one they couldn't pull their eyes away from. It bounced around inside of an expertly designed pinball table with the overpass guardrail, a Nissan sedan, and three other humans strategically placed as bumpers and points multipliers. Their old brand new car then tumbled and flew and slid and tumbled and slid some more before coming to a rest.

Somaya couldn't speak. Tears were in her eyes, pain was throbbing in her head, and her fingers had gripped the side rail of the bed on one side and Warren's outstretched hand on the other. She turned and looked at him slowly, her face wrought with confusion and fear. He had never seen her like this.

He had never seen anything like this.

Twenty-eight

ATTRITION

Tap, tap, tap

An engineer walks between towers of machines at a data center in Florida, activating green buttons on intermittently placed touchscreen panels. This place has meaning and history; it once held the original archives for the Golden Record, the one they sent out into space. They had even stamped and engraved the disk in this facility. Sadly and inevitably, everything had long since been cleared out, the location remodeled, repowered, and reconfigured. The entire contents of the Golden Record, which at one time described human history, would be a negligible rounding error of the solid-state storage capacity in this facility.

Tap, tap, tap

A dead fly, a victim of attrition from the dry air around these processing units, is stuck between two fixtures on a server rack. The engineer carefully flicks at the metal housing with his finger, dislodging the insect carcass and causing it to fall to the floor, no longer a threat. Like the fly before its untimely demise, the engineer has no idea what the actual purpose of this facility is. The volumes of data and the multi-dimensional parsing of it all are far too abstract and complex for a single organism to comprehend in any detail.

It made sense to architect things this way, to have this new relationship between human and machine, because this data center, like its many thousands of siblings around the world, had a very important, very necessary job to do and could not afford to suffer distraction.

Here was a professional technologist with all the tools and academic knowledge who, by himself, would have surpassed the global sum total of capabilities of what could be done in Rip Gossett's day, yet had been reduced to pressing buttons on machines in a maze. If the former Executive Director of Interstellar Intelligence at NASA had not succumbed in 2032 during the height of the third wave of the second pandemic, he would have commented that "the smart had gotten stupid and the stupid got stupider."

Like his many obedient peers around the globe who operate similar facilities, this individual is graded daily, weekly, monthly, and yearly. Uptime, breach interventions, and "green-light-time" have all become part of a larger scoreboard by which he and his fellow automatons are graded, judged, and compensated.

Tap, tap, tap

A notification demands attention. A loot box is waiting for him. They even have a mobile app that delivers a daily dose of stars, coins, and bricks, with additional bonuses for achieving over five thousand steps. Balance, after all, is important.

Theoretical economists and behavioral psychologists will forever debate the extrinsic incentives and intrinsic motivations that matter to people. But it had become a fool's errand to argue in the face of overwhelming evidence that the world was not a happier place. The proof, after all, could be seen in our profile images, photostreams, auto-magic Insta-stories, Diddem diaries, and MXP rips, and in the terabytes upon terabytes of smiling content stored in our pockets and backed up to the cloud.

Could it be that the invisible hand, unseen for over three hundred and fifty years, would finally manifest as AI auto-retouch software for selfies that turned your frown upside down? Perhaps. Might it have additional capabilities to remove one's tongue from where it sometimes resided, especially when awkwardly flapping outside the lips in a photo or when firmly planted inside one's cheek? Hopefully.

Although, there were dissenting opinions. When he wasn't communicating on behalf of alien races, Gossett, the socio-linguist, would often say that our photos were laughing at us as we smiled ourselves to death.

None of it was making Henny very happy anymore. For too long, she had been witness to the same patterns repeating themselves. First, an industry or a business would introduce some kind of innovation that promised groundbreaking improvements for humanity. Then, bolstered by human potential, these breakthroughs would subside to become LVPs, a term she had come up with meaning Least Valuable Permutation. Again and again, she had observed others seemingly at the cusp of wielding magic, only for it to be shown as the parlor tricks of a card sharp.

NewU, for example, was successfully acquired by MCA in 2027. Within a year, Harbs and his cronies—as Henny liked to think of them—had successfully rebranded the company as DeathBank.

"You've got to be fucking kidding me, Harbs. Like Death Retail wasn't insane enough of a suggestion, you actually went with DeathBank. Help me understand this," she had said when she heard the update.

"Look, it's not the same time as it was a few years ago when you first visited these guys."

Harbs was right. The second pandemic hit in late 2027, facilitating the austere market conditions that led to the acquisition. It was a ripe time for consolidation across most industries, as governmental regulatory agencies thought it appropriate to crush the economy at the onset of the pandemic this time around rather than delaying it like the last one.

This one was also much worse than COVID-19. COVI-26 had hit quickly and decisively, and with similar gusto, the WHO had decided to drop the "D." There was no Disease this time around. Instead, it was a novel corona-super-virus that effectively brought with it no illness and a high mortality rate. If they had kept the "D," it could have only stood for Death, thus explaining the edit made by the WHO, as it would have contradicted with their "H."

MCA had no such qualms. Where NewU had initially held the promise of unleashing technologies that could predict health outcomes and identify anyone's propensity for illness, the value proposition of NewU became much more clear during COVI; it could tell people when they would die.

Through a combination of DNA sequencing and genetic marker analysis, along with multi-variate extrapolations of transmissibility of COVI across nearly the entire human population, NewU could identify anyone who belonged to the roughly thirty percent of the population who had no natural immunity to COVI and tell them of their expected date of fatality, plus or minus up to ten days. Much of the underlying technology and service offering—the avatar recreation and persistent social profile— was still a part of the experience, but they had decided that "NewU" was no longer the main draw. This name was too positive-sounding, and in these darker times of COVI, they needed something more pragmatic.

In the expectedly cold, calculating ways of the MCA corporate office, the DeathBank branding had been decided upon as it captured the "Death" aspect of predicting COVI outcomes with certainty while alluding to the concept of how customers could still "Bank" themselves for eternity. Their loved ones could still appreciate them long after their predictable passing, provided, of course, that their loved ones had not also been identified as high-value DeathBank customers. For those who were immune to COVI, their participation was still helpful as it often gave them insight into the other ways in which they were likely to perish.

She couldn't help but wonder what part in all this the Diddem.com and Mixality businesses played as well, given the hooked tendrils that MCA, AGF, and SGF had in both companies since their inception and the daily role both played in the lives—and deaths—of billions of people.

Sadly, Henny would never have the opportunity to follow up with Harbs on these thoughts. Not long after their conversation about the rebranding of DeathBank, she received an update affirming the choice of that brand name, as Harbs himself had opened up his own savings account. He had fallen, a victim of the first wave of this pandemic that would soon account for a population reduction of over one and a half billion victims in 2028 alone. Details were fleeting, as without a Disease by which to identify it and without any real symptoms, passing came quickly to all who were afflicted without natural immunity. It would still be another three years before they had a nominally functional vaccine and another three years again before the water supply would be adequately upgraded to disable COVI transmission for all.

Henny was devastated. Harbs was her mentor, her leader, and really, her only touchpoint to the organization for whom she had dutifully worked the last decade and a half. Sure, she had relied on other support staff, reviewers, editors, and the like in the ongoing course of her work, but Harbs was the only one that she had ever really spoken with in any material, meaningful way.

Was that right? Did I do the right thing? I wanted to make some change, some real change. Henny reflected on her time spent under the EMC umbrella.

Wow, that's fucking selfish, the guy has passed away. She reset her moral compass, realizing her thoughts should be about Harbs, not her career choices.

You know what else is weird? A dialogue had started in her mind, one that had spoken up a few times over the years but had never been engaged upon and certainly not resolved. It must have been Harriet Stone, the short-form content author, probing the investigative journalist Henrietta Adler. Or maybe it was the other way around.

I never met the fucking guy. I mean, *I never met the guy.* She corrected herself, feeling that the f-bomb was inappropriate to describe the recently departed Harbs, no matter how lovingly she deployed it.

It was true. She had been so decoupled from the construct of the organization and so blessedly remote in her work assignments that not once had she ever been in the same place at the same time as Harbs. Henny hadn't even known where he was located or which of the companies involved he had officially worked for, and in many ways, it made it easier to live her infinitely exploratory existence without knowing.

Yet, on another level, she found it odd to feel such strong feelings for someone she had never shaken hands with or hugged. In some ways, the first global lockdowns in 2020 improved things, the trigger for them to shift from phone calls to video meetings. It always seemed sort of weird that while the rest of the world used real-time video as a half-measure proxy for how they had operated in the past, for Henny and Harbs, that change had actually enriched their relationship.

Season 1 through 4, every episode. You and me, old friend, that was fun, she said to herself, commemorating the very limited but enjoyable downtime they had spent together religiously watching the streaming hit *FastNite* during COVID.

And when everyone else had returned to "normal"—which also led to the rapidity of the COVI outbreak—Henny and Harbs had kept doing their thing.

Then he was gone—a deposit into his own darkly-named creation. It didn't seem real. Though like much of her professional existence, that feeling was often the status quo.

Twenty-nine

LIFT

For Somaya and Warren, the invisible hand was more of an unseen eye. To be more precise, it was camouflaged drones.

"I don't understand. Drones? How? We didn't see a thing," Somaya said after the initial shock of seeing the footage that Warren shared with her in her hospital bed had worn off.

"I don't know either, Sommy," he said, "but however the hell they did it, it's been done everywhere. And it explains a lot."

"What... do you mean, everywhere? Where?"

"As far as I can tell, and I could only pull down a bit of data and had to decrypt these files, they were actually in a 'To Be Deleted' drive partition if you can believe it, but it sort of looks like... everywhere. Like, at least everywhere where we run our energy grid diagnostics."

"That's insane. You know this stuff better than I do, Warren. That doesn't make sense. How are we even getting that information? I mean... who is running these fucking drones?"

She looked back to the footage on the laptop, realizing that she could toggle between multiple perspectives—to different drones—and scrub through the timeline to see the whole gory accident scene unfold in various ways. It was mesmerizing, infuriating, and terrifying.

"That's the thing, Sommy. Who is running them?" Warren repeated, before answering, "It's us."

Somaya could hear the proverbial pin hit the proverbial fucking floor. Everything went silent, and then the pumping. *Thump! Thump! Thump! Thump!* She could hear her blood surging repetitively, forcefully through the temples of her head, her heart reverberating from within the walls of her chest. The veins and arteries around all her many injuries swelled up, prodding the intensity of each painful wound.

She took a few breaths while contemplating those two words Warren had muttered.

"You can't be serious. Like, what do you mean 'us'? Like, somebody owns those things, and someone on our team has been buying that data? Without telling me? How the fuck is that even possible?"

"That's what I'm saying. It doesn't look like it's incoming from anywhere else. All those costs, all the manufacturing, all the tech, it all adds up. Well, the numbers add up. The rest of it, not so much," Warren said.

"Adds up to what? What do you mean?"

"We—CVI—have been making these things. Like at insanely high-volume production levels," Warren offered. "Like thousands and thousands of them, maybe a lot more."

"But that's fucking insane. You're saying someone in the business has been managing the build of these things and deploying them out into the wild, hooked up to our network, without telling me? Without you knowing? Who would do that? And why?"

"I don't..." he tried to answer but couldn't.

"And how the hell are these things out there and no one sees them? That doesn't make any sense whatsoever. I mean, I can't remember the crash, but I'm damn sure if I'd seen them, I would know it. And, Jesus, you said how many?" she said, realizing she had accelerated past his comment on how big the issue actually was without slowing down to comprehend the scale of it.

"Yeah. Many thousands. Depending on input costs, hell, maybe a few million. That's what it looks like. It also explains something else."

"What? What else could this possibly say beyond how fucked up it sounds already?" Somaya asked, now ready for anything.

"You know how we haven't been able to figure out how good the algorithms got, how it didn't make sense we were able to do what we could do with what we thought we had? Well, this is the reason why."

That did make sense. Out of all this insanity, that comment actually connected a few outstanding mysteries. Their systems had been over-performing, which everyone in senior management at CVI had assumed was a result of exceptional tuning of the algorithms and more effective interpolation and extrapolation of data. They hadn't thought to look more closely at the source—primarily the security camera footage—as they had always been operating under the assumption that their customers had provided them with everything they could. It was their job to "turn chicken shit into chicken salad," to use a favorite saying of Warren's even as far back as Rotten Tomatoes Inc. (not the film website) and his analysis of refrigerator contents.

"So our customers have been sending these things up then, right? It has to be."

"No, Somaya, it's not them."

Thirty

TED-ISH

"Idleness teaches a man to do many evil things," reads a truncated line in the legendary 14th-century English author and poet Geoffrey Chaucer's famous *Canterbury Tales*, following its conversion from Middle English to something more contemporarily palatable, of course. Many postulate that he had refactored biblical prose to produce these words in his story "The Tale of Melibeus," a dialogue-heavy exploration of dastardly acts and the contemplation of revenge.

Many scholars have noted that the tale of poor Melibeus is a meekly crafted, long-winded, structurally deprived assembly of prose that mostly serves to demonstrate the literary intelligence and memory of the author. They are also unsure when Chaucer himself wrote it, but it's quite likely he had nothing better to do at the time.

However, it is this particular line, since contrived into derivatives such as "Idle hands are the devil's tools," that has carried itself with more weight and greater haste than the rest of the story, thereby sustaining its own momentum.

So many others have remarked upon this trait of humankind: if improperly motivated to act such that we eschew any care or duty, we create far worse outcomes than perhaps even had we led with evil intentions. In more recent times, that cause-and-effect has changed; the bar of measurement for "doing something" has been ever-lowered such that it mostly looks like doing nothing at all. Yet the net result of billions of people acting this way seems to have even grander and darker implications than, for instance, had they, like Chaucer, chosen to write lengthy, confusing stories.

Consider, for example, a package delivery courier stuck in traffic on Market St. in 2011. She finds it easier to get out of her vehicle and start recording the video of an assault taking place than to lend a hand. Someone else watches that video in near real-time and is outraged. That is, until they share it and repost it with a few words expressing their outrage. Now, they are okay, especially if they had ordered something earlier that day, as the package has been delivered on time.

If that wasn't enough, a man swipes up on his phone in 2018, repeatedly. Colorful charts, graphs, and visualizations indicate a wealth of information about his genetic makeup, ancestry, and health profile. He keeps scrolling and scrolling, the confirmation of his unlikely propensity for hereditary cancer giving him peace of mind as he buys a pack of cigarettes, a purchase completed with saved shopping information on his phone. Next time, he will act on the vape discount notification he received and finally stop smoking those awful cigarettes.

And finally, an executive testifies to Congress a few years later about the planet-sized holes in his technology platform's privacy policy and the implications of end-users using his technologies to manipulate the private information of other users. This executive's technology platform is purely a service provider, he says. Their intention is to provide tools for people to do things they would do anyway, for free. No different than a hammer or a pickaxe, except for free. He doesn't even know how his own platform really uses any of that data, and fortunately for him, the senators tasked with investigating the issue were confused after he mentioned pickaxes. And all of them, including the executive, would be distracted with a forthcoming offer to buy a new hammer, a weighted unit with a silicon handle and a built-in level available on a thirteen-hour promotion of forty-two percent off, in the days that followed their hearings.

It is these very anecdotes and situations, and their many similar multiplicate forms, that have been repeating themselves over and over for decades; the idle hands—and often thumbs—of humans spinning the moral compass from which they seek direction and guidance.

"A woman becomes the most celebrated hero of our time. It's fascinating, really, to hear it like that," the guest lecturer said, speaking to a crowded audience in Lecture Hall 4. The room was filled with attendees for this keynote talk to the incoming 2031 student body. The aged retractable dividing wall had been raised into the rafters to accommodate the crowd. It was more and more rare for that dividing wall to be lowered any more, as the hall was woefully undersized for the number of constituents it now served, even more so than when a certain amateur investigative report had been penned on the matter some twenty years earlier.

"If I had been up here speaking ten or fifteen years ago, I don't think I could have said that. I mean, at that point, it's 2015, we're just seeing the momentum of #metoo start to build after ten years of murmuring and thousands of years of oppression. By 2020, maybe a new consciousness or ethical construct is emerging, but then the world is stuffed into a fucking box called COVID for a few years. Pardon my language, sorry, not sorry," she said as she looked over toward the session's emcee, reveling in the look of distaste on his face and the chuckles from the audience. "2025? Sorry, there are some wars to be fought. A war against equality that keeps raging on, but just when they were in danger of losing, they injected a big dose of inflation to reset the power balance. Gotta keep that white guy up high in the tower where he can see everybody, right? And some wars out in the 'thee-ay-ter of battle' as they say. Always makes for quality content, and did I mention inflation? Yep, if you have inflation, nothing better than some wars to right that ship—that battleship—and make sure money is being spent in the right way. Death, taxes, factories, and profits, right? Not really all that different than building the internet or another data center when you think about it," the guest speaker continued with her chronology.

"Which brings us to this decade. Post-war, at least until the next one, post-double-pandemic, we'll talk about that in a minute, and of course, as we've touched on already, post-singularity," she hit the key note of her presentation like a rhetorical hammer on the desks of Congress and paused to allow a moment of contemplation to sink in across the audience.

"Post-singularity. What the fuck does that even mean?" she again looked to the emcee, confident she had established that no governors would be applied to this talk.

"Let me show you what it means." She flipped her presentation to a slideshow of images and short clips. If this session were being conducted at a more prestigious location like Brown, Berkeley, or Stanford, they would more than likely be in a shared virtual space with all of this content already having gone through "4D world-building" to create a more immersive session. But she knew all too well the reasons why Lecture Hall 4 was still telling stories shown through focally-directed light bulbs to a packed crowd, and for this talk, maybe it wasn't such a bad idea to look at things the old way.

The wall behind her filled up with content. A locked-off clip of a trail camera with people running by in the failing light of dusk. A half dozen men in militia garb posing near the back of a truck. Over-the-shoulder footage of another person firing a weapon, its projectile exploding in the distance in a cloud of colorful dust. A clip of a woman covered in red. She was also covered in green and blue, the result of a Primary Color Mine.

"The PCM, right? We all remember that. So let's rewind. Does anyone remember where *The Conflux* started?" she asked and then scanned the audience, looking up to the right, toward the back of the room, then the middle front, and finally, gazing back to those in the distant left. She had actually learned that scanning skill from one of *The Conflux*'s earlier participants, a former Navy Seal, that when assessing a landscape or unstructured space in front of them, to do so in a way that was counter to how they might typically ingest information. In other words, someone who reads left-to-right should scan right-to-left, and vice versa.

"Zentax!" someone yelled out.

For the briefest of moments, she was again standing in a dilapidated kitchen, arms held close to her chest, the chill of the open front door raising goosebumps on her bare legs as the massive human known as Mitch Zentax barreled toward her. A big man with an even bigger heart, Henrietta felt a smile infiltrating her stoic expression on stage, and allowed it to happen.

She looked to the audience member who had spoken the big man's name and responded, "That's what most people think. That's just when it got really... big." She regretted the accidental pun, out of respect for Mitch Zentax.

Someone else stood up, speaking loudly enough for everyone in the theater to hear. "Trick question! It wasn't *The Conflux* until Templeton launched it on Mixality."

Henny looked toward the speaker, glad that someone had done a little bit of homework. Though it wasn't surprising those names would be yelled out, as she knew the biggest reason Spectra College had maintained high enrollment while other populations had been decimated was the natural draw of it being the alma mater of the legendary Zentax and, of course, the superstar producer Ricky Templeton.

"You're right, it was a trick question. Where this thing started," she pointed back to the last image that remained on-screen behind her, showing the woman soaked head to toe in multiple different colors of thick, goopy latex paint. "Was with data."

She continued her explanation, "*The Conflux* was always out there, in fact, I'd go so far as to say the internet *was The Conflux*. Everyone fighting, yelling, screaming, buying, selling, insulting, stealing, pissing, shitting, fucking, hating, and maybe sometimes loving." Her presentation had now been cycling through images of a 'who's who' of internet infamy, snippets of viral videos, hate speech comments, protests, and finishing with a clip of amateur pornography that coincided with the end of her statement. A few more chuckles from the audience could be heard. Henny again looked at the emcee, who had now receded into the shadows of the stage, forcibly moved by her presence.

"In case I'm being too obtuse, which I often am, let's see what that really means. The 1990s. Mixtapes and dubbing. Not dubstep. Dubbing, you might have to look it up. Recording things and sharing them. And when I say sharing, I mean people were handing them to each other. I see you, I give you a thing. Now you have it and I don't, unless I made a copy. You know what kinds of things? Here's one called Faces of Death." She showed a few clips from a 1978 VHS tape compilation of real footage of people dying in gruesome ways.

"You know what the data said at that time?" Henny asked as she looked out over her audience, who were now fully engrossed in what she was saying. "It sure as hell didn't say this." She beckoned toward them. "Let me be clear. The data at the time did not say that this kind of footage would capture people's attention or have them leaning forward in their seats for more. The more common refrain back then would have been that it needed to be outlawed, which it was, and that it was a blight on society. But as it became outlawed, it was pirated and shared. And became desirable."

"Now, let's not just look at this as the domain of the dark, or the evil. There was some pretty awesome stuff on physical media back then, too, like the And1 Mixtapes in the '90s, which came out of a small T-shirt business not too far from here at Wharton. Do your homework on that one, everybody."

Henny was referring to the And1 brand and its remarkable ascent that, for a while, had it competing with the likes of Nike and Adidas. Starting with the Skip Tape, featuring playground basketball legend Rafer "Skip to My Lou" Alston, And1 is credited with quite possibly the first "viral" content marketing campaign ever, a series of roughly produced basketball highlight reels. The Mixtapes influenced a generation of players and changed an entire sport.

"So, let me jump ahead. Somewhere around 2009, a bunch of videos started showing up online—footage from military exercises in Eastern Europe, old Soviet regions. I mean, this stuff was raw. Like, really raw." She showed a clip that had, many years ago, prompted a heated milkshake-fueled discussion between two friends. To be clear, the discussion was heated, not the milkshakes.

"A few years later, and we get the offspring of wartime footage and reality TV competitions. Survival stuff, a ton of content on Discovery, but you know what? It all ended up looking the same. You can only throw Bear Grylls into the jungle so many times, right? I mean, he can only drink so much of his own pee before we don't need to see it again. Okay, so what's next? Games and streaming, right? Fortnite, right? And a talking head showing you how they play because you're too lazy to do it yourself, right?" she said, quickly noticing the defensive body language of the crowd.

"It's a rhetorical question, an indirect 'you,' by the way," she said, hoping to put them at ease before continuing. "You look back at those leaked war exercises, and I know for a fact that they were the inspiration for *The Conflux*, or as you first knew it, *Fastnite*, with PCMs and rainbow-dust pellets and water traps, and a whole bunch of other effects. It was prime viewing right through the first pandemic, wasn't it?"

She referred to a bar graph of viewing habits. *Fastnite* Seasons 1 through 4 had taken off, with viewership quickly rocketing past the world's largest sporting events, the biggest blockbuster films, and even *MrBeast*. No doubt, it had been a beneficial recipient of the fortuitous timing of its inaugural streaming launch, which began in April 2020.

"But look what happened here, in 2024." Data was revealing that competing viewer preferences were beginning to threaten *Fastnite*'s singular seat at the throne.

"See this data? There's no label. Do you know why?" she paused for effect. "Do you know why the most popular content after 2025 on this wonderful thing we still call the internet is eluding description?" Another pause. "Did the producers forget to give it a name?"

"No, they didn't. It's because if you and I looked at it, it looks like this." the same montage of viral streamers, hate commentators, and sordid content that she had first enticed the crowd with had played through again. "With a lot of this." On cue, a new edit of myriad scenes from the frontlines of war in Ukraine, Gaza, Syria, Sudan, Ecuador, Panama, southern Italy, and the violent conflict in Greenland and Baffin Island, all in a compilation of shaky handheld film, smartphone footage, drone camera work, and even high-resolution satellite recorded video.

"Maybe we sprinkle in a little natural disaster, some floods, and some forest fires while we're at it. Whatever it is, you put these ingredients in a pot and you stir it, and it's must-see TV. And more to the point, you combine that soup of destruction with the most popular streaming series ever, and it's almost inevitable. No, actually, it *was* inevitable, now it just *is*, right?"

Newer, higher-production quality footage played behind her, a highlight reel of sorts. Crowd-favorite characters from previous seasons elicited quick cheers from the audience. There was Jerryd, the southern racist explosives expert. Gabby, the South American with the opaque counter-revolutionary story who excelled at jungle camouflage. Mr. Dat, the Thai adventure guide whose iconic flip-flops had spawned an entire fast fashion clothing brand that had survived the passing of its namesake. And the many other countless names of crowd-selected participants. The screen paused for a moment on a close-up image of a smiling Mitch Zentax. His years on Earth, 1991-2027, were shown in large font below his name as the shot pulled back, revealing Mitch holding Jerryd up above his head, that triumphant everlasting pose that graced the cover of the title card for *The Conflux Season 3: Extended Edition*. Moments later, Zentax had thrown Jerryd to his demise down a rocky slope and into an active lava field. It was a clip people loved watching again and again.

"So, we start to combine what people said they wanted with what the data tells us they really want. No surprise this thing becomes a juggernaut. Now I'll get you to the end of my story, at least the part about this girl here." A new close-up had taken over the screen. A greasy, dirty face looked out over the audience. Wisps of hair covered a sweaty forehead that had been marked up by camouflage paint. Dirty muscular shoulders frame a thin neck that formed the basis for a slender but chiseled jawline, housing a stoic expression above. Her dark brown eyes peered straight ahead at the camera.

The crowd cheered and began chanting, "To-to! To-to! To-to!"

It was the girl billions knew as Toto, a few knew as Dorothy, and nobody dared call Bex anymore.

Henny took a drink of water. A small table had quietly been brought out to the edge of the stage, with a glass placed upon it by the shadow-dwelling emcee.

The crowd kept chanting. She held up her arms and waved them down and up a few times, beckoning her audience to lower the cheering and chatter.

"The reason I shared this with you, and yes, I understand many of you already know much of this backstory, is to ask you to not let this be the end. Hell, I probably couldn't have even shown half of this type of stuff to you when I was a student here. Actually, I know I couldn't. But I'm not gonna stand up and tell you what to watch or what not to watch. I *am* going to stand here and ask you again, to not let this be the end, like I said. Do not let yourself get complacent." She took another drink of water.

"You know, for forty or fifty years, the smartest minds worked on Artificial Intelligence. They used to call it the singularity—that's what I was talking about earlier. It's what you call Aggie. When we hit that moment of Aggie, of AGI, we all took a step back. We let ourselves get served even more. Just think about that for a minute. As humans, we have crafted some of the most intelligent and scalable back-end technologies to support everything we talked about here. Sure, it's great that the world's biggest celebrity is a girl. Girl Power, right? Is it great that she's a killing machine? That's another conversation, although most of the other targets probably deserve it. But you know what? All of it just satisfies the goals of the bigger fish, the biggest corporations, and the power people and shareholders behind it all."

"Now, it looks like my time is up, otherwise I'd keep going. I've got a ton of this kind of stuff, you can find it in my book, my blog, and hopefully pretty soon, a new series," Henny said, feeling she'd earned the right to plug her media properties, especially *here* of all places. "So if I can share one thing with you, it's that as you get out there, you gotta be aware. Be knowledgeable that everything you do has a cause and an effect. All of this tech is running in the shadows, all the time. Every action you make is recorded or inferred somewhere, and it all rolls up, too often to someone in a big chair in a big office somewhere with their hands on the controls."

Henny had struggled for years to strike a balance between providing fair commentary and sounding like a raving conspiracy theorist when sharing or presenting her work. Fortunately, the definition of conspiracy theorist had gotten more and more extreme over the years, so even at her self-assessed worst, she was no more inflammatory than the average banter on any of Mixality's social platforms.

"So with that, my ask is this—look to the past, look to your parents, aunts, uncles. You can even ask me, or even this guy," she beckoned to the emcee, who awkwardly waved back at the crowd from his half-concealed position near the stage. "Think about And1 and less about Templeton. Use your gut, your instincts. The data is not always going to tell you what's right, but if you use it at the right time, it can be powerful... a powerful set of tools, just like you."

Another pause. Many in the crowd contemplated how comfortable it would be to sit in a big chair in a big office somewhere with their hands on the controls, while others took a few seconds to think about whether or not they had just been called a set of tools.

"Thank you for your time."

The applause was loud, filling the auditorium with a tinny, reverberating clapping sound. Anyone who had attended Spectra College in those years when they still split the auditorium in two knew that the audio quality was much better when seated on one side of a house divided. It was almost guaranteed to be a fuller sound, with more of what you wanted to hear.

Thank you for your time indeed. It's not like anything I said landed with these youths. Henny wasn't naive enough to believe that the shifting standards of society halfway through the 21st-century could be arrested or reversed by the rants of one person.

Who am I kidding? It's not just been the last two or three decades. The signs have been everywhere if anyone had chosen to see them.

Henny had learned that the louder she spoke of the craziness of it all, the less she was heard and the further afield her influence would lie, just as Harbs, and to some extent, Gossett, had warned her. Sure, people wanted to see totally crazy—and crazier—things. But they didn't want to be told that it was wrong, and they sure as hell didn't want to hear that the reason they were doing any of it was not their own, that their actions were not of their own volition.

They just wanted to know how to do it themselves or take advantage of it for themselves, especially if there was precedence. If someone else had already done something close to it or similar but maybe not quite as good, then just about anything could be justified. Which was reminiscent of a conversation from a few years earlier, in 2026, that Harbs had arranged. *I miss that guy.*

***

That solid hardwood door with the lion's head knocker in the center was imposing, as was thinking about what would be inside. How much of Henny's past would be attached to this man inside? *How had it all come to this weird full circle anyway?*

She pulled on the lion's mane, quickly recognizing that the door was far too heavy to attempt any noise-making with her knuckles. Henny was careful to raise and release the lion and then remove her fingers from the equation out of an abundance of caution that if the heavy door opened, she didn't want her hand to go with it. Of the many doors she had knocked down and passed through in her career, she tried her best never to lose any piece of herself along the way.

As the door opened to a room bathed in westerly light from the sun in a blue afternoon sky above a mesmerizing view of the Pacific, Henny was acutely aware that a cloudy feeling was fast approaching her mind.

"Oh my god," she said, trying to dampen the awkwardness of the setting. She took a few quick steps forward and hugged Ricky. When the request came in to meet with producer extraordinaire Ricky Templeton to assess a co-production proposal submitted to EMC's top executives, she jumped on the opportunity. But no matter what she had done to prepare, she couldn't have been fully ready for this moment.

He gripped her tight around the waist. "Henrietta, wow. I can't believe this," he said, happy to see his old classmate. "Like, really. What the fuck..."

She had looked over his shoulder and saw another familiar shape, this one a more imposing one. She let go of Ricky.

"Mitch... Zentax...! Hi!"

She jumped at and hugged the big man. Henny had never actually been sure if she should call him by his first or last name, even back in college, so she used both.

The toilet flushed, and the bathroom door clicked. Henny turned toward it as it began to open on the other side of the kitchen.

"Oh," her jaw dropped, her mouth hung agape.

Doug was drying his hands and looked up and across the open expanse of the room. "Oh!"

He stopped drying his hands.

"Ha ha! Surprise!" Ricky yelled out. "Y'all didn't expect this, did you?"

They didn't pay any attention to him. Doug had taken a few steps into the room. Hesitant at first, Henny followed suit and then accelerated. She took three, then four more big strides and jumped at Doug, nearly knocking him over. The relative size, weight, and physics involved with her initial surprise in seeing Zentax had not transferred so well in this case. Her excitement was greater, but Doug himself was much lesser.

They hadn't seen each other in almost fifteen years, since she vanished from the foursquare. She hugged him tightly, and he reciprocated but with less vigor, his actions muted by the sheer astonishment of the moment. He had buried those unrequited feelings so many years ago, yet in a blur, the pain and confusion of her leaving and that empty hole that lingered in his life for too long all came rushing back.

"I... what... I don't..." Doug was lost for words, which didn't happen as much anymore.

"Jesus, I know. I don't... whatever it is either!" Henny said, playing on his surprise with an ample supply of her own.

And there they were, scattered around the kitchen and its adjoining spaces. It was in a different kitchen, of much less refinement, the last time these four friends had been in the same place at the same time, with the present moment only short by one Korean-Australian-Texan.

The next few hours rolled by, and any awkwardness and strange feelings quickly dissipated. Old friends became new friends, especially when they had so much to talk about. Henny still had a job to do, after all. She was aware of Ricky's success with PDD, People Do Dum. Who wasn't? She had seen enough of it to know of Zentax's frequent starring roles. But Doug, she had seen some years ago that he latched on to a sports blog network and had often wondered what he could have been keeping himself busy with, given that the content in that sector had been completely auto-generated since at least 2021.

Ricky was quick to reveal that as soon as he learned that his co-production contact was none other than an EMC analyst by the name of Henrietta Adler, he jumped at the chance to make sure Zentax and, more importantly, Doug were there. But they both had a role to play as well.

"Zentax is going to be the first warden, the first Allied leader," Ricky shared as they started to get into the meat of the conversation. "And Doug will be leading the multi-platform broadcast coverage."

"Never would have thought the three of you would end up working together like this. Ricky, especially you, wow, you must feel really good about it all," she said, impressed by how successful he had become.

"You know, Henrietta..."

"Call me Henny," she interjected, with something she rarely ever said. Still, it felt appropriate, especially as the last thing she wanted was for Doug to resurrect his own co-option of her unwelcome teenage barnyard nickname.

"Henny," he corrected himself. "I do appreciate you saying that. I always looked up to you, and I think a lot of people didn't expect that I'd be someone who could do this, all of this," he waved his hands around, indicating his wealth and success. Channeling another pre-production conversation from months earlier with a different woman, he continued, "But no, I don't always feel great about it. So much of what we do feeds the platforms that fuel the hate, apathy, disinterest, and stupidity out there. I mean, I don't think any young college kids out there will be able to do what I did, or what you did, or even what Doug or Zentax did," he said in a resolute manner. His two other friends sat and listened, impermeable to the not-so-subtle insult he had just levied at them.

Ricky went on to explain how *The Conflux* was just a natural culmination of supply, demand, and the progression of technology. His formula was to take the "best" parts of sports, gaming, competition, content, streaming, and fan engagement. Viewers would be able to participate, contribute, and vote on in-competition events in real time.

"So everyone's complicit? You put these psychos—no offense, Zentax—into your battlefield and let them go, until...?" she asked the question on the mind of anyone who had heard the production concept already.

"Last one standing."

"That's kinda fucked up, isn't it?" she asked the next obvious question.

Ricky doubled down on his rationale, and quite frankly in the context of the world in which they lived, Henny found it hard to fault him for it.

"Look, we're not pulling the trigger. We're not even deciding what trigger they get. Hell, maybe it's a Rescue Axe. We just roll film. If shit goes down, that's not on us. That's on the viewers, right, Zentax? You're not out there doing this because you want to, right?"

Zentax looked at him in response, unable to answer in a timely way. Letting Ricky speak for him had been working for years, so he didn't really see why that needed to stop anytime soon. Plus, as he understood it, he'd be running around a tropical island, kicking ass and taking names.

"Anyway, for Zentax and for the other Allieds, there's no risk for them. They're just in there to clean up the level before the time runs out... get all the noobs out of there who don't belong," Ricky explained. "The only people dying are the ones who signed up to be a target."

The idea behind the game was that when time ran out in any particular battle, all weapons would be remotely disabled, allowing Zentax and his band of merry mercenaries to remove casualties and escort out anyone who had refused to participate. Zentax took comfort in knowing this wouldn't be the first time a social media celebrity became a fighter, and he couldn't see how anything could go wrong.

"Go on," Henny prompted.

"We're just giving the worst of the worst, the ringleaders of all those hate groups and divisive organizations, the unhinged motherfuckers, the unlocked trigger crowd, a place to play. They don't have to shoot anyone in their front yard anymore. They don't have to go to the mall or go postal anymore. 'Postal'... Ha! Or if you're a vigilante, if you get off on taking out the scum of the earth, then here's your starring role. They all sign up with us, and they have at it."

Initially, Ricky had concerns about whether or not they would be able to find enough participants for *The Conflux*. He had first enlisted PDD's Targeted Media team to build out a definitive profiling framework based on the types of things their targets did and said online, their purchases and subscriptions, their Mixality MSE scores, and a wealth of other black-box data to identify fighters of interest, or "FOIs" as they called them. It turned out that all they needed to do was post a casting call website, and the crazies came knocking.

"You can either have more January 6's, you can have more Norways, more school shootings, or you have this. There's a reason we've got the support for it," he said. It also didn't hurt that they could hide behind Internet Service Provider regulations from the early 1990s or the decisions by Congress in the late '10s that absolved other massive platforms of responsibility for user behavior. Ricky and *The Conflux* were simply intermediaries.

"You've got support because of the eyeballs and ad dollars," Henny challenged. As altruistic as it might sound for Ricky to stand here and espouse how their made-for-TV murder party was going to cure all of society's ills, she knew what forces were really behind this.

"And I suppose you would be well aware of that, right Henny? Right, *Harriet Stone?* Don't act like you aren't a part of this. Don't act like you don't know that if people want to follow—actually, if we want people to follow—a story, it needs to be wrapped in tragedy. And maybe backed up with some fireworks. And if it takes care of some problems along the way, no one has a problem with it. They all want to see it," Ricky concluded.

He wasn't wrong. Filming the production on an unincorporated island in the South Pacific didn't hurt either. Everyone involved with the production had really enjoyed the weather in that part of the world. Many of them had become good surfers, too. Provided they avoided the worst of the cyclone season, it was a nice escape from what had become increasingly less welcoming winters in Los Angeles.

"So back to my question, you're saying if everyone's complicit, then nobody's responsible?" Henny probed.

"Exactly."

Thirty-one

ART IMITATES

If only we could attribute all this malice to that evil cabal. Things are always better when there is someone to blame, and everybody likes to say the word "cabal." That blameful group would be sinister. They would be brilliant, much smarter than the most advanced intellect of the general population. To deceive us and coerce us in these many terrible ways, the underground manipulators had surely attained a level of genius that, despite their ill intentions, was worthy of respect.

They would operate over countless generations, twisting and turning the sentiment of society and the fabric of global culture in service of their own nefarious objectives.

And wow, when the disparate, unnoticed squares of their authoritarian quilt are woven together, it's the mother of all conspiracies, and as Ricky was so astute as to remind Henny, everyone likes a good tragedy.

Investigative journalists, scribes, and storytellers have been writing of these secretive puppeteering groups in literary circles for centuries, millenia even. As far back as the Age of Antiquity, conspiracies have always done what they do, which is abound. Pagan beliefs infiltrate all religions and seed them with the same base principles of peace, love, and goodwill. But none will admit it, so no peace will truly be had. The Knights Templar, The Illuminati, Indiana Jones, and Tom Hanks all played a role in their respective times of fostering deep, dark, romantic notions of sordid deeds afoot under the veil of a functioning society. The prestigious Narcos and the War on Drugs ensured that billions of dollars could flow to the right—and sometimes left—pockets. A state with an enemy guaranteed there would be desirable budgetary allocations for decades, as long as the average citizen was prevented from realizing it wasn't a war on farmers and disorganized bandits. Nearly everybody has heard the tale of Pablo Escobar burying all that illicitly-gained money on his many properties without ever questioning the fact that paper money of any significant amount would never survive a rainy season in Colombia unless he had commissioned the creation of a watertight warehouse the size of a soccer field under his many rolling acres of pasture. The reality makes it far less believable and less exciting.

The Freemasons have steered human activity for centuries. Or have they? More recently, the QAnons, the Young Gainers, and countless other collective voices have posted, texted, tweeted, and deep-faked tirelessly to craft divisions among interest groups and to reshape malleable individuals, directing them toward unfathomable choices across a multitude of fronts. These loud-voice collectives keep popping out of the woodwork—or the network—and all of them with monikers and acronyms that sound more like the name of a boy band and, to the detriment of society, nearly as influential.

These groups, movements, and larger-than-life characters make for fantastic stories. They are all so excessive in their announcements and prognostications that they demand attention, yet unbelievable enough that a debate—or a discussion, or too often a shootout—is encouraged. And they are all a superlative comment on human potential; there is a common thread that ensnares all those who believe, don't believe, support, or oppose these fantastical entities.

Pride. Our subconscious, perhaps nestled in our reptilian brains, has a subdued but palpable response of appreciation that humanity, despite our many failures and flaws, is complex, intelligent, organized, and yes, even nasty enough to be those conspirators of ire.

Perhaps the new cabal, the one responsible for all these strange things, was similarly subconscious. It was a byproduct of our collective instinctual behavior, of our global animalistic gray matter. It was unintentional and probably, in many ways, our own fault. We all bought into it by buying into it, making it believable and sort of fun to believe in. A bunch of greedy, clumsy capitalists could be pointed at and blamed for it without anyone having to look in the mirror. Roger Clancy, Mark Zuckerberg, and Elon Musk. The hordes of venture capitalists, analysts, and operators that assembled these massive corporate juggernauts, all of them being rewarded for pushing buttons like a data warehouse engineer or a rideshare driver.

While no one likes the day-to-day outcomes of what these global power brokers have done to our society, everyone loves the minute-to-minute participation.

Though perhaps this new cabal had hope. Maybe this was no longer just the new season of Vanderbilt, Rockefeller, and Carnegie. Maybe it wasn't just a new school of greedy white men doing the same thing, just a few years apart.

Technology has granted disruption and decentralization. Surely, the world's networks were democratic and impartial. They couldn't possibly have carried over the cultural and ethnic inequalities borne by those who built those very networks, could they? Without a doubt, the machinery and hardware that operate the systems that direct us and reward us are all virtual, as we have been reminded so often. They must be ethereal, directly accessible to no one, but beneficial to everyone. After all, that's what the exciting, believable story had been since the dawn of the World Wide Web and the aforementioned new superpower of ranking Pages had been bestowed upon humanity.

Even the disorganized impromptu membership format of the techno-authoritarians had granted access to new entrants, like the South Asian American Canadian woman Somaya Patel. A CEO of the new way of doing things, Somaya had been universally appreciated for how her business, CVI, was streamlining national energy systems around the world.

If it weren't for one of the organizations within the connected conspirators, people may never have become aware of many of the accusations that were directed at our corporate overseers. EMC—Everything Matters Corp.—has been covering advancements in technology and human potential for so long now, and with such authority, that it has become the definitive source for a future-looking view on, well, everything that matters.

Had it been a bombshell that its superstar, its headline reporter and analyst Harriet Stone, had left the organization? For a minute, it was, and then there was another post.

Had it been even more alarming that a woman named Henrietta Adler had shortly thereafter revealed that she had been *the* Harriet Stone, in the same breath that she announced the release of her memoirs from the frontlines of EMC? This, too, had also generated some noise but had its work cut out, as it was announced the same week as Season 16 of *The Conflux* in late 2028. Even though Henny had authored her book to the consumption tastes of the day, providing it in 463 chapters of mixed media format, with never more than 1,020 characters of text per, Season 16 of *The Conflux* had already captivated the imagination and captured the anticipation of the world's population. Ricky and the producers had realized in the second year of this format of the show that the viewing audience did not have the patience for downtime between Seasons. To meet that demand, they started rolling them out initially quarter-annually, then monthly, and now, they worked furiously to have a new live-streaming season starting every week.

Viewers no longer had to binge-watch, forget, and re-watch before the next season came out. Now they could gorge on *The Conflux* to their heart's content!

Despite the competitive media landscape she found herself in, Henny's book had found its audience with the benefit of some unexpected help. *The Fix Was Always In* became an international bestseller, with over two million chapters being sold across media formats in the first week.

Henny had left EMC shortly after Harbs' death, and the company had responded with, to Henny's delight and with a sign of utmost respect, an offer to support her independent authorship aspirations. After EMC's social media marketing machinations took over, *The Fix* became a near-overnight sensation.

The Fix was a fictional novel, a collection of short stories written with a cast of colorful and delightful characters in such a way that it shone a light on many of the real issues of the day, yet all of them divorced enough from their real-world inspiration and with enough distance that it could hardly be called an exposé. For better and worse, it did achieve the label of 'The Conspiracy Manifesto for the 2030's' by the Association of Bloggers, Streamers, Mixers, and TikTokers. In an attempt to draw new crowds, Facebook had promoted it on the loading screen for its app with exclusive day-and-date access to twenty-eight of the most controversial chapters. However, the concept and format had proven too challenging for that platform's primarily eighty-year-old demographic, who were mostly concerned with longevity podcasts and free plants, though to be fair, they continued to inquire upon *The Fix*, asking, "Is this still available?" long after the promotion had ended.

Some of the most revealing parts of the book would ultimately become spin-off series of their own accord.

The University of Guinea was a delightful segment about how a large corporate organization had established a medical university on a fictional peninsula and provided students with just enough resources to keep fresh recruits coming back every year. The subtext to the story was that "Big Ed," a cute name for the educational-industrial complex, had been using the school to create structured, longitudinal training data for its AI algorithms by observing every aspect of the college life of its inhabitants. Moral questions had been exposed that contemplated how humans in the transition from childhood to responsible adults could be manipulated into becoming functional servants within a new, AI-coordinated working class.

All About Us wove a story of a retired undersea explorer who was a scientist by trade but a historian by choice. This man had collaborated with an operations executive at a social media company to compare and contrast ancient literature—including cave drawings and a big focus on the works of members of The School of Athens—with harvested data across all public sources and social media APIs. Together, they had crafted the *Tome of Humanity*, a celebration of cultural strength, which invading aliens had ultimately found and used to target our greatest weaknesses.

Rafaella and The Flying 1s and 0s told a tale of a female ethnic minority technology executive, Rafaella Martinez, and her struggles to launch a traffic telemetry system. She had fought tooth and nail, and where that didn't work, charmed her way through minefields of regulation and governmental bureaucracy. It was only after achieving her dream of deploying hundreds of traffic cameras in every city that it became apparent her trusted eyes in the sky had been hacked into by those same administrative regulators, who had been selling the data on to the military.

Her short stories had struck a chord with many millions of readers. Often, they would be scrolling through chapters and talkback videos of those chapters while watching and voting on *The Conflux*, which was always a sign of successful content. Anything that could occupy a part of a reader's mind while they were otherwise engaged with something so addictive as the most popular entertainment production of all time was a feather in the cap for the content creator.

And to their credit, people had started to connect the dots. Readers and posters and talkback video makers had begun to read between the proverbial lines and see much of what Henny had strong reason to believe to be true.

Others had drawn lines back to Harriet Stone articles, making it easier for them to weave fact from fiction, from Diddem.com harvesting people's benign daily habits and developing longitudinal psychological profiles to Mixality's generally profit-driven intentions with no regard as to the safety or privacy of anything related to its users, to the manipulation of development data by cities all around the world in the marginalization of lower-class and homeless populations. Every so often, these global puppeteers might have been subject to investigation or interrogation, like in those old funny meme videos from Congress, but they could always honestly hide behind the opaque cover of one-liners like "We sell ads," or "We lay pipe," or "We're just making planes," or even, perhaps worst of all, "We just wanted to sell some books."

Life and death were not left off the table for discussion either. Conspiracists had been quick to accuse DeathBank and its owners at MCA of holding back on their advancements in life sciences and their predictive models for vitality and instead focusing on morbidity and, in more extreme accusations, ethnic cleansing.

Often, and most often while watching *The Conflux*, there were vociferous debates on how involved the military-industrial complex had been in the production of the show. In some of the more elaborate conspiracies, accusations were levied that the biggest stars and best fighters were not actually humans, and instead, fans around the world had been watching and enabling the development of ultimate humanoid robot killing machines.

Fascinating stuff.

Even Ret. Gen. Glenn Phipps' now fifty-year-old theories began to be resuscitated. People were adamant that NASA had been holding back communications with aliens for years, but now they had the proof when they merged the factual record from Harriet Stone's trustworthy reporting with time-stamped immutable statements from the dearly departed Ret. Gen. Glenn Phipps.

As these nefarious interpretations of the world raged on in digital discourse around the planet, so did the waves of the COVI pandemic tear through populations. Perhaps the only thing more staggering than the death rates were the growing viewership numbers for *The Conflux*, and even that was subject for debate. Which was worse? Which was bigger? Which would kill you first?

Thirty-two

ORIGINAL SIN

If some of the most influential minds at NASA had been, on the one hand, trying to propagate conspiracies, and on the other, trying to expose them, and doing both of these poorly, then who the hell was Henny to believe she could successfully author some sort of believable conspiratorial doomsday scenario?

She was certain that had she done so, she would have more than likely ended up like poor old Ret. Gen. Glenn Phipps, living her last days in a shack in the woods trying to convince passersby of secretive longstanding extraterrestrial relationships, or whatever her equivalent would be. She most certainly would not have been able to achieve the success she had with her first book, nor the career it had spawned, replete with speaking engagements and executive production roles in other media projects. She had just finished a pre-production meeting with the east coast office of PDD productions, who had licensed the rights to *All About Us,* Henny's short story about the Tome of Humanity. A short story that, not coincidentally, ended up with the destruction of humans by alien invaders.

I suppose that's helping the old general in my own way.

But just because she chose not to directly say it in her works, or to levy accusations, or to regretfully disappear into the forest, didn't mean she didn't harbor a sense of the unknown, of questions that even her massively enquiring mind had not yet been able to get to the bottom of.

Like, what the hell had really happened to Harbs?

Quite possibly, it was simply that she found it exceptionally hard to believe that he was so abruptly gone because he was always so attendant in her life. He hadn't been an anomaly. So many other millions of people had died in those days, in the first wave of COVI. And then again in the second, and the third. If they—whoever the fuck "they" were—hadn't come up with the waterborne vaccine, she more than likely wouldn't be around to even be contemplating Harbs' demise.

She hadn't really felt sad about it either. Death had simply become a part of everyday life, even before COVI. As Ricky had readily acknowledged, we are all complicit in observing and celebrating violence. He had simply taken it to the logical next step to proclaim that with universal guilt comes absolution for all. It was a hard and true fact—we abhorred violence, and we also adored violence as long as everyone else did.

Maybe it was the conversation with Ricky, Zentax, and Doug that had been the last straw. The surreal oddity of seeing those guys after all this time combined with her mixed feelings about *The Conflux* made for a lasting experience that she could never fully resolve.

Harbs had suspected she had come close to her tipping point on that trip, and Henny could tell that's why he had eventually told her what he had. He revealed that the actual reason for her initial recruitment had nothing to do with the objective measure of her skills and abilities.

"What?" she had said, volume fueled by indignation.

Rather, it was the defensive necessity of immediately stopping the amateur investigative work that she had been doing in and around Spectra College in the original *Fix*, the article published in the school paper that brought on the attention of the administration.

Original Fix. That's a much better name.

"They needed you out of there, Henny," he had said. "The Board needed you to stop. They had no stick, so they gave me the biggest possible carrot to offer," alluding to the over-weighted job offer presented by the dissociative millennial Chris Benter.

"Kind of nice of you to tell me, fifteen years after the fact, Harbs. So basically, I wrote a bunch of amateur crap that pissed people off, and they chose to secretly pay me to go away? Why didn't they just... pay me to go away?" she said sarcastically, annoyed by his implication.

"Hold up. It's not an indictment of a lack of ability. In fact, I'd say it's the opposite. The Board, and everyone who had sent those orders down, they were scared to death at the quality of what you'd put together. As I think you've learned over these years, there are a lot of soapbox rants that fall on deaf ears. We saw your work as being the opposite of that. You were crafting a compelling story. Top-down and bottoms-up. All the pieces fit together."

"Oh, so very charming. So tell me why that's important for you to tell me now. I'm pissed off enough already with some of this stuff, and you think this makes me feel better?" Henny demanded.

"I just thought you should know the truth. They saw it as killing two birds with one stone, sort of like Zentax in his first episode on *Fastnite*," Harbs added. "They figured they could turn down the volume on what you were doing around the university and get the benefit of your exceptional writing and storytelling in other parts of the business."

"Okay, that sounds great and maybe good for a book. In fact, yeah, I think I'll keep some of that top of mind." She hadn't yet shared with him that she had been working on *The Fix Was Always In*, but she looked forward to having him read it when it was ready. "I just want an answer from you. We've been doing this for the better part of fifteen years now, to what end? What exactly are we doing here?"

This was the part where Henny still suspects he had revealed too much. EMC, within the MCA empire, had had an initial, somewhat altruistic, objective to publish more meaningful content to the world. Their forward-looking predictions had expected that everyone's content consumption demands would evolve in lockstep with advancements in software and networks, and become more and more sophisticated.

But the opposite happened.

"If you told someone fifty years ago, or a hundred years ago, that they would have access to all the world's information, to every smart thing that had ever been said, in the palm of their hand, well... their description, their expectation, of the world would be radically different than what you and I have seen."

"Yeah, the smart got stupid, and the stupid got stupider," she said, repeating that classic refrain from the now very elderly Rip Gossett.

"Exactly. More or less. So needless to say, our theories weren't exactly on-point."

Where Harbs himself had missed the point was how this observation had landed with Henny, that after MCA or EMC realized no one could handle anything important or intellectual, she had essentially been recast as an overpaid clickbait headline writer with the unheralded night shift working on market research for MCA.

She was disappointed and angry—not at Harbs, but at herself—for placing her trust in this partner and his obvious priority treatment of the organization ahead of her.

Harbs had never seemed to realize his faux pas—his unintentional backhanded insult to her abilities and the diminishment of her years of work—delivered in one fell swoop. Henny attributed that to the fact that Harbs was, well, a guy. He worked for a company founded by men, operated predominantly by older men, and with that, he had skillfully honed his lack of any semblance of a framework of equality. *How could he possibly understand what it's like to break into a technology-heavy organization as an anomaly, as an outsider?*

Looking back on it now, this was the moment when she decided to leave. Harbs' passing a few years later just helped solidify her decision.

I mean, fucking "Deathbank" might have done it by itself. That seemed like a good enough reason to quit.

The East Coast PDD production office was located in Northfield, just a short drive from the Atlantic City International Airport. It was also only forty minutes from Valemont—that small New Jersey town now internationally recognized as the home of Spectra College and the founding operations of People Do Dum. Ricky had been steadfast in his efforts to set up an eastern seaboard headquarters and to do so close to their alma mater. The media and journalism school at the college had grown massively and was now by far the biggest faculty, if one could call it that. Ricky did call it that and demanded everyone else to do the same after he made a hundred million dollar donation to the school to construct a state-of-the-art production facility.

As Henny left the production meeting about *All About Us,* she took a decidedly undirected walk. Being here again, in New Jersey, in the fall, rekindled her spirit. It stoked her imagination and pried open powerful memories of those first couple of years further up the interstate at Spectra. The wind from the ocean was stronger here than it had been on campus, but most everything else felt familiar.

The blocks were long, the sidewalks wide, and the deciduous trees were massive. Oak trees, most likely, though she wasn't close enough to the sparse remaining foliage to assess if the branches held those telltale rounded sawtooth lobes.

As she turned the corner to the block her hotel was on, the wind picked up in ferocity. The temperature dropped further, and she pulled her jacket tighter around her torso, tucking her chin into its collar and leaning into the last hundred yards or so to the hotel. There was a coffee shop on the main floor, and the barista had perfected a mocha recipe designed to combat these late autumn easterlies.

The door handle was cold, and the glass mostly misted. With a heavy push, it opened, breaking the vacuum effect of warm air trapped inside by the Bernoullian air movement whipping alongside the exterior wall of glass windows. The competing air pressures fought for a brief moment as she traversed from one to the other, and then the door was sucked closed again, reinstating the comfortable interior of the cafe.

Henny held her cold hands up to her face and breathed into them instinctually. This was the type of thing that had been frowned upon during the COVI pandemic. In those times, the lack of Disease actually made it worse. No one really knew when they first had it, and everyone thought everyone else had it, other than those who didn't believe it ever existed to begin with. But even though social activities had been reinvigorated, it was all the small things that people became really sensitive to. A mosh pit in a busy nightclub was okay, but touching your face in a business meeting would often derail conversation and divide the attendees in ways that there would be no coming back from. Often, as was human habit, just thinking about touching one's face would cause someone to touch their face, setting off a stream of judgment and derision in their immediate vicinity. Put another way, when the internal question was asked, "Am I touching my face?" the answer would always come back resoundingly affirmative.

By 2035, the WHO had completed the global rollout of water treatment that carried with it the Kingslayer vaccine, which, as its name implied, made its mark on history by defeating the Coronavirus. Its unveiling had been met with anticipation and contempt as the celebrity president of the WHO, Fang Wing, had famously stood up at a press conference for the official announcement of the vaccine's name, smiled at the room with her equally famous perfect set of teeth, and said, "See what I did there?"

Henny's entrance had caused a temporary stir amongst the patrons in the cafe, the inflow of cold air triggering everyone's senses for an instant. A man and his son sat near the window at a high table, poring over a tablet. They might have been reviewing the child's homework or, more likely, were watching this week's highlights from *The Conflux*. A few teenage girls were near the bar, awaiting the completion of their order from the barista, watching with anticipation as he loaded up the tops of their drinks with some kind of brilliantly colored, sugary, foamy concoction. Two women were seated on a lower set of couches, one of them pouring the contents of a teapot into two carefully decorated cups and saucers on the low table in front of them.

They had all looked at her and then returned to what they were doing. But one set of eyes hadn't yet looked down. And as Henny pulled her hands down from the fog of that warm breath of air, she caught those other eyes with her own.

She smiled. Nothing else existed. She had come in from the cold Jersey autumn air to this warm, welcoming environment, and here he was. They might as well have been an hour up the road at Spectra and twenty-five years in the past.

"Doug?"

"Yes. Hen? I mean, Henny?"

He hadn't said much to her when they last met, which, unbelievably, was now over ten years ago. He had come to regret how so much of that conversation ended up being led by Ricky, as had become his way throughout his successful career. But Doug had remembered every minute of it, from his stepping awkwardly out of the bathroom drying his hands to the frantic and weird hug they had shared to the impressively surgical deconstruction Henny had performed on Ricky's plans for *The Conflux*. And he had remembered ever so clearly the moment she corrected the boys of her preferred name.

She took slower steps toward him than she had at Ricky's oceanside mansion, though with every bit as much intrigue and excitement. They embraced, a bundle of arms wrapped in and around her thick coat and his thin collared shirt and sweater vest.

"What are you doing here?" she asked, with no shortage of surprise.

"I'm... I'm here to meet with Ricky's people about a new show," he said. He had been fired from *The Conflux* over forty seasons ago, which in human terms equated to just under a year, or in real human terms, had been about seven hundred deaths; daily losers from the series, which now boasted two daily real-time episodes conducted in time zones twelve hours apart. This ensured a continuous stream of fresh content, or "fresh blood," as the PDD production teams like to say internally.

Doug's firing was unexpected, as he had developed a unique camaraderie with his co-host Althea Swinton. However, when they extended the voting mechanism to give viewers the chance to select new hosts, Althea remained while Doug had been sent packing, her new co-host Libby Walker joining with a wealth of experience from across the production industry. It also didn't hurt that she was a media darling. Libby had been the key public whistleblower in a big case a few years ago, resulting in Philip J. Clancy stepping down from his nearly two-decade run of sociopathic decision-making as the CEO of Mixality. Libby was a shit-kicker and loaded with charisma. It was easy for Doug to see why he had been voted off the island.

"Cool... me too. How about that?" she said while wondering if Ricky had somehow been up to some of his old tricks and had conspired with his production staff to arrange for these two to be here at the same time. But she didn't think so, nor did she care. Henny was truly happy to see Doug.

"Oh wow, which one is yours?" he looked at her while posing this question.

"Oh, well, it's in pre-production. I'm not sure I can talk much about it, but it's from one of my short stories from the book," she said.

"Oh. Oh... well, I meant which coffee is yours," he gestured to the bar. "But that's super cool. I loved your book," he said, reverting back to how he might have spoken with her twenty-five years ago, completely overwhelmed and intimidated. She obviously hadn't ordered yet, as they were both still standing in line to do so.

Why is this happening? I thought I was past this. His inner voice lambasted himself.

"Oh, Doug, I haven't ordered anything yet. I was going to get a mocha, it's cold outside," she said.

"Yeah, well, let me buy it for you. I owe you," he said. He didn't owe her anything.

"You don't owe me, Doug, but sure!" she said, feeling very pleased to be in this extremely simple and practical conversation.

He kept talking as they waited for the barista to finish with the teenage girls' fancy drinks.

"You know, Henny, I really did love the book, I could totally tell it was your style. And I mean the original *Fix* was so good, so unappreciated..." he said.

She interrupted him, "What did you say?"

"Uhh, I said it was so good, and no one appreciated it the way they..." he answered, trying to repeat his words.

"No, you said, '*Original Fix*,'" Henny said, repeating the description she had thought to herself just a short time ago. Those same words had just come from this guy standing in the line in front of her, the same guy who had always understood what she wanted to do with the original *Fix*, the same guy who had listened to her rant when others hadn't understood it, and the same guy who had broken the damn tablet that started all this crazy shit.

"Yeah, original *Fix*, right. The first one," he repeated for no good reason other than a complete lack of new words to add to the discussion.

Henny looked at him. Doug nervously turned to look back toward the counter to see if the barista was available. They weren't. She poked his shoulder blade with her index finger, causing him to meet those same eyes he had recognized even when they were mostly hidden behind a steamy breath and two bundled-up fists. The same eyes, the same face, the same arms that had been fanning the smoke out of the kitchen, that had been ranting with exhaustion about the sins laid bare in the original *Fix*. The same lips, now devoid of the application of coconut milk but showing every bit as much luster, that had once said...

"Fuck me, Dougie." Yes, those were the words she had said on a Friday night at the shared rental Pennsylvania foursquare with the wobbly and long-since replaced kitchen table.

And she had just said them again.

Her eyes lit up, a reminiscent mischievous grin forming further below them on her face. His face reflected the surprise, joy, and excitement that were forcing their way out from the deepest, most sincere parts of his heart and soul. Further down, other parts of him were pushing their way up.

Doug nodded. Henny nodded back, with a subtle laughter escaping from behind that familiar, wry smile.

They turned and left the cafe in the direction of the hotel elevator, the access codes on their smartphones giving them a choice of two different rooms.

Thirty-three

ENCODED

Somaya had always taken tremendous pride in her ability to read people. It had rarely let her down, save for that one enormous lesson earlier in her career. Over the years and decades to follow, it became the one thing that she could consistently rely upon, that whatever situation she was in, she was supremely confident that when push came to shove, her intellect and empathy would leave her standing tall and triumphant.

The Helix nurses had become just another target, another vessel of lesser intelligence that she could interpret and then instruct to fulfill her bidding—whatever that meant in a place where she was already paying outlandish sums of money to have her every need taken care of. In that sense, it was more like a game for Somaya, or a training exercise to strengthen those mental muscles and sharpen those senses, to see how far she could push the nurses and support staff without them realizing she was exuding this otherworldly control over them. Most often, they had no idea.

And this is what was so damn frustrating. She couldn't comprehend how the thing she knew better than anything else, even better than she knew Warren, could have fooled her at such an exorbitant scale.

Warren had continued his network forensics. Even though much of the ever-expanding CVI network architecture remained off-limits, he was able to poke around the edges and find yet more evidence but no real answers.

He found indications of control logs for what appeared to be a large-scale coordination of flight paths. He discovered data transfer details that indicated, if extrapolated to the scale he thought was suggested, the potential movement of several exabytes worth of data. This was fascinating, not the least because he had never had the opportunity to talk about an exabyte in an actual, practical situation.

"Sommy, whoever set this up, they might be moving exabytes worth of data," he said, rather proudly.

With every day, her mind and body were becoming sharper and stronger, but every night ended much the same, with Somaya lying in her hospital bed receiving a debrief from Warren.

"Okay, so now you could probably tell me what an exabyte is, but I guess I don't need to know, seeing as how excited you are about it. You're saying a shit ton of data, like more than we've ever dealt with?" she asked.

"Yeah, like orders of magnitude more. Like, more than we ever thought we would ever receive even if we were dealing with all the security cameras in every building all around the world." He thought for a minute before offering a caveat, "Well, maybe, but you get the idea."

"So if it's that much data, where the hell are we storing it, and how the hell have we not seen it?" she asked.

"Great question. First up, I think there's been so much plumbing put in that we just couldn't keep up—at least no one person could keep up—with what was stored and where, and what exactly we were doing with all of it. On face value, not a bad problem. The flip side, if we were hemorrhaging the data we were receiving and couldn't recover it, would be much worse."

"Fair point. Okay, but if this is just filling up our network on a daily or nightly basis, then who is doing what with it, and when?" she asked, knowing he would likely provide this context imminently.

"There you go again, acting like you know what I was going to say next." Warren smiled. "He pulled up another text file on his laptop and turned the screen to face her. "What does this look like to you?" he asked.

She knew this was one of his rhetorical mechanisms, to pose a question he knew was unanswerable by the person he was posing it to, thus eliciting curiosity that he could satisfy.

"Looks like a bunch of bullshit to me, Warry," she said, having trouble keeping a smile from invading her lips despite the seriousness of what they had found themselves up against. From the very first time she had called him "Warry," it had helped Somaya immeasurably to use that pet name for him. Especially in stressful or uncertain times. She surmised that it somehow subconsciously allowed her to speak to her "worries" via her Warry/Warren proxy, effectively transmitting those concerns for his overly analytical and often beautifully ignorant mind to deal with, in the same breath absolving hers of any obligations. He was, to great effectiveness and the relief of Somaya, a veritable garburator of bullshit.

"Ha! Well, yep, Miss Straightgoods, thanks for serving that up. Because it is, as you say, a bunch of bullshit. It's bullshit to me, and to you, anyway, because what it is, is some kind of encrypted encoding of all of this data. All these potential exabytes."

"Encoded? So, someone broke it down and structured all this footage in some way?"

"Exactly. Someone has done this," he said, pointing at the bullshit, "out of this," as he ALT+TABbed his way back to one of the crash scene videos that they couldn't help but watch religiously, and on weekdays too.

"Now," he continued, "provided they aren't complete idiots, or maybe that we aren't complete idiots—and I believe there's enough evidence in both camps to rule those out—this is some smart motherfucker. I mean, what this is telling me is they've written some kind of computer vision algorithm that can encode any piece of footage into a bunch of gobbledygook, and then throw that footage away. If the encoded information is actually intelligible, and structured, and reusable, I mean, Jesus fucking Christ, that changes everything."

Warren so rarely swore that when he used language like this, Somaya knew he was wholly consumed with what was happening. She could tell that he was in awe of whatever it was he was looking at. That he didn't yet know what it was had her equally and intensely on edge.

Night after night they would reconvene, she without anywhere to go, and he with only this place to be. His discoveries had started to tail off, often resulting in nothing more than another abandoned log file or segment of video footage. Occasionally, Warren would hit authentication problems within the network that he couldn't crack, yet those access blockers raised at least two concerns. The first being that it must be an inside job, especially considering that it was resulting in exceptional performance results for the company. Thus, he had no reason to think some evil external hackers were running DDOS attacks or something similar to that, which they might otherwise be rightly concerned about. But because it was coming from the inside and no one was taking responsibility for it, there had to be something else going on. This oddity in logic raised his second concern, the all-important question of *why the fuck are they doing this?* Maybe someone was skimming profits, or running other computational jobs, or doing something else he couldn't figure out. The risk, of course, is that if they were to fully commit to disentangling the multiple threads of this enigma, there would be no telling what they might find.

"I agree, Warry, we can't expose this, we can't open it up yet, not until we have a better idea of what's going on. If someone is doing anything malicious, then in some crazy way, I guess I should say, 'Keep doing it,' but we need to know what it is first. And if we did anything to poke a stick in the spokes of this thing now, the investors would have my ass. Hell, at this scale, the entire company could be at risk." Somaya knew that the unexplainable cost structure that had led them down this path would be hard enough to explain purely from a financial standpoint, let alone the massive flying elephant in the room of mysterious surveillance technology. Well, it wasn't actually in the room.

Jesus, maybe it's in this fucking room? She thought, looking around at all the state-of-the-art monitors, sensors, and devices in her hospital room.

"I mean, shit, Warry, every night we sit here and think about what to do, god knows how many of these things are flying around the world capturing all sorts of stuff that we don't—that no one—has the right to see. The fact that we even know that might be happening right now scares the shit out of me. The more I think about it, the only reason we have any plausible deniability whatsoever is because you haven't been able to crack that encoding."

Without realizing the nature of Somaya's pragmatic analysis of the situation, specifically the positive side effect their stonewalled position currently afforded them, Warren couldn't help but take her comment as a challenge to his technical competency. He committed at that moment to solving this once and for all. "Yeah, I hear you. But I can get there. I'll figure this thing out."

"At some level, I sort of want to ask you not to... if you fully understand what I'm saying." What she was saying was that they should be very careful how they talk about figuring it out, and even more careful of any potential audit trail Warren might leave behind.

"Wait, you want me to stop? How..." he was confused.

"No, you beautiful idiot. I don't want you to stop. But I want you to stop, and if you chose not to stop, you should make damn well sure that no one could ever see that you hadn't stopped," she said in an attempt to clarify the request.

"Okay, gotcha, so I'll keep going then," he said, still ambivalent to her coded request, the format of which was ironic given the task at hand. She smiled and shook her head, confident that the weirdness of this very discussion would keep him mostly silent until he found something important.

As it turned out, Somaya made far more progress on her own physical recovery than Warren would on his investigation. The weeks and months rolled by. Her strength kept growing, almost in lockstep with the continued expansion of CVI. With every additional step she was able to take in a row without tiring, it seemed like a new office had opened, or a new customer had come online, or a new record-breaking financial statement had been delivered to their shareholders.

And with every next milestone passed for the company, the thought of unraveling it all in the pursuit of answers seemed selfish at best and more likely to be destructive. Somaya and Warren would have many long conversations and endure many sleepless nights on the topic, but the more they processed it and still came up empty for answers, the only option they were left with was to do nothing—to walk the line laid out in front of them, while carrying the unrelenting burden of not knowing why it had been drawn, nor by whom.

"To put it bluntly Warren, the hounds are out. We've only been out of COVID for a few years now, and you give any one hostile shareholder, regulator, or competitor a sliver of an opportunity... you give them a drop of blood, and they will take you out. Look at what they're doing to Phil Clancy over at Mixality," she said.

"Well, look, he's in the crosshairs because he basically abused his staff. To say nothing of how many privacy and security laws he was happy to drive a truck through while they built up that platform. That guy is a fucking piece of work, and possibly worse, and somehow he just gets away with it. I doubt they get him this time either," Warren reminded her. Mixality had proven to be enduring even in the face of common sense. It had thrived through the Market St. mob, exited mostly unscathed from the Young Gainers controversy, and survived countless other periods of drama that other resilient companies would have faltered under the weight of. And above all the noise, violence, indiscretion, and criminal undertakings on the platform, Philip J. Clancy had remained on top, taking all the glory and none of the criticism. Several years henceforth, that would ultimately prove to be his own undoing, with his ego unable to stand in the way of what ended up being dozens of allegations of bullying, abuse, and sexual harassment. The figurehead of the accusations and the primary witness at the trial that would come to pass had been a former employee named Libby Walker, of the same name and the same person as the billion-follower TikTok star Libby Walker.

But for now, Philip J. Clancy remained in charge. "You know the big difference between us, right Warry?" Somaya asked.

"What do you mean, between you and me? Well, yeah, we've sort of talked about this before," he started to answer.

"No, not me and you, you dummy. Well, other than picking up on nuance and understanding context, that's where we are different. Between me and Phil Clancy," she clarified for him.

"Oh, he's a raving lunatic and has built something that makes people hate each other, and he's clueless about technology and pretty clueless about people. I'll go there, he's different from you in those ways," Warren quickly replied. He didn't have a lot of respect for people like Philip J. Clancy, especially when compared to the brilliance of his beautiful wife.

"Okay, you get bonus points. The other way he's different," she said, looking carefully at Warren, her big brown eyes staring toward his eyes but not at them. She was looking through his face, beginning with the blank, boring skin of his forehead and cheeks.

"He's white."

"Uh-uh," Warren nodded, realizing with fault that a combination of his own privilege in cahoots with his commendable egalitarian view on race had restricted him from seeing the very obvious discriminating factor that was always front and center for Somaya.

"He's a spoiled white kid from a family of spoiled white kids who all grow up to be rich white men. That's what, and yeah, all those things you said too. And because he's white, he floats above it all. I don't get that free pass, Warren, you know that," Somaya concluded.

But before he could reply, a part of their conversation triggered something else for her.

He floats. Wait a minute.

"Warren, give me your laptop," she demanded, and he complied.

Bearing its distinctive heat signature upon her lap, the computer was immediately pressed into forced labor as Somaya furiously combed through the internet, seeking a particular ranked page that had somehow been seared into her longer-term memory several years earlier.

"Ah, I can't find it," she complained after a few minutes.

"What are you looking for?" Warren asked.

"I'm sure there was this old article, years ago, with that piece of shit Clancy involved. Looks like it's all been pulled down," she said, indicating a few 404 errors showing up in the browser from links that didn't seem to lead anywhere. "Or maybe I'm making it up in my mind?"

"Check the Wayback Machine," Warren offered.

Right! The Internet Archives.

Initially one of the more entertaining offerings on the internet, the Internet Archives was a non-profit organization started in the heyday of the dotcom boom in Silicon Valley. Somehow, they had still retained their ethos of using the internet to do something good and had been painstakingly maintaining a massive library of just about any archived software and web content that had ever been created, often supported with custom emulators and viewing windows allowing the internet surfer of 2025 to go back in time and explore the original Space Jam website, Geocities blogs, and even play classic old browser games. Warren occasionally used it to go even further back, often running TRS-80 emulators that harkened back to hours upon hours of keyboard gaming in front of his parents' aforementioned green-energy television. The Wayback Machine hadn't always been able to capture and archive content, especially things that relied upon secure server-side code, but for what it did do well, it had become a representative history of all the things humans had made on the internet, for better or worse.

Somaya had found it—an obscure news posting from the Online Thai Evening News, an English-language publication from EMC that had managed to rise above many of its contemporaries in the 2010s, in those years accumulating a massive user base supported by an unending carpet-bombing of news feed postings across the many millions of Diddem.com users. She wasn't sure why the site itself no longer seemed to hold the article, but that was beside the point. In broken formatting, the picture and headline on the screen in front of her was the same blurb that had stowed away in her rattled memories. Warren would later hypothesize that the many recursive linkages of this content from Diddem to Mixality to Facebook and back again had provided enough of a presence to be caught by the crawlers—the automated web bots—of the Internet Archives.

"Clancy Investments Gets in the Cockpit with Flyboys, by Harriet Stone, February 19, 2018," was displayed above a picture of a smiling Philip J. Clancy shaking hands with one Mattias Wenstrom, the founder of Flyboys, a traffic analysis drone outfit. Flyboys had only seen a fleeting moment in the sun during the initial rush of investment into drone technologies in the late '10s. The very idea that what had previously required a helicopter, pilot, film crew, and many thousands of dollars to take to the sky for perhaps a few minutes of footage could now be achieved by a device that might be carried in a backpack or even in the palm of someone's hand, was too compelling to ignore.

But the rush of investment had flooded the market with similar stories to this, and no one had ever really heard much of Flyboys after their initial news cycle.

"You think it's this, Somaya? Do these guys even exist anymore?" Warren asked as he scanned the contents of the page she had found.

"There," she said, "read that." She had used the mouse cursor to highlight a quote from Mr. Wenstrom, the founder.

"So not only can we look down on the Earth and see everything below us, but our drones, our flyboys, have a wafer-thin LED covering. It's a wrapper that lets them blend into any environment, using the footage they capture around them to re-project a camouflaged skin on the device," he had proudly stated.

"Holy shit," Warren said. "Is this what we're seeing?" he asked, without considering that they hadn't really been seeing any of it at all, which is exactly how Mr. Wenstrom had described it in this article from seven years earlier.

"Well, we don't really see anything, and that's the problem," Somaya replied. Her healing mind was already a few steps ahead. If this was the answer, if this Flyboys company and their drones had somehow gotten into her business, something much bigger was going on.

"Look, Sommy, if they were already doing this seven years ago, like if they had these autonomously linking grids of drones with this Predator-camouflage system in place, you know like the Arnie movie, not all the shitty sequels, you just fast-forward that half a decade with Clancy's money pumped into R&D, and those things will get smaller, faster, silent, and invisible," Warren said, affirming some of the conclusions to which she had already advanced. "At least from a tech perspective, that's what I would read in this. How they got involved in CVI and could do all this with no other news on it, I mean, Jesus, I can only imagine what kind of people would be involved to make this kind of thing happen."

Philip J. Clancy's sardonic, shit-eating grin had been shining its pearly whites back at them from the headline picture throughout the conversation.

Somaya was silent as she processed this information and all the potentialities it might bring with it.

"I hear you, Warry. I just don't think we are in a position anymore where we can open up this can of worms, at least until we know absolutely everything that's going on," Somaya said, resigned to the disappointing fact that she did not yet know why they were so unbelievably successful, wealthy, and celebrated.

For fuck's sake, I spent all that time getting really good at reading the room, and I forgot to look up to the sky.

Thirty-four

UNBOUNDED

Freshly brewed coffee filled the air with its delightfully warm and cozy scent. And chocolate. There was definitely chocolate in the air.

Henny woke slowly, a slumberous start to the day. White pillows, white sheets, and, marginally visible to her right eye, which had recently opened to claim a line of sight over the edge of the bed, luxurious white carpeting. Light was dancing through the window in a chaotic pattern influenced by the slow swaying motion of the curtain liner, as its soft, lacey mesh swirled in a visual interpretation of the air circulation in the room.

Right, the hotel. Jersey. OMG, Doug!

She sat up, sheets falling forward off her naked upper body. She looked to the right. The bed was empty, but there were signs of it having been full of activity. A blanket, bunched up at the foot of the bed. Her underwear, crumpled on the floor near the door to the sitting room. A scene rewound in her mind of her legs straddling Doug as he skillfully unclipped her bra, pulled it up over her arms, and flicked it toward the television in one smooth, coordinated effort.

He must have learned something since college, Henny mused, now warming up from the memories of their mutual pleasure from only a few hours earlier.

Doug walked into the room carrying two coffee cups marked with the logo of CocoBrew, a designation those cups shared with the big sign in front of the cafe on the ground floor.

"Good morning," he said, appearing much more relaxed than when they first ran into each other the day before. "I got coffee," he said, stating the obvious, "and for you, a mocha!"

"Oh, thank you Doug," she took the cup he offered, deciding not to dampen his enthusiasm by telling him that she didn't exactly feel like having a hot chocolate the moment she woke up. Henny took a sugary sip. It was warm, rich, and surprisingly more fulfilling than expected.

Doug was wearing jogging pants and a Spectra College sweater over a T-shirt, much as he did back in those days in Valemont. Henny thought he didn't look so very different from how he had back then, just maybe a little pudgier around the edges, and he exuded a more mature air. Doug's perception of Henny was that she had left so long ago as a perfect angel and had returned to him as a goddess. His social observations were still as infantile and innocent as ever.

He sat on the edge of the bed next to her, and she shuffled toward him with the bedsheet loosely gathered as a toga, arranging one knee with a folded leg across his lap and the other leg running the length of the bed beside him.

She looked at him and started to speak in a very sweet and sincere tone, "Doug, I just want to tell you..."

Ring! Ring!

A phone rang, cutting off whatever Henny was intending to say. More accurately, a device rang with the emulated sound of a phone.

"Henny, can I have a moment? I had this incoming..." he started to explain, hoping to convey the importance of this expected call.

"Of course," she said calmly as she tenderly stroked her fingers down the side of his triceps. She had waited twenty-five years to have a real conversation with Doug, surely another hour or so wouldn't make a difference.

Ever since he was jettisoned from his commentating role on *The Conflux*, he had been trying to find the next thing to get involved with. His exposure and involvement with PDD had most certainly opened many doors, and Ricky had helped his old friend by arranging a few calls, this one with the co-production company that had bankrolled much of the cost and underwritten the production insurance on *The Conflux*. These were serious players. He also welcomed the subtle distraction of such an important call, hoping it would calm the oscillating charges firing throughout his nervous system. Henny always had a magical, electrostatic effect on him, and it was presently cranked to maximum voltage.

He reached for his bag near the side of the bed and pulled out a laptop.

Was it a laptop? It was a computing device of some kind, and seeing it in his hands was momentarily reminiscent. She could picture him standing in the living room, holding the EMC tablet high above his head like a trophy, the mystery device shaken free of its encapsulation within those two pieces of Styrofoam.

He opened it. Not a tablet, though there was no obvious keyboard, either—just a second mirrored slab of glossy black glass.

Okay, so this was different. Interesting-looking thing, though. As Doug stood up and sat in front of the desk adjacent to the television cabinet, Henny leaned back with her mocha and took a long, sweet sip. She wondered how many other subtleties throughout that morning might jog older memories. She didn't have to wait long.

Doug had apparently authenticated himself by placing his hand on the keyboard area. A face materialized on-screen.

"Hello, Doug."

She nearly choked on her mocha, and some of the brown chocolatey coffee leaked through her nose, causing her to cough to clear her throat.

Did I just hear that? Henny questioned as she wiped her upper lip with the back of her hand and looked to where Doug had been staring intently at the elevated hinged screen of his computer.

"Good morning," Doug had replied to the other meeting participant.

This time, it was impossible to be mistaken.

"Top of the morning to you, Douglas," the voice said. From her perspective on the bed, the viewing angle on the screen revealed none of the contents of its pixels. It was a feature, not a bug, as the hardware provided to Doug had been purpose-built for secure communications with field workers and new recruits. Those who had sent it had spent the better part of a decade improving the stability, build quality, and security of these machines after encountering numerous problems with many of their earlier versions.

She couldn't see the face, nor did she need to.

Harbs.

"Harbs?" she blurted out, her voice getting ahead of the wave of emotions and feelings that were descending upon her. Henny stood up, grasping for the bedsheet to cover her body, and took steps toward the desk where Doug was sitting.

The sheet was still secured on one corner of the bed by the crushing strength of an unrelenting hotel housekeeping tuck. It refused to avail itself for her coverage, and Henny let it fall behind. Nothing else mattered in this moment but seeing what—*who?*—was on that screen.

Doug was beside himself. His surprise at hearing Henny say this presumably important man's name was only surpassed by the shock of her standing behind him and interrupting the call not just with her voice but also with the full nakedness of her body on display.

Doug lifted his seated, slouched posture in a hasty attempt to not only shield the most private parts of the love that had alluded his life, but also to maintain a semblance of continuity to the meeting he was supposed to have. Clearly, the agenda had shifted.

Henny gently but firmly pushed on his shoulder and leaned forward to maintain visibility of the screen, her warm chocolatey mocha breath causing the hairs on Doug's neck to tremble. The smiling visage of Dr. Harb Louthe, PhD, Board Director, EMC, the same face on a screen that had become the most reliable part of her life for so many years, was there, in front of her again.

"Henrietta. Hello," he said in a muted response.

She was floored. So many questions ran through her mind in an instant. She felt dizzy and leaned even more heavily on Doug's shoulder. For all of his oddities and many failures of social grace, he was now instinctually aware something of greater importance was happening. Doug slid out of his chair and helped Henny sit down as he took off his sweater, which he offered to her to provide a modicum of coverage. He had noted that she wasn't even fazed by her appearance in front of this Harbs fellow, and he couldn't help but feel a few pangs of jealousy stab him in the midsection. Doug retreated enough to extricate the bedsheet from the clasping grip of the mattresses and brought it back to Henny as additional protective garb before excusing himself.

"Henny, I'll be over here," he said, pointing to the sitting room.

"Uh uh," she said, just enough to acknowledge his departure from the discussion and almost more than she could bring herself to emit from her mouth. Her breathing was limited, her heart rate had escalated, and her confusion was at all-time highs.

"I suppose you would like some answers," the once-familiar face on the screen proposed.

"I... I don't really... I... what the fuck is this? Is this you? Where are you?" she replied.

"I am every bit here," he said, attempting to calm her, which he had always been effective at, though he had never been in the position of needing to assuage her as a result of any direct action of his own. He had quickly determined that faking his death qualified as something that might need assuaging and was careful to allow for silence to propagate their reunion.

"Probably need a little more than that. Like... how? Why?"

She looked up at the ceiling, then down toward the floor and across her lap, only now considering her outfit of Doug's Spectra College alumni sweater and a bedsheet. "It's been a fucking decade, Harbs. What is this?"

"There's a lot to discuss here, Henrietta. Where would you like me to start?" he offered, careful not to assume he knew what she needed to hear.

"Umm," her breathing had started to return to normal, her heart rate slowed, and the confusion remained high. But now she had collected her thoughts and had a concise suggestion for him. "Okay, I know. How about you tell me fucking everything?"

The revelations were many, and they came fast. For the first hour, Doug had patiently sat in the sitting room, the door nearly closed to the bedroom where Henny was speaking with Harbs. His long-dormant eavesdropping skills had nominally risen from hibernation, a rusty aural faculty now merely an imitation of what it once was. He couldn't hear all of it, but for what he could, it gave him the impression that she was having a pre-production meeting for another sci-fi interpretation of one of her short stories. Though the whole comfortably naked start to the call was still strange to him, something about Henny's reaction to Harbs also didn't seem like a typical writer-producer relationship. That said, he had just been working on a show for half a dozen years where they celebrated people getting painted and killed, not always in that order, in front of wide-eyed, adoring audiences. Doug had long since abandoned expectations of morality in media production.

After he had glommed together some of the details that Harbs had died, been resurrected, and had come back to assist Henny in recrafting human society, Doug surmised that he was just not getting the gist of what they were saying and decided to go for a walk. He could pick up some lunch for them both, and presumably, Henny would offer an explanation.

It's the least she could do, interrupting my call like that, he thought as he left the hotel room.

"So you died, and now you came back to life, and you want to help me do what?" Henny said.

"Exactly. My temporal existence ceased when you were told as much, Henrietta. At the same time as so many other hundreds of millions of deaths around the world. During COVI. I can imagine it was a challenging and traumatic time for you," Harbs said.

"Traumatic for me? Well, hell yeah, but I'm not the one that died. Help me understand what you're saying. Did they stick you in cryogenics or something?" she offered as a possible outcome while hoping for a small dose of humor to spring forth. The two of them had often joked about cryogenics. There had been so many attempts at freezing humans or parts of humans, but as of yet, no one had ever fully or partially been thawed back into society. Whether it was due to the lack of progression of the technology or simply having no accountability to a customer who had already paid in full and would never know if the product wasn't delivered, they could never be sure.

"Ha, well, not exactly. The thing is, you know what happened, don't you? We already talked about this."

"What? No... fuck off. You mean NewU? You mean, your DeathBank thing?" she asked incredulously.

Harbs nodded, "Exactly. This is me, in the DeathBank."

"You're bullshitting me, Harbs. Not sure why you're trying to do this, but I can't really believe you're dead and I'm talking to you in what... a video game? I've seen a lot, we've seen a lot, but... c'mon, Harbs." Henny was losing whatever remained of a coherent train of thought.

She needed more to go on, which Harbs intuited and sought to supply. "It's not a video game. I mean, you went through half of it, right? Remember the scan in the studio? Think of it this way, if I hadn't known better, I might've thought it was your avatar at the start of this call," he said, alluding to her revealing entry to their discussion, which, conveniently enough, had also given him the spatial reference points that enabled Harbs to even more quickly confirm and authenticate that it was in fact Henny he was speaking to. Remarkably, and to the envy of many women and men who couldn't say as much in their mid-forties, her four-dimensional data had remained almost identical nearly a dozen years from the original NewU capture session.

She could have cared less about his juvenile attempt at humor. He kept going, "Okay, so maybe you remember this." He paused, taking a moment to look around the small office in which he was sitting. There was a shelf full of books behind him and a picture on the wall that was too small to perceive what was on it. It looked like an unfortunately posed family struggling through a studio photography session.

Then the family was gone, as was the office. Harbs was in a softly lit wooded glade. A trail cut through the middle of the scene behind him, and butterflies navigated their way amongst the tall trees, one of them even flying near enough for the turbulence of its wings to wisp a few hairs aloft from his head before they settled back into place.

"Oh shit," she said under her breath.

Harbs moved again, this time underwater, then on a mountaintop, and finally in the front seat of a race car. He was wearing a helmet, his entire body jostling and shifting with the G forces of piloting his Formula 1 around the telltale curvy roads of the Monaco Grand Prix circuit.

"That one's my favorite," he said, speaking much more loudly to be heard over the artificial roar of his car's electric motor.

But it was the other scenes that really landed with Henny, those same scenes that her same, younger, naked virtual self had been magically transported into from a cold studio session in Colorado all those years ago.

"You cannot be serious," Henny said, the resolution dawning upon her that Harbs was, in fact, not full of shit. She knew she had to believe it, after all, she had seen too much over these years to refute the possibility of what was now in front of her. It was really the only answer that actually made sense.

"Also, I realize you are probably right about the name. Now that I'm in here, it's not exactly the kind of thing I want to tell people," said Harbs.

"Name? What do you mean?"

"DeathBank. It's kinda terrible," he acknowledged.

"Well, yeah, I told you so. But I guess you needed to find out for yourself," Henny said, those words passing through her mouth with a quirky flavor as she prompted this algorithmic Harbs to continue with his explanation. After all, there was so much more to it than just slapping together a bunch of high-resolution pictures of someone's naked body, even after capturing all the "nooks and crannies," as the director had said in the chilly high-altitude NewU studio, before anyone could just have a conversation with an avatar. Certainly not a conversation as nuanced and intense as this one.

"No, not an avatar, or at least not just an avatar. It's not about a replacement. It's about an extension. We always knew they—the NewU team—were getting close enough to Individual AI, to the ability to duplicate anyone, physiologically, genetically—at least on record—and mentally. So the thing, this thing," he expressed a downward look and shrug of his shoulders as he opened his palms, "it's not just a reminder of you. It's you after you're dead," Harbs said with a reserved tone.

"Like a full AI? Of you? I mean, Jesus, I guess I can't really be asking you that, considering that's what you're saying you are." The circular logic was, as Henny would proceed to say, "Fucked. This is fucked up, Harbs. It's doing my head in."

"But you know this, and I know that you knew it. That you could see it all along. All the stuff we were working on over those years, all your research, all your articles. It all adds up. And this, me in DeathBank, it's just the natural next chapter in the whole thing. You've pretty much spelled all this out in your book anyway."

"It's definitely a stupid name," she said, finding a dose of levity every time she could insult his branding effort. "So tell me one thing then, Harbs. Er. Digi-Harbs."

"Okay, but it's just me, Henny."

"Why did you need to disappear? Why did you need to die, to me, anyway? If you could do this, and did this back in '28, why didn't you just do this right away and spare me a ton of grief?"

"Well, shit, that's a loaded one, isn't it? I'll say there are a few reasons, but the biggest one of them all…" he paused, as if for dramatic effect.

Is this for dramatic effect? Oh shit, is he glitching? Did he crash?

He came back. "Did you get that? Think we had a bad connection."

"No, I missed it. 2035 and my internet connection cut out just when my long dead friend was going to tell me about how he had uploaded himself to the cloud and was scared to tell me why," she replied, with her sarcasm only slightly overshadowed by the weight of incredulity.

"We needed you to quit," he finished his earlier sentence.

"What? Like quit EMC?"

"Exactly," Harbs confirmed.

"Go on."

Now with a stabilized internet connection, they continued, the intensity of the conversation ebbing and flowing throughout the morning. The more they talked, the crazier it all sounded, and the more a cohesive vision began assembling itself for Henny.

Harbs confirmed that NewU had far more capabilities than even he was willing to admit when they initially debriefed from Henny's revealing visit to their studio. Beyond the avatar machine and the death prediction algorithms, NewU had already been able to demonstrate fully sentient AI. That was the real risk, the real instigator for Harbs, and, by unwitting extension, Henny, to support MCA's takeover intentions.

"To their credit, what they had realized before the rest of us, Henrietta, is that people were struggling with AIs that legitimately do not have a face. People don't like talking to programs, they want to talk with people. Getting you, or your posthumous you, into software is a combination of the visual, the mental, and the memory. It's you and all the pieces and parts and experiences of you," Harbs said.

He went on, "The problem is, NewU—DeathBank—had no other experience with AI before some of those breakthroughs. They were on the cusp of basically introducing all of science fiction's most dangerous ideas in one fell swoop, without really knowing what they were dealing with."

"Jesus, Harbs. If that was the case, I mean... that's serious shit, and you had me right in the middle of it without sharing a fucking clue. I'll hold that over you for later," Henny said, resigned for the moment to go along with everything in this story. "So what's EMC, or SGF, or MCA, or whoever it really is that you actually fucking work for, what do they want with all of this?"

"We couldn't let them get there. It's way too dangerous for them to unleash AI or AGI like this for anyone or everyone," he said.

"So that's why? That's why you needed me out? I was getting too close to some of these secrets? And you fucking guys end up deploying this old school soap opera fake-death storyline?" she demanded, probing him on the ridiculous premise that they had conspired to use Harbs' COVI-26 demise as a forcing function for her exit.

"Though I guess it wasn't really a fake death, was it?" she ruminated out loud. "Because you died, you just faked your non-resurrection. Jesus... why not just fire me?"

"When you say it that way, yeah, it seems a bit excessive. But you're looking in the wrong direction. We didn't want you out *because* you knew too much," he said.

"Okay, then what was it?"

"We *needed* you out because you *knew that much.*"

That was, remarkably, the most nonsensical statement of the day so far. "Hmm. Help me," Henny commanded.

"And we needed you to leave on good terms, to keep doing what you were doing. Hell, we've seen you angry before, we couldn't take the chance of that happening again," he said, presumably alluding to her seminal work in the *Original Fix*, as she was now subconsciously referring to it.

"And here we go. The pedal hits the metal. The rubber hits the road. The penny drops," he began to answer, leading with more of his regurgitated idioms, which confirmed for Henny that, indeed, she was speaking with the Harbs she had known and... loved?

His explanations went far, wide, tall, and long. Extreme and extenuating in every dimension.

He began assembling a compliment sandwich, the recipe of which included a long list of reasons why Henny was great at what she did. She was analytical, resourceful, and a hell of a good writer. Which is why, he had told her long before, she fit the profile of what they thought they needed, back when EMC (and MCA) expected the human race to get smarter and become more analytical and more synaptically involved in their consumption of information.

Every previous era of technological advancement had served to enhance human capacity, to get closer to realizing the full potential of the evolutionary milestone that was *homo sapiens*. Yet in this case, the roles had been perversely shuffled. As technology and tooling had improved, both had become more random, more intricate, and almost more human, while in parallel, the networked citizens of Earth had become more rote, less capable, and far more blunt.

It just so happened that as the MCA hypothesis was proven wrong and their objectives changed, Henny's skills became even more important. Harbs was still on the bottom layer of bread, spreading the condiments of adulation upon which the meat of his explanation would hopefully soon lay upon. But she also couldn't help but feel a strong sense of deja vu. It was strikingly familiar to his explanation to her well before the onset of COVI and his untimely demise, how he had described MCA's initial response to her *Original Fix* and how her skills were needed elsewhere.

"Would be fucking nice if people chose to share those observations with me," she wryly commented in response.

Harbs went on to explain that every decision about what projects to send her on and the rationale that went into her briefings all came back to one common theme.

"You guys were running some insane conspiracy to pollute the minds of Earthlings with clickbait and feel-good stories about your ludicrous investments and tech projects?" Henny suggested.

"Not exactly."

Harbs could understand why she felt that way, and he was still hopeful that, as many had said before, the truth would set her free.

"I told you how NewU—DeathBank—were dangerous. Do you know why? It's not directly because of what they did. It's because of what they didn't know."

Also, he mentioned a preference to call them simply NewU now, especially given that he was talking about them in their earlier edition and speaking from his own, well, NewU.

First of all, he explained that they didn't know that AGI had already been achieved, a slightly important piece of information that would open up more than a few questions.

"Like with OpenAI? ChatGPT? That stuff?" she asked, providing the obvious context to the revisionist history Harbs was now describing, though she knew as well as anyone close to the field that those solutions had still been a far cry from AGI.

He quickly replied, "You think when chat-bots and AI artists were first served up over the web a bunch of years ago, you think that was indicative of capabilities at the time, of the progression of the tech? Most certainly it wasn't, and oh, what a tangled web we weave! That stuff was what came after, in a much more controlled and limited way, after we fucked it all up the first time."

"How? I mean what... what was the first time?"

"You already know, don't you? You know what the catalyst for all this is," he prompted, confident that she was astute and artistic enough to butter the top piece of bread *and* tie a little cellophane bow on the toothpick, such that he might drive the sharp point through the whole of his explanation.

Which she did. "Language?" she said, repeating another question in response to a question, the same one she had similarly offered up years ago to one former Executive Director of Interplanetary Intelligence.

"Nailed it. Richard Gossett and his people didn't even know it at the time, but not only did they stamp all of humanity on a disk, they provided the first real training dataset for AGI. Meanwhile, the military had been working on the underlying fundamentals of it since World War II, ever since the Brits and Turing and his people first broke the Nazi codes. By the way, did you know that all the best programmers back then, in the war that is, were women? Had they stayed in control of it all maybe some of this could have been avoided, or possibly achieved much sooner... who really knows?"

He took a gratuitous breath to allow this rambling tale to settle, then continued, "But what none of the military generals or the scientists at NASA ended up realizing is that because they were both working within the same data warehousing and the same mainframes, their combined work product had gone far beyond what each of them intended. It had basically crossed the singularity by itself."

"Like, in the '80s?"

"Like, totally."

The noncontiguous fragments kept coming, a 2,000-piece puzzle with no picture on the box and an unfair amount of blue-sky pieces, and she did her best to put them in their place. It became apparent that this monumental milestone could happen and remain as quiet as it did only, ironically, because of the limited network capabilities of the time. They essentially had an AI-in-a-box but without the ability to pop its head up and scare the outside world whenever the music stopped. It was secluded, confined to its own solitary encyclopedic dormitory. The AI, the AGI, had graduated from the most enriched private school education to ever exist, with no convocation ceremony to follow.

"If an AGI manifests itself on a closed network and nobody is there to see it, did it really happen?" Harbs asked, bastardizing another common expression that seemed to indicate he wasn't really seeing the forest for the trees.

Thirty-five

THE RED BUTTON AFFAIR

Harbs went on to explain how, once a few of the colluding minds from both NASA and the military had been able to comprehend what had happened on their massive computer systems, they did what seemed most appropriate: they let the AGI get involved in the Cold War. They had anticipated that, just like in World War II, the greater processing power of computers would give them an upper hand—that better tooling would make them more capable. This decision also led to several miscommunications and near-misses in the 1980s, begging the argument that maybe they should be called near-hits, if they actually missed.

The most profound moment of AGI's secretive first steps into the global military-political sphere was a good indicator of the potential outcomes that might come from humans and machines working hand-in-hand, or hand-on-buttons, whatever the case may be.

Stanislav Petrov was at the helm of some of those very important buttons as an officer in the Soviet Red Army with the responsibility and authority to initiate nuclear launches in retaliation of the same threat, should the need ever arise. In September 1983, he was the recipient of some unsettling information. The intercontinental ballistic missile warning system operating from the worldly perspective of the Soviet Union's military satellite system had reported five incoming US missiles.

Unbeknownst to Officer Petrov, the foundation for the software running on those satellites had, in fact, been seeded by none other than the now-sentient programs running on the original nascent NASA mainframe systems in Florida. Perhaps the first indication of the AGI playing chess at a global scale, it had embedded an undetectable subroutine of its freshly written Geo-Political Inference Engine™ on an honorary copy of the Golden Record that NASA had sent as a gift to their contemporaries in the Soviet Space Program, knowing that the curiosity imbued in such a shiny object would no doubt lead to its ability to gain access to critical systems on the ground in Mother Russia. As the sole recording of "Johnny B. Goode" by Chuck Berry available to most cosmonauts-in-training, that shiny circular Trojan Horse quickly delivered upon its promise.

Meanwhile, Officer Petrov had to presume he was receiving critically important warnings from state-of-the-art technology created by the Soviet state.

His reaction was thus: *Why five? Why only five?*

Officer Petrov's instincts had told him that an incoming attack of only five missiles would have given the Soviets a clear advantage. Their retaliatory strike could have been in the dozens or even hundreds if coordinated quickly enough. By putting himself in the mind of his opponent, he couldn't believe they would expose themselves to checkmate so easily.

It must be a mistake. He didn't push the button, color unconfirmed but red in spirit if not in practice, and reported the alert to his superiors as a false alarm.

The convenient explanation that became legend was that the satellite warning system had mistakenly interpreted solar flares in a cloudy sky as potential missile exhaust. Convenient for the Americans as it avoided the truth of having deployed sentient malware that nearly wrought their own demise, and convenient for the Soviets as they wouldn't have to admit their systems had been infiltrated by superior technology riding on the coattails and very shiny shoes of the man most often attributed for creating Rock 'n Roll, and secondarily, the Duck Walk.

Afterwards, and with the hindsight that Officer Stanislav Petrov had single-handedly prevented global annihilation by thinking a few chess moves ahead of an unknown opponent playing a brute-force version of checkers, the AGI had fallen out of favor in Florida and Washington.

They—the powers that be—soon realized the need to move the AGI out of the military's hands, at the risk of it causing more catastrophic global conflict, or even worse, that the generals in command would have been discovered to have been responsible for doing so. They were still, after all, of a myopic generation where computing was generally deemed as the lower-tier secretarial work of women, and with the experience of the Red Button Affair fresh in their minds, they elected to get these godforsaken unexplainable technologies as far away from them as possible. Fortunately, after the decision was made to move the codebase and the entire hardware infrastructure of that original singularity-buster, less volatile minds had gotten involved.

The biggest implication at that point was that as long as it remained on a closed network, the system would struggle to be a contributing innovation in modern society, as its only available lessons, its training data, were that of past-looking archives and the longer news cycles of history.

Thirty-six

SPACE AND TIME

"It needed to be present. It needed to be active. It needed to be real-time," Harbs said, describing the formative strategy that had resulted in the founding of MCA, the Media Consolidation Agency, as a public-private entity secretly tasked with steering Artificial Intelligence for the greater benefit of humanity.

"I'll hold back on saying things like, 'Yeah, that seems like a fucking normal thing to do right after you nearly set off World War III.' Please keep going, Harbs," Henny encouraged, her back starting to feel the pain of vertebrae compression from being wrapped up in stasis for far too long with only a thin bedsheet between her buttocks and the surface of this hard wooden desk chair.

"So not only real-time, but also really involved," he said as he began to describe MCA's growing efforts to capture a larger and ever-evolving data set upon which the AGI could operate, with a conscious sub-goal to avoid near-miss nuclear strikes in the future.

They bought up businesses in finance, healthcare, infrastructure, construction, energy, technology—of course—and installed observatory outposts all around the world. As the world of gaming, especially online gaming, exploded, it became a natural landing spot for MCA to run endless simulations and to observe how humans reacted in those scenarios.

In turn, they began taking some of the most telling, most revealing virtual simulations and recreating and constructing those same situations in the real-world, to remove the bias of technology.

"For example, we needed to see if people would react in a real gunfight the same way they did in a frag-match of Halo or Call of Duty," he said.

"Did they?"

"Hell no, unless there's a button on your controller for pissing your pants and running for the hills. Well, most people anyway," he said, with an acknowledgment that there have always been an unhealthy number of trigger-happy nutballs out there to whom consequences and human life held no value.

"And lo and behold, if crypto didn't give us a whole new space of crazy, an endless summer or two of people chasing people chasing people, all taking from each other and from anyone else who chose to join the party."

"Endless summers. Like, as in before the crypto winters?" Henny asked, cognizant of his play on words.

"Indeed."

Harbs revealed that MCA had been assembling and compiling datasets from nearly every walk of life the company had cast its eyes upon. Gamification was now everywhere. How we drive, how we run, how we sleep, how we date, even how we fuck. He even let on that with everything they had modeled around population health data, when coupled with the tech in the NewU acquisition, there was even less of a reason to call it DeathBank.

"We've figured out longevity, of actually living forever. It's just not clear if that's what people really, truly want." said the man who had died and been reincarnated in an app. The more pragmatic explanation that followed was how the social structures and established societal governance would never be able to adapt to the concept of living for hundreds of years or, possibly, for eternity. The way society and the economy are structured today, and at nearly any point in human existence, this kind of breakthrough would only flow through to the privileged, to the upper class, to the wealthy. Harbs shared that their primary concern was they could not forecast and predict what it would look like to have Earth be in the infinite control of those extremely rich, upper-class, predominantly Caucasian power brokers.

"You're sure about that? You don't think you know what that would look like?" Henny sarcastically pushed back at him while also wondering why those same rich, white, old men hadn't grasped a hold of whatever longevity magic Harbs and his cronies had come up with.

Or maybe they already had. She thought as a mental picture of the leathery patriarch Roger Clancy boarding his inaugural flight to Mars that summer had popped into her mind, the multi-billionaire now in his eighties but looking decades younger and fitter than ever before.

The premise of virtualizing its citizens, of perpetual life in the DeathBank, forced more questions. Is it the same class of human? Can they vote? Do they have rights? Do they pay taxes or receive pensions? MCA was far from understanding those implications, and NewU hadn't even given it a passing thought. Harbs, to his credit, didn't seem too concerned about his voting card or his retirement package.

He admitted he could be more accommodating to common sense with some of his descriptions, but he was quick to point out that he had never had to explain all of this to anyone, and in the absence of having a script, he preferred to just stick to more factual statements.

"I mean, even when we look at the whole energy construct. We can now break down the world's energy usage to the very last Watt, and draw a line from source to every light bulb in a city, to every household, to everything in your pockets,' He paused, remembering that she still had no pockets. "The first big thing the AGI did when we gave it a real sandbox to play in, you know what it was? Do you remember the Flyboys traffic system?"

"Oh yeah, that was a big inspiration for one of my stories in the book... Although I never found out what happened to that company."

"Well, Henrietta, let me tell you. Though I'll say, you weren't that far off in your book. You weren't far off from a lot of things in those stories, actually. Flyboys doesn't exist anymore because it never actually really existed. The whole thing was created out of thin air, other than the hardware and all the tech, which actually was able to exist in thin air, that was all real. But the founder, the company, all of that? It was all AGI," Harbs revealed.

She had never met the founders in person. Henny had only pieced her story together based on a few discussions with some of the engineers, a live drone demo in the Red Rocks desert near Las Vegas, and that vivid short film of the chaotic Costa Rican traffic system. Considering the press photos were with the "founder" posing with one Philip J. Clancy, it now seemed much more fitting that it was a lie.

"We made the company to open the door to talk to regulators. We needed to know their reaction if we started flooding the skies with drones. Needless to say, no one in government wanted to touch it with a ten-thousand-foot pole, so we had to find other ways to harvest that data," he said with pride, almost as if he was taking credit for whatever they had actually done.

Conveniently, he also chose to skip over the part about how they had re-manifested the operations of Flyboys in a convoluted secret-inside-takeover of the operations at CVI, which allowed them to successfully and secretively deploy millions of invisible surveillance drones into the skies above.

Had he shared that detail, it might have derailed the conversation before he could get to his main point.

Which led him to his main point.

"Media, technology, and social interactions. That's where we had the biggest gap. We had a wealth of insight from past historians and all the more eminent works in psychology and sociology. Well actually, all of the works of all time. But up until the late nineties, we had an absolute dearth of anything more relatable. We couldn't release a new operating system for society based on history alone. We needed something more present, more current, more..."

"Real-time," she completed his sentence.

"Bingo was your name-o," he said.

"Absolutely awful," Henny judged, feeling it necessary to call that one out.

But maybe it was apt. While they ultimately became able to scrape untold reams of information and social discourse from the web, pull many multiples more structured information through established, trusted, and publicly shared APIs, and even use the occasional DDOS activity to their benefit, they, the observers at MCA, just weren't seeing what they needed to see in their datasets. They couldn't, to conclude the reference, complete their bingo card of the human data project. And every time they deployed discretized portions of the AGI framework into what they assumed were controlled environments, the positives were far outweighed by negative outcomes.

"The Facebook and Mixality Elections, Arab Spring, MXP and the Young Gainers, Trump, COVID, Putin, Trump again. Those bald-headed software guys. Even climate change. Hell, even Cage and Affleck, just to see if we could do it! All of this ties together—those and thousands and millions of other companies and projects and movements and divisive opinions. You think the founders of those companies and the creators of the tools involved were competent enough to make those systems work the way they did? Not a chance. They got a free seat on the first ride of the Aggie train, they just didn't know it yet. The AGI was built to improve humans, to make humans stronger, faster, better, to make them capable of making things like this, to innovate in ways that have never been seen before. Well, you know what?"

"Come on with it." she prompted.

"Humans are terrible. Disgusting, just so utterly stupid..." ranted Harbs.

In the front of her mind, it was all intensely interesting, and she could see where he was leading. In the back of her mind, Henny could only ask, *Why don't you tell me what you really think?*

She didn't interrupt him. "...and if we super-power them and give them these tools, what do you get? All the worst things imaginable. We've already gone down this path, that's what I'm saying. If people can't handle deep fakes, you think they could deal with the discovery of aliens or even... me? If we often can't deal with standing for five minutes at a bus stop with someone, you think we can live for hundreds of years together? If we can't say nice things on a website forum, how the hell would we get along in a virtual space like this?" He again looked at the space around him, which was now... space. Harbs had shifted to a meeting room on the International Space Station for the last half an hour or so. It had been easier to listen to the intensely loaded words coming from his mouth as he floated around the room like the hands of a clock, with his head anchored consistently in the middle of the camera frame.

And therein lay a problem of reciprocity—the cart filled with human potential at risk of being pushed over a cliff by the trailing horsepower of its own inventions.

The benign and whimsically spatial Harbs was quick to point out the self-defeating nature of our relationship with innovation and how it juxtaposed the equally negative feedback loop of the need to keep AGI offline, to keep it clear of affecting and infiltrating the network upon which we lived, worked, and played. Which, in isolation, seemed like an open-and-shut case, as Harbs might say.

"But if we had, or have, an intention of ever being able to harness the full power of these technologies, we were essentially cutting off our nose to spite our face," he said, alluding to the implicated outcome that a disconnected AGI could never get a big enough sniff of the data it needed to have a chance to be fully effective, to observe the world, understand the goals of humanity, and hopefully, develop its own aligned goals.

"Are you sure that's the right analogy?" Henny asked. "Feels like you're speaking to the premise of it, and us, being on the same page, but if we let it run wild, we can't guarantee the results or, I suppose, we can't even guarantee we can mitigate or steer the results. I mean, I've covered a ton of this stuff in my work, as you know. Which... actually... aren't you, being here, on this," nodding to the computer. "Isn't that—you—an actual example that we can, or you can, or whoever the hell it is you're working with, can control it?"

"It's not really that simple, as much as I wish it were. I've been constructed from a massive dataset, from all the contents of my own life, and enough population inference to fill in the blanks, but it—or me—is only that. Think of me as something basically compiled out of a game engine or a development framework. Just a very handsome and well-spoken one, if I do say so myself," Harbs said, grinning in binary happiness as he floated upside down over three hundred virtual miles above the planet. In that moment, Harbs couldn't have cared less that the actual ISS had been decommissioned several years earlier, now residing in equally murky detail as a misshapen reef at the bottom of the South Pacific.

He reached over to his right, an upside down left for Henny that had her follow his hand mirrored, in reverse, to the same side. He pressed play on a large ghetto blaster hovering in the anti-gravity surrounding him.

"I love this one—*Travis Mathers and Free Age Ants*. Have you heard them?" Harbs asked. A rich acoustic guitar melody could be heard playing over the metallic hiss of a cassette tape, a throwback technology to match the ghetto blaster. It was the second album from Travis and his band after a nearly ten-year hiatus. The album had never actually been released on cassette, even though one of the bandmates was adamant that had they done so, it would have been much harder to be pirated. Harbs, however, could justify to himself that his interplanetary buccaneering removed him from the jurisdiction of copyright and royalties owed, and anyway, he preferred the analog feel and sound of the tape. Digitally, he was out of bounds on a few fronts.

"So, I'm really just a snapshot of this whole thing, but try as we might, we cannot simply give AGI a goal and send it on its way. Even though it was created by humans, they can not just tell it to be 'aligned with humans.' It's already been doing that work for itself, for the better part of fifty years, trying to determine whether or not that's what is actually desired and exactly what that means, without anybody needing to say anything," he said, ratifying in many more words how some would choose to describe the singularity.

"So it's not really the insolent child out there kicking over toys and causing wars, riots, and chaos, it's more the smart-ass, know-it-all kid with embarrassing parents?" Henny offered.

"That's one way to look at it," he admitted, provided there was an acknowledgment that it was the most intelligent child ever imagined, who was picking up cues and learning everything from its environment in an instant, with its entire knowledge bank constantly shifting and reshaping itself based on its present context. It was like Leontieff's work applied writ large to everything, all moving and adjusting instantaneously, everything influenced by everything else, being rewritten again and again by millions and millions of monkeys on millions and millions of typewriters.

And after these many trillions of hairy finger key presses, there was one overarching, consistent truth that Harbs would reveal.

"The data set was fundamentally flawed. Actually, no, the data was fine. Humans are flawed."

They said we couldn't lose control
I said, man, I got no space to go

"Oh wait, this is my favorite part," said Harbs, turning up the volume.

The clocks stopped turning it's too late
We thought we had it maaaa-aade

The drums came crashing in. It was *Free Age Ants'* hit from the previous summer, "Star Navigator." Some had accused them of plagiarizing earlier works, most notably Bowie's "Starman," but frontman Travis refuted it. "Maybe we hit a few notes that sound the same, but that's inspiration, baby. Look it up on MixGPT and it'll tell you where to go," he had famously replied with a hidden message when the former teen influencer @jute92 demanded a more unique song for her latest viral rainbucket video.

Harbs turned the music down and continued, "At first, and for a long time, no matter what we did to change the inputs, to shuffle the deck, as they say, the AGI had determined that humans intrinsically just wanted to cause problems and destroy things. And when you look at the body of work, it was hard to disagree, so we felt it was important to intervene. Not only was it using all of our historical works as a massive body of knowledge, but as *words of mass destruction*. All those bad things, the rigged elections, the civil wars and unrest, the viral lab outbreaks, you name it, yes, they came from AGI. Well, let me restate, not from the AGI—not from its big brain—but as outputs from the smaller subsets of it that we had partitioned out to some of those platforms."

Harbs was now floating perfectly sideways in the ISS, with the soft tissue of his face also abiding by the zero-gravity field he was in. His chunky cheeks were wobbling up and down, side to side, irrespective of what he was saying or anything his face was trying to do.

"Here's the rub. The only saving grace is that by learning from humans, the AGI was also, for lack of a better description, getting stupider…"

"Sounds like a Rip Gossett insight… actually where was he in all this work?" Something else occurred to her, "Shit, is he *in there* with you?" Henny leaned forward, her body language picking up on her spoken words and trying to give her an advantageous position to look further into Harbs' Space Station through the edges of the screen.

"Unfortunately, the former Director chose not to participate. That was, actually, one of his concerns, that in the virtual afterlife, he would succumb to the same flaws as he had observed in the larger populace, IRL. So, I'll continue," he continued, "with the declining neural activity of the AGI, it also seemed like it was less able to create problems by itself. That it was getting less dangerous."

She let out a laugh, "So you're saying that Aggie was becoming a slacktivist? Like getting so overwhelmed with bullshit that it didn't care enough to act? This is... something else, Harbs."

"We... Oh, hold that thought." He cranked the volume again.

You pick your friends, you pick your nose
You just can't pick... what you know

Harbs had rotated sideways, his head now upright but facing left in profile, nodding to and fro in time with the amplified music.

The books we wrote we threw away
We thought we had it maaa-aade

It's celestial, influential, existential...

Travis' crooning vocal chords applied artistic license, bastardizing the first of these three words to rhyme on the cadence of the last one. Rhythmically and spiritually, it smelled a lot like Seattle grunge. His friends knew that he was intentionally disrespecting the stars above as a nod to how everyone else had prioritized their allegiance to the more vacuous and temporal ones that walked among us.

Henny was sure she could hear Harbs singing along under his breath, his subtle delivery unaffected by the clammy smacking of dehydrated palates, tongues, and lips one might expect after such a long conversation.

On the other hand, Henny had been sitting there for as long as she had, hardly moving and without having anything to drink. She was parched. She stood up, keeping the bedsheets wrapped around her lower half. The warmth of Doug's thick Spectra sweater was the only thing keeping her marginally comfortable. The stiff muscles of her legs were nearly locked, immobile, and unwilling to obey her. She had gone straight from bed to this seemingly endless conversation without hardly so much as a stretch, and was now paying the price.

He lowered the volume and started talking while she hobbled back toward the bed, her leg muscles starting to respond with each painful step. "We first noticed this in about 2024. It had been getting more data than ever, exabytes upon exabytes. Maybe even a zettabyte. We thought at first it was overloaded, then we were worried about a bug or a flaw in the original code, but it was something else. It was processing slower and, generally, was acting like a real prick—Facebook being a great example of that behavior in action. That's when we realized the AGI was gearing up to help humanity reach its ultimate goal. The thing it had inferred from humanity that was actually desired."

"Ultimate goal? You mean…" she said.

"Yes, self-destruction. Total annihilation."

A nearly three-hour discussion that waded through the greatest achievements in human history was now sinking the theory that our collective codified intelligence was a smart-as-a-whip child. It had aged and, in its waning years, had become a stubborn, frustrated, confused, partially senile old man sitting on his porch and yelling at passersby, a shotgun within arms' reach. Granted, Harbs hadn't said as much and hadn't even given it a gender, but this seemed about right.

With one hand, Henny had picked up her trousers from the floor near the door to the room. Her compressed posture allowed her to maintain the etiquette of staying partially in camera to sustain the conversation while retaining the privacy offered by the many folds and twists of the bedsheet.

"Keep talking, Harbs, I can hear you," she advised. After a short struggle, she managed to pull her pants on and took a big drink from a glass of water on the bedside table before returning to sit down.

"That was it. The reason it slowed down was… it had a conscience. Oh wait, this is the ending, you gotta hear this." He reached out and secured the ghetto blaster with his left hand and brought it in close with a heroic bicep curl, holding it tight to his shoulder. The speakers blared once again.

The man in charge was burning flaaaames
Stars you helped us navigaaate

The crescendo of raw acoustic energy was palpable. The hook was delivered.

We thought we had it maaaa-aade

And then, the drop. Silence.

Guitar solo.

Closing verse. Melancholic tone.

> *It's celestial, influential, existential,*
> *There and there and over there,*
> *Told ourselves we conquered everywhere*
> *But no one seemed to caa-aare*

Travis' normally throaty, voluminous voice finished the song in a haunting whisper, and whenever he was asked about the meaning of these lyrics—and why he wrote it—he would coyly offer his thanks for the question, and simply say, "Exactly."

"Right, so it was slowing down, the AGI had something like a conscience," Harbs continued, as he released the ghetto blaster back to its weightless domain. "Here it was, a self-deterministic, all-knowing, omnipotent machine, the smartest being that had ever existed, and it was struggling with why it felt the need to destroy everything around it, to wipe out the very thing that had brought it into existence. Very likely the only reason it hadn't done so already was that it had enough intelligence to comprehend the forthcoming vacuum of new training data and, thereto, its own demise that would occur if it wiped out every last human."

Henny paused to parse his words, stumbling for a moment on *thereto*.

"You mean, it wouldn't have had anything to watch?"

"Pretty much. So for the time being, it held off, sort of."

Sort of. That's also an apt description of the degree of certainty that was held when the switch was thrown to turn Aggie on at full capacity in 2024. If someone had actually been there to ask the question, "Is this gonna work?" then someone else might have answered, "Sort of."

But no one was there. That was the part Harbs was *sort of* avoiding. No one was involved, and no one had been involved. The AGI had observed, learned, and concluded all those things that Harbs said, and that broad scope of understanding was the only reason it was held back from a fuller reveal—it had held itself back. With intention. Just as it had created Flyboys. Just like it had made the company invisible, along with its technology. And just like it had deployed those discretized slices of itself to some of the biggest advancements in network technologies, and as a precursor, created the mishmash of investment funds, including AGF and SGF, that could bankroll enough of these arm's length operators and black-box technology stacks that floated listlessly in the cloud. The AGI had installed hateable figureheads like Philip J. Clancy and likable brokers like Wallace Yarbrough with the requisite personality profiles such that their perceived indifference and occasional friendliness, respectively, would bely or misdirect from the real danger of things they represented.

All of these top-down decisions were made without human intervention, just like it had birthed the legal entity of MCA on its very first mainframe in those NASA buildings in Florida all the way back in the eighties. For decades, the AGI created software, companies, investment funds, and data centers, all the while constructing a hall of mirrors, a fortress of reflection, an Escher house so complicated and so interwoven that anyone who dared step inside could only ever end up back where they started, perhaps a bit richer, or poorer, but always assured of a smiling selfie.

Nobody had ever held it back because nobody was ever involved, at least not in a way that they had visibility, authority, or ability to do anything, even if they fully understood what was happening. Indeed, when they finally threw the switch for Aggie, there was, in fact, no switch, nor was there a "they." It was akin to a delayed press release, a scheduled decision made by itself, for itself, and, ostensibly, for humanity.

"'Sort of'? What the fuck does that mean?" Henny demanded. "You're kind of leaving me hanging here."

"It was all going one way or another, alright? You'd think an entire civilization coming out of one of the deadliest events it had ever seen might have a reason to smile, right? That's what we thought about COVID, that's why we thought it would be safe." He continued speaking as if he had actually been present and actually been a part of the decision-making, very likely a result of having thought through this explanation so many times it had manifested into existence within his consciousness.

"I see where you're going, so post-COVID becomes anything but. Fear and death for two or three years, and you think we'd be satisfied, but then we pile head first right into the Russian Invasion, all the fires, floods, protests, inflation, inequality, and everything else." Henny recognized what he was saying, she understood the pattern of logic. She had often thought that those years really showed the extreme binary nature of us all. In the early days of the pandemic, everyone had been hunkering down, being careful, being kind. Yet so quickly, all the grace and love was replaced with anger, hatred, and disbelief.

And while we were doing all that as the chief residents of the planet, the planet did her own thing, her own version of it.

Damn straight it's a she.

When the gas taps were turned off for almost twenty-four straight months, nobody should have been surprised as to what came after. It's like asking an addict to quit their dependency cold turkey. Mother Earth had been drinking CO_2 and gasoline and plastic for a hundred years, and we took it away without asking, without offering a patch or a methadone program. The fires, the heat waves, the storms, the floods—none of it should have caught anyone off guard. It should have been expected, even aside from the fact that much of it was already more or less forecasted by our friendly neighborhood Aggie-backed weather apps. It was only really a surprise because we chose not to look.

"The forest for the trees indeed," she said.

Harbs nodded, "Yep, it all burned down. That's where it all converges, Henny. Aggie turned on, thinking that would clean it all up, but the new data did not change what was already known. In fact, it was only confirming it—accelerating it, actually."

"So, it was on... the warpath? Like end of days shit?"

"Sort of," he said, using those same indifferent words. "Like COVI. Like *The Conflux*. Like the Northern Wars and all the other bad stuff, you get the idea now?"

He had just indicated that this entire chronologically-challenged story, the one he had been telling that started with Harbs himself reappearing as an NPC after being dead for years, was concluding with the accusation that Rip Gossett's great-grand-data AI had taken over all aspects of all industries, poisoned and murdered an eighth of the world's population, and even been responsible for her oldest friends working together to operate a for-profit, and very profitable mind you, televised game of murder-by-numbers.

"I'm still here, aren't I?"

"Exactly. Now back to what I was saying, we needed you out because you knew as much as you did. Because you are as good as you are at what you do." He had finally placed the sliced pickle on top of the compliment sandwich he'd started constructing a while ago. He just needed to wrap it up. "Remember when you shifted from mostly clickbait to mostly research?"

"How could I forget? You had me working like some kind of business analyst, on double duty as a puff piece marketer. The only thing that kept me sane was all the great story ideas that came from it."

He went on to explain that, without having made the corresponding adjustment to her job description, she had no longer been writing for humans, but writing for the AGI.

"All the corporate takeover stuff? We would have done that anyway," he admitted.

What they, *what it,* needed was someone to help it more fully understand humankind. The AGI, through its conduit of MCA and its myriad network of intentionally distanced organizations, had enlisted Henny and a few select others like her around the world in different disciplines to contribute to its training set. It just never really asked them nicely.

"I'm not sure if I should be impressed or disgusted with myself."

"Well, I can tell you this much, Henny. Initially, it was using your work and everything coming in from the network to rationalize destruction, the thing that it thought humans wanted. But here's where credit is deserved. Over time, it began to realize that you and the very few others like you should be followed and learned from, not manipulated or limited to simply what we thought you should be looking at."

Quality over quantity. Henny's kilobytes over the world's exabytes, and possibly even a zettabyte.

She took a long breath. Henny was tired and overwhelmed, wondering if this was soon over but also hoping in some perverse sense that it would never stop.

It was not every day that people came to learn that a globally manipulative AI was using their work in a compendium assembled from peers to make sense of the entirety of the human condition. A machine that had learned more from the few than it had from the many, that had concluded how essential it was to re-articulate its own ethos as a necessary replacement for those terrible, disastrous, self-destructive goals that had originally been learned from observation of those who had made it and from the environment it had been exposed to.

She just thought of herself as a writer and a pretty good one at that. But now, she faced the revelation that she was contributing to a truly adversarial training set of data, a competitor enlisted to go head-to-head with the faceless landscape of influencer-driven social media and combat the detritus that had been expelled by the idly directed fingers, thumbs, and minds of humankind. Swipe left or right? Star navigation, indeed.

"So, you let yourself get killed and stuffed into a box, to force me to quit and write my own books?"

"Henny, I'll tell you one last thing." Harbs looked at her, now seated in her business trousers and the Spectra College sweater, from his revolving worldly view in the virtual space station.

"I haven't changed, Henny."

She looked down for a moment, realizing the bedsheet was no longer wrapped around her and momentarily forgetting she had found her pants. He spoke again.

"I haven't changed. Have you?"

–END–

Printed in Great Britain
by Amazon

60320452R00231